final chapters are breathtaking – visionary, beautiful, powerful, deeply moving.'

Julia Green, *The Children of Swallow Fell*

'A captivating eco-fable with enough danger and action to please lovers of action adventure but also with the lyricism and wonder that comes from Nicola Davies' deep love of the natural world.'

Linda Newbery, *The Shell House*

'A heartsong. And a song of active hope in a dark world. Hope and beauty are a hard song to sing, but Nicola does, and this is it. This book has the feel of an absolute modern classic about it; it is layered and nuanced and contains within it a perfection that makes it shine.'

Jackie Morris, author and illustrator, *The Unwinding*

'A very special book. Inspiring, important and innovative – full of action that keeps you on the edge of your seat. Nicola Davies is a magnificent writer and this is a tour-de-force. It's for fans of *Mortal Engines* as much as it is for those who love *Watership Down*'.

Simon Fisher, Family Bookworms Wales

'How to classify this great book? Ecofiction, thriller, fantasy, parable? Page turner from the outset: tense, uncompromising and hopeful. Nicola Davies' knowledge, understanding and passion for the natural world and all that we are in danger of destroying, imbues every page.'

Eva John, literacy consultant

with thanks to
Molly Howell
Cathy Fisher
Jackie Morris
the midwives of this book

and to my husband
Daniel Jones
for unfailing love and support

THE SONG THAT SINGS US

NICOLA DAVIES

First published in 2021
by Firefly Press
25 Gabalfa Road, Llandaff North, Cardiff, CF14 2JJ
www.fireflypress.co.uk

A CIP catalogue record of this book is available from
the British Library.

1 3 5 7 9 8 6 4 2

ISBN 978-1-913102-77-7
Ebook ISBN 978-1-913102-50-0

This book has been published with the support of
the Books Council of Wales.

Typeset by Elaine Sharples
Printed by CPI Group (UK) Ltd, Croydon, Surrey, CR0 4YY

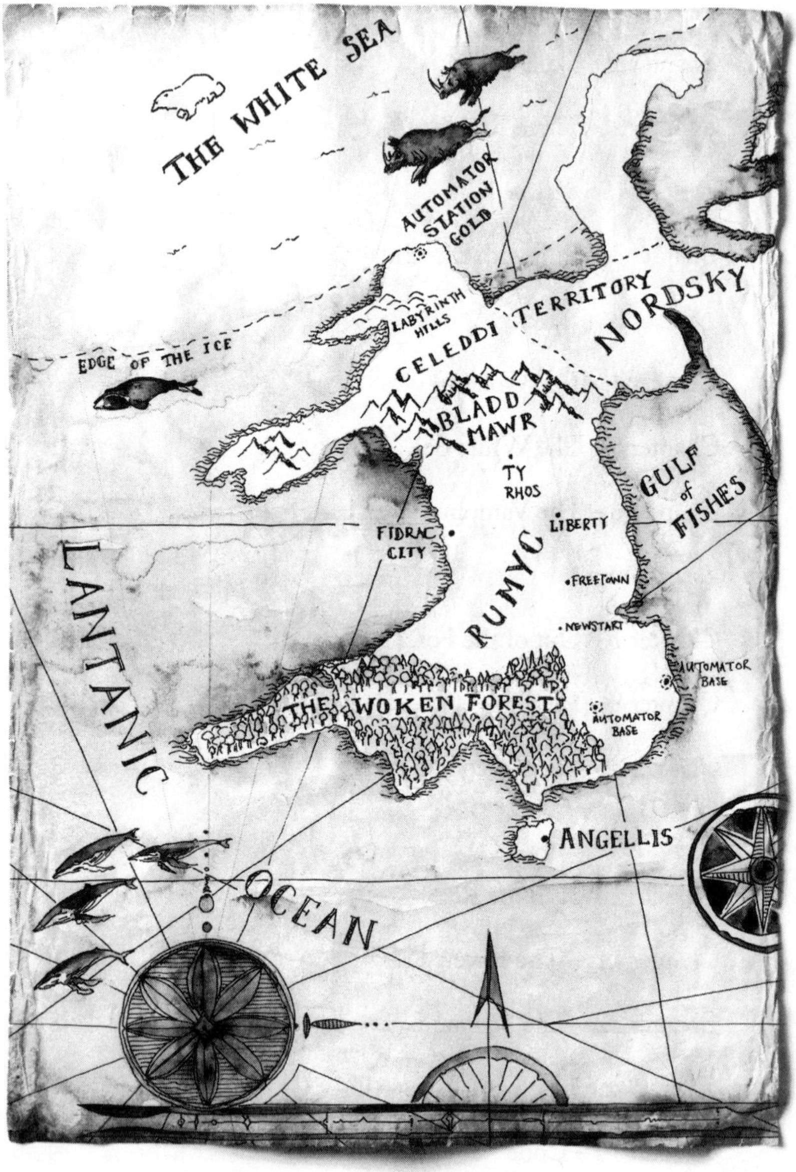
THE WHITE SEA
AUTOMATOR STATION GOLD
LABYRINTH HILLS
CELEDDI TERRITORY
NORDSKY
EDGE OF THE ICE
BLADD MAWR
TY RHOS
GULF of FISHES
FIDRAC CITY
LIBERTY
RUMYC
FREETOWN
NEWSTART
LANTANIC
AUTOMATOR BASE
THE WOKEN FOREST
AUTOMATOR BASE
ANGELLIS
OCEAN

Contents

1
Skull Gully

Harlon

 Harlon sees the lantern beams slicing up the mountainside towards her home. They've come at last, the people called the Automators. The red symbol on their black uniforms is a fist closing round the Earth and now it's closing around her family too: they've come to take her brother and her sister, Ash and Xeno. But she and Ma won't let them.

'Kill the lights,' Ma says. 'Get ready.'

They all know what to do. They've practised this routine so many times, but Harlon never thought it would be for real. Together the three children bar the front door and lock the shutters. They don't speak.

Ma pulls two rifles out from underneath the bed. She loads both then lines up more ammunition on the windowsill and pokes the barrel of the first between the shutters. She's not Ma – Breen Avvon, alpaca farmer – now but someone else, the person she was before; the person no one is allowed to talk about, who knows how to shoot straight, and knock a man to the ground in perfect silence.

'Dammit,' Ma says. 'How did they find us?' Her eyes narrow, focused on the dark silhouettes darting between the rocks and trees, getting closer. She bites her lip and Harlon sees that Ma's afraid. That scares Harlon more than anything, but she mustn't show it. It's Harlon's job now to be strong for her little brother and sister. So she listens, looking calm, while Ma tells them what to do, speaking in snatches over her shoulder as she aims.

'You'll have to snowboard down Skull Gully,' Ma says.

What? Harlon wants to answer. *What?*

Skull Gully is six thousand feet, six thousand ways to die is what Ma's always said before. But, as if she's read her eldest daughter's thoughts, Ma says, 'I've done it myself, Harlon. I know you three can do it too. Nothing will follow you down there.'

Of course nothing will follow them because it's like jumping off a cliff!

Ash and Xeno look at Harlon; she stays steady and she gives their shoulders each a squeeze to tell them that if Ma thinks they can do it, then they can. Really, she's not sure.

A bullet slams into the kitchen wall, striking sparks from the stone. Ash and Xeno cry out and Harlon pulls them further from the window. Ma pumps a volley of returning fire.

'That'll keep them back for a minute,' Ma says and turns from the window to look at her children. A dark stain is spreading through her shirt; she tries to pull her jacket over it but it can't be hidden.

'Ma!' Ash cries out. Xeno whimpers and moves towards her.

2

'No! Keep back from the window,' Ma says. 'Just listen.' She grits her teeth.

'No time to explain. Get to the bottom of the gully. Don't let them catch you. Head to the coast.'

Ma gasps, takes a few deep breaths against the pain and closes her eyes.

'You have to get to a place that's not on a map. An island lost in the deepest part of the ocean. No one will find you there. You'll be safe. Promise me you'll stay together; promise me you'll get there.'

Her eyes open, blazing, her voice with an edge like a sword. *'Promise.'*

Blood loss, Harlon thinks. It's made her crazy, but there's no choice but to make the promise.

'We promise, Ma,' they say together, like a small chorus.

Xeno starts to cry.

'Hey, little bird,' Ma says, more gently. 'You have to take our song there, alright?'

Ma takes a breath and hums the first notes of the lullaby she's sung them all their lives. 'The song that sings us' is what Xeno calls it. Xeno answers with the first three notes sung in her bird-like trill.

'Good. Now hand me that other rifle, Harlon. Quick.'

Harlon does as she is told, creeping low under the window to pass the rifle to her mother's hands.

'I'll be alright, Harlon,' Ma whispers. 'I will survive this. I'll be fine and so will you. You trained for this.'

For a moment Harlon feels about to crumble, then something flips inside her. Ma is right, she did train for this, all her life. Ma trained her.

3

'Travel like ghosts,' Ma says. 'Don't trust anyone. Take our song. Remember, lost in the deepest ocean. Now, GO!'

Ma's voice is laced tight against the pain, her sparse words only just managing to escape her lips, but still she turns to aim into the centre of the flickering torches. She has always seemed to Harlon like a dagger forced to be a spoon, but tonight she's more like herself than Harlon's ever seen her, that secret person that Harlon feels she'll never get to know now. That person whose skill and fierce love will buy her children as much time as she can, whatever it costs.

They have to use it.

Harlon steps back from the window and rubs her tears dry. She barks at Ash and Xeno.

'Ma's fine. Let's go. Right now!' And they start to run.

The three of them race down the long stone corridor and grab their outdoor gear from the pegs that line it. Their boards lean up against the wall, cleaned and waxed by Ma's long, beautiful fingers. Harlon pushes down the questions formed by Ma's words: *an island not on any map? Lost in the deepest ocean?*

She must not think right now. Their survival depends on focus: one step, and then the next. Harlon reaches for her jacket but her hand falls on Ma's old one instead. It's a man's coat, too big for Ma, but she used to wear it all the time when they were small. Harlon pulls it from the peg and puts it on. It's old, with stitching crisscrossed over its layers of lining, but it smells of Ma; that's all that matters.

Their backpacks, ready packed with camping gear, dried food and water bottles, are in size order. Ash takes his middle-sized one and catches Harlon's eye.

4

'The three bears,' he says. That's what Ma used to call them when they were little: *my three bears*. Harlon, as the biggest, was the daddy bear, Ash never seemed to mind that he was Mamma, and little Xeno, although his twin, could never be anything but the baby.

Ash smiles at her, even though he's scared, so she smiles quickly back.

'Get your backpack on, Mamma Bear,' Harlon says. 'No time to waste!' Xeno smiles too and for a moment they're those three kids again, giggling insanely because Ma called them bears. Then Xeno frowns and lifts her board above her head to show how ready she is.

'Sky will hatch!' she says and Harlon nods, even though nothing Xeno says ever makes much sense. Then there's another shot, from inside the house, and the sound of a ricochet hitting the walls.

'Go!' says Harlon, and hustles her siblings out into the pre-dawn dark.

Outside, the cold has fangs and the stars fizz with frost. Ragged clouds are shoaling round the moon like fish. It may snow, Harlon thinks, hopefully. It would be good if their tracks were covered. Their eyes are used to the blue twilight of winter nights, so they don't need a torch to find the way. Frozen snow is piled head high either side of the path that leads away from the house, hiding them from the Automators whose shouts and lights stab up into the sky. The alpacas call in alarm, like a herd of rusty hinges, as the noise reaches their stall.

Ash stops moving.

'They're scared,' he whispers. 'So scared!'

It's not just the calls that tell him. Ash can feel their thoughts, Xeno a little too, but the alpacas are Ash's special friends. Alba, the white cria who he reared when her mother died, cries out like a human baby.

There's a burst of gun shots, the alpacas scream and Ash's legs collapse under him. Xeno turns from the path and throws up into the snow. There is a horrible silence. Harlon doesn't need to ask what's happened. Why would anyone do such a thing? Shoot defenceless beings trapped in their stable?

'Alba!' Ash whispers. *'Alba!'*

Harlon feels she could throw up too. She knows every one of the alpacas by name and character, even if she can't eavesdrop on their thoughts the way Ash can. But there's no time for grief now, no time for anger even. She pulls her brother to his feet.

'We have to go,' she says and pulls at his jacket.

But Ash doesn't move. Xeno lays a hand on her brother's arm. Her mouth is a straight, determined line and her eyes shine hard as ice. She's tougher than Ash. Like a bird, small and tough, armoured with feathers. Xeno makes a sound like the first notes of a robin's song, but lower.

'Ash!' she says. *'Fly!'*

'Right,' Ash says. 'A'right.'

Harlon calculates as they run up the steep rocky track: a ten-minute climb to the top; thirty for anyone not used to climbing mountain paths at speed. More for someone who doesn't know the path, which is half hidden between the boulders and stumps of trees. Will their headstart be enough to let them get away? Harlon is not sure. She picks up her pace and pushes Ash and Xeno to do the same. The sounds of hard breathing and the scrunch of footfalls enclose them as they run. There are shouts behind, voices yelling orders, more shots. Harlon gives Xeno and Ash a stream of small orders and encouragements to stop them thinking.

In Harlon's head, her ma's voice speaks.

When you are in danger, the most dangerous thing is to wish you weren't. Accept the reality of danger, then you can survive it.

Climb, she tells herself. Get away.

Xeno is first to the top. She's waiting when Ash and Harlon reach the rocks that stand like sentinels guarding the gully, one almost overlapping the other, so the narrow entrance is hard to see. Beyond them, sheer drops hide under lips of snow. Even the most skillful skier could not go down Skull Gully; skis are just too long to make turns tight enough for the narrowest sections. But snowboards make this dangerous descent a possibility and Breen Avvon and her three bears are expert snowboarders. No one will have the slightest chance of following them.

Behind them there is a sudden boom, and the house that has been the only home they have known, becomes a cloud of red flame and smoke against the snow. The children look at each other without a word, numbed by shock. That's it. There is no going back. From this moment their past life is gone, and any future they imagined utterly changed. Harlon can't lie and tell them Ma is fine and will follow when she can. All she can say is the obvious.

'Time to go!'

Harlon bites down on fear and sorrow and cuts off their past life. A kind of reckless joy rises in her like a shiver as the three of them drop over the lip of the gully.

The light of the setting moon makes the snow glow almost blue. Thin shadows of their three bodies follow them down the slope. This first section is just steep, really steep, and narrow. There's not much room to turn; the only choice is to go straight down, a sort of controlled fall. Which means gathering more and more speed, reacting more and more quickly. But they are very good at this, they have ridden the mountain snow every day of the long winters since Ash and Xeno could walk. That means climbing every slope before boarding down it. So they're fit and strong as well as skilled.

I know you can do this.

Harlon looks round. She needs to know at all times where Ash and Xeno are. They must be close enough to keep in contact but not too close to risk collision, a fall that could be fatal at this speed. Ash is in front. He reads the snow intuitively, and he's at his boldest when he's on the slopes. To the right and a little behind, Xeno is careful and precise, naturally graceful.

A voice of doubt whispers like a mutiny inside Harlon's mind: And you, Harlon? What would you say about your skills and strengths?

It seeds panic in her heart. She doesn't really know what she can do.

Stay calm, Harlon, Ma's voice tells her. *Think. Always, think!*

Every tiny undulation, every minute change in texture in the snow is vibrating through the soles of Harlon's feet, into the joints of her knees and hips. Her whole body is reading the snow, the way Ash says bats read the night air. New information from nerves and muscles piles into her brain, more and more with every passing second as her speed increases and increases. The slightest error, a misjudgment of balance, a turn when the edge of the board isn't perfectly positioned, will send her into a cartwheeling fall. She feels she's already at the very limit of what she can do.

There's a sudden quiver in the snow. Its surface feels unstable. A glance to the side tells her Ash and Xeno have felt it too. They all know what it means. They must float over the snow without attacking it. Slopes as steep as this one this rarely slip, but now this feels as if it wants to stop being a surface and start being a wave. It is an avalanche wanting to happen.

There's no headspace for thoughts about what lies behind, or what lies ahead. There is just *this* moment of intense effort and concentration. And then the next, the next, the next. Each second so packed with what every muscle must do, every sense attend to, that time slows down and stretches.

The gully widens a little, flattens out before a second plunge into a slope that's spiked with rocks. But the flat brings another kind of risk: slow down here, Harlon knows, and they could all sink into powder over their heads. For several moments this takes every ounce of concentration, and then Harlon realises that she can't see Xeno. She's so small that if she sank here they'd never find her. When did she see her last? A second ago? Ten? Where *is* she?

9

'Chirrup.' Her voice is right at Harlon's shoulder, answering her thought.

A wind is getting up, siphoning up the gully from the valley floor, slithering over the powder and whipping it into a low icy mist, obscuring boards for moments on end. Easily enough time to hit a rock. But they can't slow down. They must keep the impact on the snow light and quick or risk starting that avalanche. Then the gully turns to the left, out of the wind but into deep shadow. Harlon's eyes struggle for a moment in the lower light and she loses sight of Xeno and Ash. When she spots them again they are fifty feet behind her and above them, almost on them, two dark shapes.

Falcons?

The birds of prey are huge and very fast. Harlon's never seen falcons so big, or willing to fly in moonlight. They are strange and menacing and very clearly chasing Ash and Xeno. But what makes Harlon's blood suddenly run ice cold is that Xeno clearly doesn't know they're there. Xeno's power of tuning into bird minds is exceptional; she can sense the presence of a bird that she can neither hear nor see, tune into a passing goldfinch a hundred feet up in the air. Yet she hasn't sensed these creatures and they're almost on her shoulder.

Just as the wrongness of this hits Harlon in the belly, the birds stoop, full of malevolent intent. Their dark bodies dive like missiles, wings part-folded, like the fletches of giant arrows. The air is fractured by their speed. There's a flash of yellow eyes and outstretched talons more like steel daggers.

Harlon screams a warning and now, at last, Xeno and Ash

see the birds too. Xeno lets out a high-pitched cry of shock. She ducks and one falcon skims her head and wheels round for another pass. Ash hasn't been so lucky. The other bird has raked him with a claw and there's a dark line of blood across his cheek.

'Trees!' Harlon yells. 'Into the trees!'

Ash and Xeno understand at once. Close-packed trees clothe this section of the slope to the left of the gully. To board between them at this speed, in moonlight, is insane but it's the only way to lose the birds. Falcons are built for high speed in open country, not for fast changes of direction in the enclosed space of dense woodland.

Moonlight, deep shadow, tree trunks, come at the speeding boarders in a high-velocity tangle. Every microsecond could smash any of them into a tree. Harlon hears the gasps of effort, the scrape and swish of boards turning at the last possible moment, as her brother and sister make split-second decisions about which way to turn. She sees them appear and disappear between the trees. In shadow, in light, in shadow again. Close, then far, close again, as if time was being cut into unconnected chunks.

Everything seems to get faster and faster. More disjointed. Senses, muscles, joints are close to overload and still the birds pursue them.

'Look out!' Ash yells a warning. One falcon is coming straight for the side of Harlon's face. But the bird is so focused on its target that it looks only where its feet will strike. Harlon jinks sideways, scrapes the tree trunk with the edge of her board, and the falcon's left wing smashes into the trunk.

11

There's a snap, loud as a rifle, as the bird shatters into a floundering mess of feathers.

Ash and Xeno crow with delight, then Xeno screams. Harlon sees her shoot past, flashing between the trees with the other falcon's foot tangled in her hood. Xeno swats at it in panic, trying to keep her balance on the slope, trying to avoid the trees. She rips the hood away and swirls it. Too late, the falcon realises its mistake. Xeno smashes it into a passing tree and its head explodes.

By then the children are a hundred feet further on, speeding ever faster through the trees and, like the birds, too focused on what's just in front of them to see the bigger picture. By the time Harlon registers the end of the trees, they are all in the air. They've shot out over the lip where the slope of trees becomes sheer rock face, and are now falling.

Harlon is aware of the quiet as they fall. She has time to see the moon setting behind the mountains, the stars, the shapes of her brother and sister against the indigo sky, against the dull pearl of the snow.

'Oh,' she thinks, 'we're going to die.'

And then they drop into snow on the slope below the rock face. Harlon thinks of Ma dropping berries into whipped cream one summer day, counting as they made a satisfying plop.

One, two, three.

They are blackberries dropped in cream. Side by side, alive, unbroken, up to their waists in the fluffiest powder they've ever seen! It seems impossible, insane, wonderful.

Harlon is the first to free her legs and board from the drift.

She stands in the stillness and silver light, the relief of survival running through her. Then, there's a sound. A low crack. It's a sound they all know well. It means avalanche. There's a dark rupture in the pale face of the slope that runs from Harlon to Xeno, and from Xeno to Ash like a jagged, pointing finger. Their luck has run out.

In the early light Ash's face is too distant for Harlon to see but she can see Xeno, though she is not close enough to grab, to touch, to hold and never, ever let go. Close enough to see Xeno's eyes fill with terror. Close enough to hear her call, for the first time in a long time, 'Harlon! Harlon!'

The snow below gives way, as if it had just evaporated. They fall into a pounding maelstrom of white.

Harlon knows the theory of what to do in an avalanche.

The first thing is: try to get out of the way. But the whole slope has turned fluid; there is no 'out of the way'. The second is: try to hold on to something, but there's nothing to hold on to. The third: try to swim through the snow to keep at the surface, but the force of the snow-wave is so great that she's turned over and over, helpless as a leaf in a storm. 'Up' and 'down', lose all meaning. Her head hits something and she's not tumbling in a white-out any more, but high up in the branches of a tree.

*

It was Harlon's birthday and they'd all come down the mountain into town. Later they would go to the baker and get

13

cake, but first Ma was delivering wool to a weaver, one of her regular customers. Harlon was to watch over the twins in the yard behind the weaver's house while Ma did business. But the weaver's garden had an irresistible tree that Harlon *had* to climb. She reckoned she could see the twins well enough from up there.

Harlon looked down through the branches and the twins were still sitting together on the back step. She'd left them with her spinning top but they had found another game to play: a row of mice and robins, live creatures, was lined up like toy soldiers at their feet. She knew the twins had done this, and she knew it was bad. Bad people called Listeners talked to animals like this. It was wrong, worse than stealing, her teachers said. *If you know a Listener you must tell me at once, even if it is someone in your family,* Madame Mollit told the class every day. Listeners were taken away to stop them being bad and came back, branded with a letter L upon their foreheads, so you could spot them and keep away.

Harlon began to cry. She didn't want Ash and Xeno to be bad; she didn't want them to be taken away like that and have a letter burned into their skins. Snivelling, she got to the bottom of the tree as Ma came out. Ma shooed the birds and mice away, scooped up the twins, and in two minutes they were all loaded in the cart and heading out of town. There would be no cake and everyone was crying: Xeno, Ash and Harlon. Ma stared ahead and didn't say a word.

Juno, their horse, lost a shoe so the journey home took ages. The twins fell asleep at last.

'Only bad people talk to animals, Ma,' Harlon whispered.

'They don't *talk,* Harlon. They have a power called siardw, that lets them *listen* inside animals' heads. Sometimes animals like the feeling, like a cat likes being stroked, and they come to take a look.'

'But only bad people talk to animals and tell them what to do, Ma,' Harlon insisted. 'My teachers say.'

Ma shook her head.

'They don't *tell* animals what to do, Harlon; they only listen. And that's a good thing. Siardw lets Listeners hear animal thoughts, sometimes even plant thoughts in their minds. It helps us understand them, so we can treat them properly. Listeners are very special.'

'Then why do people say they're bad?'

'Because the Automators don't want anyone to hear or understand other living things; they just want to use them. They fear Listeners and what they can do.'

'Are you one, Ma?'

Ma shakes her head.

'No, but I think I know about what it's like to be one. Like being able to hear a song that other people can't hear, a song that's everywhere all the time, that holds the whole world together. You should be proud your brother and sister have this special power.' She pulled Harlon close and went on.

'The Automators try to get rid of Listeners, but d'you know what? More are being born all the time. Remember the field behind the house? How it bloomed with yellow flowers when it was ploughed and the ground was broken? Listeners are blooming like flowers because the Automators are trying to break the world apart. Listeners help to protect it, so we need to protect *them*.'

Then Ma began to sing,

Oh, there was a woman, and she was a widow

Listen to the flowers in the valley
With a daughter as fair as a the bright sunny meadow...

Harlon didn't really understand what Ma said about flowers and Listeners protecting the world. But she did understand that Ma's voice was sad when she sang the word 'widow'.

They stopped going to town and Harlon stopped going to school. She didn't mind. They could learn from all Ma's books, and the space and the solitude in the mountains were better than a load of screaming children. There were soaring eagles, deer, and the calls of wolves and ravens instead of teachers. Harlon spent long summer days with Ash and Xeno, wandering the high pastures. Ash calmed the alpacas and laughed at their funny thoughts, while Xeno connected with the passing flocks of finches for news of bears. Winters were encased in a magic, white world of snow and ice, perfecting techniques with the snowboards that Ma had built and taught them all to use. Harlon sometimes thought she could hear the song that Ma had once said 'holds the world together' even though she had none of the siardw power that her siblings had.

But down in the valley things were changing faster and faster. Ma called it the Automators 'spreading their stain'. When Ma and Harlon went down to get supplies or sell their wool, they saw the forces of the 'Diacoch', as the mountain people called the Automators, more and more often. They saw Listeners taken from the streets, or dragged from their carts or houses. Adults sometimes, but more often children, and their families. Ma said they took them to Fidrac city, the capital by the sea, to the Automator headquarters. Most never

16

came back. Those that did were husks of people, able only to sit and stare, with an 'L' branded on their foreheads.

The radio signal in the mountains was unreliable, but when voices came out of the crackle they belonged more and more to Automators, telling of the bright future that waited for everyone who would leave the land and live in the city. Lots of people had listened already and there were empty houses in the small mountain town. Often Ma would turn the radio off and go outside and walk for hours, even in the dark.

The threat of the Automators was there in the lessons Ma taught them, like a shadow on the wall. As well as reading and sums and history, they learned how to survive in a blizzard on the mountain, how to travel without being noticed, how to hide. Harlon had extra lessons too: while the twins fed the chickens or tended the garden, Ma taught Harlon how to be their protector. Harlon never asked how Ma knew the things she taught: how to fight, how to use anything as a weapon, how think like a spy and a warrior.

*

As Harlon floats back up to consciousness, Ma's secrets are like the foaming backwash of a wave that melts into the sand. She wakes to find she's still tumbling in whiteness, which stops abruptly. Now she remembers the fourth thing to do in an avalanche: as soon as it stops, move, flail, struggle all you can. In seconds, the snow will change from behaving like a liquid, to being solid; it will set around her face like stone and she will suffocate.

Just in time, Harlon wriggles her whole body, if wriggle is

the right word for the huge physical effort it takes to create the smallest amount of movement. She's left gasping, heart leaping, coughing out the snow that's worked into her mouth and nose and lungs. She manages to create a pocket of air, the size of a loaf of bread, next to her face.

This makes only a tiny bubble of hope that soon pops: the snow has set, like concrete. Her left arm is pinned behind her back, her right held just in front of her face, and her legs are folded like a squashed fly. Panic engulfs her, more paralysing than cold. Who is going to dig her out? There's no one. What if Ash and Xeno are both dead?

The fear says *yes, they're dead.*

The fear says *lie still, let the snow hold you tight and take your breath, quickly. Die! Die now.*

Breathe, Ma's voice tells her.

Breathe. Just breathe.

Harlon's heart slows. If Xeno and Ash are still alive, she's not allowed to die.

'Harlon!'

'Harlon?'

Ash's voice! He's alive. Maybe he's even above the snow. The most useful thing about the air pocket is that it gives her space to yell.

'ASH!' Harlon yells with every scrap of volume she can manage, but the cold has stolen her voice and it takes Ash an agonising time to hear her.

Then he does and starts to dig her out. Ash scrabbles with his hands and says her name over and over, but there's no sound from Xeno, no bird chirp, no second pair of scrabbling hands. She's probably too chilled to help, Harlon tells herself. I'll need to get them both to some shelter soon. This thought warms her, but when she's out into the air at last, Ash is alone.

'Couldn't find her,' Ash is saying. 'No Xeno!'

Harlon stares at Ash; she is stupid with cold. He tries hard to find the words to tell her what has happened, but he too is chilled and the words slip about like bits of broken ice.

'Supside-down,' he sobs. 'Got out. Called. Searched. Poked the snow like Ma taught us. No Xeno. No Xeno.'

Xeno, little Xeno, Baby Bear, Little Bird, is alone and lost on the mountain. Or buried, waiting to be rescued. Or already dead, her mouth stopped with snow. Harlon's legs are like straws that won't hold weight.

Don't think about what you can't change; focus on what you can.

Ma's voice is in her head again, the only still point in this storm of pain and disaster.

Assess. Think. Act. The mantra that her mother taught her.

Assess:

They are dangerously cold. Soon they will lose all ability to think or move. Snowflakes are already flying round them. A blizzard is gathering.

Think:

She can't help Xeno now, but she can help Ash.

Act:

Harlon stands up and takes Ash's shoulders. She shakes him, hard.

'Stop blubbing, right now,' she says. 'We have to get to shelter or we'll die.'

'Where is Xeno?' he wails. He's small for his age and now

19

he looks tiny, more like eight than twelve. Harlon thinks of stone and ice and metal and puts them all in her heart.

If Xeno is buried, then she's gone. But it won't help Ash to hear it.

'She'll have got out, like you did,' she tells him. 'She'll find shelter. She's smart and she knows what to do. We'll find her, when we've warmed up.'

Her words work. Ash nods. He helps pull her board out of the snow. Its tip was sticking up from the snow close to where she was buried. It helped Ash to find her. The bindings are undamaged and she still has both boots. Ash's board is gone so she stands him on the front of hers where she can hold him, and sets off down the slope.

She's too cold to try to calculate how far the avalanche has taken them from where they should have been. The clear dawn has turned into a sudden blizzard. Snow drives in from all directions, biting and scouring, wiping out all lines and shadows. The world has turned blank. Gravity is the only guide and shelter of any sort, a rock ledge, a fallen tree, anything, is the only destination.

Time too goes blank. Has Ash been leaning on her legs like this for minutes, or for hours? When did she begin to feel this sleepy? Just as she's about to stop and dig a snow hole to keep them both alive until the blizzard's over, something brushes past them, dark and low. Instantly Ash wakes up.

'A Gula!' he says. 'A wolverine. It's come to find us!'

Harlon can tell at once from Ash's voice that he's not just looking at this animal, he can *hear* it. How has Ash 'tuned in' to the Gula, the way he does with the alpacas, when his siardw, never strong, has got weaker as he's got older?

The wolverine lopes easily beside the board. Harlon catches the glitter of a dark eye. She's never felt such concentrated power from any animal before.

'There's shelter,' Ash reports. 'She's going there. She says we can follow.'

She says we can follow? That's not eavesdropping that's a conversation. Harlon's skin prickles. Why would a gula come looking for them like this? Harlon can think of a reason at once: gula aren't big like a bear, just a kind of hound-sized weasel, but they have a reputation: they'll eat anything, alive or dead. Perhaps this gula's just waiting for them to die so it can make a meal of them. Perhaps they smell of death already.

Harlon pushes the board to gather speed and the Gula ups her pace to run in front.

'She says it's not far,' Ash reports.

The creature's shaggy outline swirls like ink into the paper of the blizzard and, just as Harlon is considering jinking away from her, she's gone and the corner of a log cabin looms out of the whiteness. The board hits it hard, tumbling Harlon and Ash into a drift.

Ash sits up. 'She tuned out,' he says sadly.

She tuned out? Harlon looks at Ash. She wants to ask *How did* she *tune out, if* you *were in* her *head? It should be the other way around.* But now's not the time for questions. She's too tired, and too relieved: this cabin means they won't die in the blizzard after all.

Fumbling with frozen fingers. Harlon gets herself out of the board's bindings. Together they feel their way around the cabin searching for a door. They find one shuttered window, a bank of solars poking up from underneath the snow, then finally the door, unlocked. They fall in through it and kick it shut behind them. The howling blizzard still goes on but now it can't get them. Harlon sinks down onto the floor. The relief of being safe from the cold and snow feels almost unreal. Is this a hallucination? Or worse, some kind of trap? She signals to Ash to be silent and they creep about, exploring.

A solar lantern, almost out of charge, shines just bright enough to show a room with thick beams holding up the roof. There's a stove, still warm, a high bed, table, chairs, jars and tins of food. Not a hut, but a home. Is the owner here somewhere? Or lost on the mountain?

They hold still, listening for signs of life. A sudden soft thudding has them almost jumping into each other's arms. It's coming from a cupboard in a shadowed corner of the room!

Thud, thud, thud.

Then a pause and…

Thud, thud, thud again, in quick succession. It's almost like someone banging out a code.

Again, and then again. They creep closer to the cupboard.

Harlon's thinks that whoever it is must be tied up and gagged, knocking their head against the door to get their attention. Maybe the people who set the falcons on their trail have tied up the owner of the cabin?

Thud thud thud thud…

Pause.

Thud thud thud thud.

The pace is becoming more desperate.

They stand either side of the door. Harlon puts her hand on the latch and looks at Ash.

One, two, three, she mouths, then snatches the door open.

A woman is sitting in the cupboard, squished between sacks of flour and large jars of pickles. She is tall, with a huge complicated mound of gingerish hair, a sort of fortress of plaits and twists and pins. The hair twitches a little, like the surface of a pond rippled by the wind: there are many insects using the hairdo as a home. The woman is comically folded, with skinny arms wrapped around long, thin legs, in striped leggings. Her eyes are open, but blank, like the windows of an empty house. Harlon reaches out and gently touches her arm.

'Madam? Can we help? What's wrong?'

The woman turns to look at Ash and Harlon. Her eyes come on like lanterns in the dusk: warm and kind. She puts a hand up to touch the place on her head where it banged the cupboard door.

'Oh,' she says, a little dazed. 'I wonder, could you help me up?'

There are streaks of white in the braid-mountain but there's something in her eyes that seems too young to call her 'old'.

Ash takes one long arm and Harlon the other, and they pull her up and help her to a chair. The woman passes her hand over her face as if reminding herself of her own features.

'I am a little out of sorts,' she says. 'The death-watch beetles in my beams, you see, their voices when they hatch are…' she shakes her head '…quite overwhelming. They use their banging to call to each other. Insects do not think many things but what they think, they think very intensely.' She smiles apologetically. 'Sometimes their thoughts catch me unawares and I have no choice but to join in!'

Ash and Harlon exchange a glance; it is clear to them that what she's taking about is siardw. Although speaking so openly about this forbidden power makes Harlon nervous, it almost certainly means that there's not a threat from the Automators inside this little cabin.

'We could make you a cup of tea?' Ash offers. It's clear he is fascinated. He's never met another Listener apart from Xeno before.

'Thank you,' the woman says. 'My name is Mayo by the way, Mayo Mayer.'

Before Harlon can tell Ash to be cautious he's introduced them both. Mayo looks at each of them in turn.

'Welcome, Ash and Harlon,' she says. 'I am more glad to see you than I can say; human conversation is the best antidote to the beetles, I find. I am quite recovered! I think *I* should be making tea for *you*.'

Together Harlon, Ash and Mayo relight the fire, assemble cups and teapots. Mayo directs them to a store of honey underneath the bed; the reason for its unusual height, it turns out, is a hoard of jars, crocks and tins, all *full* of honey. Ash chooses a jar with dark honey, like a giant, amber bead. There is comfort and distraction in these homely tasks but the horror of Xeno's absence and Ma's fate howl just outside the door with the blizzard.

While the tea brews Mayo assembles salves and dressings for the cut on Ash's face. But she understands that Harlon wants to dress her brother's wound herself. Harlon cleans the

24

blood away and underneath it's just a scratch that doesn't need a dressing.

'There,' Harlon whispers, 'good as new.' She wants to kiss the hurt place, but Ash is too big for that stuff now. She turns away to drink the tea laced with honey that Mayo's poured for them.

'Honey is most restoring!' Mayo tells them. 'Honey helps and heals!'

Harlon wraps her fingers round the cup and sips. As the warmth and sweetness flood through her, Harlon's body sighs in gratitude. The honey is like nothing she's ever tasted before. It is the taste of summer and suddenly Harlon finds she is flooded with memories of Xeno running with her trail of finches through the flowery mountain meadows. Tears prick her eyes and Mayo sees them.

'Ah my dear!' she exclaims. 'Honey memories! They can be powerful. You have been reminded of a person you have lost?'

Lost? Harlon struggles to regain composure, to be strong for Ash. But this time, he is strong for her instead.

'My twin sister,' Ash explains, quite calmly. 'When we were caught in the avalanche, we lost touch with her. But she's very clever. She will be fine.'

Harlon stares at her brother. The panicked child wailing on the mountain has gone. He sounds so convinced, so calm. He leans close to her.

'She's alright, Harlon,' Ash tells her. 'I *know* it. She isn't dead, Ma neither, they're alive. I *feel* it in here!' He puts his hand on his chest and looks into her face. Harlon nods. She wants so hard to believe him, to believe Ma.

I will survive this.

Madame Mayo shakes her head at them in dismay.

'Oh my goodness. You poor children, it seems you've had quite a time of it.'

She looks keenly at them both, her eyes saying more than her words.

'I won't ask anything about your story that you don't want to tell. But I can guess why you were caught in an avalanche before dawn. You have nothing to fear here. I am a Listener and the Diacoch are no friends of mine. While the blizzard blows and while you are in my care, you are safe.'

She gets up.

'Now,' she says, businesslike and practical, 'if there's one thing I know, it's that young grubs need feeding.'

Mayo fetches jars of pickles from her cupboard and lines them up along the middle of the table. She has preserved every flower, leaf, fruit and seed that the mountain has to offer. The lantern light shines through their colours: greens and yellows, oranges and reds, like the seasons spiced and caught in glass. She cooks up sheets of flatbread on the stove and piles them on a plate. Mayo shows them how to roll the pickles and preserves inside the sheets of warm bread. With each one, they try new combinations from the rows of jars. And then they make dessert with rolled-up bread and honey. There are different kinds of that too; seasons, weathers, pastures all blossom in their mouths and run over their fingers. While they eat, Mayo's head glitters with the moving carpet of her insect friends. They come to the surface of her hair to take morsels of food from her fingers, then dive back down into her braids, like whales under the surface of the sea. They are nothing like the things that

26

usually infest human hair, more like living hair jewellery. Their movement clearly fascinates Ash.

At last, they're finished. Mayo sets Ash to do the washing up while she and Harlon make up two extra beds. As Mayo pulls blankets and pillows from cupboards, she speaks about her bees, their cleverness and bravery, how hard they work.

'They dance, you know, and sing, to tell each other where the flowers are. But it's more than that. It's joy. When a worker dances for her sisters there's a harmony through all the hive, it thrums with happiness. It can set my heart singing for days when I listen to their thoughts. The Automators will never, never understand that.'

Harlon finds her heart is racing, her hand frozen on the blanket she's unfolding.

'Is something wrong, Harlon?' Mayo asks.

Harlon shakes her head.

'It's just that I've never heard siardw talked about so easily. Our mother didn't like us to speak about it.'

Mayo looks at her keenly.

'But your brother is a Listener? Yes?'

Even here it seems a risk to say it aloud.

'How d'you know?'

Mayo shrugs.

'We can spot each other.'

'But how?' Harlon asks and as she does other questions push their way onto her tongue. 'I don't understand siardw; how can a brain inside a bony box connect with anything?'

It's a thought she's never said out loud before, not even to Ash or Xeno. But Mayo replies calmly.

'I wish I could explain to you, Harlon. But I've no idea how it works, all I know is that it *does*. I can only tell you that it feels like listening to a sound that's always there, but not everyone can hear.'

Harlon nods, remembering what Ma used to say.

'A song that holds all life together?'

'Yes!' says Mayo. 'That's it! Who told you that?'

'My ma,' Harlon begins. 'She taught me everything. And now…'

Harlon stops herself. She doesn't want to say the words out loud but Mayo says them for her.

'You don't know what's befallen her and you don't know what to do.' She sighs as if she's come to a decision long in the making. 'Perhaps I can help you. Sit down by me while I tell you a bit about me, and about you too, perhaps. But first, get that tin from the shelf above the bed. And fetch your brother over here.'

Harlon does as she's asked. She puts the worn, round cake tin into Mayo's hands and Ash joins them beside the fire.

'When I was young,' Mayo begins, 'insect Listeners like myself, and my dear father, rest his spirit, were in demand.'

Mayo starts to work at the lid off the tin. It is very stiff and she turns it round and round as she loosens the lid, telling a little more with each turn.

'Insect Listeners are rare, but very useful. You can go deeper into small minds safely, sometimes a little too deep, as you saw with me and the death-watch beetles today. But if you take great care you can do more than listen, you can *suggest and guide*.

'We made a living keeping locust swarms from fields of

maize, and making sure the peach trees all got pollinated. I had a small airship-transport, so we could travel far. Then the Automators came with their nonsense about "escaping nature's tyranny" and their machines and chemicals. We were outlawed. I kept my transport for a while. Made a living flying things to places roads didn't go. But then they outlawed that too and took all the airship-transports for themselves. When they killed my father I came up here with my bees and left my other family behind.'

Ash is transfixed. What must it be like for him, Harlon wonders, to hear his secret power talked about so openly, to hear about a time when it was valued, not feared?

'I was close to my brother's only son, Tui,' Mayo continues. He was a Listener too; horses were his gift. Another useful talent in the countryside, but both he and his employer had to keep it secret, and that was getting harder. He saw what was coming, the Automators' big tar-powered cultivators that would put horses out of work. So he enlisted in the navy: no horses on the sea to give him away. We kept in touch by letter, never long – we both had to take great care. When he was seventeen and home on leave, the Diacoch came to get him and his father. They killed my brother and Tui vanished.'

Finally the lid is off. Inside is a small notebook.

'For four whole years I heard nothing. I didn't know if Tui was alive or dead. Then this came…'

She hands the children the notebook. It is filled with beautiful little watercolours of all kinds of creatures. The first are familiar ones from the countryside of Rumyc, birds and flowers that Harlon and Ash can name, but the last pages are full of more exotic animals. Sea birds that Harlon's only seen in books, brightly coloured crabs and fishes in rainbow hues. The last page is a black and white tail, the fluke of a whale.

'He was a wonderful artist, I think,' Mayo says. 'He drew or painted every living thing he saw. Some of those were painted at the place where he grew up but the last ones perhaps in the place where this was taken.'

Mayo draws a photograph from the bottom of the box, pinned to the single sheet of a letter.

'This is the last letter that Tui wrote to me,' she says.

The handwriting is firm and clear, a rounded and generous hand, but hastily done, with a poor pen. Harlon reads it out.

Dearest Aunt,

I'm so sorry for the long silence. Forgive me. It's not safe for you or for me to tell you much, but know that I'm a father, of a little girl, and that I fight to protect my wife and my child, and to preserve the song that sings us all!

Greetings and love to you and your bees

T

The photograph is small, the size of Harlon's palm – it is a wonder in itself because the Automators have outlawed cameras too. They are the only ones allowed to have them.

They don't want witnesses to their wickedness is what Ma used to say.

For Harlon and Ash any photograph would be a piece of magic, like a fragment of the real world. But this photo turns out to be even more important. It shows a woman smiling, one long hand shielding her eyes from the sun, the other holding the hand of a small child. The background is out of focus, but it seems to be a beach and their bare feet are washed by a wave.

'Tui must have taken it, though I have no idea where they were. I know he kept his camera after the Automators made it against the law to have one. I think it's a good likeness.'

She's right. There are the intense, deep-set eyes, the quiet smile. He's captured them perfectly, even the ugly zigzag scar on her left cheek.

'It's Ma!' Ash says. 'Ma, all young. Is that you, Harlon?'

Mayo nods.

'Where are me and Xeno?'

'Not born yet,' says Mayo, 'but I think you are also in this photo. I believe your mother was pregnant with you when this was taken.'

Harlon clears her throat. It takes a moment to find her voice.

'Your nephew took this picture? So he was...'

'Your father. Yes, I'm sure of it. You are very like him. I saw it in you both at once. But I wasn't certain, until now.'

Harlon and Ash look at each other, searching in each other's faces for this father that they've never known. Harlon strokes the image with a finger. Why can't she remember this? Remember him?

'What does he mean about fighting and it not being safe to tell you anything?' Ash is lit up with this discovery of the father that he's longed for, thinks Harlon; he wants to hear that his pa was a hero.

'I think Tui and your ma were rebels. I think Tui vanished because they went to join the Green Thorn, the force who fought against the Automators.'

31

A rebel warrior! That's it! *That's* who Ma was in the time before. That's who she was in the house earlier.

'Where's our pa now?' Ash asks. 'Is he still where this photo was taken?'

Harlon knows what Ash wants. He wants Mayo to say yes, he's on an island, in the deepest part of the ocean. Then at least something would make sense and they'd have a real place to get to. But Mayo sighs and Harlon can see the news she will deliver won't be good. She takes Ash's hand.

'Not long after this letter arrived, having reached me through many secret hands, over several months, I saw your mother, quite by chance. I was in a village I don't often go to, selling honey at the market. There she was, buying supplies. You were with her, Harlon, and even in her winter coat I could see that she was pregnant. But Tui wasn't there, and she looked hunted and alone. Desperate. I wanted to help, but I guessed that she was on the run, that her survival depended on no one finding her. With my family connection to Tui I could only put her in danger. The Automators were very determined to kill every one of the Green Thorn rebels they could find.'

Mayo sighs and looks down at her hands

'I thought about her, about you, so many times. I thought about trying to find you, but I didn't know her name, her real name or any false one she might have used. I never knew you were so close. Just the other side of my own mountain.' When she meets Harlon's gaze her eyes are full of tears.

'But what happened to our pa?' Ash asks. 'Where is he now?'

'I'm not certain, but I guess something very bad happened, Ash. I never heard from him again. I think…'

She cannot finish so Harlon does it for her.

'...that he's dead.'

'You don't know that,' cries Ash. 'You can't be sure. Maybe he's still alive. Maybe we could find him...'

Ash crumbles. He's exhausted, a frightened child once again. Harlon guides him to the nest of blankets and pillows she and Mayo have made in the little loft space above the kitchen. In a few minutes he's asleep. Harlon lays her hand lightly on her brother's head; she hopes he will have a few hours of peace.

Mayo is sitting waiting for her, when Harlon returns to the fireside.

'I'm more sorry than I can say that I didn't have better news to give you,' Mayo says, 'and that in all this time I didn't come to find you all.'

'You did the right thing,' Harlon tells her. 'Ma was very careful. I always thought she was hiding Ash and Xeno, but she was hiding herself too for all those years on the mountain.'

Harlon gazes at the photo, at Ma's smile. How seldom Ma had smiled in the years that came after. She must have been afraid all the time. Afraid that they would come and find her.

'Yes, I think when the Diacoch came – which I assume is what drove you out into a blizzard – it was perhaps your mother as much as the twins that they were after.'

A thought occurs to Harlon.

'I suppose Breen Avvon wasn't her real name.'

Mayo shrugs.

'Perhaps not. I never knew her name,' Mayo says. 'Tui's photo is all I have of her.'

Harlon looks at the picture once again. Travel like ghosts,

Ma told them. Harlon can't help feeling that all these years they've been living with a ghost that called herself Breen Avvon. And now she's gone.

'I wish I remembered him,' Harlon says.

Mayo lays her hand lightly on Harlon's head.

'Oh, he's in there somewhere, I bet!'

Mayo smiles to wipe away some of the sadness.

'Where will you go, Harlon?' she asks. 'When you leave here?'

Harlon shakes her head. An island lost in the deepest ocean seems more like a dream than a destination.

'I don't know. The coast? It's probably safest if we leave Rumyc behind.'

'And your sister?' Mayo asks softly. Harlon feels her heart wring.

'If she's still buried, then she's gone,' she whispers. 'We can't wait here. I have to think of Ash.'

Mayo reaches for Harlon's hand and encloses it in her long fingers.

'If she finds her way to me, Harlon, I will keep her safe.'

'I know,' Harlon breathes. 'I know.'

Mayo releases Harlon's hand and gets up.

'You have had quite enough for today,' she says. 'Now you must rest.'

Harlon curls up round her brother. He used to creep into her bed when he was small. His familiar warmth is comforting and so is his conviction that Ma and Xeno are alive. She clings to it and falls asleep.

She dreams a familiar dream, of waves sighing on a sandy shore and her feet, very small, beside much bigger feet.

Somebody is singing in the dream. A man's voice. Her father's voice? Harlon has heard this song many times when she has dreamed this same dream. It's so familiar that it's a part of her.

I dreamed I saw my daughter dear,
Oceans, oceans away, so deep,
She came to me to sing her song
Ocean deep, away!

That song it rang the world around
Oceans, oceans away, so deep,
That song it rang the world around
Ocean deep away,
Ocean deep away.

Harlon looks up into Pa's face.

I won't forget you, Pa, she tells him, not this time and he smiles a sad smile and turns away to walk back into the sea.

2
Three Braids

Harlon

 When Harlon wakes, the dream slips through her mind's fingers, as it always does. By the time her eyes are open, all memory of it has gone, and Pa with it.

The pale light of a new day is seeping round the shutters. Harlon has slept through an afternoon and a whole night. Ash is still asleep but Mayo's up and loading food into an ancient rucksack.

'Blizzard's over,' said Mayo. 'I've got a rucksack ready if you need it. Food and blankets all packed.'

'Thanks, Aunt Mayo.'

'Hmm. Aunt. I like that. No one's called me that since Tui was a lad.'

She takes Harlon's hand.

'You don't have to leave. You can stay here if you like or I can take you somewhere. I want to help. I want to help fight the Automators. I can't just sit on my mountain any more. You know, I still have my little transport, hidden in the barn. She'd still fly…'

Harlon shakes her head.

'They'd shoot you down, Aunt Mayo, you know they would. Thanks, but I think it's safer to go on foot.'

Harlon leaves Ash to sleep and goes outside to clear her head a little. Everything is still. She loves this peace that always follows a mountain storm, the sense of life drawing in a long, slow breath. She breathes too and looks around. Familiar peaks seems to be in the wrong place. Somehow, with the avalanche and then the blizzard, they wandered much further than she thought. But it was probably a lucky mistake. They're further now from where any pursuers would expect to find them. Further from where Xeno would expect to find them, too. Is she wandering, looking? Or buried, already frozen into the heart of the mountains? Harlon takes another breath.

Focus on what you can change, not on what you can't.

Then, she hears it. The high, sweet tinkling of goldfinch voices. They are flying directly above her when one breaks away and flutters down. It lands on a fence post thirty paces away and looks straight at her. It is like every other goldfinch and yet not; it is more intense than any bird she's seen before. Purposeful. Somehow it makes her think of the Gula and its deep glance, and of Ma's mantra.

Assess. Think. Act.

The small bird looks as if that is exactly what it's doing. It flutters closer, hopping from post to post until it's right next to her. It drops three small strands onto the post right in front of her. It takes one last keen look at Harlon and flies off, leaving her to wonder why a bird would do this?

But the message the bird has delivered sweeps all those questions away. She stares at the three little threads in her hand. The first strand is hair, wayward and springy and even confined in this minute braid, unmistakably Xeno's. The second is another tiny plait: alpaca wool, spun by Ma, dyed deep blue, and knitted, untidily, into Xeno's favourite sweater. The one she always wears.

These aren't just random strands pulled by a bird from the body of a girl lying frozen on a hillside. They are carefully plaited. They are messages that Xeno has sent to say *I am alive!*

But the third strand carries the bad news. It's another carefully made braid but this time of the soft metal limunim, the stuff the Automators' flying transports are made of. This strand says that Xeno is a captive, already aboard an Automator craft, flying away in the sky. The thought of her in the Automators' power makes Harlon burn white hot. She knows at once that she must find wherever Xeno's been taken. Keeping her promise to head to the mysterious island will have to wait.

The morning sun is already melting the snow. It drips off the eaves of Mayo's cabin as Harlon climbs into Mayo's old and cranky lectric truck. It was a surprise to find that Mayo didn't have a horse and cart.

'I can't negotiate with anything bigger than a beetle,' is how she explained it.

'Ready, Nap?' Mayo says, and Harlon nods. A hasty haircut and a sacking tunic has made her into Mayo's nephew and apprentice, Nap, on his way to learn more about the honey trade in the capital. The more they use the name together, the more natural it will seem. Harlon rather likes the idea of trying out the life of a boy.

She has tried to make Ash stay behind. It will be hard to find and free Xeno, *and* keep him safe. But it was impossible

38

to persuade him, so now he's hidden in the back of the truck amongst the honey jars. If the Diacoch *are* still on their trail and they are stopped on the road they'll be looking for a girl and a boy, not an apprentice and his mentor. So Ash must stay hidden until they get to town. He too has had a makeover: his hair is the same gingerish hue as Mayo's, so if need be he can be another 'nephew', Satty.

The plan is that 'Nap' and 'Satty' will pick up a lift at the market to the transporter refuelling station at Ty Rhos, the bigger town a day's journey to the south. Mayo's heard that Listeners are held there for questioning before being taken on to Fidrac. What happens to them there, she doesn't know, but Mayo and Harlon have both seen the empty husks of Listeners returned from captivity. If Harlon can get there within two days, she may have a chance of catching up with Xeno.

And if she's not there?

One step at a time Harlon, one step at a time, Ma's voice says, but Harlon already knows she'll go the Automators' headquarters if she has to.

They bump down the track, through pools of mud and meltwater, stopping every hour or so to change the battery on the lectric and to take turns at driving. Mayo's little truck is even more rickety than Ma's old lectric. Harlon asks about Green Thorn.

'They were successful for a while. They blew up a tar station in the White Sea; set fire to Automator buildings and factories. Stood by villagers who tried to stop the smashing up of windmills and solar plants. But the Automators got too strong;

39

they killed every Green Thorn fighter they could, and then their leader just vanished.'

'Who *was* the Green Thorn leader?'

Mayo shakes her head.

'Boogam, the Ghost, they called their leader. But no one ever knew exactly who it was, man or woman.'

'Are there any Green Thorn still left?'

'A few, I think, but very few. I've heard nothing of them for a decade. Only Listeners stand against the Diacoch now, and what can *we* do when they steal us away in the night?'

The road descends from the high mountains. Down here it's closer to real spring, and snow survives only in the coldest spots. As they near the town, the fields grow wider where the hedgerows have been grubbed up to make room for the giant tar-powered machines that Automators send to cultivate the land.

'They spray these fields with poison now,' Mayo says, 'to kill the insects. This land once rang with insect voices but now it's quieter every year.'

On the outskirts of the town there are solars and windmills still standing, but there are new billboards by the road that suggest they may not survive for long.

Wind power? Solar? Why wait for the weather when you can use Black Gold?

Escape the tyranny of nature! one reads: one of the Automators' favourite slogans.

Sick of winter work outdoors? Start a new life in the city! And, *Eat meat every meal for health and strength.*

The Automators are tightening their hold, even here, so far

from the capital. The town will be more dangerous than they thought.

The last billboard shouts a chilling slogan.

Suspect a Listener? Speak out!

Mayo laughs grimly as they pass it.

'They want to cut the world to fit their shape and fill their pockets. They don't want humans listening to any voices but their own.'

New streetlights jitter on and off along the slushy streets as they reach the town. Harlon is nervous under her disguise and glad that Mayo's called her Nap all day long. They pull into a potholed yard behind the pub where Mayo says she always stays. Mayo nods toward the open back door and the saloon bar beyond, where a woman in a tall red hat is pulling pints.

'She has a sour face and doesn't do much trade,' Mayo says, 'but that suits us well.'

Mayo backs the lectric to the stable door, so Ash can climb out into the shadows and stay safely hidden. They unload the spent batteries and put them on to charge. The last still has some go in it and they leave it connected, *just in case*, Mayo says.

Two horses whicker softly in the hay-smelling dark as they scent Ash in his hiding place between the bales.

'Don't move from that spot,' Harlon tells him. 'I'll bring some food out later if I can.'

As Mayo and Harlon cross the courtyard towards the back door of the bar, Mayo staggers. Harlon takes her arm to keep her upright. Mayo's face is bleak. Horrified.

41

'What is it? Is it the beetles again?'

Mayo shakes her head.

'No. It's the silence. I've heard quiet in the fields where poison's been sprayed before, but never this nothingness.'

Mayo is distressed; it takes a moment for her to gain control of her breathing.

'There are many insects here, in the barn and the old buildings,' she says. 'Cockroaches, earwigs, beetles and their grubs in the wood. There is a chorus of their thoughts and voices that I can always hear in the background of my mind, but now it is silent! Like falling into a pit.'

She shakes her head as if to dislodge something from her mind. Then pastes a smile across her fear and pats Harlon's arm.

'I'm probably just getting old. And hungry. Lets go in.'

Harlon's stomach answers with a growl and they step inside.

'Remember now, *Nap*,' her aunt whispers, 'don't speak unless you have to.'

The place is small; there are just three tables, jammed against the wall opposite. There is a yellow light over the bar, guttering candles on the tables and elsewhere, brown shadows. Two old men curl over their glasses as if deep in conversation with the ale. The front door, with a glass panel, opens to the market place beyond, where people are busy preparing by lantern light for the trading that will start at dawn.

The landlady gives the smallest nod of recognition as Mayo and Harlon take a seat at a dark table. Harlon, remembering Ma's training, takes the seat with its back to the wall, facing out into the room with a clear view of both doors. Something about this place is already making her feel twitchy.

42

Mayo orders drinks and food and, a few minutes later, the landlady brings a loaded tray, her red hat swaying as she moves. She bangs two glasses and two full bowls down on the table and clatters out a pair of spoons.

'Eight jars of honey, for you and the boy, dinner and bed,' she demands.

Mayo puffs out her cheeks but she doesn't argue.

'I'll put the honey in the barn,' she says and picks up her spoon.

More customers come in: old farmers who hunch mumbling over their pints. Then the unmistakeable flash of black and red insignia and two Automators step through the door, one fat, one skinny.

'Diacoch!' Harlon breathes.

'Keep calm,' Mayo whispers. 'Eat, don't attract attention.'

But that is easier said than done. The food in Harlon's bowl is an unrecognisable mass of brown lumps that tastes of misery. Harlon can force it down because she's very hungry but Mayo is having more trouble. She pecks at her food with her spoon, but can't seem to swallow.

Behind the bar, the landlady folds her arms and nods, drawing the Automators' attention to Mayo's reaction to her food. The skinny one removes the uniform black mask to reveal a spiteful scowl pinned to a vague, female face.

'Something wrong with your dinner, old woman?' the skinny one shouts.

Mayo stares down at her bowl, tries to eat a bigger spoonful but gags and coughs. The Automators step across the room at once, as if this was a sign they'd waited for. They grab her by her shoulders and haul her from her chair.

43

'Can't stomach the food of a *real* human, eh?' the short one gloats, his rasping voice coming through the mask that he still wears.

'A filthy Listener that's what we have here, I think!' he says.

'Maybe two?' the skinny one says, grinning at Harlon.

Their eyes have a dead look to them and Mayo hangs limp their grasp. She mouths a single word to Harlon.

RUN!

Without warning Mayo's body tenses in a huge, convulsive wriggle of such energy that the Automators are taken by surprise and loose their grip. She leaps up onto the bar with the grace and energy of a teenager, as thousands of insects stream out of the tangle of her hair. For a moment her head is lost in a rippling glitter of iridescent beetle backs and cut-glass wasp wings. They fly around the Automators, biting and stinging. The old farmers yell and rush outside. There is chaos. No one is looking Harlon's way as she slips out through the back door.

She darts into the barn.

'Ash! Ash, we have to go.'

He pops up from the bales, and beside him is the Gula!

'What's that doing here?'

'Not a *that*. A *she*.'

'Why did you bring her?'

'I didn't. She just came.'

There's no time for explanations. They jump into Mayo's lectric truck and hurtle into the night: a girl, a boy, a Gula and a year's supply of the best honey on earth.

Harlon takes a small road heading south towards Ty Rhos. It's full of potholes. The lectric lurches and the Gula stinks and

44

Harlon feels she might throw up. The Gula looks at Harlon with unblinking black eyes and twitching nose, then turns away and looks at Ash, as if they truly are in conversation.

'Are you *talking* to each other?' Harlon asks.

'No!' Ash cries. Then, 'Yes. Sort of. She's kind of in my head.'

'*She's* in *your* head? Isn't that the wrong way round?'

'Let's not talk about it now,' Ash says. He leans out through the window.

'No one following,' he says. 'The road's all dark.'

Harlon relaxes a little. Maybe Mayo's still keeping the Automators distracted and off their trail.

'The Gula says you ate sheep. Yuk!' Ash says. 'She can smell it on you.'

'*That's* what that bowl of lumps was!' Harlon fights the green wave of nausea that rises in her. She should have guessed. She remembers the billboards with pictures of roasted bits of body on. 'Meat,' the Automators called it, hiding the idea of dead flesh behind a word. Most humans south of the White Sea hadn't eaten flesh in three centuries.

'Maybe flesh eating is a test, another way to spot a Listener,' Harlon suggests. 'Mayo gagged on it and that's when those thugs pounced.'

Ash shakes his head.

'Poor Mayo! What will they do with her?'

Harlon thinks it's likely they may beat her badly, even kill her, but that's another thing she doesn't want to say to Ash.

'She might get away. Or they might take her to the same place they've taken Xeno, I guess. That's where I have to go.'

'*We* have to go,' Ash corrects her. He seems to have grown

45

up a lot in just a day. Still she wishes that she'd made him stay safe at Mayo's. She has no intention of allowing him to come with her to the Automator holding station at Ty Rhos now.

A loud bleeping interrupts her thoughts and a red light flashes on the dashboard, showing that the battery will soon run out. At the same moment they are caught in a blinding beam of light, shining down from above: the searchlight of an Automator transport, an airship floating above them. A booming voice shakes the windows.

'Stop at once! Get out of the veekle by order of the Head of Intelligence.'

Assess.

The road behind is still dark, so this must be the only pursuit. On either side the land is flat, no sudden drops.

Think.

Ash must not be taken. They will find out he is a Listener and she knows what that can lead to. Ash *will not* be taken. They don't know he's here, it's only Mayo's 'nephew' that they're after. So they can have Nap and maybe they will lead her right to Xeno. Maybe Xeno, Ma *and* Mayo are in the skyship right above them now!

Act.

Harlon kills the lights and hits the accelerator. She judges that the veekle has enough charge for one last spurt. She shoots them out of the transporter beam. If she can outrun them for a moment that will be enough. She swirls the wheel, jinks the lectric off the road, smashing Ash and the Gula against the passenger door. Ash's startled face is lit with the green glow from the dashboard.

'Head west, Ash. To the coast like Ma said. Find that island,' she tells him, then presses the button to open the door. Ash and the Gula tumble out into the dark. She swings back and onto the road, flicks on the lights and races the approaching beam, getting it as far away from Ash as possible before the battery finally runs out and the transport catches up with her.

The skyship beam is blinding.

'Get out with your arms raised. Do not carry a weapon or we will destroy you.'

Harlon feels bleak and afraid, but somewhere, somehow she *will* bring her family back together.

The space inside the transport is smaller and scruffier than Harlon expected. Most of its huge silver egg shape is gas, of course, held inside that limunim skin, with just a small oval hold for passengers and 'cargo'. Cargo is what she is, shoved inside a cage next to a small porthole, where wisps of cloud shoot by. There's no light, but as her eyes accustom to the dark she sees boxes and boxes of tinned food, cases of rifle bullets and two other cages with the humped shapes of captives inside: one small, one large. Xeno and Mayo?

'Xeno?' she calls out softly. 'Mayo?' But there's no reply. She tries again, a little louder this time, and one of the humps responds.

'Shut your mouth, you idiot. D'you want to get us all beaten?'

The other hump whimpers and then curses.

Wherever Mayo and Xeno are, it isn't here. Harlon feels her heart fall through the bottom of her stomach. She was so sure they would be here, that this would be the key to rescuing her sister, but all she's done is break her family apart even more!

She thinks of Ash. What brought the Gula to his side? Harlon cannot guess but she hopes the creature will keep her brother safe. Oh Ash, so much for protecting him and Xeno. She's failed so badly! And Mayo, has she already suffered the same fate as other members of her family, beaten to death by Automator thugs? Can Automators simply beat a person to death in a bar without any kind of consequence? Perhaps. There's so much that she doesn't know, that Ma didn't teach her up there in their little mountain bubble.

Harlon's hands are cuffed behind her back and the cage is too small even to kneel. She lies uncomfortably on her side. She'll never sleep like this! And then she does.

Morning sun streams through the porthole. They're heading south all right but they've gone too far. The journey to the holding station would be just an hour or two at most. They've been in the air for eight or more. Every moment on this transport is carrying her further and further from Xeno. Further from Ash.

Suddenly the whole idea of 'rescuing' Xeno seems ridiculous. She's been running blind since the moment they left Ma behind. Everything is hopeless.

What can she do now?

A metal door opens in the end wall and an Automator comes in, masked and armed. A girl judging by the build, tall but quite slight. She's an ensin. The lowest rank, recruited at gun point, was what Ma said about them. Ensins were the dogsbodies who didn't even get trained in fighting. But this one clearly wants to look like something that she isn't.

'Privy time for you, Listener scum,' she growls. Only the slightest waver in her voice gives her anxiousness away.

I *do* need the privy, Harlon thinks, and I'm thirsty too, but I don't suppose there'll be anything to drink or eat.

She sits up and remembers too late that's not possible. She hits her head on the cage roof and the ensin smirks. She pulls her cudgel from her belt with a swagger and holds it ready.

'You first.' The girl's toughness is almost convincing but it cheers Harlon to think that she could take the ensin's weapon in about two seconds. Harlon replies quietly and keeps her eyes low.

Don't reveal that you are a threat. Perceived weakness can be a weapon.

Another of Ma's favourite lessons.

The girl unlocks the cage, and Harlon allows herself to be pushed towards the far end of the hold. She can see now that the humps in the two other cages are a woman with ragged black hair, and a boy about Ash's size. They've both been beaten. The woman's eyes are closed; the boy is very still. Harlon thinks he isn't breathing.

The privy is just a trap door in the corner of the floor. Above it on the wall, Harlon notices, are two parachute packs. Harlon wonders how they work and if she could wriggle through the trap door with one. Certainly not while she is handcuffed.

'You have to undo my cuffs,' she tells the ensin. 'I can't go through my clothes.'

The ensin covers her nervousness with a scowl but undoes the cuffs. Harlon rubs her wrists. She wants to keep the girl thinking she's a boy, Mayo's innocent Nap, so she starts to open her trousers and says.

'Don't I get any privacy?'

The girl blushes, the colour of it reaches the little space between her mask and her helmet.

'I've seen it all before, boy, just get on with it,' she says but turns her back all the same. Harlon lifts the trap door and squats. Warm air rushes up through the hole. Below is a forest stretching in every direction. This is the Southern Forest that she has read about but never thought she would see. What's an Automator transport doing here? There are no cities in this part of Rumyc and nothing further south but the free port of Angellis where Automators don't yet have much power. What do they want down here?

Harlon finishes, and the ensin turns to face her, smirking behind her mask.

'You just shat on some of your little mates,' she says. Harlon keeps her face blank, with no anger and no question in it, but the girl goes on and this time her ferocity isn't faked.

'Down there,' she says, 'there's a load of you lot. But not for long. We're going to put an end to all of it. The forest, the Listeners and the rebels. We're...'

But she doesn't get the chance to finish her explanation because the transporter lurches suddenly and drops, smashing the two of them and the cages against the wall. The cage doors buckle and fly open and the woman and the boy roll out onto the floor. Harlon springs towards the parachutes. Through the trap door Harlon sees the craft has dropped much closer to the treetops. A vast flock of birds of all sizes and colours is rising up around the craft, gleaming like fragments of rainbow.

Their cries surround the ship as they start to peck and claw at its thin silver skin, through which little eyes of blue sky begin to appear.

The ensin seems to think that there's some point to putting the prisoners back into the broken cages. She tries to hit Harlon with her cudgel. Harlon wrenches it from her and shoves her to the floor. Then she pulls the parachutes from their hooks. They are easier to understand than she thought. She throws one to the woman.

'Put it on and hold the boy,' she tells her.

She shrugs her way into the other. Just in time. The compartment begins to break apart. For a split second the woman, the boy, Harlon and the ensin seem frozen in the air as the floor beneath them peels away. The ensin is very close, her helmet and her mask stripped off by the rushing air, her eyes filled with terror. She's not an Automator anymore, just a kid, alone and frightened. Like Ash. Before Harlon even knows she's done it, she's grabbed the girl and slipped the harness round both of them. In less time than a heartbeat, the ship is merely wreckage and they are falling through the tattered ribbons of its silver skin to the green canopy below.

The Gula Speaks

Trail is all things
Nose, eye, ear, skin, all attend it, deep.
Paw, hold the ground
pull running from the body,
Claw hold the ground
pull climbing from the body,
with no rest, no cease,
to follow it.
On rock, ice, thorn, root, mud, blood.
In dark, blaze, freeze, dry.
The trail gives hunger, food
The trail gives thirst, drink
The trail gives loss, finding
The trail asks
The trail gives
The trail is and is and is.

Fear is on *this* trail, also.
Dark is on *this* trail, also.
Alone is on *this* trail.
Pain is on *this* trail.
Sorrow also.
Breaking on *this* trail and blood.
Unmaking maybe on *this* trail.
Ending maybe on *this* trail and death
I see it

I smell it
I hear it
I know it.

No other Gula on this trail
Human cub is on this trail
Cub *is* this trail
I follow this trail that is this cub.
It shines with stink and bright-dark;
It calls in the night
It bites deep in bone.
It beats in the heart
this trail, this trail of all things, all things, all things
this trail sings against
no smell
no sight
no sound
no touch
this trail is life against unlife
this trail is and is and is
all and all and all
while I still live
I follow, follow, follow,
to an end where everything begins again.

3
Run with the Gula

Ash

Inside Ash's head the Gula is talking.

Cub, she says. *Cub!*

It's what she calls him.

Run, Cub, run!

Neither 'cub' nor 'run' are really words, the way the Gula uses them. Run is more like the rhythm that her paws make as she lopes between the trees. It beats inside him, helps to keep him going, along the valley side, away from the mountains.

They head west, the way Harlon told them. The way Ma said. Towards the sea. But the choice of direction is the Gula's and Ash tries not to think about the island that isn't on a map or the promise he made to get there. It doesn't sound real. He doesn't think of anything much. Not Xeno or Harlon. Certainly not Ma.

He just follows the Gula. Follows what she calls 'the trail'. She showed it to him in his mind, a thread as fine as spider silk that leads them on. It glows. Not just with light, but with everything, touch, sound, smell. It sings with life, with purpose. Now, sometimes, Ash can feel it singing as they run. He doesn't understand why it seems important, but it does. And anyway, he can't think of anything else he can do.

The way Ash hears the Gula isn't the way he's used his siardw to listen in to other creatures' thoughts before. It's not eavesdropping. He isn't doing the listening; she's doing the talking. She *wants* to speak. She's in his head, not the other way around, but while she's there he can sort of talk back to her.

It's a new feeling. Before, being a Listener has felt like being a spy. Sneaking in amongst the thoughts, in dark and silence. Sometimes not really understanding what you hear, sometimes not even really hearing. Ash was almost glad as his ability diminished as he grew older, glad it was just his friends the alpacas that he listened to, and then only to try and make their lives more comfortable.

But the Gula *shows* her thoughts, or what she smells or sees. She digs around in his brain to find things she can use to speak to him. She finds words and chews on them like bones, to get their meaning, spits them out in a sort of raspy wheeze that Ash hears inside his mind.

Sister gone, the Gula told him when he saw the transport airship leave, although it was too dark and too far to tell if they had lifted Harlon or left her in the lectric.

Smell it, the Gula said.

Ash ran to the abandoned veekle anyway, because he wanted the Gula to be wrong. But she wasn't wrong. He sat in the dark in the truck and cried then. He didn't feel tough or clever anymore, the way he'd felt hiding behind the honey jars with the Gula. He just wished with all his heart he had stayed in Mayo's cabin like Harlon had wanted.

The Gula had pushed a jar of honey towards him.

Eat, new sun, maybe nothing.

She was slurping her way through jar after jar. He guessed

'eat today in case you can't eat tomorrow' was pretty central to the Gula's thinking. Ash felt too sad to eat, too lost and too confused. Ma's words about the island and destruction of their home blew around his head and made no more sense than flying snowflakes. He did force down a handful of Mayo's dried fruit and nuts and felt a bit calmer.

The back seat of the lectric would have been a good place to sleep, but they could hear other veekles moving around on the roads leading from the town. It didn't feel safe to stay.

Go, the Gula said. *Go, get safe.*

So Ash picked up Mayo's pack. The Gula held it with her teeth and growled.

Slow, she said. *Heavy, heavy,* and tugged the pack in time with the growly words inside his head.

Ash pointed to the blankets and tried to speak to the Gula in his head. Using words the way *she* did felt awkward, like trying to draw with a blindfold and thick gloves, the pencil in your wrong hand.

No fur, cold, he managed. He rattled the remaining tin of nuts.

Food.

The Gula snorted.

Eat now! she said.

Belly full, no run, Ash told her. He pulled at the pack and at last she let go with a disapproving *snufff.* She barged out of his head the way she'd barged in. In spite of everything being so terrible, his home and family lost, Ash smiled: who would have guessed that you could argue with a Gula? It made him feel a bit braver.

Snow has turned to sleet and freezing rain as they head along the valley side between the trees. Nothing stops the Gula. She lopes along in front of Ash just close enough so he can see her dark shape against the forest floor. Just far enough to keep him running. They have run for hours. Ash didn't know that he could run for so long. The Gula's paw beat has taken up the empty space that the last days have left inside him, driving any other thoughts away.

When light shows between the treetops they stop. Gulas are night animals so Ash will have to be nocturnal too.

She nips into his head again to say, *Eat,* and then she's gone. She scrabbles in the rocks beside the little stream that they just crossed, and drags something long, long dead out of a hole. She chews on skin and crunches bones. The smell is beyond disgusting. Ash tips Mayo's dried berries straight into his mouth. He eats the whole tin. Harlon would lecture him about rationing. But he's a Gula now. He uses the tin to scoop up water, making sure it's upstream from where she found her meal. Harlon would approve of that.

The Gula wriggles into a big pile of fallen branches.

Sleep, hide.

Ash follows, dragging the pack in after him. Inside, the pine needles make a dry bed, but a prickly one, so he pulls Mayo's blanket from the pack. An envelope is tucked inside it. The letter from Pa to Mayo with the photo of Ma and Harlon on the back. Mayo must have slipped it in the pack. He doesn't look at it but puts it inside his shirt, right next to his heart and closes his eyes.

He tries to think in a straight line about all that's happened, trying to make it all add up, but his thoughts keep jumping about. If Xeno was here, the half of himself that's missing, thinking would be easier.

Xeno. Thinking of her hurts. Not thinking of her hurts. It is somehow his fault that she's been taken, because he never told Ma about the starling thing that happened, the day before the Automators came...

They'd been about to snowboard down a favourite slope, him and Xeno. She was up ahead, chirping at him to hurry up.

'Make snow sing!' she called. 'Snow sing loop sky-blue!'

It was the kind of thing she always said before a descent. For Xeno everything sang. As she waited and he struggled through powder towards her, a starling had dropped out of the sky. It landed on a rock right close by. Ash wondered what a lone starling was doing up here? Where was its flock? It wasn't unusual for Xeno's siardw to attract a bird's attention, so one would swoop down to take a look. Mostly, once they'd checked it out, they'd fly off. But this was different. Xeno and the bird were too still, as if they were frozen.

As Ash got closer he could see the starling was more like a thing than a bird. Its beak looked as if it was made of metal and its head was bald. Xeno screamed at the bird, 'No!' then picked up her board and swiped at it. It took off and wheeled into the sky.

'What was *that?*' Ash asked, as he reached her. She said nothing, just picked up her board.

'Are you alright?' Ash insisted. 'What happened?' Still she didn't answer, so Ash caught her by the arm. She shook herself free and glared at him, but he could see she was afraid, very very afraid. The sight of her fear was so shocking that Ash had stepped back, as if he'd been slapped. Xeno jumped on her board and raced away. She didn't wait for him and beat him to the bottom by minutes. She *never* did that. When they got in, she went straight up to her room and shut the door.

He knew that there was something not right in it all. But Ma was always telling Xeno to be careful about using her siardw.

'Don't talk to strangers!' she would say, half joking. 'Humans or birds.'

That starling had certainly been strange and he didn't want to get Xeno into trouble. But now he wishes he *had* told because the next night the Automators came and he was sure the starling had something to do with it.

If only there were someone here to answer questions. To tell him what he should do. Is it right to just trot after the Gula? Or should he try to find his sisters? Or head home; maybe Ma is waiting. Waiting in the ashes. Yeah, Ash, yeah.

He stares at the sleeping Gula. How can she spend so long inside his head, whole hours sometimes? If he spent more than minutes inside Alba's head he'd feel weird, like a dislocated toe standing straight up, the way a toe should never, ever be, wrong. Is the Gula feeling like a dislocated toe? Everything is wrong: lonely, broken, horrible. He wants it to stop; he wants to wind back time, to go home, to…

Cub. The Gula's eyes snap open and she pops up, back inside his head.

Cub. This is trail. Gula trail, Cub trail.

We follow.

See, this trail?

The glowing line shimmers to life in his heart again, winding off to the west, toward a setting sun.

Follow, only follow.

Follow is enough now.

For some reason the Gula's trail makes Ma's lullaby rise up in his chest. Is he singing it or is it singing him?

Follow, only follow.

Follow trail is all for now, the Gula says.

Sleep sleep. It's like a paw covering his eyes. *Sleep, Cub, sleep.*

The Gula puts her snout into his face to wake him up. Her eyes are like beads of glass shining in her face.

Wake, go now, Cub, she says. Ash stows the blanket in the pack and wriggles outside after her. It's not raining or snowing and the sun is sinking between the trees.

He stretches, lifts the pack onto his shoulders. Immediately the Gula's in his head. She has a picture to show him. It is of himself running with the backpack jog-jog-jogging on his back. It looks ridiculous. She shows it again. And then again. And now she starts to make a noise with her outside voice, and sort of coughing: *chuck chuck chuck, chuck chuck chuck.*

She's laughing. The Gula is laughing at how he looks carrying Mayo's crazy old pack! He's so astonished that he does something he didn't know he could do; he shows her a picture in his head. It is the Gula chewing on that stinky *thing* she pulled out of the hole, the sound is very, very loud: crunching, slurping, sucking.

The *chuck, chuck chuck* sound gets faster and faster, and then

Ash is laughing too, until his belly aches. So you can argue with a Gula *and* tell jokes!

She is right about the pack. It rubs his shoulder and slows them down. The blanket is pretty wet now and the food's almost gone. He puts on the jacket Harlon left behind – Ma's old one, the one that's too big – and leaves everything else. The Gula approves.

Cub fast, she says and Ash sprints off ahead of her.

Gula slow, slow, slow, he says.

This is the right thing, Ash thinks. Just head west is what Harlon said and that's what he's doing. That's the trail and it's enough.

They run on and on, loping between the trees, under a frosty sky. They rest somewhere near midnight on the edge of a clearing, where the Gula has found an old deer carcass. Ash has one handful of nuts left. Shooting stars fall between the dark branches and owls call. Ash catches the fearful shiver of a mouse's thoughts. Strange, he hasn't been able to do that since he was small. Being with the Gula is making his siardw stronger, sort of waking it up, as if a part of him has been asleep for ages.

They set off again and once again the rhythm of running takes over. It's already getting easier. Still, he'll be glad of the rest that dawn will bring.

But at first light the Gula doesn't stop.

Run, Cub, run is still beating and keeping Ash's feet pounding on, even though he is more tired and hungry than he knew a person could be.

61

And then quite suddenly the paw-rhythm stops.

HEAR! The Gula says.

All quiet, no birds, no nothing.

Ash listens. She's right. Yesterday the treetops were awash with the bird songs of early springtime, but here, there is silence. Ash reaches out with his siardw. It's not like the beacon of his sister's power but still he should pick up something; there are squirrels here, little red ones with tufts on their ears, and beech martens – the Gula's cousins – hunting them. And mice of several kinds. In every part of the forest they've passed through Ash has picked up faint echoes of their nervous scurrying thoughts: little snatches of life, tastes of nuts and new shoots, the warmth of the inside of nests, the joy of branch scrambling.

Here there is nothing. Nothing at all. And as they walk on they discover the reason.

The forest ends abruptly in a tree graveyard. All around, the bodies of great noble trees lie toppled on each other. Ash has seen trees destroyed by wind and avalanche, trees whose branches have been harvested for wood, but never a whole tree killed. Never a whole forest destroyed.

The first huge trunk Ash comes to is almost twice as broad as he is tall. It has been brutally severed by sawing. Ash lays his hand on the old tree's rough skin and shuts his eyes. He's glad it's only early spring and the tree will have been more than half asleep when this was done to it. But still he can tell it has suffered, is still suffering. So are the trees around it. Their distress prickles underneath his feet through the web of roots and fungi that connect them. Ash has never felt anything from trees before, but this feeling is so strong, it makes him want to cry out.

The Gula is horrified too. She stands in the wreckage of the tree, looking at him, sniffing the air. For the first time, Ash can see that she's afraid; she doesn't know what to do. He wants to tell her *let's go, leave this dark place*, but she has left his head and he has no idea how to get into hers. So he starts to move, and, to his relief, the Gula follows.

But the silence only gets worse. They reach the edge of a slope, recently thickly forested and now a mangle of felled trunks and ruined branches. Below them smoke fills the valley and now the sound of distant human shouts and screams drift up with the smell of burning and breaks the horrible quiet.

The Gula barges into Ash's head. *Closer, closer?*

She's said it twice before he realises it's a question. She's never asked him anything before.

Closer, he agrees. They both want to find out the reason for this carnage.

Danger! the Gula warns. *Stealth, stalk, hide.*

Together, they move down the valley though the maze of trunks and branches. The Gula seems to flow between, under and over the wreckage of dying trees. Ash creeps low, sometimes even dropping to his belly. He's good at this. It's one of the drills that Ma and Harlon set that he enjoyed. There is a small pulse of approval from the Gula. There, Ash thinks, you didn't know I could do that!

Just before the felled trees run out and give way to meadows and small ploughed fields, they stop and peer over the trunk of a young beech. Now they can see what's going on. Between the curtains of smoke that the breeze shifts, there is a village. It's a bit like the places where Ma and Harlon went to trade their wool. Ash knows all about those because he often stowed away without his sister or Ma knowing, and took a quiet look around.

But this village isn't really a village anymore; it's just a bonfire, set alight by Automators. The black and red figures of the Diacoch move amongst the buildings, making sure the fire spreads to every one. The school and the healing house are already blazing, and now the roof of the meeting house is lit. The windmills have been toppled and the solars have been smashed. The uniforms move slowly. They don't need to hurry; no one is going to get in their way because the people have already been rounded up.

At first Ash thinks it's a trick of the smoke. Or that he's so tired and hungry that he's seeing things. But the Gula's low growl inside his head confirms it's real.

The terrified villagers – parents, children, old people – are being herded from their village by *giant dogs*. Not just big dogs like the mastiffs some mountain people use to protect their flocks from wolves. These are twice that size. Almost as tall as a man, with huge muscled shoulders and heavy heads. They are a sickly white, with thin, stubby tails that hang down like rope. They make no sound, just grimace silently to show their gleaming metal teeth.

The Gula sniffs the air.

No smell, no sound, unlife.

Both Ash and the Gula are so caught up in the horror of it

all that they don't sense the Automators that have crept behind them. The Gula's warning, *Run, Cub! RUN!* is too late. A whip cracks and its leather tentacle is round Ash's ankle, pulling him over the roots and rocks to the black boots of the two Automator officers. They are fighting ranks, with the ivory fist badge on their collars. To get that you have to have a talent for brutality. One of them, a skinny man, grabs Ash by the hair and pulls him to his feet.

'Look what we caught!' he cries.

In panic, Ash looks around. If they catch the Gula they'll kill her. But she's disappeared, melted into the shadows. All that's left of her is a thought reaching out to him.

Cub, it says.

CUB!

Ash is tied and bundled under the arm of the larger officer who smells much worse than the Gula. There's no point struggling. He can't escape so it's best not to draw any attention to himself. They mustn't find out that he's a Listener.

They walk through the cordon of dogs. Up close they are even more mechanical. They don't react to their Automator handlers, except to move and let them pass. Their eyes are black, like holes, and don't reflect any light. Ash picks up nothing, not the slightest pulse of life from them. But something is controlling them, some one. In the middle of their line are two small figures in Automator uniforms with a different badge, not the fist but the bared teeth of a red dog. There are unmasked so Ash can clearly see their faces. One of them is a child, as dead eyed as the dogs, a girl, with a large L branded into her forehead. She says nothing but she watches every move the dogs make. The other, a young woman, speaks quietly into the child's ear, and every time she does, a moment later, the dogs react. The Listener child controls the dog; the woman controls the Listener. This is what happens to Listeners who are taken by the Automators: they are turned into tools of the Automators! Will that be Xeno's fate? Ash cannot bear the thought of it.

Ash is dumped just the other side of the rank of dogs and he scuttles away like a crab, in fear and horror. He mingles with the crowd of crying, distraught villagers who are too frightened and upset to pay him any mind.

Ash glances up towards the hillside. He knows he won't see the Gula, perhaps he might feel her? But there's nothing. Just that 'less than silence' feeling. How would she rescue him anyway? It's hopeless.

The dogs, under the control of their two minders, pace back and forth, herding the people down the middle of the valley. Behind the dogs, a crowd of Automators, all fighting ranks, are swaggering and barking orders. They're done with their burning and smashing now. They walk on, their rifles slung over their shoulders. Ash is very afraid that this will end in all the people being felled like the trees. He can imagine such a terrible thing quite easily now.

Then Ash sees where they're being taken: two skyships, transports, squat where the valley flattens out, tethered to the ground by ropes. *Harlon*, Ash thinks. Harlon? Maybe Xeno too and Mayo, even Ma. They would be captives but together.

Ash looks at the big black numbers on their sides. One has

a four and a six the other, a line of three twos. What were the numbers on the transport that took Harlon? It was dark but the craft's own lights shone up the side: 2, 1, 7. Ash can close his eyes and see them still. Neither of these transports has Harlon in it.

There are more Automators at the entrance to the transport holds. They have stripes on their arms, capos, the highest rank of fighters. Ash has seen them on village streets, pulling Listener children from the arms of screaming mothers. They enjoy their jobs. There are higher ranks Ma once told him, controllers and commanders, but they sit in warm offices behind desks and don't get blood on their hands.

They are sorting villagers into adults and children. They take the children and if the parents resist they beat the children, or threaten to throw them to the grinning dogs. It works quite well. Even though the Automators' faces are mostly covered, Ash can see that they find the screaming and the crying simply boring, they've done this many times.

Ash can't escape. A line of dogs and other Automators form a barrier of eyes and teeth and weapons. But he is so overloaded with the shock and horror of it that he wriggles his way a little to one side, just so he can have a moment away from what's happening.

Now he's standing very close to two Automators, ensins, who do all the other dirty jobs: mending engines, loading cargo, washing floors. One is older, judging by his belly and the wrinkles round his eyes; the other is just a kid, maybe Harlon's age. He is skinny and nervous-looking. He fiddles with the ropes that anchor the smaller of the transports. He too is trying to avoid what's happening. They're talking quietly, but Ash is close enough to hear.

'Did you hear about transport two one seven?' the old one says.

The boy immediately looks alarmed.

'Did you say two one seven?'

The old one is gruff and impatient.

'You deaf as well as useless? Yeah, *two one seven.*'

The old man says the numbers very slowly. Neither the boy nor Ash can mistake this number now.

'My sister's ensin on two one seven.'

It has never occurred to Ash that Automators might have sisters. Ash holds himself very still and quiet as the boy asks.

'What happened to it?'

The fat man looks down. He can't look the boy in the eye now.

'Caught fire over the Woken Forest,' he tells the boy. 'Went down with all hands. No survivors.'

The boy just stares. Ash sees tears filling his eyes, just like the ones that are filling his own. The fat ensin looks over his shoulder, at the higher-ranking Automators busy sorting villagers.

'Pull yourself together,' he hisses. 'If the capos to see you blubbing like a baby we'll both catch it. Look on the bright side. It went down with all the Listener scum they caught up in the mountains.'

Ash feels like his heart has stopped. He hardly notices as he is shoved into the hold, with dozens of other wailing children, packed into wooden crates ten at a time, like cargo, like *things.*

The number on the side of the transport that took Harlon throbs in Ash's head. Xeno and Ma were probably in there too, and Mayo.

All the Listener scum they caught in the mountains.

He doesn't feel that they are dead, but maybe that's how it is; people feel alive to you even though they're not. Until Mayo said that Tui had been killed, Pa had felt alive to Ash, even though he'd never seen him or even heard his name.

So, now they're *all* dead. All his family.

The cargo hold is closed, shutting in the darkness and the crying. Ash feels the transport leave the ground. He's never flown before. It's what Xeno always wanted, to fly. That's why she wanted to be a bird. Somewhere far below is the Gula. But the trail is broken; he can't see its golden thread. Everything is lost. Unlife has swallowed him.

The Elephant Speaks

These are words.
They are not my way. Our way.
But I have learned to use them.
I learned this over long times.
They are small and go in one direction.
Many things I live will not fit in them.
But they are all that humans have. And so I use them.

It is raining.
The wetness falling. Dripping from the leaves. Making secret
pathways to the river.
Water has its own thoughts, no being may oppose.
Water tells its thoughts to every wrinkle of my skin.
And my skin is very great and very wrinkled.
My skin hears the thoughts that travel in veins of trees, my
sisters,
My skin hears the thoughts that water brought down from
the clouds;
These thoughts have travelled from the far-off blue.
The blue that is Great Grandmother of all the land, and in
her live her swimming children.
I will never see them, the tiny ones more in number than the
leaves
or the great ones, bigger even than my kind
but the clouds bring to me the echo of their singing
thoughts and being.

Through the rain I know them.
Through the rain I know many things.

Through the air I know many things also.
The speaking of the plant people
Asking for help
Offering reward
Sending warnings and alarms.
Their scents are strands that twist and blow inside my trunk.

Through my feet I know things also.
The crackling in the long fingers of the mushroom people
that reach into all things alive and dead.
Their meanings are deep, deep and old,
sometimes hidden, always bigger than the sky
with ends and edges beyond my understanding.

There are little pebbles underneath my feet also.
Sweet with smooth roundness,
small with age and history, yet tender, like baby-things.
They tremble with the deep business of the rocks
the long crush and grind that has made them
and the slow dance at the hot melted heart of the world.
They tell news that runs long back in time, and forward also.
This I feel and know.

In all things there are voices.
The raindrops in the river
The ocean into cloud
The leaves fallen on the forest floor

The sand made rock and sand again.
The blood, the bone, the muscle and the skin
The wood, the sap, the petal and the seed
The mushroom veins that lace together life and death.
Connected one to another in
a long singing, singing, singing;
that holds all life as one.

Without the life there is no singing;
without the singing, there is no life.

Yet now there comes a dead silence.
It spreads and spreads;
It has been brought by some of human kind.
It creeps in every place,
into earth and water:
silence in the rock and wood and bone,
silence in the bodies and the minds.
Silence that undoes all singing
Silence that can undo all life.

All my kin, sisters, daughters, have been taken by that
silence.
Taken in blood and burning and death.
Made more than dead.
Made nothing.
Ended.
Empty. Gone. Silent.

Their low voices do not shiver through my feet, sing in my
tusks, roll in my belly.
We do not say *move to new water*
We do not say *find the best fruits*
We do not say *rejoice a calf is born*
We do not say *these are the tusks of one who was living*
We do not talk in the touch of trunks
We do not speak in the stink of musth
We do not sing
We cannot sing
We *are* not *we*
We are not we.

I is all that remains.
Only I.
But without we, what is I?
Without we what can I be?
Where is the song for me?

I have wandered broken, half alive.
In that long pain and brokenness
I found another kind of we to be.
A new kind.
A we that has never been in the whole of life's long story
A we made of *different kinds of kin.*
A we with four legs, six legs, eight legs, two legs,
A we with wings,
A we with roots and leaves and branches.
A we with words.

73

Every day I build this new we;
I put my thoughts inside new minds and feel the strange fizz
of other livings,
to make a song strong enough to sing through the silence.

I put my thoughts also inside humans.
Sometimes in fear
for there are shadows there.
Still I go,
for humans minds brought forth the silence and the
nothingness,
in human minds the singing must begin again.
In human minds the change must begin.

Can I make these minds kin to me,
and kin to all?
This is what I try:
to make a new we of all beings;
to make a new singing of all life together.
One kin, one song!
If not, the silence will take all things,
life will be unmade, undone to nothingness and
never-ending quiet.

Although I am afraid.
Although you are full of words and shadows,
I sing
I sing
I sing.

4
The Woken Forest

Harlon

Sound returns to Harlon out of a long, long darkness. Trills, plinks, buzzes, hums, booms and hoots. Many different rhythms that twine and overlap and separate again. It reminds her of the music Ma liked to listen to on the radio.

Symphony, that was the word for it.

Beneath these sounds is something else.

It is a sound, but a sound so low that her body feels it like her own heart beating. It grows louder. Rumbles, growls. It resists the pull of the dark silence that wants her back. It rolls her up and lifts her to where the trills and plinks run in endless twirls and twists in the air.

Harlon opens her eyes.

A dim green light blooms around her, and around a huge shape that looms above her. From the middle of the shape an eye looks out, surrounded by ridges and wrinkles and a tangled fringe of eyelashes. It is tawny gold with seams of chestnut, rimmed with the blue of dawn. She tries to sit up, but pain shoots through her body. Something presses on her chest with a force both gentle and utterly irresistible, keeping her still. Harlon reaches her right hand to find out what this thing is and touches skin as rough and ridged as the deep ruts in a muddy winter track.

It is a trunk! An elephant's trunk!

Even though she has only seen them in books, she knows that the creature looking at her, holding her down, is an elephant!

The rumble that is too low to be heard runs through her once again. It is coming from the elephant, vibrating through her body, echoing through her mind. Suddenly she sees herself as if she were looking down from the height of the elephant's eye. She is lying on a floor of beaten earth, with great trees all around. Even from up here, she can smell herself, a very bad smell of mortal fear and grief. Harlon never knew before that emotions had a scent. And she can tell, somehow, what is going on under her skin, all the battering and bruising that doesn't show from the outside. She watches her own head turn and gasps to see that part of her scalp is burned, the hair is ash and the skin has blistered.

A rush of pain and panic overwhelms her and she finds she is once more looking up into that tawny eye in its landscape of crinkled skin. The rumbling, soft as dust, deep as oceans, calms her racing heart. It begins to take on a texture, a rhythm. Yes, there's a pattern in it.

It's a song! A song she hears through her joints and the soles of her feet, a song that sings away the pain and takes her on a journey, down, down into the deepest layers of her senses and her perception, using an old, old part of her brain. She moves through the million smells of the different trees, the sepia, ochre, umber scents of their trunks, the complex green cocktail smells of their leaves, the perfume of their flowers, ravishingly beautiful. Everything sings layers of meaning that Harlon can sense, but that will not fit into any part of her mind that uses words. Even the dark soil is singing, millions of tiny coiled stories that twine and curl and dive to make a vast library. She can feel the touch of fungi everywhere; their soft persuasive communication runs under, through and over everything, binding, uniting, ancient and solemn. The song sings touch and smell, those comforts that lie at the roots of her being. Harlon feels safer and more alive than she has felt since before she was born. Warm and dark and also somehow flooded with the purest light. It is a wonder!

She sleeps and sleeps, for a long, long time.

Voices. Human voices. Speaking Standard but with two different accents. Harlon keeps her eyes shut and pays attention.

'They must have been in the transport that the birds brought down.'

An older woman's voice with a strange accent.

'Madame Mavulu you can't believe that!' This voice is younger, a girl not much older than Harlon herself. 'We cannot *know* that the birds attacked the transport. They just happened to be there when it crashed.'

'Cavan, this forest is *my* forest, my home, and I tell you it is fighting back!'

Harlon can hear that this is an old argument, a good-natured tug of war that neither side expects to win. The younger voice sighs.

'If they came down with that transport, how did they survive? How have they stayed alive for four days in the forest?'

There is definite defiance in the younger woman's voice. There's a little more edge to this part of the argument, it seems.

'You know how, Cavan,' the older voice responds sharply. 'You said yourself that Enkalamba's footsteps were all around the hut when you arrived this morning and found them. She has healed them and cared for them. So they won't need much more of your time. Check this one over, and put her in the recovery tent with the other. There's plenty of other work to do.'

The older voice is heavy with authority now, squashing the opposition.

'Yes, Madame Mavulu,' says the younger one, Cavan. 'I'll finish here as quickly as I can.'

'And try to find out who they both are. I don't think Enkalamba would have brought them this far if they were Automators but we can't be too careful.'

There's a rustling, a bead curtain being pushed aside, and Harlon senses she's alone with the girl, Cavan. She opens her eyes just enough to see her surroundings.

Harlon is inside a round hut, on a sort of low bed. Slivers of bright sun slice through the gaps in the thatch and sunlight gushes through the bead-curtained door. The air is soft, humid and warm, full of the scent of growing. Birds call close by and, at a distance, human voices are talking urgently and hurrying feet slap on soft ground.

The girl is at her side. She's dressed in an ancient T-shirt and shorts that have been patched a hundred times. She's sturdy and strong, with long dreadlocks bound up with a cloth. Her face is broad and open, with huge dark eyes.

'Ah, you're awake,' she says, and puts a cup to Harlon's lips.

Harlon never knew drinking took so much energy. But after two cups of water she feels much better, like a plant that's recovered after wilting.

'Do you remember what happened to you?' Cavan asks.

'I'm not sure. But I'm not an Automator, or a spy,' Harlon says, groggily.

'Ah, you were awake. Apologies. We are under attack and we must be cautious.' The girl looks at Harlon keenly. 'So, tell me who you are, and how you got here.'

That is quite a question. Harlon finds she hasn't got an easy answer. She thinks hard. An avalanche? Ah, *the* avalanche! Xeno. Ash. The Gula. Mayo with her cloud of insects. Ma's words; the island, and the promise; the falcons. It all comes back at once, like being punched.

'I'm Harlon. I was taken in a transport by Automators,' is all the reply she can manage before her racing heart and shallow breathing take all her attention.

'It's alright,' Cavan says. 'Lie still while I check you over.'

Cavan's touch is gentle but precise and expert. She examines Harlon from toe to top and only pauses when she reaches her head.

'When did you burn your head? It's nasty, but it's healing well. Has it been treated?'

Harlon knows about that burn. She's seen it for herself, looking down from far above. How can that be?

'I don't know. Maybe when the transport crashed. There was fire, I think.'

'What else do you remember?'

What else does she remember? Harlon tries to remember more about the crash. There were birds, she thinks, but perhaps not? A woman and a boy! Yes. And then her mind recoils at the image of their bodies, no more than tattered ribbons caught in the branches. Their parachute was faulty, but ours... *Ours?* Yes, now she remembers.

'I shared a parachute, with a girl,' she says.

Cavan whispers. 'With an Automator?'

Harlon thinks, then nods.

'You are an Automator also?' Cavan's voice is suddenly sharp.

'No, I told you. I was taken by them.'

'Then why did you share your parachute with one of them?'

This questions irritates Harlon and the anger clears her mind of fog. She pushes herself to her elbows.

'She was very young and very afraid. I couldn't leave her to die.'

Cavan puts a hand on Harlon's arm.

'It's alright, I believe you. Lie down, please.' Gently she presses Harlon back onto the pallet.

'I found you together outside this door,' Cavan adds. 'Mavulu would not like it, but I am a healer not a judge. You are a Listener then?'

'No, they thought I was. But I was looking for my sister...'

Once again Harlon finds it hard to breath.

'Alright, no more questions,' Cavan says, 'but I will tell you what I know. Enkalamba brought you both here, and for Mavulu at least that counts for a great deal.'

'Who is Enkalamba?' Harlon asks.

'You don't remember?'

'All I remember is a dream about an elephant.'

'That was no dream,' says Cavan. 'That was Enkalamba. She is the last elephant in this forest.'

Somewhere deep inside Harlon the elephant's voice echoes faintly, calming her heart, her breath, clearing her mind.

'She took care of me?' Harlon asks.

Cavan shrugs.

'Mavulu says that Enkalamba protects the forest, and helps all others who protect it. I think that's superstitious nonsense. But that burn on your head has had a healer's touch and though I can't see why or how an elephant would do that, she did bring both of you here, four days after the transport went down. Alone in this forest, injured as you are, you would not have survived.'

But I was not alone in the forest, Harlon thinks, not at all alone.

'Where is here?' Harlon asks. 'I know I'm in the Southern Forest, but where?'

'Of course,' Cavan sighs, 'you don't know where you are. You are close to the eastern edge of the Southern Forest or the Woken Forest, Mavulu would say, in a Green Thorn camp.'

'Green Thorn?' Harlon interrupts. 'But I thought the Automators put an end to them years ago.'

'That's the story that they spread for sure,' Cavan replies. 'But the rebellion has never stopped and now the need to fight is greater than ever. A few miles from here our fighters are making one last attempt to stop the Automators from cutting down the forest with their great machines, their Monsters. We hide here under the trees so they can't find us. But the odds are not in our favour. They have many more fighters and more powerful weapons. I'm sorry to tell you, but you were probably safer in that transport!'

Mavulu calls from outside, 'Cavan! Cavan!'

81

'Coming!' she calls back. She points to a pile of ragged garments on a box.

'I saved your boots, but your other clothes did not survive. There are clothes for you and for the other girl here. I burned her uniform. It seemed the safest thing to do. Few here would shelter an Automator, no matter how injured or how young. But I'm not sure any Automator can be trusted. Watch her for me? She's in the recovery tent just next door. When you feel ready, you can go in there to rest. It should be quiet in camp – for a while at least.'

With that, she's gone.

The effort of remembering the crash has been exhausting. Harlon lies still and listens for the deep rumbling voice that seems to have left its imprint on her bones. It's there inside her; it makes her feel a little stronger. Cavan is right. The frightened little ensin should be watched. Harlon dresses slowly. Cavan has left two pairs of ragged combat pants with string to hold them up, and two huge T-shirts. Her boots are worn and singed, but still like old friends. Outside the door of the hut, she can see she's in a little settlement, hastily put together but well ordered. There are portable solars up on poles to catch the sun that slants between the trees. There's a mess tent with pots and pans and other tents and shacks set up between the trunks of huge trees. People hurry around carrying trays of medical gear, bandages and bedding. They are a mixture drawn, Harlon guesses, from all over Rumyc, perhaps even further. A few are especially small, dark and neat, with close-cropped hair; she tries not to stare at these, the Forest People that Ma's books said had died out long ago. All

82

are dressed, like her, in worn-out T-shirts, patched trousers and carefully preserved boots, held together with tape, glue and string. In the branches above, a large flock of small green parrots chatters and purple crows strut about on the ground looking for scraps. It seems so peaceful that it's hard to imagine this place is about fighting.

Walking takes much more effort than she expected, so Harlon's glad to find the recovery tent. She ducks through an open flap and steps inside. It has windows covered in fine green net that lets the air flow through, so the space is pleasantly cool. As her eyes accustom themselves to the dimness, she notices the low pallet beds that run in two rows on either side. In one, at the very far end of the hut, a human shape lies curled.

Without the stiff uniform and the pretence of aggression, the ensin looks small and very young. Perhaps not that much older than Ash and Xeno, Harlon thinks. She winces as she calls to mind their names. It hurts even to think of them, how she has failed to protect them. What will she do now? She has no idea.

Focus on what you can change not what you can't.

Harlon sighs. Right now her ma's advice seems pale and thin. But it's all she has, so she steers her mind away from Ash and Xeno and crouches down to look into the face of the unconscious ensin. It is scratched and bruised just as Harlon's is, but she is not burned. She seems oddly peaceful and her breathing is deep and even. It reminds Harlon of how very, very tired she is herself. She lies down on the pallet next to the ensin and soon she too is deeply asleep.

Harlon goes to the same place she always goes in her dreams and which she never quite remembers when she wakes. But this time the elephant's deep singing has left every cell of her brain and body vibrating, like the shiver of a great bell that lasts far beyond the chiming. So the dream is brighter and unfolds further than before.

She is looking up into her father's face. Tui's face. He has an untidy beard and tangled hair. He looks afraid. He's carrying her. She wants to speak to him and tell him not to worry but she can't because she's very small and very sick. She can feel the fever racing through her tiny body like a madman, burning her to the bone. Beyond Tui's face, little clouds dance along the horizon and the mast of the boat moves steadily through the sky.

Harlon feels the rise and fall of the water underneath them grow deeper and longer. Tui holds her closer, then holds her out, away from him and puts her down onto something smooth and wet and living. A whale's back! She knows this. She has seen whales in this sea before. On the whale's back she is carried away, so now she sees Tui far off on the boat staring after her.

The whale rolls in the water, very slowly, and she rolls too until she is under water, gently held beneath its vast flipper. She can feel the way the whale is using only a fraction of its strength, so as not to crush her. She's not afraid, even though now she has to hold her breath. Above is blue, below is blue, around her are other whales. She sees their grooved tummies and knobbled heads, their long white flippers like oars, and eyes like the starry sky.

hur-whoop, hur-whoop, hur-whoop

Their voices sweep from low to high and dive again to deep rumbling rolls.

They are telling her a story, about where the oceans came from, about whales who once swam between the stars.

Swirling, roiling, growling, popping, louder and louder.

They are telling her about their song and about its power.

A power to make the whole world ring.

A power to make the whole world shake.

A power to make the whole world break

and make again anew.

A power bigger than the whole night sky and smaller than a grain of sand.

It sets her shivering, vibrating in every nerve and bone and muscle until she shivers free and swims up, up to where Tui's arms are waiting to pull her up into the light and air. The stalking heat of fever's gone; she's wiped clean, made strong. But the power of the whale's song is inside her now. For when she'll need it again one day.

Tui holds her up and looks into her face, smiling. He doesn't say her name or speak because, Harlon understands, her pa has become a whale.

The bright trails of her dream slip away to nothing and Harlon's eyes open. She sits up. She's slept for hours. It's dark and a lantern lights the recovery tent with a yellowy glow. The ensin is dressed in the trousers and T-shirt Harlon left her. She's sitting cross-legged on her pallet, and scowls at Harlon. The ensin is about to say something but she's interrupted as Cavan's face appears around the flap of the tent door.

'You're awake, good. If you two are feeling strong enough,' she says, 'we could do with help.'

Harlon nods. The pain and tiredness that she felt before have gone and she would like to be busy. Ma trained her with some basic field medicine; she knows she can be useful.

'We'll be there in five minutes,' she replies.

Cavan drops the flap and hurries off.

'*We* won't!' says the ensin. '*I'm* not helping any filthy rebels.'

The girl's snarl seems half-hearted, but all the same it's irritating. By saving her, Harlon now realises, she has made herself responsible not only for the girl's safety but for her behaviour. As if the situation wasn't bad enough! It doesn't make her feel kind towards the girl. Harlon swings her legs out of the bed and reaches for her boots.

'The *filthy rebels* saved your life,' she snaps. 'That girl you just saw? She's Cavan, the *healer* who tended to you. She burned your uniform so nobody but her and me know what you are.'

The girl's eyes drop, but her voice is still angry and resentful.

'Why'd she do that?'

Harlon wonders if kindness is something this girl has never met before.

'Because she's a healer,' Harlon explains wearily. 'And if she hadn't then you'd probably be dead.'

The girl chews her fingers. The bristle of bravado drops a little. She doesn't meet Harlon's eyes.

'Why did you ... share your parachute?' she asks.

Looking at this grumpy, sullen girl Harlon asks herself, well, why *did* she? When the Automators have almost certainly killed her ma, stolen her sister, and seem intent on ruining the world, why *did* she save one of them? Harlon sighs.

'Because I couldn't do anything else.'

'That doesn't make any sense.'

'Well, it's all the sense you're going to get.' Harlon tells her. 'Now get ready because I want you where I can see you. And if you don't make yourself useful, I won't keep quiet about who you are.'

Harlon pulls on her boots and stands.

'You aren't a boy!' the ensin says crossly, as if this is the final insult.

'Well observed,' Harlon replies, 'and *you* aren't an ensin while you're here, so you'd better give me a name I can call you.'

The girl looks up and for now the scowl has gone. She's just a frightened kid again.

'Tollara Flix is my full name,' she says, 'but Tolly, that's what people *used* to call me.'

It is a long night. From the moment she and Tolly step from the recovery tent the camp is enveloped in a storm of furious activity. Stretcher-bearers run in constantly with the wounded, carried through the forest from the fighting at the Bai, the clearing in the forest where the Automators have landed their transports. Mavulu and two other doctors work on the most seriously injured. They stitch together broken bodies, save limbs where they can and, where they can't, make neat amputations.

Cavan leads a team of healers like herself who deal with the less serious injuries, stemming bleeding, dressing wounds and tending to those in the recovery tent. Two large stretcher-bearers, Budly and Tink, relentlessly cheerful young men, lug the wounded from tent to tent. Harlon and Tolly do everything else, tearing strips of cloth to make bandages, boiling water to sterilise instruments, stewing up medicinal herbs as painkillers, antiseptic and anaesthetic, ferrying tea from the kitchen to keep the exhausted doctors and healers awake and working.

Harlon had feared that Tolly would be as useless as a sulking child. But although more and more Harlon is convinced that the girl is very young, Tolly surprises her. She doesn't talk much, she certainly doesn't smile, but she's hardworking and capable. Like Harlon, she doesn't need to be told what to do. She sees a job and does it. After an hour or two, they are working well as a team. But Tolly is clearly upset by some of the injuries, and more than once Harlon sees her turn away to breathe down a wave of nausea at the sight of something especially bloody. It doesn't stop her though. There is clearly real grit somewhere inside this narrow, pale little person.

Although Ma taught Harlon basic first aid and 'field medicine' – how to stitch wounds and treat breaks and burns – Harlon has never seen real injuries like the ones she's seen this night. But unlike Tolly she doesn't have a moment's squeamishness. The blood and pain don't touch her. She's tough. She's numb.

The flow of casualties waxes and wanes, but never quite stops, all through the night and into the following day. The hours are so long, so full of work and struggle that they seem like days; the doctors, healers and stretcher-bearers begin to feel like people who have been in Harlon's life for years. Tolly is a kind of comrade even though they hardly speak but only work. The camp feels like a sort of home and she is aware that even though the work is sad and bloody, it is full of purpose. In some strange way Harlon is enjoying being part of it all.

The wounded who can speak bring news about what's happening at the Bai. At first things go well for Green Thorn. During the night they completely destroy one of the huge tree-felling machines, that they call Monsters. But at daybreak the Automators retaliate with full force and pursue one group of rebels into the forest. For most of the next day they are able to turn that to their advantage and while the Automators chase one group, another attacks the remaining Monster. The reports of how this has turned out grow hazy as some of the most seriously injured wounded come from this point in the struggle, and there's simply too much to deal with every second to think of anything else. But as darkness falls again it becomes clear that some kind of great reverse has occurred and that, at least for now, the Automators have been driven back decisively. But it's only towards the end of this second night that the nature of the change in rebel fortunes becomes clear.

There is a lull in the stream of casualties and Harlon and Tolly are handing out tea and flatbread to the doctors and healers. A skinny man, a boy really, talks as he is having his leg wound stitched.

'The last lot of explosives we put on the Monster didn't go off. Must've been the rain, I reckon,' he says. 'So we had to leg it. By then the Automators were close. They could have just picked us off. They got me, sure, but then they just stopped firing. Couldn't really see what was happening but it looked like they were all running, running back to the transports. Couldn't understand why. Then Tench says look, points at the ground; it's covered in army ants. Like a *carpet*. Took no notice of us. Then we saw the mosquitoes, caught in the torch beams. So many, like smoke, they were. They swarmed round the Automators. Other things too: moths and beetles and I dunno what. Ignored us completely, just went to the enemy, sent 'em screaming.'

He shakes his head, smiling in delight in spite of the pain and blood loss.

'It's really happening isn't it, Doc? What they always said about the forest, it's true.' He beams at Mavulu who smiles back through the grey of her exhaustion.

'Who knows,' she smiles. 'Perhaps.'

'No perhaps about it! Is not called the Woken Forest for nothing. All the Listeners in my unit say so and *they* should know.'

'Enough talking now, young man,' says Mavulu. 'These two will help you find a place to rest.'

Tolly and Harlon get either side of the boy who, although skinny, is much taller than either of them. His arms droop across their shoulders. He's already drifting off with the pain-killing draught he's been given.

'It's happenin',' he mumbles to himself, 's'really happening!'

'What's happening?' Harlon asks.

'The forest. S'fighting back, *all on its own*. It's like it knows who its enemies are.'

Tolly's face in the lamplight is fearful.

'Shuddup. A forest can't *know* anything. It's just trees,' she hisses. 'Keep walking, alright?'

They put the boy in a makeshift bed on the floor of the recovery hut and hand him into Cavan's care.

'Thank you for all your work,' she says, and tries to catch Tolly's eye, 'both of you. I think we'll have some peace for now. Maybe for quite a while. Go and sleep! Should be some spare hammocks next to the mess tent.'

Harlon and Tolly, almost asleep on their feet, feeling their own cuts and bruises now for the first time in hours, totter past the mess tent to the open-sided tent beyond where hammocks are slung like so many moth cocoons. Snores are already coming from most of them where healers are snatching rest while they can. Right at the end of the hut, only just under the protection of the roof, are two unoccupied hammocks, hanging very close together. Now that the work has stopped, Harlon can feel the awkwardness between them once more. She wishes that the hammocks were not touching like this but she's too tired to try to do anything about it. So there are a few self-conscious minutes while she and Tolly move round each other, trying to get into the hammocks while having the least physical contact with each other. At last it's done and Harlon sinks back and shuts her eyes. But Tolly is very close; only the thin fabric of their hammocks separates their two bodies, and Tolly is a wriggler.

When Tolly has changed position for the fifth time, Harlon loses patience.

'Just keep still,' she whispers fiercely.

'There's a hole in my hammock,' Tolly complains. Their heads are so close together that they can almost whisper into each other's ears.

'Just lie still and go to sleep,' Harlon hisses.

'Alright!' Tolly snarls back.

For a moment Tolly manages to be still and Harlon thinks she might finally get some rest.

Then the girl wriggles in her hammock *again*. This is ridiculous, Harlon thinks, she's practically sharing a hammock with an Automator, who actually helped to put her in a cage! It's almost funny.

'Tolly! For goodness sake, lie still.'

'You sound just like my brother,' Tolly breathes.

Of course, thinks Harlon, Automators have family too. Are Automator families like hers? In fact are *any* families like hers? She has no idea; all she's ever known is Ma and Ash and Xeno and their isolated life on the mountaintop.

'Where's your brother now?' Harlon whispers.

'Dunno.' Harlon can feel Tolly shrug and she drops her voice very low. 'He's, you know, in the *same business* as me.'

'Oh. What about your parents?'

'Dead.'

'How?'

Tolly holds very still. Harlon understands. She wouldn't want to talk about her family right now either.

'I'm sorry. You don't need to talk about it,' she says, but Tolly replies all the same.

'It was a fire. In the veekle factory where they worked. They said it was Green Thorn that started it. We got chucked out of our apartment after that. So it was the streets or … join up, not much choice.'

Is that what's kept the Automators going? Green Thorn killing the mothers and fathers of kids like this?

92

'What will you do now?' Harlon whispers.

'Don't have much choice, do I? Stuck with you lot now, aren't I? My brother probably thinks I'm dead. I might never see them again.'

Harlon can't think of anything to say to this, because she's in the same situation and she doesn't know what to do either.

It feels as if she's only just got to sleep when sunlight wakes her, slanting through the trees. Harlon swings out of the hammock straight into her boots. It's still early and the air is cool but all the other hammocks are empty. A jolt of fear runs through Harlon; where is Tolly, what might she have done? But as she hurries through to the mess tent she sees her, sitting alone at the far end of the long table where a few medics and healers are sitting in a huddle. Harlon grabs two mugs of tea offered by the cooks and slides onto the bench next to her.

Tolly takes the mug Harlon hands her and wraps her fingers round its warmth.

'Thanks,' she says. She tips her head towards the people at the table's end. 'I've been listening to what they say,' she reports. 'The Automators have retreated; the transports left the Bai at first light. So I'm stuck here.'

'I'm stuck too,' Harlon admits.

'But these Green Thorn are your lot!'

Harlon shakes her head.

'There isn't really a "my lot". I'm just here by accident. Same as you.'

Tolly frowns; Harlon can see she wants to ask more but Cavan comes into the tent and sits beside them.

'You've heard about the Automator transports, I guess?' she speaks softly. 'Good news for us. I think we have a few days before they'll come back to the Bai and repair their machines and mount a new attack. We need to move to a new location before then. But we need medicines for the wounded and more dried food before we can do that. Our friends outside the forest have arranged a delivery to the hills in the north. It's not so far but everyone here is too busy with the wounded, so Mavulu wants to send you two to get it.'

Cavan's face is tense. She looks like she hasn't slept at all. She leans in closer to make their conversation more private.

'Look, I know this isn't great for you. You're both still injured. It's not great for us, you know, having to rely on *someone like you*, Tolly. But...' she spreads her hands '...there aren't any choices. We need this delivery.'

Harlon looks at Cavan.

'What do you mean by a *delivery*? Dropped from the air?'

Cavan nods.

'Two nights from now. It'll take you that long to get there. Mavulu will explain.'

Tolly too leans in and whispers.

'What about the forest animals. Don't they attack, I mean, *people like me*?'

'You won't be alone,' Cavan smiles. 'You'll have a guide who knows the forest really well. And as for the animals attacking: you don't want to believe all the silly stories about "the forest fighting back". It's superstitious nonsense.'

Tolly shakes her head. A hardness comes into Cavan's eye.

'It's only a matter of time before people here find out about you, Tolly. Someone will ask you where you got your Automator boots, or you'll make some slip that gives you away. And if they suspect Tolly, they'll suspect you too, Harlon. This will prove whose side you're on.'

'What if I don't want to help you?' Tolly says.

Cavan's face grows grimmer.

'We need help and I don't have any choice but to ask for it. But you don't have any choices either. Do this and what you do after you get back, that's your business.'

Cavan gets up.

'Mavulu's tent is the blue one at the north end. Finish your breakfast and get yourselves there.'

They watch her stride off through the camp. Secretly Harlon thinks Cavan's toughness is a sham. It just shows how tired and desperate she is. Probably. But her words have set the wheels of Harlon's mind whirling for the first time in days.

Assess.

If the Automator forces come back to the Bai as Cavan thinks, Tolly will return to them. The Automators probably don't know exactly which ensins were on the transport that crashed.

Think.

With Tolly's help, Harlon could get accepted as an ensin and get on board the transport. That might get her to the capital. If Automator HQ is where captured Listeners are taken then that's where she has to go to find Xeno. It's the longest long shot, but it's all she has.

Getting Tolly to agree will be tricky. But the journey through the forest will give Harlon time to work on her. She's pretty sure Tolly doesn't have an Automator's heart.

Act.

'You know Cavan's right, we don't have much choice.'

Tolly sets her mouth in a determined line.

'I'll do it. But if *my lot* come back to the Bai afterwards,' she whispers, 'I'm off.'

Harlon nods. Well, that's at least one part of her plan in place.

Breakfast is grey stretchy goop that they agree can only be called food because they are so very hungry. It doesn't take long to eat and with no gear to get together the girls are soon on their way to Mavulu's tent. People greet them kindly, thanking them for helping during the night.

'If they knew who I was,' Tolly whispers, 'they wouldn't be so nice.'

'Just smile,' Harlon says. 'Whatever you were *thinking* last night you still helped save people's lives.'

'*Rebels'* lives.'

Tolly grumbles, but her grumpiness seems false to Harlon.

'People, Tolly,' she tells her. 'Just people, same as you.'

Mavulu's tent is at the edge of the clearing where camp gives way to forest. She's standing outside, at a table made of cardboard crates, giving her healers their tasks for the day. Somehow her small stature makes her personality seem even bigger and more powerful. Surely, Harlon thinks, she must be exhausted and yet she is infusing all the people who surround her makeshift desk with energy and resolve. At last the morning briefing is complete and Mavulu steps forward to greet them.

'Thank you for agreeing to do this,' she says. Tolly scowls and Harlon is ready to kick her if she starts to say that she didnt 'agree'. Mavulu continues: 'Let me show you where you'll be going.'

She spreads a rumpled sheet of paper over the cardboard desk. The camp is marked by a red circle at the bottom end. A wavy line or two show streams leading across the blank space that is, Harlon supposes, the forest. Towards the top of the paper is a row of bumps. It really isn't much of a map.

'These are the Bird Hills,' says Mavulu pointing to the bumps. 'There are seven of them. The tallest, the one in the middle, has a good flat top, grassy and free of trees. This is the drop zone. You'll need to be there by tomorrow night and make a signal fire to bring them in. Then carry the delivery back here.'

'What will be making the delivery?' Harlon asks. 'I thought only Automators had transports?'

'That's something I can't tell you,' said Mavulu. 'Our friends outside use whatever means they can. All I can tell you, is that you will know it when you see it!'

'How far do we have to go?'

'The distance to travel is not great. Perhaps fifteen or sixteen miles but the trails are hard to follow and the forest is very dense. That's why you'll have a guide. Ah, and here she is.'

A deep rumble that seems to rise from their own feet is the only sound that the 'guide' has made as she approached. It seems impossible for so large a creature, but the elephant has come out of the forest and crossed the clearing to the tent without a sound. She stands now right in front of the three humans, very close, very large, her vast body a whole landscape in itself. Her ears flap gently and her trunk reaches out past the girls to where Mavulu extends her arm. Trunk and arm entwine for a moment and Mavulu closes her eyes.

There is a stillness which makes Harlon want to hold her breath, and she can see that Tolly feels it too.

'It wasn't a dream,' Tolly breathes. 'I thought it was a dream.'

'No, it really wasn't,' Harlon whispers. 'None of it.'

Mavulu untwines her arm and smiles, a real smile that Harlon hasn't seen her give before.

'This is Enkalamba,' she says. 'But I think you two already know her.'

The elephant rumbles again and inspects each of the girls in turn with the end of her trunk. She starts at Tolly's feet, taking great in-breaths over her boots, skimming the girl's slight body and face, then resting a hand's length of trunk end on Tolly's head. It takes moments but leaves Tolly looking confused and dazed, as if she's just woken up.

And then it's Harlon's turn. At the touch of the trunk, almost as gentle and delicate as a fingertip, Harlon feels again the healing calm that the elephant brought the first time that they met. Harlon shuts her eyes and thinks her thanks, knowing that even if she were a Listener she could not make the creature really understand. And then, with a shock like a sudden light in utter darkness, Enkalamba is in her mind. Harlon cannot see her, or even hear her voice, and yet she feels the elephant's presence and knows that Enkalamba is speaking to her. It's a little like the voice of her own self, speaking in her head, but very *unlike* that because Enkalamba is so very, very different from any human being. Her presence in Harlon's mind is huge and strange. Harlon's brain fizzes with the effort of trying to comprehend what's going on.

Words are small, says Enkalamba.

Hard to use.

But I can speak them, here in you.

You also may speak words to me

if you want this.

I hear your thanks,

but healing is like breath.

Part of the song.

And then she's gone. Harlon breathes out, opens her eyes. Mavulu's expression tells her the medic knows what has just happened.

'I don't understand. I'm not a Listener,' says Harlon. 'I have no siardw.'

'You may not be a Listener, neither am I. But Enkalamba is a *Speaker*. She has a rare gift to enter human minds as she chooses. And it is her choice, and her skill, to enter your mind and communicate with you, to help us.'

'Why?' Tolly asks.

Mavulu shakes her head.

'I am a doctor and a scientist and I don't know why or how. I have to put aside my science and accept what is. I know this forest well enough to know that there is much here I will never understand. I am just grateful. Enkalamba will keep you safe. She knows where to lead you; she will help you. Now, go. Cavan has prepared packs for you with food and water bottles, and nets and ropes for Enkalamba's back so she can help to carry the drop back to us.'

And that's that. There's no more to be said, only a journey to be made. How many more times, Harlon wonders, will she set off on an unknown path with a bag packed by someone else?

5

The White Sea

Ash

In the dream Ash runs and runs. All four paws bite the ground. He climbs a rock face in a blizzard, swims a river in the dark. The trail gleams in front of him, it fizzes in his feet, beats in his heart. He shakes rain and snow and frost out of his coat. He follows, follows.

But the alarm claxon goes off at 5am and the dream is gone. Ash is in his own body again. Aching. Tired. Sad. If he feels this bad after less than a week here, how will he feel after a month, a year? He doesn't want to open his eyes. He doesn't want to begin another day, but there's no choice. The routine is already familiar. In twenty minutes the huge doors at the far end of the hut will be thrown open and the temperature in the dormitory will drop to the same as the temperature on the ice outside. Any part of his body that isn't covered in clothes when that happens will freeze.

All around, other people are crawling from their bunks. They're all young, kids or teenagers, but they move like old people. Ash calls them 'tortoises' inside his head. A hundred tortoises creeping out of sleep. He's spent all his life with Ma, Xeno and Harlon, and now he shares a hut with a hundred others and it's quieter than home. No one sings; no one even speaks much. Their guards don't like it when 'tortoises' speak and anyway everyone is mostly too tired to bother.

Except for Mabbet of course. She can't seem to stop talking. Especially when she wants something. She sleeps in the top bunk, above him. She leans down now and whispers, 'Hey, got any string?'

String is important. You need it to tie things round your body, under your snowsuit, to keep warm. Anything will do, rags, paper, moss. But Mabbet's always asking for his string. She's older than him. Bigger. But he won't give in just yet.

'Find your own,' he growls at her. Growling. He never used to growl, did he?

'C'mon,' Mabbet whines. 'I got to tie something round my face today.'

She points to her nose, which is scabbed and turning dark with frostbite. Ash knows what it's like and, anyway, if he doesn't give her string she'll hit him. He hands her a length of twine but as she reaches down to get it, she sees the envelope. Ash keeps it hidden under his head at night, and inside his snowsuit by day. But this morning he is extra tired, and he got careless.

Now, Mabbet's quick fingers snatch it up out of sight into her bunk.

'Give it back!' Ash's voice is louder than he meant it to be.

'Shuddup,' Mabbet hisses back. 'You'll get us into trouble.'

Mabbet leans down and waves it in front of him, jabbing at the image of his mother.

'You've got a photograph,' she says. 'That could get *you* in a lot of trouble.'

Ash tries to snatch it back but Mabbet whisks it away and slaps his head.

'Who's in the picture? Tell me!' she orders.

'My ma and my sister,' Ash mumbles.

'How'd your ma get that scar on her face?'

'I dunno. Just give it back!'

'No. It's mine now,' she says and disappears back into her bunk.

The Ash of just a few days ago, the Ash who existed before he came here, would have cried. But the now-Ash doesn't feel much at all, and doesn't care about anything except food and warmth. Any second now the doors will open; he must be ready. Ash gets back to stuffing his clothes with bits of newspaper and scraps of rag. Then he puts on his boots and wraps Ma's jacket carefully around him. It is his armour: the last little thing that holds him to the life he's lost. Finally he puts on the bright-red snowsuit and pulls up the hood. He's lucky he is quite small, so there's lots of room inside for extra insulation.

Icy air floods in. Light bounces off the ice and snow, so bright it hurts. Everyone pulls their goggles over their faces, strips of cardboard with two slits cut in, tied on with string. Just enough to see out of. With their lumpy red suits and cardboard-slit goggles, they all look the same, red tortoises, hardly human at all.

Three other huts spew out goggled red tortoise-people. Guards hurry them into trucks that chug black smoke. Everyone coughs. Like every machine here the trucks run on what the Automators call black gold. Tar is what everyone else calls it. Other names too, a lot less polite. The stinking fug of tar hangs around the base, staining the snow a greasy grey. The smell is everywhere; it clings to your skin. Ash thinks he'll never wash the smell off, even if he gets away from here.

When Ash arrived in this place they call Station Gold, he wondered if he had died and that this was some horrible afterlife, like the Hell people once believed in. He couldn't work out why humans would spoil the beautiful snow and sea and mountains with this stink and stain. All around the Station is the silence that was in the felled forest. A silence not of death, but of unlife. He hasn't seen or sensed a single creature since he's been here. There should be snow bears here, white foxes, woolly rhinos, seals and whales in the ocean and many, many birds. Creatures he's seen in books and longs to see in life. But there's never anything, just a few sad patches of grass struggling through the tar and human rubbish that litters the tundra. Not even any mice in the food stores, because the Automators spray poison in there to kill them. The sea is covered with the black scum that runs out of the station, over the water. This fills Ash with a terrible loneliness, every bit as bad as the longing for his family.

Even though there are no living things to listen to, the Automators seems as worked up about Listeners as ever. There are posters about them everywhere.

Listen out for Listeners!

If you suspect another Volunteer (that's what they call the tortoises, Volunteers) *you must report it at once.*

So it's safest not to talk to anyone, especially as he's only really used to talking with his family and any kind of 'tortoise' conversation can attract a beating from the guards. He's glad he still has his false name, Satty Meyer, to hide behind.

But Mabbet seems to get away with talking. She's always asking questions, especially when new children arrive. The day he got here she leaned down from the bunk above and told him what Station Gold was all about, when he was lost in a daze of confusion.

'The Automators use tar for veekles,' she told him, 'so nobody needs to bother with batteries any more. Tar veekles don't run out of battery.'

Later Ash saw the posters on the walls.

Freedom! Travel without a recharge.

With pictures of people driving one of the little tar-powered veekles called 'karz' and smiling, smiling, smiling.

'Wouldn't you *love* one of those?' Mabbet said dreamily. 'I would. I think I want a red one. I'm gonna get one, someday, when I get away from here.'

Some of the posters showed solars and windmills torn down.

Escape from the tyranny of nature! they said.

Why wait for wind to blow or the sun to shine? Be free! Use Black Gold instead!

Ash didn't get it. Why bother with black gold, tar, when the sun *did* shine and the wind *did* blow, pretty much all the time. But, finally, he did understand: wind and sunshine were free, but the Automators owned tar. This didn't seem to bother Mabbet. Ash decided she really wanted to *be* an Automator.

Station Gold was all about tar. The Automators had made huge machines to suck it up from far beneath the ice and sea and rock below. They pumped it into giant tanks, bigger than a house. But then they had to get it south, to the cities they were busy building.

'That's where we come in,' Mabbet told him cheerily. 'They're using us to build a giant pipeline to take it there.'

'Us' was the children snatched from villages, just like the one where Ash was caught, separated from their families and brought here to do the Automators' labour.

'Most of these got relatives down south. If anybody makes trouble, their family gets it.' Mabbet punched her fist, grinning, as if this was a good thing.

'Not me though,' she added. 'My family's all dead. Nobody makes me do anything. I'm going to be a self-made woman. You just wait!'

Would having a dead family make him into a self-made man? Ash wasn't sure he liked the sound of that.

Today Ash is trying not to think or talk; he's concentrating only on surviving. He shuffles forward with the other tortoises and takes the chunk of bread he's handed as he climbs aboard the truck. But Mabbet is thinking, and talking. She jostles closer. She's trying to be nice. That means she's after something.

'Who wrote that letter?' she whispers.

The fat capo of the guards, the man they nickname Dough Boy, is watching as they're loaded onto the trucks. He doesn't come out of his office often and when he does someone usually gets beaten. Ash doesn't want it to be him. So he turns his head, as if he hasn't heard her. But Mabbet goes on whispering.

'Well? *Tell me!*'

106

She can get into trouble if she wants to. But not him. If the Automators find out he's a Listener, things could get even worse than this. Ash shoves his bread inside his snowsuit so it won't freeze solid.

'Shuddup,' he says. *'Shuddup.'*

The truck rumbles over the ice and out onto the faded, tussocky grass of the tundra. It scrunches to a stop next to the huge pile of metal pipes. Today's work will be rolling them, lifting them. The guards will shout and whack and grumble. Somebody will probably get crushed when a pipe rolls out of control. And then, at the end of the long day, they'll all be taken back to the dormitory, given some more bread and soon it'll be another day, just the same.

Ash has already found a way to escape, so only his body has to endure the cold, danger, and bleak boredom. He's found that he can leave his body behind, and run with the Gula in his mind. Over the ice he runs, between the trees, with the rhythm of her paws beating in his heart and the line of her trail gleaming like a lectric spiderweb in front of him.

Just as he's about to leave his poor, tired body to the day, a flock of birds flies up. Pale as snow, with little black caps and red beaks. These are the first living things Ash has seen or sensed in any way since coming to the station. At once, Ash knows what they are, he read about them in one of Ma's books: snow terns. They fly between the ends of the world, from here, around the White Sea, to Diwedd Pawb, right at the bottom of the world.

They look too delicate for this hard place. They wheel around as if trying to work out what to do next. They are beautiful. Ash thinks they may be the most lovely thing he has ever seen. They open up his heart, which he has so carefully kept closed, and his siardw unfolds like a dry leaf after rain, open to connection from *any* sort of life, not just alpacas and mice!

Thoughts of Ma, Harlon and Xeno rush out from where he's kept them locked away.

He feels suddenly as soft as a snail without its shell. So when the guards lift their guns and start to shoot, he thinks for a moment that the bullets are entering his own body.

The guards are laughing, as if this is the best thing that's happened for a long time. The birds cry out. Some fly off, but some are hit, and their small bodies blow apart, spitting blood and feathers down onto the snow. Everyone is looking up as the birds tumble out of the air, but Ash looks down, he cannot bear to watch. He cannot help but sense the wave of pain and terror that spreads from the falling birds. It hits him like a blow. He's reeling.

A tern falls at his feet. It looks almost unharmed, just dazed, but if he leaves it here it will be crushed by someone's foot. He can't do that, any more than he can decide to make his heart stop beating. He glances round. Everyone is still looking up even though the guards have already put away their guns. Good. He pretends to refasten his snow boot and scoops the bird up, tucks it in his suit, stands up again. Through the forest of people Mabbet catches his eye. Did she see? He thinks not, but all the same he's glad when she's directed to another team, and Ash is lined up with tortoises he doesn't know.

Every move he makes, he feels the tern's small body inside

his snowsuit. He tries to calm it, the way he could calm the alpacas, but bird minds are Xeno's territory, not his. He's not sure he's doing any good, until the bird snuggles against his body and its breathing slows. It falls asleep. Almost at once, Ash feels the bird's dreams! This is not like listening in the dark on the sidelines of the alpacas' minds; it's more the way the Gula came into his head. It feels as if the tern is *choosing* to share its dreams, speaking to him.

All day, as he lifts and struggles, the tern sleeps a long, healing sleep. Its dreams wash through Ash, like tides and currents in the ocean. It dreams of stars and wind over the sea. Of the shape of coastlines, the smells of land and regions of the ocean, like different countries. Lines of magnetic force stripe its path and zing like a scratched itch as it flies across them. The stars shine in patterns like a language; they sing about paths and routes and directions, about food and danger. The wind and light harmonise, adding more detail about every route and place and season.

Ash learns that whole oceans fit inside the tiny, fragile body, not just oceans now, but oceans past; all the long journeys that the bird has flown are stored inside like stories. The tern is a living map of space and time, a feathered device for way-finding. It is the ever-changing answer to the question its spirit eternally asks: *where? Where? Where?*

There is so much power and purpose in the tiny body that nestles against Ash's chest. It brings him back to life. To fearing. To grieving. To wanting.

Close to the end of the working day, the bird begins to wake and starts to struggle inside his suit. The guards mustn't see. Ash bends over and clutches at his stomach as if he's got cramps. A guard waves him off.

'Don't do your business where we'll tread in it tomorrow. Hurry up.'

Doubled up still, Ash rushes behind the pipe mountain out of sight. Then he gently lifts the feathered body out. Its wings push hard against his hand, but when he unlaces his fingers, freeing it, it doesn't fly at once. It paddles its small, red feet, and tilts its black-capped head to look into Ash's face, first with one eye, then the other. Then, it flickers up into the air and Ash feels its mind fire up like a struck match with the smell of the breeze, the position of the sun. It is fizzing with direction, a gleaming path is looping into a sky striped with blues that Ash's eyes don't see, that humans don't have words for. Before it vanishes, Ash picks up one last thought; it is the bird's view of him from above as it flies off, his face looking upward seen through its eyes. Then, like the Gula, it finds words in his mind to use.

Wayfinder me! The bird says inside his head.

I follow a new trail, a trail where all trails shine, where the salt sky loops blue.

All trails there made new. You go also.

Greeting Wayfayer you.

The guards yell abuse at him as he runs out from behind the pipes and scrambles into the nearest truck. The other tortoises give him filthy looks for holding them up and making their food five minutes further off. But Ash doesn't care. He's alive again, really alive.

When night comes, he can't fall asleep. He listens to the snores and whimpers, the muffled sobs, the coughs around him. The tern has brought him back to life and he knows he cannot stay in this place, just surviving until the day he dies of cold or a giant pipe crushes him into the dirty ice. He *has* to get away. Even if everyone else is gone, then *he* will find his way to Ma's lost island. The Gula's trail, the tern's path, twirl and dance in the dark before his eyes.

All trails there made new. You go also.

What did that mean? It's the kind of thing Xeno would say. If only he could understand things the way she did, if only he could see his trail the way the Gula and the tern see theirs!

'Satty?' It's Mabbet, of course, but whispering so quietly Ash can hardly hear her.

Silent as a snake, she slithers down into his bunk.

'Here,' she says and hands back the envelope with the photograph and Pa's letter in. 'Sorry I took it.'

Why is she being nice to him? Is she his friend now? Ash has never had a friend, apart from Alba and the Gula, so he's not sure.

'I saw you with that bird today,' she whispers, 'and I bet I'm not the only one.'

There's no point denying it. Ash says nothing.

'Reckon they'll come for you tomorrow, so you need to get out tonight.'

'How?'

'There's a way. But you have to come with me right now, yeah?'

This doesn't feel good to Ash. He thinks once more of the

111

dislocated toe, of wrongness. But if Mabbet's right, what other hope does he have?

'Alright.'

She presses her finger to her lips and beckons him to follow. They cross the floor like shadows and enter the latrine. It's just a patch of wire mesh grids over a deep hole with a security light above that burns all night. In the far corner is a metal drain cover, inset in the filthy floor. Mabbet pulls it open and gestures to Ash to slip down through it. She follows and lowers it shut behind them.

They slide down a muddy slope in perfect dark. At the bottom Ash feels Mabbet reach past him to the wall, where she must have a torch, because now its dim beam shows where they are; a narrow tunnel, just high enough for them to walk almost upright, leads off into dimness. All this time Mabbet has known about this escape route. Ash's mind races with so many questions he doesn't know where to start. As usual Mabbet just talks anyway and she pushes him along the tunnel in front of her.

'This is how I get all the Listeners out,' Mabbet says. 'I'm a sort of secret agent. Yeah. And I'm a Listener too o'course. I didn't tell you before.'

Ash would stop still in astonishment if it wasn't for Mabbet's finger jabbing in his back. How would Mabbet shut up long enough to *hear* anything?

'Yeah. Always chatting away to animals, me. Morning, Mabbet, they say, chat about the weather. Just like a person really.'

For a moment Ash thinks that Mabbet is making some sort of joke, and then it dawns on him: she is just lying, making it up. Why would she do that?

She pushes him up a short wooden ladder, and through a trapdoor, and there Ash finds his answer: he's in an office and Dough Boy sits behind the desk, his pasty face sweating gently in the stuffy atmosphere.

'You took your time, Mabbet,' says Dough Boy. 'I've missed my dinner.'

He rubs his belly which pushes against the buttons of his uniform jacket, as if it might like to escape and have a life all its own. Ash has been betrayed. Mabbet is a 'sort of secret agent' but she's working for the Automators.

Standing beside Dough Boy is a small man with a beard, wearing a very clean, white apron over an Automator uniform. Dough Boy heaves himself from his seat and together he and the man in the apron force Ash into a heavy, metal chair. His wrists are strapped to its arms and another strap holds him round the waist.

Ash struggles, but there's little point.

Dough Boy pulls out a pad of official-looking forms. His big hands make the paper and the pen look like toys. He looks up at Ash.

'Right, Listener scum, what's y'name?'

Mabbet jumps in and answers for him.

'Name's Meyer, sir, Satty Meyer,' says Mabbet, standing straight as if she too were an Automator. 'Saw him talking to a bird.'

Dough Boy is hardly listening. He waves a hand at her.

'Alright, Mabbet. Pop off back to your hut now, will you? Don't want any of your little friends getting suspicious do we, or you won't be very *useful* to me any more.'

'But sir, there's something else,' Mabbet blurts. 'He's got a letter and a photograph. Suspicious documents.'

So *that's* why she was so interested in the letter and the photograph. She thinks they'll get her something. Ash is shocked at how much she's planned this.

'Oh yeah,' says Dough Boy, bored. 'Where is this "document"?'

Mabbet bites her lip, summoning her courage.

'What will I get if I tell you?'

Up close Ash can see there is intelligence in Dough Boy's eyes. He's a thug, but not just a thug like the other guards. He wants more than this little office. Poor Mabbet's bitten off a lot more than she can chew by challenging him. He steps from behind his desk with some agility for a bulky person and lifts Mabbet off her feet.

'Don't think you can bargain. If he's got something suspicious then I'll find it without your help. Now get out.'

He drops her in a heap and she almost slithers back through the trap door. This, Ash thinks, is how Dough Boy got to be a capo.

Slowly, Dough Boy sits back down. Beside him the man in the white coat is fiddling with a contraption of wires and dials. It doesn't seem to be going well. The wires have a mind of their own and his glasses keep slipping off his nose.

'Satty Mayer.' Dough Boy writes it on the form. 'Seen … talking … to … a … bird.'

'I didn't talk to the bird,' Ash says. Ash has always found lying difficult but this is perfectly true; he didn't, it talked to him.

'Oh shut up, scum,' says Dough Boy as if swatting a persistent fly. 'Dr Zebber here knows exactly what to do with the likes of you.'

He tips his head towards white-coat man and his misbehaving wires, and taps the top of the contraption.

'Know what this is?'

Ash shakes his head.

'This here is a Turner. A new model. Just been sent from HQ.'

Dr Zebber looks up from his fight with the wires.

'Turner Mark 6,' he says, as if describing a new and particularly delicious variety of cake that he has just taken from the oven.

'Yes. A Turner Mark 6. It'll test your brain for all the nasty bits that make you the dirty animal lover that you are. If you're lucky, they'll just burn away and you can be made into something more useful. In that case we'll send you south and you'll be working for one of the new dog units or one of the falcon units.'

Ash thinks of the dead-eyed girl in the village, making those 'dog' things snarl and bite, and of the falcons that chased them down the gully.

'But it doesn't always work. So you might just be a human cabbage. If so, we'll slap a nice big L on your head and leave out on the ice to freeze like any good vegetable.'

Dough Boy seems to think this is very funny.

Dr Zebber has finished his battle.

'I'm ready, Capo Vellum,' he says.

Dr Zebber is no more than skin, bone and jumping nerves inside his white coat. His hands flutter like moths as he attaches wires to Ash's head with little sticky pads. Ash goes blank with panic. He struggles wildly against his bonds and Dough Boy gets up to squash him firmly into the chair.

115

'No more wriggling,' he commands.

Ash wants to cry. Or scream. His heart and mind race. Fear sits on his chest like a dead weight so he can't breathe. He closes his eyes. He thinks of the Gula, and of Harlon, Ma and Xeno. Slowly but surely he pushes the fear off his chest and clears his mind.

Surprise is almost the only weapon he has, so Dough Boy and the doctor must be made to believe that he won't resist. Ash goes limp while at the same time very gently pressing his feet into the ground. He gauges the weight of the chair: not too heavy to lift, but heavy enough to do some damage if he swirls it round. He just needs to hold on until the right moment.

Dr Zebber stands with wires in his hands looking at Ash as if he is a poo that might bite. Dough Boy picks his fingers and stares into space.

'Um, Capo Vellum?' Dr Zebber says. 'I must put these on the skin of the chest.'

'Oh, right!' Dough Boy says, and leans across to rip open the layers of Ash's clothes. There, stuck to Ash's chest by dirt and sweat, is Pa's letter and the photo. Dough Boy snatches it up like a bag of sweets he's found to replace his lost dinner. His belly wobbles as if it too is rather excited.

'Mabbet's suspicious document, I suppose.'

Ash watches carefully as Vellum pulls out the letter and the photo and examines them under the desk light. He is finding the photo *very* interesting. Astonishing, in fact. Dough Boy looks up, his brow furrowed. He's trying to remember something.

'Meyer, did you say your name was?'

Ash nods. Dough Boy looks back at the photograph and a slow, sly grin spreads over his plate of a face.

'Well, well, well. Look who it is! This your ma, then?' Dough Boy asks.

Ash nods vigorously as if he was still mad with fear.

'Well, well, well,' Dough Boy says again and returns to gazing at the photograph.

Ash would like to know how this man seems to recognise his mother but he can't think of that right now. Ash is sadder than he can say to lose the only pieces of his father that he will ever possess, but they might help to get him out of here. The photo is taking all of Dough Boy's attention and fiddling with the very uncooperative new machine is taking all of Zebber's.

Now! Ash thinks.

NOW!

Ash pounds his feet into the floor with all the power he can muster, lifting its heavy metal legs and then swirling them round. He catches Dr Zebber in the shins, and the man crumples like straw. Dough Boy is entirely caught by surprise. He leaps up but the Turner has been knocked off the desk and lies on the floor, its wires, like octopus tentacles, tangle Dough Boy's legs. As he tries to reach out for Ash, they trip him. He falls heavy as a sack of potatoes onto Zebber who screams as if every bone in his body has been crushed. Which, given Dough Boy's size, is probably true. Ash keeps swirling and this time the chair legs hit Dough Boy in the face, blinding him with blood and pain. He and Zebber are left scrabbling on the floor entangled in a mesh of springing wires. They are both calling out for help, but it's late and there's no one else about.

Ash crashes through the office door and runs down the corridor. He's running doubled up with the chair still on his back so it's hard to see where he's going. He turns a narrow corner and the chair jams. For a second he's held, legs running to nowhere, and then the straps snap and he shoots forward, down the corridor, past darkened doorways.

Something's going on outside. There's shouting, banging. A smell of tarry smoke snakes in under the main door of the building. Ash doubles back to find another way out. He can hear footsteps and shouting inside now too. Dough Boy and Zebber have got out of their tangle and are coming after him. He darts down a smaller, darker corridor and finds a door marked 'danger', bolted on the inside. Danger? Well it can't be more dangerous on the other side than it is on this. He pulls back the bolts and slips through into total darkness.

He feels around the doorframe. There are bolts on this side too. Good. He slides them home. Now at least for a moment he is safe. He can't quite believe what he's managed to do. Harlon would be proud. No, Harlon would be *astonished*. As small low laugh escapes him as he thinks of that. The sound his own voice makes in the dark make him jump. It's magnified, distorted. He snaps his fingers and the echoed sound tells him he's in some huge space.

There are footsteps, shouting getting loud behind the door. He needs to move. The bolts won't hold against someone who really wants to get through. He moves left, following the wall. It's curved. *Curved?* Could he be inside a tar tank? It doesn't smell like it? Where is he? Panic's begins to work its way upward again.

What if he's stuck in here?

What if he isn't?

Where is he going to go if he does get away?

He won't survive for more than a few hours outside without a snowsuit.

What if…

'This way.' A voice! Fast-moving feet.

'No, *this* way!'

A whispered curse.

'Shhhhh!'

Ash freezes.

Somewhere on the other side of this big, empty space, two other people are doing the same: holding still. Holding their breath. They can't be Automators. They'd be loud, they'd have torches and there would be a lot of them. Very slowly, making no sound, Ash moves forward, touching the wall with one hand to keep himself on course.

He stops. Listens. Creeps again.

Have they gone? He has just convinced himself that his anxious mind invented the voices and footsteps, when he is jerked onto his back and a foot presses on his chest. A light blazes in his face and out of the blinding glare comes a torrent of language he doesn't recognise, in two voices. And then, in Standard, 'Are you alone?'

Ash nods. The foot presses into his chest, menacing.

'What are you doing?'

'Escaping.'

There's another exchange that Ash can't understand. Although the foot still pins him down, the light is taken from his face. It shines on two people, with spears and crossbows strapped to their backs. They are dressed in sealskin parkas, leggings and boots. Ash know this because Ma showed him pictures of people like this. They are the people of the Frozen Sea, the Celeddi, who came to the north with the ice. Ma said that all Celeddi were born as Listeners and could hear all the animals of the White Sea. Ash forgets his fear in his excitement.

'Is it true that you can all speak to snow bears and woolly rhinos and horned whales?'

For a moment the two faces just stare at him and then they burst out laughing. The younger one, who Ash thinks is probably a girl says, 'You are taken by armed strangers in an abandoned oil tank and that's the first thing you want to know?'

Ash feels a little foolish.

'I never thought I'd meet people like you!'

The other person who is perhaps also female, though obviously much older, smiles at him.

'We may have time to speak of this. But not *this* time,' she says and glances at her companion. There is another flurry of words and it seems they have reached a decision.

'You will come with us,' says the younger one. 'I am Amliq and this is Tarth.'

'Now, we go,' says Tarth. 'Run!'

They dim their torch and start to move.

They follow the curved wall until it meets a massive, open pipe, big enough to run along without stooping. They set off down it with their footsteps and breath bouncing off its cold metal walls. The Celeddi run like the Gula, with a steady unbroken rhythm. Ash tries to find the beat of the Gula's paws to help him, but he's struggling. They stop to let him rest and share some water.

'You have been long time at the tar station?' Amliq asks.

'It seems long. We don't get much food.'

Amliq and Tarth shake their heads.

'They are wickedness made flesh,' says Tarth.

'But tonight they will suffer!' Amliq sounds triumphant but Tarth shoots her a warning glance. Seeing it, Ash grins.

'What's funny?' Tarth asks as they start to run again.

'You just looked at Amliq the same way my big sister looks at me sometimes.'

Her smile flashes at him and they run on.

They haven't gone far when the pipe carries the sound of Automator voices and footsteps behind them, distant but heading their way. Ash doesn't understand the words that burst from the two women but he knows that they are not happy or polite. It's clear they didn't expect to be followed.

Amliq dims the light.

'Where have they come from? They can't have followed us from the well head!'

Tarth looks worried.

'Hmmm. Let's hope not.'

'Where did they join our trail?'

Ash interrupts. He wants to help these women who could so easily have left him behind.

'I think it's me they're after, not you. There was a door close to where we met, I bolted it after I went through, but they may have guessed I went that way.'

'Ah! That would make sense!' says Tarth. 'That means they won't pass the bomb or the fuse!'

'Do we wait and attack?' Amliq says.

'No. We must get clear. We run. The rhinos will be waiting.'

Ash likes the sound of rhinos. Woolly ones, of course! But bombs and fuses? If that's how the Automators will suffer, won't many starving tortoises suffer too?

'Fast! Faster,' Tarth urges, and Ash no longer has the breath to say, or even think, anything.

They race down one long curve and there before them is the end of the pipe and an oval of silver-blue sky and moonlit tundra. Ash has the strange sensation that the mouth pipe is expanding, rather than just getting closer. When it's almost big enough to fill their field of view, Amliq lets out a sharp, lilting cry and Ash's siardw tingles as it senses something living, coming close. The ground rumbles, and two massive silhouettes fill the pipe mouth: woolly rhinos, creatures from the pages of Ma's books come to life! The women give their lilting cry again and the animals answer with a high whistling that Ash would never have guessed could come from an animal the size of a cart and covered in a mad tangle of woolly hair.

It clear that both humans and animals are very glad to see each other, but there's no time for introductions. Ash is pulled up onto the back of one of the giant beasts. Amliq sits in front, just behind the great hump of the creature's shoulders. She hands him a strap that runs around the rhino's body, somewhere amongst the sea of matted coat.

'Hold this,' she says. 'Don't grab the wool, they don't like it.'

A bullet hits the wall close by, making the metal ring like a bell; another zips past Ash's ear.

'Keep low!' she says and Ash leans down into the chaotic carpet of woolly locks. This must be what it's like being a louse he thinks, hiding on a dog's back.

The rhinos pick up speed and in no time they're moving too fast and far for their pursuers to think of following.

Ash looks out from the waving fronds of fur to see they aren't alone. Other rhinos and their riders join them from points around the station. A whole band of Celeddi, whooping and triumphant, surrounds them. The rhinos' wide feet make a soft thunder on the silver ground and the aurora shimmer with spring green above them. But behind them, great red and yellow blossoms of flame bloom over Station Gold, and the deep muffled booms of explosions roll out into the night.

The tar tanks will burn for days, flames will lick the posters in the canteen and maybe eat up Dough Boy and his friends and Mabbet too, but what about the tortoises? The tar station wasn't their idea. When the whooping stops, Ash calls out over the rush of cold wind, 'What will happen to the children?'

Amliq answers at once.

'We did not destroy their living huts or food stores. They will learn to survive. They will learn the lessons that the Celeddi had to learn.'

Ash isn't sure those tired, sad children are ready to learn

anything. How will they travel south to see their families again? Feelings twist like the tar smoke in Ash's belly as they rush on under the hard, cold, glitter of the stars.

6

The Vampire of the Fang

Doada

 In the splendid glass and marble foyer of New Dawn Tower, headquarters of the Automators, Doada Sisal waits for his guest. The 'guest' is Merit Fane Cubit, the Chief Merit of the House of Governors, who believes herself to be the most powerful person in all of Rumyc. She is expecting to be greeted by Director Herick Lazit, founder of the Automators. The Cubits and the Lazits are old families, with alliances running back through centuries of power and privilege.

But things have changed. No one calls Director Lazit Head of the Automators anymore. People know that real power belongs to Doada Sisal. No one calls him *that* of course. He is Head of Intelligence, Commander Eye or to the people of Fidrac, the capital city, he is simply the Vampire and the tower that is his throne they call the Fang.

Tall, thin and bespectacled, impeccably dressed, the Vampire of the Fang crosses the floor to greet the Merit. He is coated with a glossy charm that deflects perceptions as the glaze on a porcelain cup deflects stains. On his lapel he wears the ivory badge in the shape of a fist that denotes high-ranking

Automators; she wears the symbol of the House of Governors, a flame of truth cast in brass. Doada considers his symbol the more honest, as a fist more truly represents what they both stand for.

'My *dear* Merit Cubit,' he says, in the languid drawl he's taken a lifetime to perfect, 'how *thrilling* to meet you!'

Like Doada, Merit Fane Cubit is elegantly dressed, in quiet, dark clothes that speak of power and wealth. She has a pleasant, even attractive face, capable of conveying great sincerity. It is only when he looks into her eyes, as Doada does now, that he recognises the same cold cunning that is hidden in his own.

'Senior Lazit has asked me to extend his sincere apologies,' Doada explains as he takes her hand, 'but he has been unavoidably detained.'

She looks at him with a cool, assessing gaze.

'Yes, Commander Eye, I gathered from his message that there has been another rebel outrage. I'm hoping that Automator forces will soon rid us of this new Green Thorn scourge.'

Doada smiles, an expression that can only be described as being like a grin painted on a knife.

'*Dear* Merit Cubit, one of the purposes of my little tour today is to reassure you on that *precise* matter. Shall we proceed?'

They step into the Ascender – a new and necessary addition in such a very tall building. It clanks and trembles as it begins to move.

'I think we'll go straight to our Engineering and Architecture Floor,' Doada explains.

'Splendid!' the Merit replies, with a cold, professional smile.

126

The tour Doada plans is selective. They will *not* be visiting Floor 3 – the Education Centre – where newly 'acquired' Listeners are *turned* from subversives into useful tools, or disposable husks: too much screaming. Nor Floor 4 – the Development Centre – where special breeding and training are carried out to create animal-machine hybrids, weapons controlled by turned Listeners: too much stink.

She *certainly* won't be shown the floor that lies between between Floor 4 and Floor 5, which is reached by its own lift, on the other side of the building. Here, Doada's special project, the Greenhouse, is being completed by a handpicked team of scientists that Doada calls the Gardeners. These benign labels conceal a new weapon that uses a revolutionary new principle, Cellular Ignition Resonance. This makes the cells in living things vibrate so fast that they burn, causing bodies to self-ignite. With the power of CIR, all living things within range of the active Greenhouse will be reduced to ash in no more time than it takes Doada to snap his fingers. It will put an end to the Listeners, the Green Thorn and all their nonsense. It will make the Automators invincible. It will make Doada unstoppable. Soon. Very soon.

The Ascender has reached its destination, the Engineering and Architecture Floor.

Merit Cubit hears about the huge machines that can cut down a hundred trees in an hour and turn them into timber. She sees demonstrations of the Sea Harvester that can suck all the life from miles of ocean to make it into 'Freedom Burgers'. Merit Fane Cubit's smile becomes a little warmer; she understands how much money all this will make and into whose pockets it will be inclined to flow. She comes from generations of lords, generals and Merits of the House of Governors, used to taking things away from others to make their own lives more pleasant.

In Architecture, smartly dressed young people show the Merit plans for tall buildings packed tightly together, like the bristles of a great brush.

'We are making progress in showing rural communities that their future lies in these new cities,' Doada explains.

Merit Cubit is very pleased with this.

'So much easier to govern and care for one's population,' she purrs, 'when they are so neatly concentrated. And when they are housed in these excellent ... what do you call these buildings, Commander Eye?'

'Tower blocks,' Doada explains.

'In these tower blocks,' Cubit continues with growing enthusiasm. 'The ideas of the Listeners and their supporters will seem like so much primitive nonsense.'

'Exactly so, Merit Cubit, exactly so. In cities they will be free from the need to tend crops and so on, or have any contact with *animals*. People will no longer be obliged to work together, with all that planting and harvesting. They will be free to devote themselves to ... other activities.'

'Such as purchasing your excellent Freedom Burgers, Commander Eye,' Cubit remarks.

They step into the Ascender once more.

'What we offer,' Doada continues, pasting an earnest expression on his face, 'is a new kind of revolution. Freedom from the cruel tyranny of nature, a new future for all of humankind.'

Cubit raises her elegant eyebrows.

'Come, come now, Commander! No need to repeat the message packaged for the masses. You and I know what the *real* aims of the Automators are. A return of power into the hands of people who know what to do with it.'

'Like you and me, Merit,' Doada replies.

Fane Cubit nods.

'The First Revolution took our power and we want it back.'

Cubit leans a little closer now, as if they were already conspirators.

'There is a lot of work to do,' she says. 'We must cut the ties that hold people to the land and to each other. They must be made to understand that animals and plants are resources to be owned and used; that they have no rights. The Listeners and their filthy hocus-pocus stand in the way of progress.'

'I see you understand our task *so* well.' Doada smiles.

'And then there is the matter of expansion,' Cubit continues. 'Our country needs more room. We must spread the advances of our civilisation beyond our borders, to lands where the scourge of primitivism and Listener culture still reign. In time, I hope you will tackle this issue also, Commander?'

Doada looks at her sharply through his artificial smile. This is just greed and ambition talking, surely? She cannot *know* about the Greenhouse and how it will allow Rumyc to dominate the world, and make the Automators quite invincible, even to the Board of Governors.

'In time, perhaps, dear lady, in time,' he replies, with artificial modesty. 'But for now: the last stage of our tour. My speciality you could say: our surveillance and intelligence operation.'

The Ascender grumbles and screeches its way to a stop, and they walk out onto the top floor. The view is extraordinary. On this clear, bright day, every part of the city lies at the foot of the Fang, every street and park is laid bare. The surrounding landscape spreads like a map to be read, with the ocean stretching to the west and the distant blue of the mountains to the north.

'From here we monitor all that goes on in the city and far beyond,' Doada explains. 'Day by day our powers of observation are growing.'

Fane Cubit shades her eyes. The brightness through the glass walls and roof is so intense, the shadows from the supporting pillars so dark.

'If you give your eyes a moment to accustom themselves,' advises Doada, 'you will see the high-powered telescopes that point in all directions. They are staffed around the clock by diligent officers taking notes.'

Cubit drops her hand and squints at the telescopes, which are aimed, like weapons, at the city. Each is staffed by a pair of black-and-red uniformed people, an observer with their eye constantly to the lens and a notetaker, copying down their quiet commentary on what they see. Occasionally, if something of particular interest is observed it is passed to the team of senior intelligence officers who occupy rows of desks in the centre of the floor.

'Our telescopes could look into the eye of a Listener halfway to the White Sea,' Doada boasts. It is an exaggeration but not *so* very far from reality.

'Impressive,' Cubit says. 'What do you do with all the information you gather here?'

130

'It is safely stored under lock and key, Merit Cubit,' Doada replies. Cubit's eyebrows once more raise in a question.

'If someone wished to access that information for the sake of, shall we say, national security?'

Doada has long ago calculated just how much of a fee political sharks like Cubit would have to pay him for even a small amount of what he knows.

'It would be available,' he replies with his most open and innocent smile, 'for a fee, of course.'

Cubit's eyes flit to the raised balcony that surrounds the top floor on two sides, where seated figures receive a near constant traffic of visiting birds. Her expression transforms suddenly to one of disgust.

'What are those birds doing? Are those persons *Listeners?*' she almost hisses. 'You are *harbouring* Listeners!'

Heads turn at Cubit's raised voice. Doada will have to work a little harder than he expected to win her round.

'Let me explain further, dear lady.'

He steers Cubit expertly into his luxuriously furnished office and invites her to sit down. She perches stiffly on the edge of the blue brocade sofa, while Doada closes the door behind them.

'I can see you have been discomforted by our use of birds,' he says, his face full of sincere concern.

'Shocked, I think would better describe my feeling,' she says. 'Shocked to see Listeners *here*. As I'm sure you know my family have been without that stain for a hundred years and more. No Cubit has been born a Listener for five generations!'

'Yes, of course. Your pedigree is impeccable and you are naturally offended by the unnatural presence of Listeners.'

Doada's facsimile of grave respect is most convincing. Cubit softens a little; Doada continues.

'They are not really Listeners anymore. They are reformed, *Turned* as we call it, so their power is ours to use. They are in fact our masterstroke: the means to defeat the primitive old world with its own distasteful weapons!'

'How can they be reformed?' Cubit frowns. 'The possession of the power of siardw is a scourge, present from birth. Only death can remove its stain.'

What terrible hypocrites these old aristocrats are, Doada thinks. Happy enough to use the talents of Listeners when they needed quiet horses to draw their carriages or compliant oxen to plough their fields. Happy enough to betray them when they think it's their route back to power. What a pleasure it will be when he will do away with Cubit and the Governors and take all their old powers for himself.

But for now he requires their cooperation, so he leans towards her, smiling.

'My research has shown that with just a small lectric pulse to one region of the brain – almost completely painless of course – they become very compliant. *Controllable.*'

He can see she is ready to be convinced.

'Would a demonstration perhaps reassure you, dear madam?' he asks.

Cubit gives a curt nod.

Doada steps from the room and returns moments later with a child, who allows herself to be steered in front of Cubit, as if she were a doll. She stands, pale and dead-eyed, staring at nothing.

'This child came from a village in the east,' Doada explains, as if describing from where he has acquired the brocade sofa or his handsome desk. 'We discovered it whilst we were relocating a community.'

'The countryside is a hotbed of rebel activity, the hiding place of enemies of the Governors,' Cubit replies. 'We entirely support your resettlement programmes.'

Doada smiles and continues.

'This child specialised in communicating with birds. It cared for a large flock of geese with *unnatural* success. But now, she works for us.'

He turns to the child and commands her coldly.

'Report!'

Like a light whose switch has been flicked, the girl responds.

'Siardw currently in use on the roof of 95 Marletti Street. Male human in contact with flock of starlings.' Her voice is a clear, expressionless monotone.

'Report from earlier today.'

'Siardw used, south end of Red Lily Lake. Two users, female, in contact with a flock of migrating curlew.'

'And have you submitted descriptions of persons detected to your monitor?'

The girl nodded.

'That will be all. Return to your position.'

The girl walks out of the room, quiet as a ghost.

Cubit is impressed. Already calculating how this can be turned to her advantage.

'But the real masterstroke of our work here,' Doada explains, 'is that all creatures that have been connected to a Listener, retain the impression in their minds of *that* Listener. The Turned can access those impressions and pass them to us.'

Doada beams as if he had just baked a fragrant cake and placed it before the Merit for her admiration.

'And where there are Listeners,' he adds, 'you can be sure there will be rebels. Through the power of the Turned we will subdue this new wave of Green Thorn activity in no time. A team of operators is already on its way to 95 Marlettti Street with the description of the Listener identified. They will detain all they find there.'

'Impressive!' says Cubit. 'Very impressive.'

Cubit is clearly once again on side.

'The power of this technique has great potential, I see,' she says. 'Perhaps you will succeed in finding the Boogam. Many in the House of Governors are convinced that our old enemy is behind this renewed Green Thorn activity in the capital.'

Doada smiles and only the snap of his cup against his saucer betrays his agitation.

'Ah dear lady, you must not believe all that you hear. We have no real confirmation that the Boogam has returned from the dead.'

'I always thought it was rather in the nature of ghosts to do just that,' Cubit replies, 'after all that *is* the meaning of the name in the language of the civilised.'

The very last thing Doada wants speak about right now is the wretched Boogam. He decides their meeting has served its purpose.

'Please forgive me, Merit Cubit,' he says, getting to his feet, 'but I have a most demanding day.'

Cubit rises, smooths her immaculate jacket and pins the professional smile back to her face.

'Of course, I don't wish to detain you. Do keep me appraised of any interesting developments with regard to the Ghost. I will, for my part, make sure the Governors support the excellent work you do here.'

Doada gives a small, stiff bow.

'We are most grateful, Merit Cubit.'

When she is gone, he shuts his office door and punches his desk with a bony fist. The Boogam! Of *course* the recovery in rebel activity is because of her. He might have known she wasn't really dead. Why has she come back *now,* at this most delicate stage? The last pieces of the old world not yet entirely destroyed, the threads that bind humans to the land and the beasts not yet completely severed, the Greenhouse not quite ready. Everything he's worked for could still come tumbling down!

He takes a deep breath. Anger will not help him catch her. Only information can do that. Is there something that he's missed in any recent operations?

Several reports are stacked on his desk. He picks up the one about the most recent and least successful of them: the operation in the Blaidd Mawr mountains. His personal spy bird had found a child with exceptional power. Potentially a very useful tool. So he'd sent a *very* competent force to capture her and her sibling – who also had some small power, his spy reported. The officers' bungling incompetence had been shameful. Two steel falcons, his latest and most expensive weapons, lost and five men (five!) brought down by some woman at her kitchen window. They had at least managed to capture the exceptional child and reduce the house to ashes, but had let the other child slip through their fingers *and* failed to confirm that the woman had been eliminated.

Doada sighs. Something about this niggles at him still. He will question his spy again. Perhaps there's some detail she holds that another interview can uncover. He'll talk to her at once. He locks the office door, draws down the blinds and pulls out a small key, hanging from a chain around his neck. It opens a narrow door, concealed by a framed plan of one of the new cities. He slips through and closes it behind him.

The room is small, no more than a cupboard. There is a window high on one wall, unglazed, open to the air. In the centre of the room hangs a cage and in it is a single bird. Once it was a starling, with iridescent feathers like a dark rainbow, and a quick, joyful wit. Now it is the shell of a bird, coloured like dust. Its beak and feet have been cunningly replaced with more durable, metal parts; its head is covered in a leather cap. As Doada enters, it turns to him with dull eyes, and opens it beak.

'What?'

The bird speaks out loud with a small, sharp voice, rough edged like a toothed knife left to rust. It sounds weary.

'Tell me again,' Doada commands.

'What?' The bird repeats.

136

'The mountain, the girl. Tell me again.'

'Power. Power,' the bird rasps sullenly.

'Yes, you've told me that already. What else? *What did you see in her?*'

Now the bird does not reply at all. Doada stares at it. If he could only search its mind himself, see exactly who and what it saw! But his siardw is long dead. He burned it from his own brain, and traded that power for one he wanted more.

'The mountain. The girl. Tell me again, what did you see in her?' he insists.

Still there is no reply. Doada knows the bird has more words she could use. He put them in there when she was a fledgling. Her mind had inborn talent for communication in a flock of thousands, but was still soft, like unfired clay. Doada placed the iron cage of human words into that brain, squeezing the softness small enough to fit the tight, hard mould, cutting its connection to everything but him. The bird has been his secret servant, his spy, for many years since. Her silence now enrages him. He reaches into the cage and encloses her body with his fingers.

'Speak!'

She turns to him, and her eyes gleam with a life they've never had the chance to live.

'The seeds are singing,' she says, *'singing, singing singing. The earth will hatch again.'*

Then, for the first time in her life, she sings: a glorious, vital, liquid chaos of notes that is the starling's gift to the world.

Doada is afraid and it makes him squeeze tighter, tighter and still she sings and sings. Only when there is nothing but a ball of crushed feathers left, does her singing stop.

He looks at the remains on the floor.

The seeds are singing. The earth will hatch again.

Those were not a starling's words, a starling's thoughts. They have been put there, put there by that brat from Blaidd Mawr, he's willing to bet on it. He will not endure such an outrage, such an invasion of his instrument. He will not be made afraid by some scrap of a Listener, just a remnant of the primitive past. No matter what her power, he will burn it away; he will find what hides in her mind by force. He will do it himself. Now.

Doada seldom comes to the education centre. His handpicked staff take care of everything and he leaves them to it. They scuttle around him now, like children trying to please their teacher.

'We are most honoured, Commander Eye,' says Officer Fallen, almost touching the floor with the top of his head as he bows. Doada conceals his irritation with a smile.

'Yes, yes,' he says. 'If you could just show me to the correct cell, I would be *most* grateful.'

It takes them some time to locate the child.

'We have so many Listeners to deal with. So many more every day,' Fallen laughs nervously. 'There's a veritable tide of them these days.'

He consults a list. 'I'm afraid this child has not yet been entirely processed.'

'Then I will do that job myself,' Doada tells him, 'dear boy.'

The man glances round at his two assistants, one of whom is actually wringing her hands.

Fallen swallows, adjusts the collar of his uniform.

'She has proved quite impervious to our methods so far. She…'

Doada cuts him off and gives up on civility.

'Just show me the cell, NOW!'

She will not be impervious to me, he thinks.

Fallen looks like a retreating cockroach as he sidles down the dark corridor. Doors line the walls and sounds of human misery echo in the dimness. Behind the last door there is quiet. Fallen fumbles with the lock, pushes against the creaking hinges and lets Doada in.

The child stands with her back to him beneath the high window, staring at the sky as if what goes on in this room doesn't interest her at all.

'Prisoner. Attention,' Doada commands.

She takes no notice but continues to stare up at the distant silhouettes of speeding swifts. Really, Fallen has done nothing with the child!

'Prisoner! Attention,' Doada repeats in a voice that usually has captive children quaking.

Still she does not respond but instead lets out a thin cry, so exactly like the screaming swifts that it stops Doada in his tracks. A prickle of fear runs up his spine. How can this child, so small as to seem almost transparent, make him afraid? He can crush her like a starling if he chooses. He steps towards her, resolved to subdue her, as Fallen and his minions have failed to do.

But when she turns to face him, Doada tumbles backwards through his life. He is suddenly in his parents' garden long ago, where another girl turned towards him. She had *these*

139

clear, dark eyes, *this* heart-shaped face, *this* wayward hair and *this* strength somehow hidden by fragility. *That* girl and the one who stands before him now are identical.

Doada feels the need to sit. While the girl returns to studying the swifts, he slumps in the metal chair that stands beside the dials and batteries and wires of the Turner, the device he invented for turning the power of siardw into his servant.

Is the resemblance some odd coincidence?

He pulls the report of her capture from his case and pores over it again. Intelligence from a schoolteacher had given them the names Breen Avvon, the mother, and the eldest child, Harlon. There had been two others, twins the teacher thought, but couldn't remember their names. Names – almost certainly false ones – helped very little.

He reads on, and finally there it is, the telling clue in the medical report that he never bothered to read. There are the details of the injuries that put five officers out of action.

Gun shot wound, upper left thigh, trauma to femur.

Exactly the same injury, five times. Breen Avvon wasn't just a protective mother with an old gun underneath her bed, she was a professional. Not just any professional. Doada's seen a list of wounds like this just once before, in the reports of Green Thorn raids fifteen years ago, attacks lead by the Boogam, the Ghost.

GSW upper left thigh, trauma to femur.

This isn't a list of injuries, it's a *signature*. A message from the Ghost herself that says *I'm back, beware!* The mother of the Listener child who stands right in front of him is the notorious rebel leader that he thought dead. The girl's looks are no coincidence; she got them from her mother, the woman who was once a child who turned to him to say: 'I won't tell them you're a Listener, Doada,'

The woman who was once his sister, Toren Sisal.

Doada's always known what his sister became. It's the dangerous secret that he's kept for years. How would it look for the Automator's Head of Intelligence to be the brother of the rebel queen? But he believed the danger to be passed and Toren long gone, shot as an unnamed rebel by the prison capo in Liberty City. By the time her photograph had crossed Doada's desk and alerted him to the fact that Toren had been captured, her body had been incinerated. Doada remembers how apologetic the capo was.

'Was the prisoner of especial interest, Commander?' the man had asked.

'No, no,' Doada had replied, 'just routine checking that all rebels are dealt with appropriately.'

At the time it had seemed like the perfect outcome: his sister destroyed, anonymously. But the capo had lied, almost certainly to cover up the fact that Toren had escaped.

Too late to speculate. Too late to wonder where she has been all this time. So many secrets of Toren's life it would be good to know. But here is one he does know: that she has children and he can use them as a weapon to bring her down. She won't slip through his fingers this time.

He looks at the child before him, so exactly like Toren at the same age. *This* is the means by which his sister can be lured, trapped, destroyed, and all those dangerous secrets buried at long last. This time he won't trust anyone to do it but himself.

Before the child can be bait she must be made malleable, and that tricky siardw burned into a useable form, the sooner the better. He decides to prepare the equipment, and is so absorbed that he doesn't notice that the girl has moved silently across the room, to stand right beside him.

'The seeds are sown,' she whispers. 'You sowed them. The sky will hatch; you cracked it. The ocean will ring; you struck it. It has begun; you cannot stop it.'

Her voice is quiet and musical, but Doada does not find it pleasant.

He grabs her wrists. She is puny, breakable; she can't begin to struggle against his strength. He forces her into the chair and straps her down. He attaches the pads to her skin, and flicks the on switch. A powerful wave of lectric is now concentrated to the very part of her brain where her power lies, enough to change its nature and make it into a tool to be used. Doada has refined this method greatly since he first used it on himself but he knows very well the pain that this will cause. The child's eyes close, tears squeeze from under her lids, her hands clench into balls.

Good. It's working. Doada waits, spectating the suffering with cool impatience. Next, he expects her body will lose all tone, she will be as limp as a rag as all her resistance crumble under the crushing pressure of the current. Then her eyes will open and look at him, and they will be as blank as stones. She will be his creature to be used as he chooses.

But she does not go limp. Her hands open and close, open

142

and close, like wings flapping hard, to take off. She begins to sing. Quietly, falteringly at first, then growing louder, surer, the same unruly tumble of notes as the starling. Louder and louder she sings as Doada turns his dials higher and higher to a level that would not just turn her, but *destroy* her, leave her an empty husk or a corpse.

But the singing does not stop. It fills his head until he wants to scream.

Then, with a small pop and an apologetic curl of white smoke, it's all over. The machine is dead. Doada flicks its switches, turns its dials, but to no avail. The child slumps onto the table, silent at last.

Doada's moment of triumph is over very quickly because Xeno lifts her head, just enough to look at him. Her eyes are pools of liquid light and dark fire, not at all like stones.

'Song is hard to kill,' she says.

The screams of the swifts fall into the cell like arrows.

There is sudden commotion at the cell door and Fallen rushes in, flustered all over again.

'Forgive the interruption, Commander. A message from Senior Lazit, Sir.'

He hands Doada a note.

Have just received telegraph reports of a serious rebel attack on Station Gold. Possibly Boogam? Pipeline completion threatened. Depart for the White Sea soonest. Red Blade team and airship await you. Warmest regards, Lazit.

Doada thinks quickly. He could refuse to go. The time is fast approaching when Lazit must be openly challenged. But not yet. For now he'll keep the old guard sweet. In any case, there have been enough bungled operations to thwart the rebels. He'll oversee this one himself. But, in his absence, the child and her secret must be secure.

'I must leave at once,' he tells Fallen. 'Double the security on this cell. The child is not to be spoken to by *anyone*. She's far too dangerous. Anyone at all. Feed her. She's no use to us dead.'

Fallen nods and glances at the burnt-out Turner. It's the fifth the girl has done for in a week.

*

Doada turns up the collar of his cat-skin coat. He chose the skins himself and its beauty is a comfort. He needs comfort on this miserable mission. Station Gold is a ghastly place at the best of times, dirty and primitive. It has not been improved by explosives and fire, or by the fact that the cold makes his glasses steam up continually.

He sits behind a makeshift desk in what remains of some greasy little office behind the canteen. On the other side of the mercifully closed door, the surviving guards and the officers who have come from HQ are trying to restore order to the chaos the rebel strike has created. Tomorrow the Automator elite force, the Red Blade, will get to work. They will find the rebels and their filthy animals and crush them all into a bloody stain on the snow.

This attack was not the Boogam's work. He saw that at once. Too crude. Fifteen years ago when she and her Green Thorn cronies attacked the first version of this station, the guards hardly knew they'd been hit until the drilling rig had dropped to the bottom of the ocean and the oil tanks had leaked their contents onto the ice.

But there are clues here he must unravel if he is to return to Fidrac as quickly as possible. Where did the Celeddi get explosives? You can't make bombs of ice and seal fat. So who helped them? If there are traitors amongst the guards, he will weed them out.

There's a knock and his aide, Mattock, pokes his narrow face around the door. Mattock is the perfect balance of ambition and stupidity, packaged in the sort of good looks that will not last beyond thirty; he is useful, decorative and too dim to ever be a threat.

'One of the station guard staff to see you, Commander Eye sir. Says he's got "information".'

Doada rolls his eyes.

'The only information I really require now would be where in this awful place there might be something *remotely* edible.'

'Ah yes, I'm onto that, sir.' Mattock risks an enthusiastic smile. 'I have an ensin scouring the remaining food stores. Shall I send this capo in?'

Doada nods wearily, and Mattock holds the door aside for the man to enter. He is large and unwieldy with a pale, soft face that is a mess of cuts and blossoming bruises. His uniform encloses his body in the same way as a mould encloses a jelly. He doesn't look as if he could possibly have information of any kind in his head. Expending charm on him is, Doada decides, a waste of energy. It's not worth the bother of asking his name, or even looking at him properly.

'Alright. Sit down,' Doada snaps. 'Tell me what you have come to say, then get out.'

The capo clears his throat.

'The Boogam, sir,' he says. 'I think she was behind this attack.'

'*Really?*' says Doada. 'And what leads you to this shatteringly intelligent conclusion?'

'Her child was here, and that can't be coincidence. Little brat did this to me.' The man points to his bloodied face. 'Posing as one of the volunteers. One of my associates picked him up.'

The Boogam's child! Doada is suddenly very interested but he doesn't want to show it. Slowly, he allows his gaze to slide from the paperwork on the desk before him to the capo's face. Could this mess of a man be useful? Is he dangerous? There is certainly something vaguely familiar in these doughy features. Doada turns on a little charm.

'Given that no one knows who the Boogam is, dear boy, how can we possibly know that some random child belongs to her, or him?'

The man reaches into his filthy uniform and pulls out a photo.

'The boy was carrying this. He admitted it was his mother and his sister.'

Doada looks at the photo and has to restrain his desire to gasp. This is indeed Toren Sisal, his sister, taken some time ago, over a decade he'd guess. About the time when she was supposed to be a scrap of ash in a prison incinerator. But where was it taken? That is *not* a mountain scene. The skinny child beside her must be the older daughter, though quite changed now, he's sure. How is this man in possession of the dangerous knowledge that the Boogam looks like this? Doada must tread carefully.

'Really, Officer. This is *mos*t far fetched,' Doada says quietly, as if dissuading a favourite child from eating the last piece of chocolate.

The capo looks keenly at him from his broken face and Doada notices a dark glimmer of cunning in his eyes.

'It might seem that to some,' he says, 'but not to them that *know.*'

Doada spreads his hands.

'What *do* you mean, Officer … I don't believe you gave me your name.'

'I don't believe you asked for it, *Doada*. I'm Vellum, Cat Vellum; we grew up in the same village.'

Doada stares and for the second time in less than thirty-six hours is tumbled back into his past. Cat Vellum, the useful thug who did Automator dirty work back home. The one Doada had given certain *information* long ago.

'Do you remember me now, Commander Eye?'

Vellum sits a little straighter now and looks boldly into Doada's face. Yes, he does remember, although the flesh the man has gathered over the years has changed him. Doada remembers Cat Vellum and what he did. But he won't give that away.

'Yes. I think I *vaguely* remember you.'

Vellum nods toward the photograph in Doada's fingers.

'I know who that is because I knew your sister. *And* I know who she became when she joined the rebels.'

147

There's a clear threat in Vellum's voice.

'Well, *dear boy*, as I'm sure you remember, my sister disappeared seventeen years ago,' Doada hisses. 'She was the top military graduate of her year. More likely to have been a victim of a rebel assassination rather than ... anything else.'

Vellum is stony faced and determined now. He always was a nasty, cunning piece of work, Doada thinks.

'You and I both know who your sister is,' Vellum continues. 'You don't need to know *how* I know. Only that I do. And so does my old dad, happy in a place where you could never find him. And we'll keep quiet, same we always have. I'll even help you track down her son, because I daresay he'd be useful to you. But there's a price.'

Doada cleans his glasses on his silk kerchief, then examines Vellum closely. Two of Toren's three children in his power would be excellent. But it won't change the fact that Cat Vellum and his father may have to be disposed of, however they know what they know.

'Well, Cat, what a very clever chap you have turned out to be.' Doada smiles. 'But not so clever as to hold on to this interesting asset. Where is the boy now?'

'Escaped with the raiders. Riding one of their stinking beasts. But I know where they've gone.'

'You do?'

'I do. And I'm pretty sure no one else on the station does. Not to their usual camp on the ice. Further south.'

Doada has no doubt that the Red Blade can track the rebels without Vellum's help, but they will simply kill everything they find. He needs this child alive, and taken anonymously. So, for now, he needs Vellum alive too.

'Alright, Vellum. You and I will lead a small advance force to retrieve this child. We will have a short window of opportunity to take the child alive before my Red Blade grind the rebels into the snow. But we need to act quickly.'

'Agreed. But I need some advancement in my career as my reward.'

'Oh, you do? Well, I'll make sure you are *amply* rewarded. Shall I hang onto this photograph for safekeeping?'

Doada puts the picture in his case.

'Please yourself,' Vellum says calmly. 'I've got copies.'

It's a bold lie, of course. Who locates a camera in the chaotic aftermath of a rebel attack?

'Of course you do,' Doada answers. 'Of course you do! Now, ready to leave in an hour, shall we say, *dear boy*?'

Toren's Story

1

 'Graduated top of her class in everything!'

Toren Sisal could hear her father's voice all the way from the hall.

'He's boasting about me again,' Toren said. 'I wish he wouldn't.'

'Then you shouldn't be so clever and such a good shot.' Aylie was always a straight talker. Nobody would have dared to call Aylie a servant. She took Toren's cap, with its new badge of rank, and the rifle case, and set them on the cabinet by the front door.

'You can't greet guests wearing a gun,' Aylie said, with a wink, 'no matter how much you dislike them. Go on in, you're late.'

She gave Toren a little shove toward the receiving room. 'I'll get your brother out of his laboratory.'

'What's he doing in there?'

'The usual. Something disgusting with dead birds and lectric.' Aylie rolled her eyes. 'It stinks.'

Toren stepped into the room, which was flooded with evening light. It would show her every detail. She pulled her uniform jacket down and hoped that Mother would not notice that it was a little snug. What would her mother find most unacceptable about the fact that Toren was pregnant at seventeen? That the father was a Listener? Or that he was the son of their ostler? A servant's boy, she would say and roll her eyes. Well, she'd never know now. Toren took a deep breath and smiled at her parents and their guests. She would give nothing at all away. She would be as calm and as confident as ever.

Toren took the glass her mother offered and sat with her back to the light, looking into the room. It contained all she loved and all she hated about this life she was about to leave behind. She loved her father, Borden. He had been a captain in the navy and fought Nordsky pirates in the Green Sea. Toren didn't want to tread the same path but she had wanted to make him proud. That was the reason she had entered the Academy to train as one of the Vipers, the elite fighting corps. She loved her mother, Tailer, too: fierce and fearless in spite of all her vanity. She hadn't been much older than Toren was now when she'd married the naval captain twice her age.

But she hated her parents as well. They talked about how much they disapproved of the way the Automators were changing the world, but what was the good of talk? Talk wouldn't stop them. They turned a blind eye to Doada's dealings with the bunch of uniformed thugs that the Automators called their 'security force'. And as for her parents' guests tonight? The Reeven Dopp family? All five of them as bland and empty headed as each other. How could her parents ever think she would one day marry their eldest boy, Stoode?

151

He'd irritated her quite enough when they were children and now he was the shining-light new recruit of the Automators.

Toren answered their questions about her training politely.

...Yes, all Vipers were trained to kill with any weapons, including a tea cup.

...Yes, it was true she had won the Academy prize for target accuracy.

...Yes, they had to run, swim and climb every morning before breakfast; and yes, even when it snowed and yes, sometimes blindfolded.

It was like playing ping-pong. How she longed to tell them all the truth. That the way the Vipers were being used to serve the Automators disgusted her. She would not have her skill used to destroy Listeners and break communities apart. Now they were to be used in the White Sea to crush the tribes people who opposed their filthy tar well. Their slogans about *the Tyranny of Nature* were utter nonsense. Nature was no tyrant, it was the provider of all that human beings needed, if only they could see it. No, the only tyrants were the Automators; Toren Sisal would never serve them. In fact she'd been working against them since her training began. Building a network of trained fighters who would soon stand up to them.

But for now she kept her face composed and her voice pleasant. She was trained in all kinds of warfare and this was merely another.

'I have been posted on secret government business,' she informed the room calmly. 'I leave in the morning and I cannot say when I will return.'

It was true enough. She *was* going and but she wasn't

going as a Viper and she had no intention of ever coming back. She was leaving to join the rebellion in the White Sea. Tui, her baby's father, would follow in a few weeks. It was all planned.

Into the consternation that her announcement had created – Father disappointed, Mother furious and the Reeven Dopps all clucking over this piece of gossip like hens over a fat worm, came Doada. He entered the room looking dazed, his normally tidy hair on end and a large sooty mark on one temple. He smelled of burnt flesh. He fidgeted between two seats then finally came to sit beside Toren, staring intently at her.

'Do you agree that it's time to eradicate Listeners?' he asked, in a voice that everyone could hear. 'That they tie us to the primitive past?'

His eyes were wide, burning, and he didn't seem able to keep still. What was the matter with him? Was he ill, or just trying to get attention? Whatever it was, Toren wouldn't let him make a drama. She smiled sweetly and said, 'Well, big brother, it's delightful to see you too!'

Doada's face went pale, his eyes bulged and he poked Toren in the middle of her chest.

'Answer. My. Question!' he demanded. Toren held her brother's gaze. He had almost succeeded in making her angry. The secret that she knew about him sat on the very tip of her tongue. How easy it would be to tell it, to say: *but you're a Listener yourself, Doada, why would you want to get rid of them?*

She shut her mouth and kept her words safely inside. The background chatter ceased.

'Answer. My. Question!' Doada said again. Tailer laughed nervously.

153

'Doada! You haven't greeted our guests,' she said, trying to defuse this awkward situation, but Stoode broke in, rudely.

'No, Madame Sisal. I'd like to hear my comrade's question answered. The cancerous scourge of Listeners affects us all.'

Toren glanced at Stoode, his mean, pinched little face. Just the sort of narrow-minded idiot the Automators loved. He'd been appointed to recruit more lawless thugs to join them. She saw a look pass between Stoode and her brother. What were they up to?

An answer came immediately in the form of thunderous banging on the front door. Aylie rushed in, white faced.

'It's the Automators!' she said, shocked. 'They say we're harbouring Listeners!'

Borden strode towards the door.

'Well, we'll see about *that!*'

But Toren saw another look pass between Doada and Stoode. This was their doing.

A gang of black-and-red-uniformed men and women stood at the door. In spite of their masks, Toren recognised most of them: a selection of the meanest people in the county. Their leader stepped forward; Toren knew him at once. Cat Vellum, one of her brother's new gang of creepy friends. Vellum was good at looking threatening so, although his voice was polite, his body gave a very different message.

'We have reason to believe, Captain Sisal,' he began, 'that you are harbouring a Listener in your employ.'

'Well, Cat Vellum,' Borden replied. 'I know you in spite of your mask. I remember you as a small lad, playing in the mud. Looks like you're still playing there. But I'm a good citizen as you all know, and I believe in progress, so I don't know why you're here.'

Vellum shifted the grip on the iron-tipped staff in his right hand and his thugs did the same with theirs. They were contemptible but Toren was certain it was all show. Borden was too respected, too well loved for them to risk real violence.

'I'll explain, shall I?' Cat said. 'Your ostler, Meyer and his boy, Tui ? *Especially* good at the job. *Very, very* good with the horses. *Too* good. It's obvious they're Listeners. We've come to take them for re-education; we'll take you too if you don't cooperate.'

Borden didn't raise his voice, or get angry. He just seemed to grow in all directions. Cat Vellum took a step back.

'Well, in that case,' Borden said quietly, 'you'll have to wait, because Ostler Meyer is visiting his sick brother. And as for Tui. Perhaps your spies didn't tell you that he's gone to sea: Apprentice Naval Artist on the *Bowhead*, currently painting pictures a hundred miles off Angellis. Not too many horses out there, I'd say.'

That took the wind out of their sails. Never mind that it was a bending of the truth, it wasn't what they expected and they weren't sure what to do. Toren could tell how much Cat wanted to dispense with words and just get down to hitting people.

'When is Meyer expected back?' he snarled.

'He'll return tomorrow,' Borden replied. 'So I'll thank you, Cat, to take your friends off my property *right now*.'

Borden turned as if the conversation was at an end and that's when Vellum struck, hitting him a crack on the side of the head with the iron tip of his staff. The blow was so sudden, so entirely unexpected that, even with her training, Toren failed to see it coming. The moment that it fell, she saw she had been foolish; this was what they'd planned all along. Borden fell to the ground.

'Step back,' Vellum told Tailer, 'or you'll get the same. As will all who obstruct us in our duty. We will search Meyer's accommodation and I'll thank you, Master Reeven Dopp, to direct us.'

Stoode came forward, unable to hide his glee in how this situation was playing out.

'With pleasure,' he said and led Vellum with his thugs across the yard and between the trees to the stables.

Tailer dropped to her husband's side, he was bleeding and unconscious but still breathing. Toren was frozen with shock. And it took Aylie's scolding to make her help carry Borden inside. The remaining Reeven Dopps had already retreated, scuttled off like startled crabs into their odd little lectric veekle, and banged off down the road.

While Aylie and Tailer tended to Borden, Toren came to find Doada sitting at the bottom of the stairs where he had been from the moment they had opened the door to Cat Vellum.

'How could you, Doada? See what your betrayal of the Meyers has done? Go and look at Father! Go and *look* at what you've done.' She knew that she was screaming at him now and she didn't care. What she really wanted to do was hit him.

'You have to stop this!' Toren yelled. 'You have to stop them. You *know* what they'll do to the Meyers.' She lowered her voice and leaned closer. 'If you don't, *I'll tell.*'

Doada slowly raised his eyes to her. There was nothing in them. No shock. No remorse. *Nothing.* He hardly seemed to be human any more. He shook his head and smiled a thin, joyless smile.

'But you see, *dear* sister, there's no longer anything *to* tell.' He raised his thin hand to point at the sooty place on his temple. 'Because today I've done it; I've burned that part of my brain clean away. I'm free. Free of that tyranny, of listening, forever. I can't listen any more, but I can *dictate.* I can *order.* I can have my *will.'*

Toren stepped back from him then in horror and watched him walk, like a dead thing, out of the door and towards the stables to join the others.

She stood in the dimness of the hall trying to calm herself. It was true that Meyer was away, but her father had lied, Tui was home on leave. They'd find that out soon enough and come to get him. Right now she knew where Tui would be, at the far end of the property, at the little outlier stable and paddock where he kept his own two horses. If she left at once she would have time to get there and warn him before Cat Vellum and his thugs got wind of it.

Toren was suddenly overcome with what she must do; leave without goodbyes, right now and forever. But there was one thing from this house that she had to take. She crossed the hall into the small book-lined room that was her father's study. She pressed the end of the seventh floorboard from the window, levering it up and revealing the cavity beneath. Hardly a subtle hiding place. Certainly not enough to keep Doada foxed. She reached in and pulled out the wooden tube inside.

She unscrewed the lid to check that the map was there and resisted the temptation to pull it out and run her fingers over the blue of the ocean and the green of the little island, the island not on any other map. She hoped her father would understand why she'd taken it, out of love for him and the deep desire to keep it safe; to keep hidden whatever secrets it held. She screwed the lid back on and closed the study door behind her.

Back in the hall quiet voices from the receiving room told Toren that her father was still unconscious, but Tailer and Aylie were there with him. He would be all right. She would never see any of them again. She grabbed her rifle and an old coat of her father's and ran down the track to the furthest paddock with the map inside its tube bouncing on her back.

Tui sat in the long grass. Patch and Ochre, his favourite horses, rested their muzzles against his shoulders. Tui's eyes were closed but the horses' sharp ears picked up Toren's quiet approach and his eyes snapped open. He smiled at her, his happiest and most relaxed smile. Toren bit her lip and delivered the bad news.

Tui was only two years her senior but he had the calm of someone much older. In spite of his composure, he understood the danger well enough.

'We'll have to leave with what we have here.'

He took an old sacking jacket from a peg in the stables and packed a tarpaulin as a makeshift tent. There was a can that would do to carry water and a horse blanket for a bed. Then they saddled Patch and Ochre, and left.

'Pa's no fool,' he told Toren. 'He'll see them waiting in the yard for him from the road and he'll just turn round. He'll go to my Aunt Mayo's in the mountains. With things as they are, it was only a matter of time before he'd have to run.'

Tui's presence calmed Toren's raging heart. They rode down the valley, and crossed the river in the dusk. The water soaked their legs and the horses' flanks but in the soft evening the chill didn't matter. Owls called and bats wove patterns over the pools and through the treetops, as the wild night took over from the tamed human day. When they reached the moor, nightjars churred in the half light.

Inside Toren the baby was only the size of a bean and yet, through it, she felt her connection to the life of this place more keenly than ever before. Her soldier's training would not hold back the tears.

'I feel as if everything is singing!' she said. 'It's so hard to leave it all behind.'

Tui's smile flashed white in the gloom, and he reached across and took her hand.

'Don't worry,' he said. 'One thing the sea's taught me is that singing is *everywhere*. As long as you feel it, you're not leaving anything behind.'

Toren dried her tears and smiled back because Tui was right. It was suddenly clear to her that the thing that mattered most of all was to protect this singing that connected everyone and everything together. No matter what the cost.

'We're going to need new names, Tui,' she said, as they rode on through the dark.

'Oh yes?'

'I have one for you already: a brave Viper captain whose portrait I looked at every time we had a formal dinner in the women's mess room.'

'Was he handsome?'

'She. Oh *very*.'

'Then I accept her name!'

'I name you … Faro Elmly! Now you have to name me.'

'Hmmm…' Tui scratched Ochre's mane. 'My great, great grandfather was a famous insect Listener. I'm sure he'd be happy for you to take his name.'

'Can I hear it first?'

Tui shook his head. 'Who ever gets to hear their name before they're given it!'

'Alright!' Toren laughed. 'Alright, I accept!'

'Then I name you Breen Avvon!'

7

Out of the Forest

Harlon

 Enkalamba places her large feet carefully on the bare earth of the narrow path. Each footstep is quiet and precise, like the full stop at the end of the loose, rolling sentence of her walk. While they have been travelling, Harlon has got to know the details of the elephant's movements very well: the sway of her fleshy tail, the pattern into which the wrinkles of her skin fall as her hind legs move, the lazy flap of her large ears. Occasionally, her trunk flips out to one side to breathe something in, or twines round a tasty snack-sized plant that is delivered to her mouth.

The path winds between and around trees that are three times bigger than any trees Harlon has ever seen before. Each one is draped and decorated with a thousand other smaller plants, using the trees' branches to steal a place in the light. The tree trunks dwarf Enkalamba and stretch up as if they truly were holding up the sky. Its blue seems very far away down here in the deep green of the forest floor. Tolly's fears about being set upon by forest creatures have proved unfounded. In the hours since they left the camp behind, the elephant and Tolly are almost the only living things Harlon has seen, apart from the

161

leeches that wriggle over her trouser leg in search of skin and a few huge butterflies that flash their wings in the patches of sunlight and are gone. But the invisible evidence of life, nurtured by warmth and rain, is everywhere. Insects and frogs call from the tangle of leaves and stems that surround them, bird and monkey voices echo through the canopy high, high above.

Enkalamba hasn't 'spoken' since the morning when they set out. In fact no one has. The longer they have gone without speaking, the less Harlon can think of what to say to Tolly, who plods on doggedly in front of her without comment or complaint. Harlon is beginning to think that the trees too have voices, that what she hears is more than the sighing of the breeze through their leaves. She listens harder and harder, trying to hear through the noise of her own breath to catch a sound behind, below, between the ordinary range of things that her ears are used to. She's sure she hears it one moment, and the next it's gone.

In fact, she is so busy listening that she almost walks straight into Tolly, who is standing still on the trail. For the first time all day Enkalamba has stopped. The elephant raises her trunk in an enquiring 's' shape, reaching up and turning the end like a periscope, searching the strands of scent that stripe the humid forest air. She steps off the path, gives a short rumble and, in just a few paces, has vanished into the green.

'What's going on?' Tolly asks, immediately anxious. 'Where's she gone?'

'I don't know,' Harlon replies, 'but I think her rumble meant "rest and eat something". So I'm going to do as I'm told.'

That almost manages to make Tolly smile. They find a tree root to sit on and rummage in one of the packs to find something to eat. Harlon pulls out a slab of the drier version of grey goo, wrapped in paper.

'I don't know what I was hoping to find, but it wasn't this!'

'If you saw what they serve up in the camp where I did my training, you'd think that was your ma's home cooking. C'mon, just tear a bit off.'

Harlon does as she's asked and they sit side by side, chewing.

'Actually,' says Tolly, 'this is even worse than the stuff from the training camp kitchen.'

'Mmm,' Harlon replies thoughtfully, 'I think this could be about the most disgusting thing I've ever eaten.'

They look at each other and giggle.

'This is mad,' says Tolly, though another chewy mouthful. 'I'm sitting in the Woken Forest with an enemy and a talking elephant!'

'On the way to who knows where, when something will be delivered out of the sky,' Harlon adds.

'Like angels,' Tolly says.

Harlon frowns, she's never heard of 'angels'.

'What are angels?' she asks.

Tolly smiles. 'People with wings and magic powers. Folk used to believe they lived in the sky and protected ordinary humans. My ma had a little plaster angel beside her bed. She said it was called Michael.'

'Michael?' Harlon says. 'Doesn't seem like a very magical sort of name.'

'Well,' sighs Tolly, 'didn't do much magic for her, that's for sure.'

'I'm sorry about your ma,' Harlon says. 'What was she like?'

'Quiet. She loved birds. She used to feed the pigeons on the balcony of our flat. She never liked what the Automators said about Listeners. Not like my da. "Nature's a cruel master," he always used to say. "Those Listeners, they want to take us all back to the dark".'

'What do *you* think, Tolly?'

She shrugs.

'Doesn't matter what I think. I haven't got any…'

There is a sudden torrent of sound, a cacophony of bird calls, and Enkalamba steps into a patch of sunlight on the path ahead. Her shape is indistinct, hidden by a cloud of wings: electric-blue forest kingfishers, tiny jewelled sunbirds, the slow, smooth flap of green turacos, the swoop of bee-eaters. They flash in and out of the dappled patches of sunlight, a rainbow-chaos, their calls are a storm of noise, even at this distance. Then, at the same moment, they all fall utterly, completely silent, and form into an orderly stream, an aerial procession that flies over Enkalamba. As each part of the flock passes above her, the birds touch down on her back or head, just for a moment, and then disperse in all directions, back into the invisibility of the forest.

When all the birds have gone, the elephant looks over her shoulder at Harlon and Tolly. She rumbles once, then sets off at such a pace that the girls have to race to catch up with her.

'What was *that?*' Tolly asks.

Harlon can only shake her head.

The next few hours are hard going. It rains, the path grows steeper and the humans make slow progress along a trail that is, in many places, liquid mud flowing over hidden, slippery rocks. There are many falls and there are leeches and mosquitos of several kinds that *do* find skin and have to be persuaded to let go. Enkalamba is silently patient, waiting while they scramble along behind her. And every time she waits, she has what Harlon and Tolly quickly come to call 'visitors'. In one spot a flock of swifts with rain sparkling and splashing off their wings cut paths around the elephant as fine as embroidery, before melting back into the canopy. At another, a crowd of small green lizards carpets the path then flows all over Enkalamba's skin as if they were a new set of clothes. At another, beetles materialise out of the forest and settle on Enkalamba's back like encrusting jewels, before vanishing as mysteriously as they arrived.

Not all her visitors come in a crowd. A family of monkeys, with dark, solemn faces and beautiful white and russet bands on their sides, step delicately into the elephant's path then climb onto her back and sit for long minutes, like people taking tea. Two large, long-necked creatures with striped legs and skin like chocolate-coloured velvet steal through the shadows.

'What are *they*?' Tolly breathes.

'Okapi!' Harlon replies. 'I saw a picture in a book once.'

They stay only long enough to let Enkalamba touch them with her trunk and then they're gone.

The rain stops and, late in the day, they reach a river. The sky opens up above them in a wide ribbon of blue and orange where the sun is sinking. Above the trees on the other side, the purple outline of the Bird Hills is visible for the first time. They still seem a long way off. It's obvious they are going to have to cross this river, which is swollen with the rain that has fallen steadily all afternoon.

'I think we'll have to swim it,' Harlon says, 'but I'd like to wait until morning. The sun sinks fast here. I don't want to be crawling out on the other side in the dark.'

Tolly peers fearfully at the roiling water.

'I bet there's all sorts in that. Monsters. *And* I can't swim.'

Enkalamba takes no notice of their fears. She has clearly decided that the crossing *will* be made right now. But she isn't expecting them to swim: she kneels down in the mud in front of them and points her trunk first to each of them and then onto her back; she will carry them across.

The prospect of riding on an elephant is exciting, even if it means a dangerous crossing of a river in flood. Harlon decides that if ever she sees Ash again, this is one of the first things she will tell him. But for Tolly this is one strain too many and it takes Harlon a while to convince her that she will be safe and that there are no 'monsters' in the river. At last they are both on Enkalamba's back. Tolly in front, close to the back of Enkalamba's head, with her feet tucked underneath her ears, and Harlon right behind her. With a purring rumble, Enkalamba starts to move into the water, feeling each step carefully, huffing the air with her trunk and flapping her ears.

At first the water is only up to the top of Enkalamba's legs. Tolly tucks her feet up to keep them out of the water and Harlon has to tell her that holding on is more important than dryness. Reluctantly Tolly pushes her feet below the waterline and back to their notch behind the ears. With a sudden downward step they are into deeper water. It flows over Enkalamba's back so that just the top of her head and the end of her trunk are out of the water. Harlon can feel the push of the current against her legs and body; the problem is there's nothing to hold on to, all she can do is grip with her legs, but trying to wrap them tightly to the elephant's body is like trying to grip a giant ball that is now slippery with muddy water. Tolly cries out in fear.

'It's alright, we're nearly there!' Harlon reassures her, even though they are barely halfway across and the water could so easily get even deeper.

What will they do if the water gets so deep that Enkalamba's feet don't touch the bottom? Can elephants swim and, if they can, how do humans cling to one while they are doing it? Ma's voice pops into Harlon's head again. It seems darkly funny in this situation: *you trained for this.*

No, Ma, Harlon thinks, I definitely *didn't* train for this.

Harlon wishes that Enkalamba would use her Speaker skills to tell them how she thinks this crossing is going. But all that comes from the elephant is the usual low rumble that both girls feel through their desperately clinging legs which communicates very little.

The sun is low, shining straight down the line of the river and turning its surface gold. It silhouettes a shape moving fast against the current. And then another and another. Logs? No, logs can't move upstream. Tolly points, her eyes wide and white with fear.

'What are those?'

Harlon doesn't answer, although she knows quite well what they must be. Crocodiles. The way they are moving tells her that these are not some more of Enkalamba's visitors. But with her eyes beneath the water, the elephant can have no way of knowing that they're there. If she can smell them, then she's giving no sign of it.

Five of them hang in the water, just downstream. They must be working hard to hold their place in the current, but all that Harlon can see above the water are their rough snouts and the unblinking yellow eyes. They don't come close, just shift back and forth across the current, waiting for one of Enkalamba's passengers to fall off and be delivered to them by the river.

The water swirls and washes. It's so hard to hold on. Tolly's legs slip and she slides sideways. Immediately, the crocs react, moving fast to where the current would wash Tolly downstream. Two of them fight over position, showing their teeth. Harlon grabs Tolly and brings her upright. Finally, they really are almost there. With a great effort that shakes her whole body, Enkalamba pulls herself up onto some underwater ledge and lifts her head clear of the water. At last she can see the crocs. She gives a small trumpet of alarm, flaps her ears at them and sends a rumble like a growl out through the water. The crocodiles move lazily a little further off, and with the far bank within reach, Harlon's heart stops racing.

But the downstream crocodiles aren't alone in the river. Without any warning, another shoots from upstream and clamps its jaws around Enkalamba's trunk. She trumpets in alarm, and pulls against the croc's strength. She steps sideways and falls back into deep water, rolling over and sending Harlon and Tolly floating free. The elephant's struggling body gives them a little shelter from the current for a moment and Harlon reaches to grab some part of Tolly before she is swept away. Her fingers close on the strap of Tollys pack, but it breaks under the strain and Tolly is caught in an eddy and disappears, spluttering, under the water. Harlon can see nothing under the surface in either direction. Upstream, Enkalamba snorts and trumpets as she tries to find firm footholds. A croc's white belly flashes at the surface, but it's impossible to see what's really happening amid the splashing and struggling. In any case, there's nothing Harlon can do to help. While she's in the water she's at risk and, as a crocodile dinner, she'll be no use to anyone. She swims, kicking her legs with all the strength she can muster, makes it to the slippery bank, and crawls out.

When she's finished coughing up water, Harlon looks up and down the river. The golden light is fading; soon it will be properly dark. Enkalamba is no longer trumpeting but backing steadily from the river, dragging the crocodile onto the bank. She has her trunk wound around its jaws, clamping them closed and lifting the front end of its body up, so that its front legs flail and its fingers spread helplessly, clawing at the air. Its tail and back legs continue to thrash and it's obvious the elephant is using all her strength to hold it. But gradually, its struggling subsides. It hangs limp in her trunk. Slowly, Enkalamba lowers it so all its feet are on the ground. She lifts her trunk and steps back. For a split second the crocodile gazes at the elephant, its eyes gleaming in the last light, then in one panicked movement it's back in the muddy river and beating its tail in retreat. Without a moment's hesitation,

Enkalamba wades back into the water and moves down stream. In moments, she's vanished into the growing shadows. Harlon waits and watches as the last light fades. She listens for the sound of rumbling or of splashing: for Tolly calling out. There is nothing but the indifferent voice of the river.

Harlon sinks down on the bank. She's wet and cold. She knows she should build a fire, take off her wet clothes, see if any food has survived in the pack that somehow made it with her to the bank. But she just can't make herself do any of that.

In the trees above her there is chatter as birds and monkeys find shelter. The strange and otherworldly sound-symphony of night starts up. The stretcher bearer, Budly, told her when she asked last night that the sounds were the calls of many creatures: night birds, insects and frogs. In the trees a little upstream, fireflies begin to flash where the branches lean over the water and stars blossom in the rain-washed sky. But the peace and beauty just make Harlon feel even more bleak and alone. Her heart is full of rocks: sharp and jagged. She wraps her arms around her folded legs and all the tears she's held back come at once. No one speaks inside her head. There's no comfort. She is all alone.

Into the hollow left inside her as the tears subside comes a strand of melody. Huskily, she begins to sing and, as she does, words come to meet the melody on her tongue.

That song it rang the world around
Oceans, oceans away so deep
That song it rang the world around
Ocean deep away,
Ocean deep away.

170

Where did this song come from? She cannot think, but it doesn't matter, it's warmed her up. Not enough though. Yes, a fire would be good. Her flint and steel are in a dry bag in the pack with a little kindling, and perhaps food. There is just enough starlight for her to find some twigs and leaves dry enough to burn. Soon she has a tiny fire. Tolly and Enkalamba may come back by morning, she tells herself. Perhaps Tolly has been injured and washed far downstream. There is still hope. More than that, there is a job to be done and Harlon can still do it. She peels the sodden dressing from her own head; the burn will be fine, she decides, better to be open to the air. Curled around the meagre warmth of her smoky little fire she coaxes back her toughness and her strength and, at last, falls asleep.

Enkalamba's rumble comes faintly into the side of Harlon's body where it rests on the ground. She sits up and looks around. The sky is growing lighter by the second and tails of mist wind up from the river. Birds of all kinds fly down to drink. But there's no sign of the elephant or the ensin. The rumble comes again, this time more strongly, no longer through the ground but through the air too. Harlon stands and looks downriver into the dazzle of the sunrise. Splashing through the shallows, in the deep shade under the overhanging trees, is Enkalamba and, sitting straight up on her neck, is Tolly.

Tolly shouts, Enkalamba trumpets and Harlon waves and waves, unable to make any sound squeeze past the lump in her throat. The elephant bends one knee to let Tolly slither slowly

171

down. Harlon would like to throw her arms round Tolly and crush the breath out of her but instead she asks, 'Are you hurt?'

'Bit battered is all. But fine. Really.'

'Good, well, there's some of that delicious grey stuff in the pack. I'll make a fire and tea in a minute.'

They stand facing each other; suddenly neither of them know what to do with their arms or faces.

'Right,' says Tolly. 'I'm starving.'

She goes to rummage in the pack, while Harlon turns to Enkalamba. She wants very much to hug some part of the huge body but instead she reaches out her arm and touches the ridged curve of the elephant's trunk, looking carefully for the injuries she's sure the crocodile's teeth must have caused. Unsure if the elephant can understand spoken words she asks, 'Are you hurt? Can I do anything for you?'

Immediately the end of the trunk reaches for her head, tweaking gently at the stubble of hair, hovering above the healing burn. Enkalamba turns a little, to fix Harlon with one eye and Harlon feels her come into her mind.

My skin is strong. Log-tooth is weak, she says. *Your friend is also strong, you are strong, strong. There is big song in you and much, much kin-making.*

She removes her trunk and begins to turn away.

I go now to feed. The other will tell all of the night's doing.

Harlon can feel Enkalamba fading from her mind. She wants so much to convey gratitude, relief, her gladness to be with this extraordinary being once again. Her mind scrabbles for a word that might do and finds the one that Tolly gave her: *Angel! You are an angel.*

Enkalamba grows back in Harlon's consciousness.

172

Angel? Yes, this was also in the other's mind. Angel! Two legs, two wings! Good kin!

And then she's gone again, leaving Harlon bereft for a moment, as the great, grey form sways away into the trees.

In daylight, it's easier to find firewood, even if everything is a little damp. Harlon builds up the fire and fusses over Tolly, toasting the grey slab until it has a sort of appetising crispness on the outside. Tolly engulfs it, then empties the water from her boots and steams, happily, before the flames.

'So,' asks Harlon. 'How come you aren't in a crocodile's belly?'

'Luck,' says Tolly. 'First time in my life, luck. I just washed past 'em. I hit a rock and crawled out and then she found me.'

'And that's it? Then how come you were away all night? I thought…' Harlon takes a breath she doesn't want to show Tolly the dark place to which she went.

'It took a while to find me, I think, and I couldn't move when she did.' Tolly narrows her eyes, trying to piece the events together. 'She had to carry me out of the river. That took a while.'

Tolly's face is glowing underneath the dirt and scratches, she seems very different from the scowling child who sat biting her nails on the edge of a pallet just two days ago.

'When Enkalamba picked me up off the rock,' she goes on, 'I was half drowned. She wrapped her trunk round me and carried me, through the water, and then up the bank. She put me down, and sort of inspected me all over. I think she did that after the crash too, but I was too out of it to know.' Tolly frowns, staring ahead of her as if trying to peer through a mist. When she continues, her voice is low and shaky.

'She spoke to me inside my head, Harlon. I'm not a Listener, I don't even really *believe* in what they're supposed to do, but she still spoke. It was like…'

Tolly struggles and fails. Starts again, reaches for Harlon's hand and presses it between both of hers.

'I can't say if I could see her or hear her. Both. It's so hard to explain. Anyway, she showed me this, thing… A song you can see, a thread you can hear? It sings and shines and it joins everything together. I could see it in my head as clear as I see you now. If the song-thread thing is destroyed everything, *everything* will die. Do you think I've gone mad?'

Harlon shakes her head. It's not mad at all. It's almost as if she already knew this. She squeezes Tolly's hand.

'Before,' Tolly continues, 'when I was working in headquarters, I heard the talk about how the top brass wanted to cut down the whole of the Southern Forest. I thought it was just so they could, I dunno, have a lot of planks to sell. But what if they want to do it to destroy the song-thready thing?'

She trails off, unconvinced now by her own words.

'It was so real when Enkalamba told me, but saying it out loud I just keep thinking what my da would say: "Listener mumbo jumbo".'

But Harlon feels that something has clicked into place.

'Perhaps that's what Enkalamba's visitors are all about!' Harlon says. 'Making the song thread stronger so the forest can fight back, like that injured boy was talking about.'

Tolly nods. 'Yeah. That makes sense. But what if Enkalamba's

174

not enough on her own? What if the forest *is* cut down? What then?'

Harlon shuts her eyes. Her gut tells her that this fits with the half-remembered song that trickles from her dreams, and the lost island Ma rambled on about. But her head can't make sense of it and now there's no more time to think, because Enkalamba's rumbling announces her return. They have a journey to make and a job to do.

Gradually the land gets steeper. It's harder to see which path to take, as many different animals have crisscrossed these slopes with their routes. Amongst the trees it's difficult to keep the summit of the hills in sight and Harlon is sure that, without Enkalamba's guidance, *this* is the place where they would have got lost.

They climb a rocky path for about two hours, Harlon wondering at the ability of Enkalamba's feet to get a hold on the small, step-like ledges. Sometimes the path won't take her weight and there's a little landslide. It's slow going. But eventually the path levels, the trees thin out and they step from a final ragged line of bushes onto an undulating ridge, covered in waving grass, green and lush with the rains. Enkalamba twines her trunk around clumps of it and passes it to her mouth, chewing slowly and with evident pleasure.

Now that they are up in the hills, everything is easier to see. Below them the forest stretches in all directions, in a thousand different shades of green.

'I never knew that places like this were real,' whispers Tolly.

'My ma and pa never even took us to the park!' A wide smile of wonder spreads over her face.

'It's like a green sea,' says Harlon, 'and every little ripple is a different kind of tree.'

Beneath the green surface of the canopy there is so much life, so many living things entwined, so many voices! The elephant flaps her ears and stretches out her trunk, as if reading the scents in the air. Harlon wonders what she hears and smells. Perhaps she can sense every one of those million, million lives, hidden now amidst the leaves and branches. As if in answer to her thought, Enkalamba's presence glows briefly in her mind.

The forest sings
one kin
one kin, growing, she says. She lowers her trunk and turns to lead them on.

Their goal, the highest hill, is clear. All they have to do is keep to the ridge and they'll get to it. Walking through the grass in the breeze and sunlight is a delight. Clouds of little butterflies swirl around them, and from time to time birds with long dark tail feathers leap up from the cover of the grass and bob up and down in the air.

'What are they doing?' Tolly asks. 'They look daft!'

'Probably showing off to attract a mate,' Harlon guesses. Tolly shakes her head, and laughs.

'Nature's a bit mad, isn't it?' she says.

Halfway into the afternoon, Enkalamba takes them on a detour down a wide gully. At first it seems that she had a simple, practical reason for this: there is a stream bubbling from the bottom of the gully with good clean water. Enkalamba drinks and the girls refill their water bottles. But the elephant wanders further and rumbles at them to follow, and they find she had another reason for coming here.

Hidden in the grass are the bleached bones of many elephants. Rib cages, thigh bones, skulls and jaw bones with grass and flowers shooting up between them. Some are huge and some must be the bones of the smallest calves. Enkalamba walks delicately amongst them, touching the bones, huffing deeply in her trunk. Harlon and Tolly look at each other.

'D'you think this is her family?' Tolly asks.

Harlon nods.

'And something killed them, all at once.'

Harlon bends to take a closer look at one skull and finds a rusted bullet lodged just below an eye socket. She feels the elephant move close and her trunk touches Harlon's shoulder, pushing her over to where Tolly stands, next to a large rib cage poking from the ground like a picket fence.

Head on head, hand on bone, Enkalamba tells them, flowing into Harlon's mind like a warm wind. With one hand on the ribs and their heads almost touching together, the girls hear Enkalamba tell her story.

My kin, here, all my kin, Enkalamba says.

Sisters.

Ma.

Daughters, all three.

Grandsons, four.

Sisters' calves, there, there, here.

Humans came here from the sky with guns, killed all.

177

Also all the forest.
Other kin.
Took away our tusks in terrible blood and blood.
Burned the rest.
I escaped. One other also. Sister, she died soon.
Here now is no sound or singing.
Empty. Unlife.
Here now I am only I.

Through the place where her fingers touch the bones, and through the great warm being of Enkalamba herself, as she stands inside her mind, Harlon feels a weight fall on her, a weight of grief and sorrow, of unimaginable depth. Here, amongst this grass are the bones of *her* mother, *her* sister, *her* brother and *her* father too.

'She's no different from us,' Tolly whispers. 'When Ma and Pa were killed, I felt this.' Tears cascade down her face.

Enkalamba stands close and touches them each in turn with her gentle trunk.

We are kin, she says.
You, I,
one kin,
one song,
tell your humans, tell them all.

When they walk back up to the hilltop to resume their journey, Harlon walks on Enkalamba's right and Tolly on her left. Each has a hand touching the beautiful folds and wrinkles of the old elephant's skin, trying to offer comfort, trying to be comforted for the shared trials and pains of living.

They reach the summit of the highest Bird Hill as the sun sinks. Enkalamba goes to find food, leaving the girls to search the hilltop for fuel for a signal fire. It's almost dark by the time they have enough. Harlon gets her spark bag and starts to strike sparks from her flint and steel onto a little knot of dried moss.

'Could you teach me to do that?' Tolly asks.

Harlon breathes the tiny flame to life.

'I *can*, but don't Automators just have a machine to do this?'

'I'm not going back to them. I want to join the rebels.'

Harlon looks at Tolly. Her plan to reach Xeno relied on Tolly going back to be an Automator. She's unsure what to do.

'I want you to help me burn off my number,' Tolly continues and pushes up the left sleeve off her shirt to show a finger-sized tattoo of six numbers on her forearm. 'This is my unique number. Everybody gets one when they sign up. I don't want it anymore.'

'It'll be too painful, Tolly,' Harlon says, 'and it might get infected. And what about your brother? Don't you want to see him again?'

'Of course I do. But...' Tolly stops and looks at Harlon. 'You're just making excuses,' she says. 'Why don't you want to help me get rid of this number?'

Harlon sighs as Ma's voice whispers in her head.

Don't trust anyone.

Ma, Harlon thinks, it's just not that simple.

'I need to get to the capital, Tolly. My sister's a Listener and the Automators took her. I let them catch me because I thought she was on board your transport. I *have* to find her. And then...' Harlon hesitates. 'It's not just about me and my sister. I made a promise to my ma. I don't really understand it, but I think it might be important somehow. Maybe connected to the song-thread thing? But I can't tell you anymore.'

'So it's kind of a secret mission?' Tolly looks excited.

Harlon nods, glad that Tolly doesn't want any more details.

'Yeah, I suppose it is. But I really need your help.'

In the firelight Tolly's face has lost its softness, she seems older.

'You want me to get you on a transport, don't you?'

Harlon nods, glad she didn't have to spell it out.

'Yes. I want to pass as an ensin, like you were.'

'Right,' Tolly says. 'Then you'll need to look like *your* number got burned off when your head got burned.'

Harlon swallows.

'Alright,' she agrees. 'Let's do it now. The steel from my spark kit will be perfect. Put it in the fire.'

Enkalamba has returned, bringing with her two large dry branches that they feed onto the fire. Harlon looks up into the sky where the sparks fly up and hopes that the airdrop happens soon. She would like to be busy to take her mind off the throbbing pain of the burn on her arm, that Tolly pronounced 'very convincing'.

'D'you think it will be a transport?' Tolly asks, peering into the sky.

'I can't see what else they could use to deliver something by air. Did you hear of any transports being hijacked?'

Tolly shakes her head.

'Only crashed or destroyed on the ground. There was a Green Thorn attack a couple of weeks back. It torched one that landed in a village up country some place.'

'I just wish we knew what we were looking for.'

Enkalamba tilts back her head and reaches her trunk up as if she were using it to breathe above the surface of the river. She huffs in a long deep breath then lets out a small squeak of greeting.

'There!' Tolly points. 'What's that? It's like a flock of birds. Really big birds.'

Really big birds in a really big flock. Perhaps five hundred pairs of dark, beating wings show against the starry sky. But their beating isn't like any bird Harlon has ever seen.

'Flying foxes!' Harlon cries. 'They're flying foxes!'

The big bats wheel in slow, wide circles, getting lower and lower and then, still a hundred feet above the ground, the flock parts to reveal a transport! It is nothing like the Automator airships, not a huge silver egg but a small green bubble, not much larger than a garden shed, with a wicker gondola slung below it. It has just one crew member – the pilot – who can be seen as a dark shape moving in the cockpit window. The pilot throws packages from the gondola, which rain down into the dark beyond the reach of the beacon fire's flames. It doesn't take long, but as the dark figure leans out to wave a hand in goodbye the fire flares and light falls on its face and a complicated piled-up hair do.

'Mayo!' Harlon calls. *'Aunt Mayo!'* But the transport is already rising high and enveloped once again in its camouflage of flying foxes. The flock and the transport move high and fast and are soon lost in the starry sky.

'Did you know the pilot?' Tolly asks.

Harlon nods.

'She's my aunt!'

Tolly raises her eyebrows.

'I thought you said Green Thorn weren't *your lot?*'

'I did,' Harlon replies. 'Maybe I was wrong.'

Tolly's full of questions but Harlon doesn't want to talk. She wants to keep the little flame of hope that seeing Mayo has just lit burning quietly inside her.

'Come on,' she says. 'Let's pick up that cargo and get going. The moon'll be up soon.'

It takes a while to get all the packages gathered up. They pull the netting bags from the backpacks and arrange them over Enkalamba's back.

'Huh!' says Tolly. 'Wish we'd remembered these before we crossed that river!'

The elephant huffs and wriggles as if the netting tickles her skin. Harlon laughs.

'I don't think we'd have persuaded her to put them on just for us to cling to!'

They pack the netting with as many packages as they can and stuff the rest into their two backpacks. The rising moon gives enough light for them to begin their journey. As they go they make a plan for getting Harlon onto a transport when the Automator forces return to the Bai.

'You'll need to pretend you're injured. I'll get you in. But then I'll get away. Get back to Mavulu and help them to protect the forest. I'll burn off my number and I'll be on the right side, at last.'

'You could come with me to the capital, Tolly. Finding my sister would be easier if I had a real ensin with me. Who knows, my secret mission might help put a stop to the Automators.'

Tolly shakes her head.

'I'm not going back there. Not even for my brother. I want to help protect this place.'

There is no convincing her. Harlon stops trying. It doesn't seem fair to force her to change her decision. Tolly's probably right, she'll do more good helping the rebels fight here. Harlon tells herself it's better if she works alone, but the thought of saying goodbye to Tolly is more uncomfortable than she would like to admit.

They rest for a short while at moonset, and set off again at first light. They all feel the urgency of returning as quickly as possible. They press on and find the river transformed. No longer a muddy torrent swollen by a storm, but a clear stream flowing quietly over rocks and between boulders. They wade across it in ten minutes, and agree that if they keep up this pace they will reach the camp before dark.

As the hot afternoon begins to cool, they are on the wide, well-worn path that is the last stretch before the camp. Suddenly Enkalamba stops. She moves her ears gently, picking up sounds from the air, and shifts her feet; she's listening with those too, Harlon knows, listening to deep sounds below the reach of human ears. She gives a short, low rumble that Harlon and Tolly now know communicates unease. Then an unwelcome sound reaches their ears too: the unmistakable drone of an Automator transport, close and moving closer. Instinctively, the girls crouch low as its huge shape almost skims the treetops, like a hunting animal.

'It's looking for the camp!' says Harlon.

183

'At that height they can't miss it,' Tolly replies.

All three of them begin to run.

The first bomb falls just as the tents and shacks become visible through the trees. The blast wave *kerwummphs* through the trees and knocks Harlon to the ground. She gets up, pulls Tolly to her feet and shouts at her that they must carry on, but the explosion has left her deaf and dazed. Enkalamba has pulled the net of packages from her back and is already thundering down the path towards the camp. They pick up her dropped saddlebags and follow as best they can, dragging the net of packages over the ground.

The explosion has blown a hole in the canopy and destroyed the mess tent, but the transport has vanished, so perhaps there will be no more bombs. Sound returns to Harlon's ears, the shouting of people trying not to panic, trying to save something and someone from this disaster. Medics and healers and fighters are rushing everywhere. Buddly and Tink have loaded a stretcher with two wounded who can't walk and are heading away from the camp. But wherever they are going it won't be far enough to escape what's happening, because now there is an even more terrifying sound. A chorus of screaming saws as the Monster, the giant tree-destroying machine conceived so cunningly in Doada's Fang, rolls towards them. The ground shudders, treetops vanish and sky appears. Trees with trunks that it would take a ring of twenty people to enfold, are sliced apart, ripped down like straws and thrown aside. There is nothing to do now but flee, yet Harlon is rooted in horror, her mind struggling to grasp this depth of wickedness. Tolly pulls at her arm but she cannot move.

Cavan, blood streaming down her face, runs up to her.

'Mavulu's dead,' she cries. 'You betrayed us!' she screams at Tolly and at Harlon. 'You led them here.'

Wordlessly Harlon points to the net of medicines and supplies, and slips off her pack with more inside.

'What good are they against *that?*' Cavan yells, pointing to the red-and-black Monster that has already cut a path of daylight and desolation that can be seen from where they stand. She grabs Tolly by the front of her T-shirt and shakes her like a rag.

'We *healed* you. We saved your life and you betrayed us!'

Tolly tries to say something but Cavan shoves her down. She snatches up the backpacks and hooks the straps of the net saddlebag over her broad shoulders. Anger has doubled her strength and as she staggers away under her load, she shouts at them.

'Go,' she shouts. 'Go to your friends. If I see you again, I'll kill you myself!'

Harlon pulls Tolly to her feet.

'Where's Enkalamba? We've got to make sure she's safe.'

They stare about them, at the hurricane of fleeing humanity and flame and falling trees.

'Oh no!' Tolly screams. 'There!'

Standing right in the path of the Monster, dwarfed by its grinding wheels, whirling saws and grabbing arms, is Enkalamba. They run towards her calling, shouting, pleading but she doesn't move. As they get closer, Harlon can see that her grey skin is gleaming green, covered in an armour of tiny green lizards and iridescent beetles. Above her, a cloud of birds and butterflies and beetles swirls and glimmers. They catch the wide shafts of light that rush through the wound that the machine has made and gleam above her back like two long, glittering wings.

'Angel,' Tolly breathes. 'Angel!'

One thought radiates from Enkalamba's being, so strong it must speak into the mind of every living thing in sight.

One kin, one kin,
all one kin.
One kin, one song,
without the song no life,
without the life no song.

But the mind inside the machine is too shrivelled with hate to hold so big and generous a thought. The Monster crushes the elephant in its path and leaves her mangled remains to lie under the falling trees.

Harlon's legs collapse beneath her. She feels hollowed out, as if Enkalamba's departure from the world has been scooped from her own body. Her head swims. But Tolly's thin arms are around her, dragging her back to her feet, pulling her from the murderous path of the machine. Tolly is shouting at her but for now words seem to have lost all meaning. She staggers where Tolly leads in the direction of the Bai from which the monster has come. This she understands, that the only safe place now is behind that dreadful machine. They struggle out of its way and rest against a huge ripped stump, wet with sap as bright as blood.

The roar and crash of the destruction fades a little into the distance. Words return to Harlon's ravaged mind as Tolly says, 'We have to get to the transports; we have to get aboard one of them.'

Harlon reaches into her chest and finds some kind of voice.

'You don't have to come, Tolly. I can go alone.'

Tolly drops her head.

'Green Thorn will never trust me now.' She gives a gasping sob and looks into Harlon's face. Her eyes blaze. 'And after what the Automators just did, I want to take the fight right to their door.'

8
Ice Ship

Ash

The Celeddi have proved to be as relentless as the Gula. They have kept moving almost constantly. Ash feels as if all his bones have been shaken loose by the pounding gait of Cryf, Amliq's rhino. But there has been time for talking, and Amliq has answered Ash's questions patiently.

'Do you use siardw on your rhinos?' Ash had asked.

'Of course. But only on Cryf. Rhino minds are as well armoured as their backs. Cryf and I were given to each other when we were small.'

'So you can go into Cryf's mind and listen?'

Amliq looked a little shocked.

'That would be very disrespectful,' she had said. 'No, we *share* thinking. A little bit of Cryf is me, and a little bit of me is Cryf. But our minds are private.'

Hearing that had made Ash suddenly feel very lonely, for Xeno, and the Gula.

The only thing that stopped the endless movement was the rhinos' need to browse. So, for an hour or two in every twelve, the humans rested too and ate. Amliq herself had been kind, sharing her food which, Ash was pleased to find, was not dried seal flesh, but berries, seaweed and salted gulls' eggs.

'You do kill animals, don't you?' he'd asked when they stopped on their first night of travelling.

'We do not keep other beings only to kill them, as the Automators do,' Amliq had replied. 'But we do kill, yes. And it is painful. We hear the fear and suffering of the animals whose lives we take. But their lives give us life, and through their death we are connected to Liorna.'

Ash looked at her, puzzled.

'What is Liorna?'

'It is the thread that joins all life,' Amliq told him. 'Liorna does not stand still; it flows from earth and sea to sky, and passes through all creatures, linking them.'

Then she'd placed her hand in the middle of Ash's chest and looked into his eyes.

'It sings in here. Liorna sings all around us. And the Automators would make it silent.'

'My sister used to say "the song that sings us". I think that's what she meant.'

Amliq had nodded, gravely.

'You are Celeddi in your heart, I think,' she'd said, then added, more playfully, 'but to be truly Celeddi you must learn to shoot a crossbow. Come. You can practise.'

Ash hadn't mentioned the *hours* he'd spent with Harlon, aiming pea-stick arrows from a bow made of a pine lath and a length of kitchen string. When his first shots hit Amliq's rag target dead on, she'd been astonished.

'You are truly already one of us!' she grinned.

189

But the mood of the band had darkened. On the second day after the raid, Automator transports droned over the eastern horizon.

'They will hunt us,' Amliq said and Tarth agreed.

'We must reach the caves and disappear before they strike.'

A cloud of dread had settled on them all. The rhinos felt it too, sniffing the air and turning their ears anxiously in every direction.

Now, early on the morning of the fourth day, the sense of foreboding is strong. Even though everyone is tired, the pace picks up until they reach the top of a ridge. Below and to the west is the sea, veiled with strands of dense white mist that are streaking onto the shore as if pulled in by the rising sun. There is a huge beach, a perfect semi-circle, and behind it a wide river valley with a pelt of stunted trees: humps of moss and lichen, their greens and yellows dotted with patches of melting snow. Beyond that, to the south, are line upon line of blue hills, like the worn teeth of a giant beast. At the sight of these some of the Celeddi let out little whoops. Cryf and some of the other young woolly rhinos, kick up their heels and squeal.

'There is our home!' Amliq exclaims, pointing to hills. 'The Automators have never found this place. The earth's hot heart beats just below those hills and keeps them free of ice. They are carved with caves, a labyrinth too great for any human mind to map. Once we are there, we will be safe.'

The Celeddi and their rhinos are not the only creatures on the move. As they descend from the ridge, the sky above is crisscrossed with long straggling Vs of migrating birds: geese

190

and ducks, swans and cranes, whose cries turn the air into a symphony.

'Spring is coming,' Amliq says. 'They are following the thaw north to the edge of the ice. I hope they do not find their home covered in tar.'

Ash looks up at them. Their wild music goes straight into his heart. Then, amongst the skeins of calling waterfowl, he spots a dark shape, flying in the opposite direction. Then another and another and another. Falcons, like the ones that pursued them down Skull Gully!

'Amliq! Amliq! Look!'

She shades her eyes and gazes up.

'Birds? Not birds! What *are* they?'

'Falcons like machines, controlled by Automators. Like weapons!'

Amliq grasps the danger at once and so does Cryf. He starts to gallop, even before she has yelled out the warning that sets the whole band careering down, towards the valley. Tarth gallops her rhino, Blewog, close.

'The beach!' she yells. 'The valley floor is too boggy at this time of year.'

'But we need cover to try to bring them down with bows,' Amliq cries.

'No, we need speed. *Speed!*'

'Look out behind, Ash!' Amliq says. 'I must watch where Cryf puts his feet.'

Ash wraps the strap more tightly with his fingers and twists round. The falcons are closing in. Ash counts five, then seven or more! Their flight is shockingly fast. Their metal beaks and talons catch the early light as they get closer.

The rhinos at the front have reached the beach, and are moving faster on the level ground and hard sand. But behind Cryf and Amliq, Manaq, Amliq's younger brother, and his rhino, Stor, are tiring and have fallen far behind. The falcons strike. But not singly as they did on the mountain. Three of them stoop on Manaq all at once, tearing him from his rhino's back. Stor turns and charges at them, but one clings to her head and slashes at her eyes. Bellowing in terror she gallops away into the marshland behind the beach. Tarth turns back, her bow drawn, arrows piling towards the un-living birds, even as her rhino gallops beneath her. She shouts to Amliq to keep on, to keep running, but Amliq and Cryf will not leave family undefended. Ahead, falcons have reached the leading rhinos and their riders. Two others have been dragged from their mounts, a third rhino is bellowing as talons pierce its eyes.

Tarth is lost in a storm of wings; she flails her arms, hits out with her bow, but her face is streaked with red and Blewog is trying to shake two falcons from his head. Manaq is nowhere to be seen. Amliq gallops close with Cryf then jumps down to the ground, spear drawn, and runs to defend her mother, leaving Ash to cling on to the rhino's back as best he can.

A falcon tries to land of Cryf's head, and reaches for his eyes. The rhino swipes it with his horn, and sends it spinning. Cryf gallops after Amliq, and as he does, a rush of air gives Ash just enough warning to dodge the raking talons of another bird, but not the impact of one huge wing that knocks him from the speeding rhino's back. Instinctively Ash rolls into a ball, and tumbles over and over until he hits the rocks that back the beach and is knocked senseless.

He's not sure how much time he's lost, seconds or minutes, but as he comes to there is another sound, the growling rumble of a tar-fuelled tryk. Ash can even smell its oily stink. There's the phht phht of bullets too. Racing down from the ridge are two Automator tryks. An officer is shooting from the back of one, over the head of the driver who leans down out of his way. Beside the shooter sits a grey-faced child, with two more great falcons clinging to her shoulders. Driving the other is a skinny man in a spotted coat. Seated behind him, clinging on for dear life, is Dough Boy.

The uneven ground makes shooting straight a challenge, so the first round of bullets misses Amliq and her mother and then the shooter must reload. But Cryf is a bigger target and he's been hit. Blewog gallops, bellowing in circles, blood streaming over his poor face. The falcons, it seems, have new orders. They take off from Tarth and head towards the beach where the remaining Celeddi are disappearing into the thickening milk of mist. Amliq drags Tarth behind the shelter of Cryf's fallen body and aims her bow at the approaching tryk. Quick quick, thinks Ash, before they have the chance to reload their rifles.

The lead tryk reaches the level turf behind the beach just as Amliq's first arrow flies true, aimed at the driver. But the tryk jinks on a stone and the arrow hits the pale-faced child in the chest. She falls sideways. At once, the falcons on her shoulders wheel into the air, like blown leaves and flap away. But the shooter has reloaded and at this range he will not miss. Ash doesn't hear the shot but he sees Amliq slump beside her fallen mother.

The first tryk doesn't bother to stop but rushes on, chasing the Celeddi across the beach. The second, with the thin man and Dough Boy, follows and they both disappear as another curtain of mist rolls in off the sea.

Please be alive, please, Ash begs as he runs to Amliq. He sees Tarth first, sprawled on the rough turf a few feet beyond Cryf's back legs. She is very, very still and there is too much blood on the ground around her. He doesn't look again, but continues, stepping over Cryf's tree-trunk legs to find Amliq curled into a ball, under the rhino's chin. A red stain is spreading across her chest. Ash takes the girl's hand and calls her name. Her eyes open and look into his.

'Help me sit!' she says. 'I want to see Cryf's face.'

Ash pulls Amliq to a sitting position so she can rest a hand against Cryf's wrinkled cheek. His eye opens and one ear swivels towards her.

She smiles.

'We will pass together you and I,' she tells him. Then with a great effort, as if peering at something already a very long away, Amliq looks again at Ash.

'Escape!' she breathes. 'On the shore. There is an umiaq, boat, hidden. In the shingle. By the whale jaw at the north edge. Take my bow. Go! Go quickly.'

'I don't want to leave you alone!' Ash cries.

Amliq shakes her head.

'Cryf is with me. I with him. Life moves on. Go! *Live.*'

Ash gets to his feet and looks down at her. Her fading eyes look at him one last time but what she says makes no sense.

'Paddle west and watch for ice ships, the ice ships,' she breathes. 'They will help.'

Ash takes her bow from where it fell, and the little quiver of short arrows. He throws their straps across his back, and runs low, towards the beach.

Mist is blurring the line between land and sea. It magnifies the sound of the waves hissing up the sand and rolling the shingle. Sounds of gunfire, shouts and revving tryks grow and recede, like backwash along the shore. Ash crosses the wall of stones and shingle at the landward edge of the beach. The sound of his feet on the stones seems much too loud; he moves as carefully as he can but it feels as slow as running in a dream. The relief when he reaches the hard sand and can really run is huge. The fog is thickening by the minute and already the top of the shingle bank is hazy. His plan is to go to the far north end of the beach then work his way back along the bottom of the bank; that way he can't miss the whale-jaw marker. He's not sure how he will dig out a boat, or what he will do once it's on the water or what an ice ship is, but he knows he doesn't want Dough Boy and the man in the spotted coat to catch him. For now, that has to be enough. As long as he is free, there is still a chance of … something.

The mist makes shapes that seem almost solid. Twice he thinks he's found the arched outline of the whale jaws. How far has he come? Is he already too far south? He swirls round just as a breath of breeze shifts the white fog and there it is, the arch of a whale's upper jaw, curving out of the shingle.

The boat is not buried deep, moving just a few stones reveals its hull of stretched skin. It looks fragile but it's stored upside down so he doesn't need to empty it of stones. There's a cascade of shingle as he yanks it free and turns it over. Two paddles are wedged under the seats. It's lighter than he expected but all the same it takes all his strength to move it. He has to pull, then rest, pull, then rest. It's very slow. The only boat he's ever launched is the tiny row boat that his ma kept on the pond below the house. This boat is much bigger. How will he manage it when it's on the sea? It doesn't matter; right now even drowning seems preferable to being caught.

Up ahead the waves are washing the shingle with a sigh. He makes one last effort, and gets the prow almost to the shallows, then runs to the stern where the boat is stuck in the sand and shingle. As Ash puts his shoulder to the hull, a hand goes round his mouth, another round his throat and his feet are kicked from underneath him. Ash feels himself engulfed by Dough Boy's huge hands. He struggles, but the hold on his throat tightens

'Stop struggling. Listen.'

Dough Boy holds very still and Ash does too. There's no sound, no gun shots, no tryks.

'Know what that quiet means?' Dough Boy says. 'It means we won't hear him coming. He's shot the other tryk driver, cos he doesn't want witnesses. And now he's coming for us. He'll kill me because of what I know and take you because of who you are. So you and me, we're getting in this boat.'

Dough Boy's huge right hand drags Ash along behind him as he pushes the boat into the water with his other hand. He is very strong and he makes much better progress than Ash did on his own. The boat is almost ready to float.

Phht – petcheww. A bullet whistles into the water next to the boat and a voice calls out,

'Stop right there! Take one more step, Vellum, and you're dead.' This must be the spot-coat man, Ash thinks. Dough Boy shifts his grip, putting Ash between himself and more bullets just as another stings the air and hits the water on the other side of the boat.

'I'm a very good shot, Vellum,' says the voice. 'If I wanted you dead, you'd be dead already.'

'Your specs are bust, Doada, and you're blind as a bat without 'em,' Dough Boy yells, then whispers into Ash's ear.

'He's got three more shots before he'll need to reload. When I push, jump in and lie low.'

'Let go of the boy or I'll kill you,' Doada shouts.

'Oh, yeah?' Dough Boy shouts back. 'You've always been a rubbish shot, Doada. Not like your sister.'

Another bullet phhhts uselessly into the water.

'Come on, Vellum. Hand him over and I promise not to harm you.'

'Forgive me if I don't trust you, Doada!'

Now Ash can see him, at the top of the beach, the gun held to his shoulder as he moves. He has a nasty head wound, one lens of his glasses is gone and the long coat is ripped and streaked with blood.

'Just let the boy go!' Doada shouts. 'No harm will come to you.'

'I don't trust you, Doada Sisal, you're just another filthy Listener! All those little feathered friends of yours when you were young. I remember those…'

Dough Boy's goading works, another bullet hits the water, and then another.

'Now!' says Dough Boy. He gives the boat a shove, swings Ash over the gunwale and dives after him.

But the boat is side on to the swells, it will capsize if it's not turned nose first in to the waves, or it will simply wash back onto shore, where Doada will have reloaded. At such close range, even with poor aim and worse eyesight, he will not miss.

'Paddles!' Dough Boy screams. 'Get the paddles.'

The paddles are tied with seal sinew that's dried as hard as iron, and they won't come loose. It's like a nightmare. Ash tears at the sinew knots, ripping his nails. The waves wash them back onto the beach and they are caught, grounded on the sand as Doada is raising up his reloaded gun and pointing it.

A long, low shape comes darting down the beach. Fast, but so silent over the shingle bank behind the man that he doesn't hear what's coming. So when the Gula lunges at his legs, felling him the way lightning fells a tree, the gun flies from his hands and skeeters down the beach into the water. With a snap, the sinew binding the paddles breaks and Dough Boy wrenches them free. He throws one to Ash and pushes off from the shingle, deftly turning the boat to send it shooting through the surf. Spot-coat tries to rise, but the Gula slashes his leg with her teeth, slicing through the padding of his clothes, clean through the flesh to bone. He screams and clutches at the wound, blood blossoming between his fingers. She leaps clear and plunges into the water after the boat. Two sturdy paws and a black snout appear over the side, and the Gula scrambles aboard and instantly into Ash's mind.

198

Cub! Cub! Cub, she cries. *Cub, very hard to find!*

Ash can't think of what to say, he just throws his arms around her and hugs her tight.

Humans do this? is what she says, but he can feel the joy and welcome coming from her, warm and comforting as tea and sunlight.

'Paddle!' Dough Boy yells. 'PADDLE! He's not dead and he'll find his gun.'

Ash grabs a paddle and soon the shore has disappeared and the furious figure of Doada Sisal with it.

The Gula is thin and very tired. As soon as they are safely away from the shore, she curls up and falls straight into a deep sleep. She has been searching for him all this time. Ash's heart turns over to think of what she might have endured.

'Stop daydreaming,' Dough Boy growls at him. 'Paddle. His Red Blade thugs will be here soon. We need to be long gone. Out of range.'

Ash paddles, *one side then the other, one side then the other.* The rhythm helps to shut out images that flash into his mind, of Amliq, Tarth, Cryf and Blewog, streaked in blood, shot, and ripped: attacked by bird machines. He feels as if he's just one paddle stroke ahead of being drowned in panic. His heart races and the tears rise into his eyes, but he paddles and paddles breathing them down. Inside himself Ash's being draws itself into a tight knot, resilient, tough, determined to survive. Out of all this hurt and evil good will come. Something good. Somehow.

One side then the other.

They paddle on, smothered in the quiet of the mist. Swells

move through the sea like breaths. In places the surface breaks into a crust, like fat on cooling soup, where sea is trying to turn into ice. From time to time they stop and listen. There's a faint drone of an airship far to the east, snaps that might be gunfire or cracking ice floes. But at last even those sounds fade away.

Dough Boy looks at the still-sleeping Gula.

'What *is* that thing anyway?' he asks.

'*She's* a Gula, and *she* saved your life.'

'Talk to her, do you?'

Ash doesn't reply. Dough Boy curses under his breath.

'Who was that man?' Ash asks.

'Oh, don't pretend you don't know.'

Something in Dough Boy's whiney, petulant tone makes Ash snap. He swings round and points the paddle at the man like a spear.

'You aren't at the station now. You haven't got guns or your friends to back you up. Just tell me who that man was. Why was he trying to kill us?'

Dough Boy coughs, spitting blood again into the water. His hand is bleeding into a wad of cloth. His face is a mess of bruises.

'Feisty little sod, aren't you?'

He looks pathetic. Ash could almost feel sorry for him, if he didn't distrust him so much.

'Alright,' Dough Boy says. 'I'll tell you.'

Ash puts the paddle down.

'That bloke with the gun, he's Head of Intelligence for the Automators. Intelligence is just their way of saying spying and sneaking. They call him Commander Eye, but his name is, or used to be, Doada Sisal. He's your ma's brother. Your ma, *the Boogam.*'

'My ma's not the … what you said. She's dead.'

'Just listen, will you?' Dough Boy snaps. 'Listen.' He takes a long breath and starts to speak.

'A very long time ago, when I was young, I knew your ma. That's how I recognised your photo of her. I helped out at the stables at her pa's house. She was smart and she was a soldier. She was seeing this boy, same age as her, seventeen or about that. Tui. Tui Meyer. He was the ostler's son. He was a Listener and the Automators came for him. I liked your sister so I warned him and he got away, but when they couldn't find Tui, they beat up his pa and his pa died. Tui ran off with your ma, Toren. They joined the rebels. They weren't called Green Thorn then just "the rebels".'

Ash stares at Dough Boy trying to read his broken face: he knows Pa's name, he thinks, and Ma being a soldier explains a lot of things about her. And didn't he hear Mayo telling Harlon something about the rebels being called Green Thorn and their leader being called Boogam? But as for the Automator's chief spy being his uncle, and this Boogam person being his ma, Dough Boy must be lying about that.

'That doesn't prove she's the Boogam, or that she's still alive,' he says.

Dough Boy leans forward, speaks more softly.

'Wait,' he says, 'there's more. Not long after she ran off, my pa got a job with the Automators, up here at the first Station Gold. One night, the station was attacked. Not like this last attack with big explosions. My dad was security patrol at the

201

drilling rig. The rebels jumped him. Their leader was Toren Sisal. She shot him in the leg, point blank. He managed to slash her face, give her that scar, before he passed out with the blood loss. Almost died. He told me it all but he never told another soul.'

'*Why* didn't he tell? That makes no sense. You're just making all this up!'

'Doada was powerful, by then. His sister being rebel leader wasn't something he'd want people to know. Pa knew Doada'd just have him killed.'

'What happened to your pa?' Ash asks.

'He's safe near Angellis where Doada big-shot Sisal won't find him.'

Ash stares at the slate-coloured water with the silver crust of ice. Dough Boy has sprinkled this story with truth but Ash is sure he can detect the stink of lies beneath them.

'Even if it's true that she *was* the Boogam, or whatever they called their leader all those years ago,' he says, 'she's dead. I know. She's dead.'

'You sure?' Dough Boy says. 'Did you *see* her? Dead, I mean?'

Ash doesn't reply. He doesn't want to say the words out loud or even think about them. The wound that Ma tried to hide, the burning house. Even if Ma survived the attack, she was killed with Harlon and Xeno in transport two one seven.

Went down with all the Listener scum they caught up in the mountains.

But Dough Boy is persistent.

'If she's dead,' he says, 'how come "The Boogam's Back" is

being scrawled on walls all over Fidrac? How come Green Thorn rebels are suddenly back in business, eh?'

'Doesn't prove anything,' Ash snarls, but he can't help wondering, hoping, that perhaps it does.

'Oh, she's alive alright. And Doada knows she is; that's why he wants to get his hands on *you*. Live bait, you'd be. If she was dead, he would just kill you. Easy.'

They fall silent like the sea around them. The only sounds are the Gula's breathing and the slap, slap of the icy water on the boat's skin hull.

'You and me, my little friend, need to stick together. Wait for Doada's Red Blade to rescue him, take him back down south. When we get back to the Station, I'll find a place to keep you nice and safe, make sure you get special treatment and…'

Ash isn't even listening, because the Gula is awake. She's on her feet, paws on the boat's prow, peering into the grey murk. She bursts into his head.

Hear? Listen! Listen!

Dough Boy looks at them, uncomfortable and suspicious.

'What's going on? You talking to that animal.'

'Shut up!' Ash says. 'Listen!'

Ash can feel how hard the Gula's ears are working. He shuts his eyes and tries to resolve sounds into pictures. Behind the close 'slap' of the slush on the skin hull, the sound of his heart and his breath there is … *singing?* Singing! At first odd notes and then whole phrases that resolve into a chorus of harmonising voices. There is a rhythmic splash, splash, splash also. Oar strokes and a bigger, deeper noise, a kind of sighing, sluicing sound that he can't find an image for.

But now he doesn't need to, because the sounds and the thing from which they're coming resolve out of the fog. A ship's hull, with a high, curved prow, a mast with layers of cross trees and tightly furled sails, and long oars, propelling it steadily through the water. Figures stand on the decks and sing in a language Ash has never heard before.

Trail! the Gula announces in his head. *Trail! See?*

For a moment Ash *can* see, not in a picture inside his head that the Gula shows, but with his own eyes, the fine glowing spider line loops around the curled prow and runs out like a loose streamer, vanishing into the mist ahead.

'An ice ship!' Dough Boy says. 'Well I'll be damned. Who would have thought they'd be our rescue party!'

A dozen pairs of long oars keeps up the steady swish-creak, swish-creak; their rhythm kept by the chanting song the oars-people sing. The ship is heading straight for them. In seconds it will mow them down. A voice shouts out from the foredeck.

'We tow an iceberg; we cannot stop. But we'll take you aboard if we can. Paddle!'

There isn't an alternative. Behind the ship, the huge bulk of the berg is just visible in the fog, as if a continent was chasing them. They cannot paddle back or forward fast enough to get out of its path, their only choice is to keep pace with the ship and hope they will be pulled on board.

Ash and Dough Boy thrash the water with their paddles, until they are moving alongside the ship. A dozen or more crew lean over the side, wrapped against the cold in various strange coats and outlandish hats. They shout encouragement and instructions in what sounds like a mix of several languages. Now that they are close, Ash can see that the ship is moving more swiftly than she appeared to be; the umiaq is slipping back into the inexorable path of the berg. A tall woman, dressed in a long bright-green coat and a yellow hat with ear flaps, shouts down to them.

'You must keep up!'

The crew begins to clap and shout in time with Ash and Dough Boy's desperate paddling.

'Closer!' yells the woman. 'We will pull you aboard.'

Ash can't see how that will be done but he has no breath to do more than keep his paddle pushing through the water even though his muscles burn and scream.

'Captain Skrimsli!' the woman calls out over her shoulder and the others take up the cry. 'Captain Skrimsli!' Even the rowers have stopped their singing now, and instead call out one word.

'Skrim*sli*! Skrim*sli*! Skrim*sli*.'

What does this mean? Is it an instruction that they need to follow?

Suddenly the cry of Skrimsli breaks down into cheers and the crew who line the gunwales step back. In their place is a huge tiger.

'Hold on tight!' the green-coated woman yells. 'The captain will get you aboard!'

The Gula digs her claws into the boat's wooden ribs and Ash and Dough Boy wrap their fingers round the seats. While the crew hold on to the tiger's back legs, its front paws reach down towards the umiaq. It springs claws as big as grappling hooks into the side of the boat and hauls it upward. The creature's face looms above them, fur like fire and soot, whiskers like strands of white wire, green eyes like the aurora. Its mouth opens in a roar of effort and, with one huge convulsion, boat, Gula, Ash and Dough Boy land on the deck of the ship with a giant cat looming over them.

For a few moments everyone is cheering, slapping each other on the back. Ash is picked up and set on his feet; to her disgust the Gula has her ears scratched. Ash looks around and realises that several of what he took for humans wearing strange coats and hats are actually *animals*. Not only does this ship have a tiger for a captain, but it has a grizzly bear and two gorillas in its crew! A raven circles the main mast looking as if this is her home, too.

One of the gorillas, a big male with silver fur poking from the collar of his scarlet coat, is holding Dough Boy by the arms. The man sags in the ape's grasp, his tattered uniform jacket drooping like broken wings.

'We are no friends of Automators,' the woman in the green coat tells him. 'Our bergs are tainted with your tar. Our crew is not safe in Automator ports. We won't waste space and supplies on keeping you alive. Over the side with him.'

'No!' the word is out of Ash's mouth before he knows it. The woman raises her eyebrows

'Why do you speak for him? You are a child slave of the tar station, are you not? Were Automators not your captors?'

The crew's smiles have all evaporated. They stand in a circle around Ash and the Gula now, grim and menacing. Inside his head, the Gula starts to snarl.

No!

Ash tells her.

Wait.

He draws himself up straight and steadies his shaking voice.

'I don't speak to defend Automators. They are evil,' he says. 'But I don't like killing. That's what *they* do so easily.'

There is a low growl and the crew parts to let Captain Skrimsli through. He leans down, puts his massive face very close to Ash so that his white whiskers brush Ash's cheeks; he takes a long deep breath, the pink nostrils flaring as he takes in Ash's scent. The tiger wrinkles his nose, raises his upper lip into the beginning of a snarl that shows the canine teeth, like daggers. The Gula trembles at Ash's side.

Be still, Cub, very still, she breathes inside his head.

Ash doesn't need to be told. He's spellbound. He never expected to even *see* a tiger. The intensity of the orange fur, the mesmerising pattern of the black stripes and the eyes, green fire flecked with gold! It is so beautiful that, Ash thinks, it would almost be worth being eaten.

Captain Skrimsli stops his snarl before it starts. He starts to purr, a deep rumble that Ash feels through his chest. The tiger shuts his eyes and bumps his head against Ash's in greeting. The crew gasp and laugh, then the tiger turns and springs away, up to a platform on the boat's high curving prow, where he takes up his station, looking ahead into the foggy course that the ship must follow.

'Put the Automator back in his boat, Silverback,' the Green Coat woman tells the gorilla. 'If he paddles hard enough the berg won't sink him.'

Silverback nods. He lifts the terrified Automator off the ground with one arm, and the umiaq with the other and carries them both away down the companion-way to the lower deck. As they go Dough Boy shouts, 'Give your mother my best wishes when you see her. Tell her Cat Vellum's thinking of her.'

And then he's gone. A few moments later a dull splash shows that Dough Boy is starting his frantic paddle to avoid the path of the berg.

'Everyone else,' the woman orders, 'change the watch!'

All around them activity erupts, as ordered as a square dance, and the woman guides them over to a hatch, out of the way. She speaks to Ash and the Gula quietly now, and with kindness.

'You spoke well, child. And true. We are used to harshness here and it is good to be reminded that there are other things still in this world. I am First-mate Ekar. This ship is the *Ice Maiden*, we are a crew of human and human-kin as you see; Skrimsli is our captain, we have bears and apes and birds serving on this ship. You are welcome aboard. We have seen other escaping children such as you over the years. But never one with such a companion, or such spirit. Greetings to you and this Gula!'

A small person in a red-and-blue headcloth pops up through the hatch. She is as wrapped as a parcel and her face is wizened and whiskery but her smile is broad and warm.

'This is Ray, our cook,' says Ekar. 'She will find you food and a bed. Now I must attend to my duties. Rest, and later we will speak.'

Ray beckons with a long brown finger.

'With me coming,' she says softly, her voice no more than a breathy rasp, 'this ways, this ways.'

208

She disappears back down the hatch from which she appeared and Ash starts to follow.

Cub, says the Gula in Ash's head. *We go under water?*

No, Ash replies. How can he explain about ships and their holds and cabins? All he can think of is, *Nest that floats.*

But the Gula will have none of it.

Nests not float, she says.

This nest float, Ash tells her. But she still stands at the hatch, peering down suspiciously unwilling to move. Ray pulls herself back up the ladder in one movement. She leans past Ash to look directly into the Gula's face and mimes eating.

Num num num.

'You want food?' she breathes. 'Then follow.'

Hunger always trumps fear for a Gula. There is no more hesitation. As Ray climbs down the ladder in front of them, Ash notices the extraordinary length of her arms and the russet-coloured hair that pokes from the ends of her long sleeves. She is a red ape! Ash decides there is great deal he wants to learn about the *Ice Maiden* and her crew.

With a full belly, and a warm bed for the first time in weeks, Ash sleeps for a long time. Only when the wind picks up and the *Ice Maiden* moves over the ocean like a cantering horse, does he finally wake. He lies, listening to the noises of the ship, the creaks of her timbers, the running of the water along her sides, the muffled voices. Behind and beneath all those there is another sound. A sound absent from the stinking tar station and the ruin of the felled forest. It occurs to him that it's a sound he's known all his life but here, coming from the sea just inches away through the wooden hull, it is a little

209

different, like hearing a well-loved melody sung by an unfamiliar voice.

Liorna sings all around us.

The Gula is no longer beside him in the little bunk next to the galley, and below him Ray's bunk is also empty. His red tortoise suit has disappeared and been replaced with a pair of sturdy trousers, much patched, a shirt, a knitted jersey and blue woollen waistcoat, felted with age, dense and warm. There is a green hat with ear flaps, very like the one that Ekar was wearing. Ma's old coat has been patched and brushed too and he still has the rhino wool boots that Amliq gave him. He holds the coat and the boots to his heart and thinks of what Amliq said about the thread of life that runs though everything.

Liorna does not stand still.

In this moment Ash feels the pain and the comfort in those words. Life moves on, and leaves death in its wake. Amliq would tell him to put grief behind him, but it is hard when he does not know what will come next. He dresses carefully, pulls on the soft boots and the coat so full of stories, and climbs from the dark hold to where sunshine floods down through the hatch.

The dark red sails curve against the blue sky as Ash steps out onto the pitching deck. He staggers to the gunwale where there is a rail to cling to, while his legs get used to walking on a moving floor. The sea is a deep blue, dotted with small white flecks of foam; a purplish smudge on the eastern horizon is all that can be seen of land. There is an air of quiet unhurried industry amongst the crew on deck: ropes are being coiled, brasswork polished, boards scrubbed and cracks caulked. Down on the lower deck the oars are shipped and lashed in place and a group of larger crew members, including the bear, are tending to the winches, letting out the ropes that run behind the ship to the berg.

It is like vast molar tooth, twice or three times taller than the tallest building, with one steep vertical face towards the ship and a knobbled flattish crown. It dwarfs the *Ice Maiden*. Its colours fill Ash with wonder. It is striped with deep turquoise and banded with purple-grey against the dazzling white. The waves have worn the submerged ice into a shelf that shines through the water like a huge turquoise skirt. Fifteen or twenty ropes are attached to the berg, in complex spider lines and a long rope ladder has been attached to the vertical face. From over the summit of the berg two figures now appear, Silverback and his companion gorilla. These two vast beings look as tiny as fleas against the shining body of the berg. They carry sacks which they lower to the small boat that Ash just notices is pulled up onto an ice ledge at the foot of the ladder. Then they climb down the ladder, get into the boat and are hauled back towards the *Ice Maiden* by their crewmates on the lower deck.

First-mate Ekar comes to stand beside Ash.

'This berg is not a perfect shape,' she said, 'with a nice flat top. But it has a hollow where we keep our food stores, so we have more room below decks. Also Captain Skimsli's food cannot be kept on board. Flesh is offensive to many crew members. He goes up there to eat.'

'Are you all Listeners then?'

Ekar replies coolly. 'That is not a term we use much. We understand each other.'

Ash waits for more explanation but none comes.

'Thank you for my clothes. You are very kind.'

Ekar nods again. There are so many things Ash wants to ask but he senses there are rules here that he doesn't understand. He must tread carefully.

'Where are you heading?' he asks.

'Once we sold ice in Fidrac but the Automators made it impossible for a mixed crew to dock there. We'll go to the free port of Angellis. They don't have much influence that far south. Not yet at least. And you, where do you go?'

Ash gapes like a landed fish. As usual he's bad at lying so he tells the truth. It doesn't give anything important away.

'I think my family are dead,' he says. 'I'm not sure where I'm going.'

But Ekar isn't really listening; she's looking intently at the berg again, where Captain Skrimsli has climbed down the ladder and has jumped into the icy water to swim back to the ship.

'He is from the Northern forests. Cold water holds no fear for him,' she tells Ash proudly. 'He will rest now, following his meal and then he will wish to speak with you and your Gula.'

She gives a short stiff bow and hurries to the rear deck where her captain will soon be coming aboard.

Ash would like to watch the tiger shake the salt water from his orange coat but the Gula appears at the bottom of the main mast accompanied by Ray. It looks as if they have both been climbing. Ray is smiling and the Gula is fizzing with excitement. She barges into his mind.

Cub! Cub, she says, skeeters to his feet and stands on her back legs to rest her paws in his hands.

Tall tree on floating nest I climb. You climb also see giants giants fish.

Ray is making a coughing, wheezing noise that Ash realises is red ape laughing.

'Climb?' she says and looks up the mast. 'Not so hard.' She puts out one elongated hand to him. 'I help?'

Giants giants fish? Ash wonders if these could be whales. Another thing he never thought he'd see. Climbing masts and rigging can't be very different from climbing trees and he was always getting into trouble for doing that when he should have been doing chores.

Masts, as it turns out, are much more unstable than trees. When they reach the little enclosed platform that Ray calls the 'crow's nest', the mast is swaying from side to side so much they are sometimes over the sea on one side of the ship and sometimes on the other.

The Gula puts her forepaws on the side of the nest and sniffs the cold wind that blows into their faces. Ray turns up the collar of her coat and pulls her headscarf down. Ash knows red apes are from hot, jungly places, she must find this cold very difficult. She doesn't mind the height, that's for sure. Ash clings to the mast with both arms but Ray casually wraps her fingers round a rope above their heads and dangles, swaying out one way and then the other. She points with the other hand and when Ash and the Gula look there are the *giants giants fish*, two of them.

Ash could never have imagined real creatures to be so huge.

213

When they breathe out through holes in the tops of their heads, it sounds as if their heads contain a huge echoing cave. They curve their long, narrow bodies down but they don't dive deep, only just beneath the surface, so he can still see their whole, incredible length. They have elegant pointed flippers but the part he likes best is the narrow, almost delicate stalk of the tail, just before the tapering wings of their tail flukes. What would it be like to sit inside that great head? What would he learn?

The Gula is fascinated.

Fishes?

Not fishes, Ash says as one surfaces again and the steamy puff of its blow is carried away on the wind.

Air breathe!

AIR BREATHE! the Gula exclaims in astonishment inside his head.

Why? she asks.

Long ago, lived on land.

The Gula takes a moment to think about this.

How walk? No legs.

Ash replies.

Had legs. Lost them.

Ash is almost glad that that seems to be beyond her. He's not sure he could explain about fossils. She rummages around his mind, and finds a word.

Foolish, she says.

Foolish big fishes, lost legs.

'Come,' rasps Ray, 'go down time.'

She swings to the deck in no time followed by the Gula in a sort of controlled fall and then by Ash, slow, reluctant to leave the whales behind.

Ash goes below and helps Ray in the galley. There is a mountain of vegetables to be chopped, nuts to be ground, dough to be kneaded. Ray's son Margi is there too. He is three and just discovering how much fun climbing can be. He treats the galley like a three-dimensional playground. Like Ray he can use human words in a breathy voice, and like Ray, his long hands are very expressive. He hangs from the ceiling teasing the Gula who stalks about sniffing things and chewing up anything that falls onto the floor. She doesn't seem to mind her fur being tweaked and makes the little ape laugh by pretending to pounce on stray vegetables.

Plants, she says disdainfully when she picks one up, *only plants to eat.*

Ray doesn't talk much and Ash doesn't want to reach out with his siardw in case that's considered impolite, as it is with the Celeddi. But Ray does sing, a wordless melody of soft, musical, hooting sounds, with lip smacking and table slapping that she does in time with her mixing and chopping. Margi joins in and Ash finds this infectious. It reminds him of singing with Xeno and Harlon when they were all still 'the three bears'.

'Sing slow?' he requests. 'So I can learn?'

Ray looks at him, pushes out her lips doubtfully.

'You want learn?'

Ash nods.

Very slowly she repeats each little phrase until Ash can join in.

Hoo-hoo, hoo-hoo, hoo-hoo
kiss, kiss, kiss
slap, slap.

The Gula stops her search for food scraps and watches them. Then she finds a metal bowl that makes a satisfying chink when she raps it with the claws of one paw, and joins in with the rhythm. Margi hangs from the ceiling by one hand and taps the rack of hanging pots with a wooden spoon with the other.

Hoo–hoo, hoo–hoo, hoo–hoo
kiss, kiss, kiss
slap, slap.

Chopping and mixing, even kneading bread dough in time to their music, they play with ever-growing confidence. But when Ekar walks into the galley, they all fall silent, like naughty children.

'Captain Skrimsli would meet with you and your Gula in his cabin,' she tells Ash. Ash puts his coat on.

'Thanks,' Ray says softly and smiles at him from under her headscarf.

We go? the Gula asks.

Meet the tiger.

Grrrr, says the Gula with her outside voice and then, inside Ash's head, *He will eat you.*

No, Ash teases, *he will eat you.*

Captain Skrimsli's cabin is in the forepeak, the very front of the ship, where two oval windows look out over the sea like eyes. Beneath them is a large bed with a swirl of brightly coloured blankets. A short shelf inset in the wood beside the bed carries neatly stacked and well-worn books. The wooden floor is covered with a patterned rug, showing a forest of tall trees. In one corner a log the height of the cabin stands on end:

a tiger-sized scratching post. In the opposite corner is a row of hooks on which hang two green coats, a number of yellow hats and a pair of soft, curled-toe slippers: Ekar's gear. They must share this cabin, as Ash and the Gula now share a bunk.

Ekar invites Ash and the Gula to sit on a bench against the wall. She hangs up her coat and pulls off her gloves then sits down in an elegant armchair next to them with her hands folded quietly in her lap. They wait. After a few moments the door is pushed open and, silent as a shadow, the great tiger comes in. He greets Ekar with a head bump then sits erect on the floor completing the circle made by the bench and the chair. Ash and the Gula both feel the need to sit extremely still as Skrimsli looks at each of them in turn. The Gula's fur bristles as he turns to her.

Cats, not like, she says quietly in Ash's head but she keeps still, even though Ash can feel her powerful desire to run.

Nothing moves except the end of the tiger's splendid tail, which twitches minutely. Ash feels certain that the twitch communicates something, but he has no way of telling what. At length Skrimsli and Ekar exchange a long look and seem to reach some conclusion. Ekar nods.

'The captain would like to Speak to you directly. Both of you.'

The Gula looks questioningly at Ash.

What?

Tiger wants to talk to us.

The Gula has no reply, but her fur bristles more and Ash senses her desire to bolt increase. Ekar is waiting for an answer but Ash doesn't quite understand what question he's been asked. He tries what he hopes is the polite response.

217

'We would like to speak with the captain.'

'Good.' Ekar nods. 'Then you give permission?'

'Um. Permission for what?'

'For the captain to Speak to you?'

This formal request seems strange. Ray has been speaking to them all day without any kind of permission. Perhaps it's because the tiger is a captain or perhaps it's because a big cat's voice used to nothing more complicated than roars and yowls will be hard to understand when it tries to tackle words.

'Yes,' Ash says. 'Of course.'

Ash is not prepared for what happens next. Captain Skrimsli does not speak with a voice like Ray, but with a voice inside Ash's head, like the Gula. But not just a voice, not just words and images popping up like signals in the darkness, then vanishing again the way the Gula does. Skrimsli's *whole presence* walks calmly into Ash's mind and sits down. He is bigger, brighter, more alive even than the version of himself which sits on the rug in his cabin.

Skrimsli in his head speaks with a very deep and rasping voice, his tiger mouth and black lips moving, just as human lips would move to form words.

You are surprised, I think, he says.

Ash can do no more than nod.

You have not experienced this kind of communication before?

Ash shakes his head.

You can speak, you know, the tiger says. *Just imagine that you are speaking to me in your head and it will happen. Or you may speak with your usual voice. I hear and understand this also, of course.*

218

Ash shakes his head again and then finds a voice inside his head.

This isn't like the way the Gula speaks to me.

I understand, the tiger replies.

Can she hear us talking now?

She is not present in your mind at this time. But she senses that it is good to wait. See?

Ash looks at the Gula. She has curled up on the couch and rests her head on her paws, alert but calm.

I will tell you some of my own story. It will help you to understand perhaps, Skrimsli continues.

I was born a captive. My mother also, and her mother before that. We were owned. Made to perform tricks to entertain. This is a great tradition amongst humans in Nordksy; it is called Circus. Many beings of many kinds suffered this fate, the fate of Circus. Bears, apes, birds, elephants.

Tigers were very popular because we are very powerful; we have the tools to kill at will. Almost nothing can resist us. If we wish it dead, it will be so. But our owners were what you call Listeners. They stole, like thieves, into our minds and spied upon our thoughts and our intentions. I may raise my paw to strike, but if you know before I do it, you will be ready with your whip, your spear, your gun. All my power and my strength are nothing, pulled away like flowing sand.

This is how the Listeners, who lived by displaying our beauty and our agility, controlled us. Generation on generation.

But I am of a new generation. I was born with a new ability. I could go into their minds, and look about me. Like them I was stealthy. I crept about, learning. Words. There are many words inside a human mind. I ate them up until they were a part of me.

And then I used them to make my owners afraid, as they should always have been, of my power. I killed them and I walked from that place, free.

But not free. Words had changed me, shaped me, made me into something other. I am not wholly tiger now; I am part human. At first I believed myself to be a monster. Neither human, nor anymore a tiger. I fell between the worlds and, for a time, I was lost. But Ekar found me, and I found her. She is a Listener, but not like others I have known. She does not creep about inside a mind. She listens only when she is asked to hear. I saw I was neither lost, nor bound, nor monster.

There are other crew on board our ship like me and like your Gula who can Speak into the minds of humans, to take words and use them to make you understand. We are all a new occurrence in the world, I believe. In my travels I have encountered more Speakers. As the scourge of the Automators spreads we grow more numerous. It is my belief that they are part of some great new pattern that I cannot yet perceive. But I seek it. I feel this new pattern will rid us of the Automators and restore life where they have made only death.

Quietly as he arrived, Skrimsli leaves Ash's mind. But the sense of deep connection remains, so that Ash finds he's staring into the gold-green eyes of the tiger, even as the captain has moved away and is now turning his attention to the Gula.

'I thank Captain Skrimsli,' Ash tells Ekar. 'I am so sorry that Listeners used him so cruelly. I am ashamed that I have crept around inside other creatures' minds like that.'

'But never, I think, for your gain,' Ekar says, kindly.

Ash hangs his head.

'Yes, sometimes. To keep our alpacas calm while we took their wool.'

'Do not reproach yourself. It is clear to me, to us, that your motives are good.' She glances at the captain and smiles. 'That is why we would like to offer a place on our crew, for you and the Gula.'

Never before has Ash given any thought to his life. Back home in the mountains he went from day to day as content and unthinking as the alpacas. Since then, he has fallen from one disaster to another. What will he do next? Keep chasing a vague promise made to a mother who was really someone else and who, in any case, is probably now dead?

Ekar's words offer him something real. A marvellous future, with companions like Ray, sights like whales and icebergs, and the wonder of the whole world to explore. This would be a *life*; this would fill the terrible emptiness that losing his family has left behind.

An island lost in the deepest part of the ocean. Promise me you'll get there!

It seems so long ago already, that promise: another lifetime. In any case, how else would he find anything lost in the deep ocean but by being on a ship?

He looks into Ekar's weathered face, her sea-grey eyes.

'Thank you, First-mate Ekar. I'll see what the Gula says, but, for myself, I'd be honoured to accept.'

9

The Beacon of Progress

Doada

'Good morning, Commander Eye. Very glad to see you safely returned from the White Sea, sir. Tough up there, I hear. I hope you are quite recovered?' Doada's chauffeur, Nimbus, doffs his cap.

'Soldiering on, thank you, Nimbus,' Doada replies, wincing at the memory of that horrible animal sinking its teeth into his leg.

'Good morning, Senior Vellum.'

Nimbus doffs his cap a second time, with almost as much respect as the first. Doada finds this irritating because, even packaged in a new uniform with the ivory badge that denotes all high-ranking Automators, Senior Vellum is as large and unwieldy as ever. Still very much 'Dough Boy'.

But useful, Doada reminds himself. *Very* useful. That is why Vellum is stepping from Doada's own private house, to share Doada's new, tar-fuelled, chauffeur-driven karz with its sparkling gold paintwork.

Vellum's presence has *nothing* to do with gratitude. Yes, Dough Boy *was* helpful in getting them out of tricky situation. He had paddled back to the beach and found Doada half dead with cold and blood loss, so a truce was mutually beneficial. Although Doada would rather erase the whole sorry affair from his memory (especially the taste of charred rhino meat which he fears will be with him if he lives to be a hundred) the incident *had* served to reveal Vellum's invaluable characteristics: dogged determination, cold cunning and absolute ruthlessness. He was, in short, *capable*.

This, together with the information about the ship on which Toren's son is now located, makes the man a tool that can be put to good use. Especially now that Director Herick Lazit has proved to be Doada's outright enemy. The reason they were stranded on the beach in the White Sea was all Lazit's doing, part of his plan to get rid of Doada and take all the power for himself. Lazit had recalled the Red Blade the moment that someone had informed him that the survival of his Head of Intelligence might depend on them. He had ordered them to return to the capital. So the full force of the Red Blade never arrived to finish off the Celeddi rebels and to rescue Commander Eye. Lazit's surprise when Commander Eye returned alive from the White Sea was very telling. But he was even more surprised when the chief of the Red Blade was killed in an 'unfortunate traffic accident' soon after, and was immediately replaced with an officer whom Doada had hand picked. With the Red Blade safely back in Doada's control, Lazit himself will soon be history. Doada will make sure of that.

Nimbus opens the doors for them to take their places on the back seat, which is made of exquisitely patterned cobra skins. Another of Doada's 'little comforts', reminding him that even the most venomous of creatures can be subdued to nothing more threatening than upholstery.

Vellum slides his bulk in and stretches an arm along the silky snake leather.

'Well,' he says, 'this really is *very* nice, Doada.'

'I thought I'd told you never to call me that, *dear* boy,' Doada says through his teeth, 'or should I say *Dough* Boy.' Vellum's tight smile shows that Doada's dig has hit its mark. They are reluctant allies chained together by links of time and secrets.

'Really Nimbus, are we to sit here all day?' Doada slides back the glass partition and complains.

'Having just a little trouble with the veekle starter, Commander Sir.'

'Well, sort it out. I have urgent work to do fighting this new Green Thorn business.'

Doada slams the partition back and slumps onto the seat.

Nimbus turns the starter of the veekle one more time. As he does, all four of its wheels pop off, dropping the passenger compartment onto the ground with an unpleasant bang. At the same moment the fence, that shields the front of Doada's smart townhouse from the general riff-raff passing on the road, collapses. It has been very neatly chewed through along its entire length and there are mounds of earth and broken concrete where something, or many somethings have burrowed underneath the supporting pillars.

Workers, trudging from the new tower blocks to the factories, can see in. They stop and peer at the Vampire of the Fang sitting in a wheel-less karz, looking *ridiculous*. At first they simply stare, but gradually they begin to point and laugh.

The passenger doors are jammed against the concrete so all Doada can do is glare back.

'Nimbus! Nimbus!' he cries. 'Do something!'

The karz' doors are very hard to open. By the time Nimbus can struggle out, there is quite a crowd staring over the broken fence. The chauffeur lifts the bonnet of the karz and peers in. 'There's no engine, sir!' he reports in astonishment. 'They've taken the engine.'

He reaches in and pulls out a green cardboard heart which is all that is left behind in the space where the tar-fuelled engine should have been. Seeing this, some of the crowd cheer. Nimbus holds the heart to the window to show Doada and Vellum what is written on it.

Green Thorn is sprouting!

It takes a very long time for a replacement veekle to be found and the only one available is an old-fashioned lectric. The crackling car radio reports that new karz all over the city have suffered the same fate as Doada's, their wheels have dropped off, their engines vanished, to be replaced with green hearts, pot plants or bunches of flowers.

All along the route to the Tower there are signs that the rebels are able to call on a large number of helpers, all of whom have been extremely busy in the night. There are slogans daubed on almost every wall.

Green Thorns sprouting everywhere
and
Listen to the Listeners
and

225

No stopping the green wave
and, most irritating of all,
Boogam's Back!

In places where there is no room for their slogans, the rebels have just stencilled a bright-green thorn. The windows of at least two new meat restaurants are completely covered in posters showing the symbol of the Automators, the red fist enclosing the planet, on a plate with a fork stuck in it.

Don't eat your friends.
Make a meal of your enemies
the words read.

On the site of a new tower block, construction workers are standing around scratching their heads, because the piles of bricks have vanished and a forest of small trees has been planted overnight. On the half-constructed lot next to it a long banner dangles, flapping in the breeze, announcing:

Boxes made for things, not humans! Back to the land!

'Ha!' says Vellum, rubbing his great paws together. 'Looking forward to putting a stop to all *this!* It's got Toren Sisal written all over it,' he whispers.

'Be quiet,' Doada hisses. 'I've told you *never* to mention that name!'

He knows that Vellum's right, of course. Toren's been clever enough to change her style: no more bombs and shootings now. She's trying something new; she thinks that Doada can't fight the laughter of the crowd. But he can. He'll show her!

'We must accelerate our plans,' he tells Vellum quietly. 'How soon can the ship be ready?'

'Soon,' Vellum replies calmly. 'The Automator fleet is still out of action but the conversion of the *Dolphin* is almost complete.'

Doada is confused, a *conversion*? What is Vellum talking about?

'Were no Automator ships available?'

Vellum pulls a document from the briefcase on his lap.

'A series of unfortunate coincidences, it seems, Commander.' He flicks through pages of reports. 'Sinking due to sudden infestation of weed and whelks and so on, engines clogged. Hulls holed by unusual worms. All due to poor maintenance of course. I'll take disciplinary action.'

Doada rolls his eyes, really is there no end to the incompetence of the world.

'And when will this *Dolphin* be ready, Vellum?'

'Oh within hours, Commander. *Hours!* Just a few more staff to recruit. Hand-picked Red Blade all on standby. All we need now is couple of radio operators.'

Vellum's confidence steadies Doada's own nerves.

'Arrange for the Greenhouse to be put on board as soon as possible,' Doada says. 'We'll need three of the top Gardeners to ensure things go smoothly.'

Vellum nods. If this tall order fazes him, he says nothing.

'Once the weapon is aboard we can depart. Are you quite certain we can intercept the *Ice Maiden* and take the boy?'

'Absolutely,' Vellum replies with a smile. 'There's only one route the ice ships take south to Angellis and getting the boy off a boat as slow as a bath tub, with a crew led by a pussy cat, will be simple.'

Vellum lacks the imagination to see anything but success. It is another of his *capabilities*.

'Just one thing, Commander,' Vellum adds. 'After we get the boy, where will we be testing the weapon?'

'At a location I will reveal,' Doada replies. 'All in good time.'

They have arrived at the Fang. Its commanding perfection spears the sky. Doada's confidence returns. He *will* hold his nerve. The Greenhouse *will* deliver victory in all things. As Nimbus opens the door to allow him to step out, he turns to Vellum.

'Pop along to the docks at once. There is a great deal to be accomplished.'

Vellum gives a respectful dip of the head.

'As you wish, Commander Eye. As you wish!'

Doada almost manages a real smile. Dough Boy is really not so objectionable at all.

Doada's good mood does not last. There is chaos and consternation on the top floor of New Dawn Tower. The usual quiet order of the department is replaced with utter confusion. The telescopes are left unattended, and some of the Turned are even arguing with their handlers! Doada raises an eyebrow at the Chief of Floor responsible for coordinating all the intelligence activity.

'My office if you please, Senior Emmax,' he tells her.

Emmax scuttles in behind him, pushing her spectacles nervously up her nose.

For a moment Doada thinks that his assistant Mattock has neglected to raise the blinds, then he sees that all the windows of his office are simply *covered* with bird droppings. Not just accidentally streaked down the middle by a passing flock, but *coated*. Of all the mishaps of this morning, this is the one that he finds most unnerving. He draws down the blinds and puts on the lights.

'Sit down, Emmax,' he says, pointing to the low, wooden chair that is known to all on this floor except Doada as 'the naughty step'. Emmax folds her long body onto the child-sized seat, while Doada takes off his coat and lounges above her on the brocade sofa, caressing its pattern with his long fingers.

'What explanation can you offer for this chaos? I'm sure you are aware of the delicate situation with regard to the rebels and the need for *utmost* vigilance and efficiency.'

Doada has never seen Emmax make a mistake. She is like a machine, but this morning one forefinger picks nervously at the skin of her thumb. She presses her lips together and begins to speak. Her tone is not apologetic.

'While you were occupied in the White Sea,' she begins, 'there have been alarming changes. That is to say the behaviour of both birds and Turned has become extremely difficult to manage.'

Doada drums his fingers on the back of the sofa.

'*Difficulty*, Emmax, is part of what we do here. I don't expect to hear complaints about it from you!'

Something in the woman snaps. She rises from her chair and stands before him, her voice shrill and angry.

'Difficult?' she cries. '*Difficult*? It has become impossible! Birds have ceased to visit, the Turned have ceased to be compliant. The whole system has collapsed and the city erupts with … with *creatures*. This morning, there was a herd of deer on the train lines! Something is going on and you refuse to see it.'

And with that, she throws her ivory badge of rank to the floor and marches from the office, straight into the Ascender.

Doada calls Mattock.

'Clear this floor now!' he orders.

'But what shall I...' The young man is dumbfounded.

'I don't care how you do it. Push the lot of them over the edge if you like, but I want this entire place empty in five minutes.'

Doada needs space to think. He stares at the guano-streaked windows. He thinks about the deer on the train lines, and the boats sunk with whelks and weeds and worms. He knows quite well this is not coincidence. It is conspiracy. Toren and her brats, Green Thorn, Listeners, the lot of them. But more than that, Nature itself is rebelling. Conspiring. Fighting back. Rebellion, conspiracy and fighting require one thing above all others: communication. And nature's communication relies on that primitive power of siardw. He has burnt it from his own brain, he has tried to remove it from the world by burning it from the brain of every other Listener he can catch. But that hasn't worked.

Perhaps he's been focusing on the wrong things. He stares at the speaking tube receiver on his desk. Receivers like it lie on the desks of Automators and their minions across the city, connected by networks of wires that Doada has had laid. Perhaps listeners are just like speaking tubes and there is something in the natural world like the wires that connect them. Perhaps there is even a place like the exchange in the basement of the New Dawn Tower, through which all of nature's 'wires' run! A place which, if destroyed, would wreck the power of the natural world to communicate and end once and for all its ability to resist?

He gazes at the globe that sits on his desk; if such a place existed, where would it be found? It would have to be a place through which many animals pass on their endless journeys around the globe; a mountain range perhaps? Or an island in the deep ocean, where both creatures from the air and water would meet?

An *island*. Yes! *The island not on any other map.* That old memory, out of reach a moment ago, jumps up into his mind. His father's voice comes to him as clear as if retired sea captain Borden was speaking in the room.

I found it in a ship's chandlers in Meritysky.

Doada closes his eyes and sees again his father's weathered hands spreading the ancient parchment of a map across a table.

He had been very small, only just tall enough to peer over the edge of the table in his father's little study. Toren had stood on tiptoe, he remembers. Before them on the rickety table was a map, its corners held down with two glass paperweights and a teacup and a pair of scissors. The paper was thick, almost like heavy fabric, but smooth and the colour of double cream. The colours on it had been painted by hand. They were very bright and vivid and seemed to jump off the page. His father explained what the map showed, tracing the shapes and colours with his fingers.

'Here's the deepest water, see, the darkest blue. That's where this island is, the green, you see?'

Even though Doada had been so little he'd understood what the map showed: blue water, shading from palest turquoise to the deepest velvet indigo. In the middle of the deepest part, almost the colour of the sky between stars, was a small green island, roughly crescent shaped. Borden had peered at it through a magnifying glass.

'This little island lost in the deepest part of the ocean,' his father had said, *'isn't on any other map in all the world. It's a secret place and now only we three know about it.'*

Borden had laughed at Toren's round-eyed wonder. When their mother's voice called from the hallway summoning her children to bed and her husband to dinner, he'd placed a finger to his lips.

'Shhhh, don't tell your ma.'

Then Borden scooped his toddler daughter into his arms and asked Doada to roll up the map and replace it in its wooden tube while he left the room.

But when Doada had reached to touch the map, a spark like a bolt of lightning had stabbed into his head. The memory of it makes Commander Eye call out and put his hand up to the place from which his siardw was burned. The touch of that map created a feeling more intense that the thrilling power he had felt as boy when he killed the birds he caught. His siardw had sensed a power represented in that map so great it terrified him; so great it hurt him and caused him to fall to the floor of his father's study where they found him. He could not explain what had happened because he didn't want to tell the fearful secret that he was a Listener. And he had never wanted to see that map again or even think of it.

Until this moment. Doada is suddenly quite certain that that map was important, full of hidden information. That's why Toren took it when she ran away. He'd found the note amongst his father's papers.

'Dearest Pa. Took the map. Hope you understand, Love T'

Doada reaches into his jacket pocket and pulls out the photograph of Toren and her eldest, on a *beach*. Had she perhaps used the map to find the island? Is the island on the map where she ran to before she holed up in the mountains? With that stinking little ostler's son? Of course – he'd run off to be a sailor, so perhaps Tui Meyer could have sailed her there!

Doada taps the globe, walking his fingers over the great oceans, palest duck-egg blue for the shallowest waters and darker colours for deeper. The very darkest blue, almost purple, is used in just one place, a tiny crescent which matches the shape he remembers from his father's map. He scrabbles in a drawer to find a magnifying glass to look at the tiny letters written on the dark colour in white ink like spider silk.

The Marraduka Trench

It is in the Latantic Ocean, south west of Rumyc, not even *so* very far away and surely small enough to find an island in.

What if that island really is some centre of nature's power? What if he could lure his sister there? What if he could make that place the first test site of the Greenhouse? Ah, then he would destroy it all, all the people and power that oppose him.

With the boy and the girl aboard the ship, and their position leaked to Green Thorn by regular radio transmissions, Toren may try to board the ship which will be well defended by the Red Blade. So she will be caught. Or Doada may just locate the island and lure her there. Either way the outcome is the same. Toren and her brood eliminated. And if he's right about the island, he could end this conspiracy of nature once and for all.

In his mind Doada erases all the 'ifs' and 'mays' and makes them certainties that will deliver him all that he desires.

The small green island *is* the place on which the power of siardw and all the natural world's power to communicate depends.

It *is* somewhere in the Marraduka Trench.

Toren *will* be lured there by her kidnapped children.

And he, Commander Eye, will cause all of it to be destroyed.

He will make the first test of the Greenhouse *really* count.

It is hardly even a gamble, Doada tells himself. If it turns out to be just another island then he still has a good test site for the Greenhouse and a way to trap Toren far from prying eyes.

Doada feels as though he has the pieces of a jigsaw all assembled. What he needs now is to fit them all together.

The first pieces are easy. Arrangements he can make down a speaking tube. He calls the head of RNR, Rumyc National Radio.

'I need to make a broadcast to the nation at lunchtime. A matter of national security. Have the studio ready at one sharp!'

Second, he calls Fallen, in Education.

'Listen Fallen, that girl I saw last time I visited your department? I want her put in an ensin's uniform. I don't care how you do it. But I need her at RNR by 12.45 today. It's a photo call. She needs to be clean and able to stand upright, but no more. Do you understand?'

Finally he calls the Fang's own security detail.

'Evacuate the building at once!' he says. 'Intelligence informs me there's a *device* in the basement.'

How well trained his staff are! The security klaxons sound and blue lights on the Ascender start to flash.

It will take a few moments for the building to be sufficiently empty, free of witnesses, and there is one more essential thing that Doada needs. He unlocks the small, secret room adjacent to his office. The starling's room. Why is his heart racing at the thought? Ridiculous, he tells himself, *truly ridiculous*. Light and fresh air pour in through the high, unglazed window. Doada keeps his eyes averted from the empty cage, from the floor. He reaches up, runs his hand over a spot on the far wall until he feels the slight indentation of the concealed button, presses it and the small door pops open. He draws out the box inside, turns to leave and, as he does, his eyes can no longer avoid the remains of the starling on the floor.

The cool dry air has mummified her, shrinking muscle and skin into a tight carapace that binds to the bone. Her beak, more yellow now than ever it was in life, is open, as if still singing. Her feathers have acquired a gloss and brightness that they had lost in life. Her wings are spread and her feet neatly tucked; she's flying. Arranged around her are concentric circles of feathers, from huge flight feathers taken from the wings of eagles, herons, cranes, through rings of feathers blue as the ocean, to tiny feathers, iridescent green and violet and, finally, cradling her body, a ring of breast feathers in the colours of dawn and sunset.

Doada exits smartly, shuts the door and leans on it. The room is secret, known only to him, so who laid the feathers round his dead spy?

Birds, his mind answers. Only birds could enter through that high window. He stamps the thought down. Birds did not, could not. It is the doing of a human. That child most likely. Yes. Birds controlled by Toren's little brat. A deed designed to work upon his mind. Doada breathes carefully, refocuses on his task. He's wasted time. He places the box on the desk and lifts the lid. Lying in its velvet bed is the pistol he keeps for special occasions. It dates back to the first revolution, with distinctive but effective bullets. Well, tonight it will help to start a second revolution. Its cold touch calms him. He loads the magazine; it takes six shots, but even with his unsteady aim, he will need just two. The handle of the gun is cool and heavy in his hand, a fine weapon in itself.

Lazit chose his office because of its privacy, on a half floor with its own access from the far end of the second floor. Nothing connects it to the rest of the building, not even the alarm system. The klaxons that blare everywhere else are merely a distant echo at the entrance to Lazit's special little kingdom. Doada has made sure that the guards who normally stand at the bottom of the narrow staircase are absent. Lazit has always said he likes to *work in peace*. Doada assumed that this meant merely falling asleep over a bottle of brandy before eleven, with no witnesses, apart from his loyal secretary. But now Doada knows Lazit used his privacy to plot against his own Commander Eye.

Doada slips up the staircase, the pistol held inside his sleeve, and greets Lazit's ancient secretary.

'Paro, *dear boy.*'

The old man almost jumps out of his seat.

'Oh, Commander, sir. Um, Chief Lazit is very busy just now I...'

Doada presses his finger to his lips.

'Don't worry, dear boy, I promise not to wake him. Just left something on his desk when we were chatting the other day.'

Soundlessly, Doada slips in through the door and closes it behind him. The office is, of course, beautiful: spacious, light with an exquisite parquet floor. Lazit's windows are clean, Doada notices, but he has lowered the blinds so sunlight won't disturb his rest. He is snoozing at his desk, leaning on his arms and a small, silk pillow, like a schoolchild in a boring lesson. Doada pulls the pistol from his sleeve and turns it round. He takes aim carefully, rehearsing the trajectory of the blow, then raises his arm and whacks his colleague on the back of the head with the pistol butt. Nothing much changes, Lazit simply goes a little limper. Then Doada swivels his colleague's chair around, places the barrel of the gun in the middle of his left thigh, covers it with the pillow he has pulled from under the man's head, and pulls the trigger. The shot is muffled, and Paro, slightly deaf yet still the secretary, calls tremulously.

'Is everything alright?'

'Just dropped a paperweight,' Doada calls. 'He hasn't stirred. Fast asleep!'

Even Paro won't fall for that for long. Doada checks the leg wound. It's bleeding sufficiently. Lazit will be dead from blood loss in about five minutes. He pats the man's cheek.

'Cheerio, *dear boy,*' he tells him.

Doada steps out through the door and shoots Paro straight between the eyes before he's even risen from his seat. The sound of the shot echos a little down the stairwell, but there's no one to hear it. Doada will arrange for the most loyal members of Red Blade to 'discover' the killings in an hour or so. Just as they will 'discover' the explosive device planted in the basement. Doada slips down the stairs feeling more sprightly than he has in months. Really you don't have to be a good shot, you just need to *plan*.

The journey to the radio station takes longer than expected. Nimbus finds one road after another closed or impassable.

'Whatever is the problem now?' Doada complains from the back seat.

'Toadstools, Commander Eye,' Nimbus replies. 'They seem to be pushing up through the concrete, sir.'

Doada peers through the windscreen. The smooth surface of the road ahead is bulging and cracked, so it resembles an over-risen cake, punched up by a line of fungi like pale knuckles. Along their entire route, fingers of yellow and red-spotted domes and pale umbrellas have pushed their way through pavements and roads.

'It's the rain, sir,' Nimbus says, 'and the unseasonably warm spring.'

They both know this isn't the reason for the mushroom invasion.

Doada shuts his eyes and doesn't open them until they are at the radio station.

The RNR station director greets him at the door. She is

almost panting with anticipation of the exclusive story her station will soon deliver to the whole country. The photographer shows the permit for her camera and Doada glances at it for form's sake then allows the woman to pop away as he makes his official arrival. He keeps his expression solemn. He is, after all going to announce the *tragic* loss of his best friend and life-long colleague.

Among other things.

The radio studio is a little chilly, in spite of the muggy warmth of the streets outside. He's glad of the coat; he gathers it round him. There is the slightest spattering of blood, just a few faint freckles along one side of the hem. No one will notice, and even if they do, what would it matter? The Red Blade officers are already his; Merit Cubit and the House of Governors well know on which side their bread is buttered. Nothing lies in his path now that he cannot defeat.

In the dim light on the other side of the glass, eager faces leer like vultures waiting for a death. Doada puts on the headphones and waits for the light to tell him that he has a direct line right into the heads of hundreds of thousands of his country folk. Listeners? Ha! Listening in on the barely understood thoughts of beasts? What does that achieve? This way he can manipulate the minds of humans and that's so, so, so much more useful.

All over the land, Doada's voice oozes out into the lunchtime air, warm and smooth. Surely that Vampire nickname was meant for some other person? People turn up the volume and

239

listen carefully. They can tell that something important is about to happen; they've already seen the signs that change of is on the way. Things are hanging in the balance; Doada's voice could push them either way.

'Fellow countrymen and women, I speak to you today with a heavy heart, a heart burdened with sorrow. You will all know the name Herick Lazit, Founder and Director of the organisation you have come to know as the Automators. It is my terrible duty to tell you that my friend and colleague Herick Lazit has been murdered at his desk.'

Here Doada pauses for a fraction of a second, a break of the perfect length to allow people to believe he is struggling to master his inconsolable grief.

'There can be no doubt about the perpetrator of this crime. It bears the unmistakable hallmark of our old enemy, the rebel leader known to you as the Ghost, or in the crude language of the past, the Boogam.'

He will save the juicy details about the telltale leg wound for the newspaper article. Readers enjoy something gruesome to chew on. Now to lay before them his two greatest weapons. Fear and greed. Fear will allow Doada to manipulate the citizens of Rumyc and greed will stop them making a fuss about it.

'We had all believed the Green Thorn attacks on factories and black-gold stations that cost so many innocent lives were far behind us. Some may have believed that the rebels had transformed into a harmless, non-violent group, content to daub paint on buildings and perform pranks with veekles. But make no mistake, their intentions are just as violent as before.

'In addition to the brutal murder of my dear colleague and his loyal secretary, a large explosive device was discovered this morning in the basement of the headquarters of the Automators: New Dawn Tower. Had it not been for the prompt action of our elite protectors, the Red Blade, the device would have destroyed a large section of the city. Thousands of citizens would have perished. This outrage, carried out in the heart of the New Dawn Building in broad daylight shows that the threat the rebels and their leader, the Ghost, pose to us is very serious indeed.

'I cannot lie to you. We are all in the gravest danger. The rebels would use the most violent force to return us all to the dark days of the past, when we spoke to beasts, when we lived at the mercy of nature, as the beasts do. All the gains of the last few years, the benefits that the new thinking of the Automator movement has brought to all, could be lost. We must not return to the past, to the terrible tyranny of nature. Nature is not our ruler. Nature is ours to *dominate*, to *use* for the good of all humanity, so prosperity can flow to all. I will not allow Green Thorn and their evil leader to threaten our freedoms. I pledge to take whatever measures are necessary to protect you all.

'So from this evening there will be curfew in the capital enforced by Automator security officers, supported by the expertise of the Red Blade. Rebels will be hunted down and shot like the beasts they wish us all to be. We will show no mercy to those who show no mercy to us.'

That has, Doada feels, dealt with 'fear'. Now for 'greed...'

'The roots of Green Thorn are like a weed; they spread far. The gravest news it is my duty to deliver to you today, is that these roots run far beyond our borders. Foreign powers are giving help and support to the rebels who seek to bring us down.

'As a result we, the Automators, with the blessing of all the Merits of the House of Governors, have developed a powerful weapon to keep our beloved land of Rumyc secure. It is a weapon of such immense power, that it will remove all possibility of defeat, forever. This weapon makes our small nation unassailable. In time, it will allow us to liberate the rest of the world from the dictatorship of nature and to free all nations from dependence on the land. The resources of the entire planet will be made available to you, citizens of Rumyc. Our glorious country will be the greatest beacon of progress and prosperity the world has ever seen!

'Tonight I sail with my colleagues, a crew of hand-picked brave young volunteers, to the Marraduka Trench. Here on a small, remote island we will demonstrate the power of the new weapon. Thanks to the tireless work of Automator technicians, the destructive power of the Greenhouse will then stand as a warning to all who oppose us, that resistance is futile. We will be victorious.

'Heed my message well. Be calm, be reassured, you are in the safe, strong grip of the Automators.'

Outside, on the steps of the station, Doada answers questions about Lazit's murder. He tells the story of the left leg injury that the Ghost and her minions have made their calling card. He talks about the distinctive bullets found in Lazit's body that will be easy to match to a gun. Even now, he tells the reporters, Red Blade officers are searching for the weapon. He is confident it will be found, that it will identify a Green Thorn culprit. He doesn't tell them that this 'culprit' will turn out to be a high-ranking member of the Board of Governors, a person who has long questioned the rise of the Automators. She and her family will all be implicated, of course, and dealt with accordingly. He makes mental note to hand the pistol to a trusted Red Blade officer to make sure it gets planted in the right place for tomorrow's headlines. Progress will be made, even in his absence.

Finally, he poses for photographs with the pale young ensin on his arm. Fallen delivered her as requested, but had been forced to use a heavy dose of drugs to make her compliant and she cannot be relied on to stand alone.

'This,' he tells the reporters with a noble smile, 'is just one of the brave crew of young volunteers who are leaving their families to help ensure safety for all.'

He makes sure her pale, empty face is turned to the light so that the photographers will obtain a clear likeness.

'She looks seasick already!' a reporter calls from the back.

'Not at all! She is merely overwhelmed by all this attention. But she will be ready to do her duty the moment that we sail.'

Fortunately Doada's coat partly envelopes the child so that fact that he is holding her up isn't too obvious. Not that it matters. What matters is that the face of Toren Sisal's youngest child will be on the front page of every newspaper by the evening.

The trap for the Boogam and her brats is set.

Winter, Fifteen Years Earlier

Toren's Story
2

 The raven shifted on Qimmiq's shoulder, leaning in so that two pairs of intelligent grey eyes were examining Toren as she spoke. Something was passing between the old chieftain and her bird but, as a non-Listener, Toren had no idea what it might be. Qimmiq's husband Keasik and their oldest daughter Chepi sat on either side of her, but they gave nothing away.

Outside the wind whined across the ice, and the silent conversation between the chieftain and her bird went on. Amongst the Celeddi no decision was taken quickly. Toren must stay quiet and hold her nerve.

She knew her plan was radical. A change of tactics. Hit the target stealthily, without detection, was what she'd taught the hothead rebels that had come to join them from the south. Pick off the guards with sniper shots that maimed without killing (her own favourite was the shot to the thigh), to build fear. But the tar wells still grew, gross and ugly, like a cancer, spilling filth into the sea and ice, killing life.

Now she wanted to destroy the tar station completely.

But to do that she needed the help of the Celeddi. Their

244

rhinos could cover snow and ice more quickly than any veekle. They could get forces to the station more quickly and make a getaway when the job was done. The Celeddi themselves were good with their crossbows, if they could be persuaded to use them.

The raven closed her eyes and Qimmiq spoke at last.

'Killing is not our way,' she said. 'Fire and destruction are not our way!'

Keasik nodded.

'You ask us to break Liorna, the force that runs through all things.'

Chepi leapt to her feet.

'Liorna is already broken!' she cried, voicing a passion that Toren didn't dare to express. 'The tar that spills into the ocean has killed our brother whales, our sister birds. Unless we stop it, Liorna will be undone entirely and the great silence will swallow everything!'

Qimmiq looked at her daughter.

'We may be hunters but we are not *killers*. We do not end life without good reason and we do not command our rhinos. We will not take them into such danger. This is not a plan!'

And that was that.

Cloud obscured the stars as Toren trudged back to her igloo, and wriggled inside. It still smelled faintly of Tui and of their little daughter. She tried not to think of them, but sometimes it was hard not to remember.

'Harlon needs more than the inside of an ice house,' Tui had said. She'd come back to the igloo one night, two months

245

ago, to find him loading the sled, Harlon strapped inside his parka. He wasn't angry just calm, as always, and sad.

'We'll head south for the coast,' he'd told her. 'I'll make sure we aren't impossible to find.'

There was nothing to be said. Tui was a much better parent than Toren could ever be. She was a fighter, and she'd never be a ma. But she couldn't let them go without anything of her. She'd rushed inside the igloo and pulled Borden's map in its wooden tube from her pack.

'Here,' she'd said. 'It was my father's. Maybe it'll help guide you.'

He'd taken it gently from her hands and looked at her, a long, deep look that held the memory of the night when they'd run off, like kids playing hooky. It had turned out to be the night that the Automators had killed both their fathers. Borden had never recovered consciousness and Tui's father had not spotted Cat Vellum's thugs until he found them waiting on his doorstep.

Then they'd embraced like brother and sister.

'Goodbye, Breen,' he'd said.

'Goodbye, Far,' Toren had replied. No one was outside to overhear, but somehow using their real names would have hurt too much.

Toren wrapped herself against the memories and the cold. She fell asleep thinking that if she couldn't destroy the tar station, she might as well head south to find them.

She was woken in the night by rhino voices, a chorus of deep rumbles and high squeaks. She pulled on her clothes and went out. Bright green and orange aurora shimmied across the sky and danced over the snow. In the eerie light, five woolly rhinos stood outside Qimmiq's igloo. They were not rhinos belonging to the settlement, already known and bonded to individual humans. These were quite wild, creatures that would normally be further south at this time of year, digging under the tundra snow for frozen moss and lichens. Stranger still, hanging back and pacing nervously on the edge of the group were snow bears! They would have walked an even longer way to get here, from their seal-hunting grounds far out on the frozen ocean.

A female rhino, smaller than the rest, made the loudest noises. Rebels and Celeddi emerged from their igloos and stood watching. Qimmiq came out and the rhinos fell silent. The smaller female walked towards the old chieftain until she stood so close she could rest her chin on the woman's head. The bears stopped their pacing and one walked to join the rhino, so close to Qimmiq that it could have swatted her with one of its great paws. Everything became very still. Qimmiq gave a little cry and put her hand up to her head. After a few moments the rhino and the snow bear moved away, and gradually, with their companions, drew back beyond the edge of the ring of igloos. The old chieftain spoke slowly and very clearly.

'This rhino and this bear have come into my mind. I did not enter theirs! They move inside my mind as a kayak cuts between the ice floes.' Her voice trembled with wonder; all around there were gasps and exclamations of astonishment. Celeddi and the rhinos to whom they were connected from earliest childhood shared some thoughts by mutual consent; but rhinos didn't just *enter* into human minds. No animal did

247

10
On the Red Ship

Harlon

 It isn't hard to find their way to the Bai. They just follow the path of terrible destruction created by the Monster, a trail of churned earth with the felled trees, already no more than giant logs, lying on either side. Flocks of birds fly above them, their voices full of confusion and terror, and the mashed remains of plants and animals lie in ragged heaps. They come across a baby monkey on a bed of ripped foliage, its beautiful white and chestnut fur unmarked, its delicate grey eyelids gently closed, as if it had just fallen asleep. Tolly sobs when she sees it.

'I feel like my heart's gone through that terrible machine!'

At last they reach the Bai. There is one transport left, almost lost in dense smoke but there are no rebels firing at it and none of its crew is standing guard. They are all too busy trying to drive off the clouds of biting insects that swirl around the entrance to the hold. All the same, the girls raise their arms, Tolly showing her Automator number and Harlon the healing scar where hers would have been. They call out, 'Don't shoot. Don't shoot!'

An ensin, surrounded by his own personal swarm of wasps, asks them who they are and hardly waits to hear Tolly's reply before waving them on board. Harlon's scarred arm and scalp seem proof enough for him even without any sign of Automator uniform. The transport capo asks no questions, just directs them to space at the rear of the hold.

The hold is full of gear, mess tents and ammunition, a handful of injured troops lying quietly on stretchers, their faces swollen with insect stings. Harlon and Tolly find a space behind some huge crates by a tiny window at the rear of the hold. It's the same position, Harlon notices, as her cage was in the transport that crashed into the forest. All that seems like so long ago now.

She stares out of the window. There are two more Monsters biting into the forest now and as the transport rises higher Harlon can see more and more of the devastation they are creating. How many thousands, millions, of creatures' lives destroyed, mashed up, turned to nothing? How many more by the end of a day? A week, a year? How tiny Enkalamba and her message seem against all that.

If the song's destroyed, everything, everything will die.

How long will it take to destroy the whole forest, Harlon wonders? A clock is ticking; the Automators must be stopped.

Tolly sleeps. In spite of her new loyalties, this is still a familiar place for her. But each time Harlon closes her eyes the horror of Enkalamba's death jerks her awake, back to the hold of the transport, with clouds scudding by the window and the drone of the engines.

The route the transport takes to Fidrac is not direct. Sometime in the middle of the first night they land at an Automator base somewhere in the east. The casualties are off-loaded and new crates of ammunition and weapons taken on board. Then there is an engine problem and they can't take off again until the following evening. At first Harlon is anxious, afraid that somehow she will give herself away, but no one takes the slightest notice of the two dirty young ensins stowed at the back of the hold.

They fly through the night, not straight for the capital but to another airfield in some deserted spot. They arrive at dawn and no one seems to be in any hurry to go anywhere.

'We could have walked to Fidrac!' Harlon whispers. Tolly shrugs and curls up to sleep again, as if she were a hibernating bear.

Towards evening a truck arrives with raw recruits who look too young to be away from home on their own. They are loaded in amongst the boxes and crates. Harlon overhears the recruits' commander talking to the transport capo.

'Things are kicking off in Fidrac, so I hear.'

The capo nods.

'Yes. We're going to need all the help we can get, even from youngsters like these. I'm not in any hurry to get back there!'

She certainly isn't! It takes another night and day, another two refuelling and repair stops before finally they arrive in the capital. Harlon has lost count of how long it is since Xeno was snatched off the mountain. It feels like a lifetime but is it seven days or ten? No, more! Certainly enough time for the Automators to have done something awful.

Oh Xeno! Xeno! Harlon thinks. Hang on.

Stiff, tired and dazed, Harlon and Tolly cross the giant airfield beside the Fang, under a low grey sky. All around many other

251

transports are off-loading their cargoes of new recruits. The girls shuffle though the doors of a huge warehouse with lines of others. Inside, voices echo off the walls and the only way they can talk is to speak directly into each other's ears.

'This is the Clearing House,' Tolly leans in to say, 'where you get re-assigned to a new job. But I've never seen it like this. It's chaos!'

Harlon has never seen so many human beings all together in one place. The entire space is filled with uniformed people milling about and talking. Older, more senior-ranking officers stand behind large desks, loaded with official-looking papers, shouting things no one takes any notice of. The girls are pushed and harried into a series of queues: for new uniforms, which are dirty and the wrong size, boots, ditto, and for food, which is disgusting. No one seems to know what's going on and there is a kind of crazy electricity in the place. The officers behind their desks look very anxious. One keeps dragging his hand though his hair so it has come to stand on end, making him resemble a large exclamation mark.

Harlon can feel even more time ticking away, time when she could be in the Fang searching for Xeno. It feels like a dream where you try to run, but your feet are glued down. The clamour of voices all around makes her want to scream.

At last they find a bench in a corner where they can talk more privately.

'How are we going to get into the Fang and find my sister?' Harlon says. Tolly bites her lip.

'It would be easy normally. Just go to the deployment desk over there and say you're volunteering for cleaning duty in

HQ. They only use uniformed recruits to do the cleaning in there and usually nobody wants to do it. But in all *this*... I don't know what's going on.' Tolly stares at the noisy milling crowd and shakes her head. She points to a newspaper that's been dropped on the floor.

'Maybe *that* will tell us something,' she says and darts through the sea of legs to grab it. At the sight of the front page, Harlon freezes. She can't speak.

'What's the matter?' Tolly hisses. 'Look a bit more normal, can't you? We don't want to attract attention.'

Harlon takes a few deep breaths, wills herself to stop trembling.

'That's my sister,' she breathes. 'The one they took.' She points to the little scrap of a human in uniform on the front page. 'But who is that man?'

'You're kidding?' Tolly replies.

'No, it really is my sister, Xeno.'

Tolly shakes her head.

'No, I mean, you really don't know who *he* is?

Harlon shakes her head.

'He's possibly the most powerful bloke in all Rumyc.' Tolly scans the lines of print beneath the photo. 'No! He's definitely the most powerful now. The Director of the Automators has been murdered by Green Thorn!' Tolly whistles through her teeth. 'That's what this panic is about.'

But Harlon isn't listening. She's reading the rest of the front page article, about the testing of the 'weapon', the 'brave volunteer' in the photograph and how the ship will sail tonight making for the Marraduka Trench, which is, the newspaper reports 'the deepest part of the Latantic ocean.' Isn't that where Ma said her mystery island was? But there's no time for questions: Harlon points at the long queue in front of the deployment desk.

'We have to get to the front of that right now. We've got to get on this ship.'

Harlon is ready to fight her way through, but Tolly has a better plan.

'Look official,' she tells Harlon. 'Hold your head up like you're someone really important and do what I do.'

Tolly straightens herself out, buttons her jacket, tucks her dirty hair under her uniform cap. Then she sticks one arm in the air and in a loud, official-sounding voice shouts, 'Commander Eye, official business. Let us through at once. Special commission from Commander Eye!'

Harlon copies her as best she can.

'Who's Commander Eye?' she whispers.

'That bloke in the newspaper,' Tolly breathes back. 'Most people just call him the Vampire, though not to his face, unless you want to end up dead.'

To Harlon's amazement, it works. People step back and make a path for them as if the two scratched and battered young ensins with ill-fitting uniforms are something very special indeed. But the officer sitting behind the deployment desk is *not* so easy to convince. He definitely notices their youth, their rank and their scruffy appearance.

'What's all this *special commission* nonsense? You look like you've been dragged through the mud.'

Tolly doesn't miss a beat. She seems to grow taller and straighter.

'Just back from active service in the Woken Forest, sir. Keen to volunteer for Commander Eye's special mission, sir.' She slaps the newspaper down in front of him.

'But you're not battle-trained,' he says. 'You're just ensins.'

He still doesn't look convinced, but his superior officer, a man with a line of stripes embroidered on the shoulder of his uniform, overhears their conversation and leans in. He pushes his bald head on its long stalk of a neck towards them.

'Volunteers for the special sea mission?' he says. 'The weapon testing thing?'

'Yes, sir!' Tolly replies, saluting again.

'Are you the radio operators, Ensins Kogi and…' The bald man consults a list on his clipboard. 'Um, Leezul?'

'We are, sir!' Tolly replies brightly.

'Where the hell have you been? Well, you're here now at any rate. Get yourselves down to Bay 17; there's a cab waiting to take you to the ship. She sails in forty minutes. You made it by the skin of your teeth.'

As they rush off, pushing through the crowd, Harlon whispers.

'D'you know how to operate a radio, Tolly?'

'I know Morse code,' Tolly says. 'My brother and I used to tap out messages on the floor of our bedroom. And I did the first day of the radio operators' course. I'll work it out.'

Harlon hopes that by the time the *real* Kogi and Leezul make it to the front of the queue, the ship will have already left harbour.

It's growing dark as the veekle whisks them though the streets. They both stare out through the windows. Harlon has never

255

seen a city before, but the tall buildings, the lights reaching up to the stars, the traffic of veekles, people, tryks, bicycles, and the frantic busyness of it all, is just what she expected. What she didn't expect are the trees, lots of them, saplings, newly planted. They are everywhere, poking out of every bit of spare ground. There are lines of toadstools too, bigger than any she has ever seen, pushing up through the paths and roadways. Neither trees nor fungi look as if they are part of the plan for the city, more as if they have arrived, like a message bringing news of change.

As they stop at traffic lights a cloud of birds wheels above them, filling the space between the buildings before swirling off like a storm. Both Tolly and their driver gasp.

'Guess you 'ent been 'ere for a while?' says the driver. 'All sorts been going on. Trees coming up, mushrooms poking through the pavements. Birds everywhere. Crapping on my cab all day and all night. It's the Green Thorn's doing o'course and *Listeners.'*

'They killed that Lazit bloke the paper says,' Tolly comments.

'Your boss man. Yeah. Yesterday that was. Green Thorn done that as well,' the man says. 'You know what else? They took the engines out of all the tar-fuelled karz. Including the one belonging to the Vam – I mean Commander Eye. And now I hear there's a strike at the factory where they make 'em. Boosted my trade.'

The man suppresses a smile as he catches Harlon's eye in the mirror: they may look like scruffy kids but they are still in Automator uniforms, and he knows what happens to those who criticise *them!*

'Here you go, ladies. That there is your ship and there's where you board.'

The ship is painted in the Automators' favourite colour: blood red. But as they get closer, it's obvious the paintwork has been done in a hurry. The original blue paint shows through in many places and the black fist and planet symbol is wonky and blurred. Two people stand at the bottom of the gangplank, an Automator capo in full uniform and mask, with a very official-looking folder in his hands, and a sailor in a smart navy jacket with brass buttons.

'Let me do the talking,' Tolly murmurs as they get close.

'Ensins Kogi and Leezul, sir!'

Tolly reports to the officer, who looks up from the clipboard.

'Kogi, S and Leezul, P.'

'That's right!' Tolly beams helpfully.

'Full names.'

'Saldo Kogi and Pria Leezul.'

Harlon is impressed at Tolly's quick thinking.

'Which one's which?'

'I'm Kogi, this is Leezul,' Tolly says without hesitation.

Harlon is even more impressed.

'Can't she speak for herself?' snaps the officer.

Harlon is about to say something, but the sailor butts in.

'Officer Zee, we are due to sail imminently. I must *insist* that we get these people on board at once!'

The officer scowls.

'Don't tell me how to do my job, *sailor*. Your ship and crew are under Automator command now,' he snaps. 'You two, show your numbers. Now!'

Beside the names on the officer's list are numbers belonging to the real Kogi and Leezul.

Tolly's number won't match so Harlon pulls up her sleeve to show the livid burn on her arm which, right on queue, starts to bleed.

'Burnt off by the rebel scum,' she says.

Zee flinches slightly at the sight of it.

'Does that satisfy your security procedure?' the sailor asks.

'Alright, alright,' Zee says. 'Get aboard. Cabin 37, engine deck.'

On board there seem to be more blue uniforms than red and blacks. The original crew of the hastily painted and commandeered Red Ship are running about on the decks with hardly any Automator uniforms to be seen. But the stern message that blares again and again from the loudspeakers on every deck, sounds very much like the Automators.

'Automator Security and essential crew only on deck. All others keep to your cabins by order of Commander Eye.'

Cabin 37 is a tiny hot cupboard, where the throb of the engine makes the walls vibrate.

Stuck to the door is a map of the ship showing escape routes up to the lifeboats if the order to abandon ship is given. At the top is a sticker which reads Red Ship Five. It peels off easily to reveal another name in blue letters: the *Dolphin*.

'Look,' Harlon says. 'That must be the ship's real name.'

'Ha!' says Tolly. 'No Automator is going to like a ship named after a sea creature.'

Harlon peers at the diagram that shows the ship in cross section. There are so many places where one small person could be locked away.

'What I can't understand,' Harlon says, almost to herself, 'is why they wanted to bring Xeno. I mean what's *she* got to do with testing this weapon?'

'She might have been turned?' Tolly says. 'I hate to say it but...'

'Turned?' Harlon stares at Tolly. 'What is that?'

Tolly looks away.

'It's what they try to do to all Listeners they take to the Fang. They make them into slaves so they can use their Listener powers to spy on other Listeners or control their machine creatures. Special Project is what they call 'em. It's all supposed to be secret, but...' Tolly shrugs. '...People talk.' Tolly looks up again at Harlon. 'I'm so sorry,' she says.

Harlon thinks of the falcons that chased them down the gully and of the dead-eyed husks of humans that sometimes returned to the streets of the village back home. What Tolly's said makes perfect sense. *That's* why they want the Listeners, to *use* them; that's why Automators want everything.

Harlon picks up the newspaper from where it lies on the bottom bunk and stares at Xeno.

It's true she doesn't look like herself. Suddenly Harlon cannot bear to wait anymore. She must know; she must search for Xeno, right now.

'I've got to look for her, Tolly,' she says. 'You stay here. If anyone asks, say you think I've got lost.' She slips off her Automator jacket. It might be better to look a little more like ordinary crew. Before Tolly can argue or object. Harlon's shut the cabin door behind her.

The corridor is dim. To her right is the narrow metal stairway down which they climbed to get here, not much more than a ladder leading back up to the higher decks. To her left the corridor continues, lined on either side with identical doors. She carries on, listening at every door she passes, in case they offer something, some clue. They are all closed and silent until the last door on the left which is slightly ajar. A flicker of movement inside the cabin catches Harlon's eye and she steps closer.

The room is even smaller than the cabin she and Tolly share, a storage space really, with a tiny narrow bunk jammed between ranks of cupboards. A dark boy in grubby shorts and a T-shirt sits on the floor with a bowl of water propped between his legs. He's washing something: a bird! He holds it up close to his face as he gently works soap into its wet feathers. It looks pathetic and bedraggled, but it doesn't struggle. He whispers to it, 'I know I know. You don't like it, but soap is useful. It will take the tar from your feathers. I promise they'll be good as new. I've done this lots of times before.'

The bird gives a small shake but doesn't attempt to escape as the boy pours a jug of clean water over it, washing away the grimy suds. It shakes its feathers, clean now and pearly white, with a little cap of inky black and fine red beak.

'Not yet,' the boy says as if answering a question, 'in a few days when you've got your own oils back. *Then* you can fly.'

Another announcement blares out from the loudspeaker in the corridor.

'Keep to your cabins. Security only on decks.'

260

The boy curses under his breath, looks up and, for a split second, meets Harlon's eyes. She snatches away her gaze like a hand from a flame; the door is pushed shut at once. She hopes he doesn't feel seen. But perhaps there will be some allies on this ship after all.

She reaches the end of the corridor, where there is a metal hatch with a wheel in the middle. Harlon turns the wheel and the hatch loosens in its frame so she can push it open. She glances round, then steps through, sealing it behind her with the wheel on the other side. The sound and smell of the engine is even louder here. It's like climbing down into the hot belly of an animal where its guts wriggle and churn in the dark.

She's now in a short corridor whose doors are marked with things like 'generator back up', 'lectric stores' and 'main fuses'. The light down here is dim, with just one yellowing bulb at the end of the short passage. It shows a narrow stairway, not much more than another ladder, leading down. Something tells Harlon *that's* the place! But before she can climb down and take a look, a large armed Automator strides down the corridor towards her, so fast there's no time to think of getting out of the way.

'No business of yours down here,' he growls. 'What's your explanation for it?'

'Sorry, sir,' Harlon replies. 'I got lost.'

'Oh yeah?' he grabs her by her collar. 'Well, we'll see what my boss has got to say about that.'

RADIO OPERATORS KOGI and LEEZUL to the radio room.

The tannoy blurts fuzzily above them.

'That's me,' says Harlon. 'I'm Pria Leezul, one of the radio operators.'

'Oh yeah?'

RADIO OPERATORS KOGI and LEEZUL to the Radio room at once.

'I'll be in trouble if I don't respond to that,' Harlon squeaks. He lets go of her collar with a shove.

'Good thing for you I'm in a hurry. Now scarper. Don't let me catch you down here again. Understand?'

'You won't, sir,' Harlon says, quite truthfully. Next time, she'll be a lot more careful.

Tolly and Harlon run down corridors and up stairways, and at last are out on an open deck. It's a relief to smell clean sea air, even if it is tainted with the stink of tar smoke from the two fat chimneys that belch their black breath into the murky navy of the night sky. Behind them, to the east, the lights of the city and its harbour are already no more than a sequin sprinkle on the edge of the black land. The paddles churn the water and fill the air with their deep chug. If you wanted to move around unheard out here, it would be easy. Unseen though would be more difficult. They are challenged on each deck by armed Automators, wearing the badge of the Red Blade on their jackets. They look like they've been selected for size and toughness. There are other eyes watching too, pale owls that gleam with an unnatural green.

'Special projects,' Tolly whispers, when she spots them. 'There'll be some poor Turned kid tuning in to what these owls see.'

Harlon shudders and hopes that it isn't Xeno.

The entrance to the radio room is on the top deck, up a short flight of narrow stairs.

'Don't forget you're Leezul,' Tolly whispers.

'What are we going to do if you can't make the radio work?' Harlon says.

'Tell them the equipment's broken,' Tolly says calmly.

They push the door and go inside. The 'room' is not much bigger than their cabin and packed with equipment, wires and screens and dials lit with pools of yellow light. A second door labelled 'bridge' stands slightly ajar; beyond it an argument is going on.

A forceful woman's voice says, 'As captain of this ship I demand assurances about the safety of the weapon you plan to test.' Her voice, though not loud, is not the sort of voice you can easily ignore.

'*Dear* Captain,' the second voice is smooth, almost calm, but still it sends a shiver down Harlon's spine. 'You are not in a position to demand. My colleague, Senior Vellum, could offer a simpler explanation perhaps.'

'That's him,' Tolly mouths. 'Commander Eye.'

Another voice cuts in, the man Vellum's, Harlon assumes. An angry voice, the voice of a person who would sooner punch than talk.

'Happy to explain,' it says with a sneer. 'You are paid by us to do what we tell you. We have the authority of the Automators and the Board of Governors. Bottom line? If I want to put a bullet in you, or any of your smart, blue-uniformed crew, there is no one and nothing to stop me.'

Commander Eye speaks again.

'Thank you so much, dear Vellum, for your characteristic

clarity. Now, if you would excuse me, dear lady, I have a much overdue appointment with a glass of *very* good brandy. I'll bid you good night and leave you in Senior Vellum's most competent hands.'

While they listen to this chilling conversation, one of the 'smart, blue-uniformed crew' silently joins them and quietly pushes the bridge door closed. He's wearing a cap with 'engineer' stitched on in red letters. Harlon recognises him at once as the boy with the bird, although in uniform he looks much older. But he gives no sign that he knows *her*, perhaps he didn't spot her after all.

'I'm Third Engineer Colt,' he says. 'Pleased to meet you. My job's to make sure all the radio gear is working. I guess you're the operators?'

'Yes,' Harlon says hastily. 'I'm Kogi,' she says.

'No, you're not … that's me, you're Leezul.' Tolly gives a small nervous laugh. 'So sea sick she can't even remember her own name.' She rolls her eyes. Colt tilts his head to one side,

'Right,' he says and points to them in turn. 'So *you're* Ensin Kogi?'

Tolly nods.

'And *you're* Ensin Leezul.'

'Yes,' Harlon replies, 'that's me. Bit tired, that's all.'

Colt pushes his cap back and scratches his head.

'Yeah, looks like you've had quite a time of it, the pair of you,' he says, eyeing Harlon's head and the scratches that haven't healed on Tolly's face.

'Alright. Who's the senior radio operator?'

'Me,' says Tolly.

'Pretty young to be a senior operator, aren't you?' Colt says.

'I guess I just learn fast,' Tolly replies. She slides into the operator's seat and puts the headphones on as if she knows exactly what she was doing.

'You'll need to tune the oscillator before you start,' Colt says. 'You know how to do that, right?'

Tolly shakes her head. Colt sits on the edge of the table and looks at them both his head on one side.

'Alright then,' he says, thoughtfully. 'Let's start with basic, shall we?'

Colt is a good teacher. After two hours Tolly has remembered all she learned before and some more besides. She really does know Morse code and now knows enough to operate the radio room and look very convincing. Harlon is still struggling.

'Leezul, all I can say is don't try to do anything without me, or your mate here. Pretend you're sick if you have to.' Colt gets up. 'My watch in the engine room starts in two hours. But put a call on the tannoy for me if you need me,' he says.

'I've got one thing to ask you both before I go…'

He leans on the desk between them and speaks very quietly.

'Have either of you ever operated any kind of radio before?' he asks. 'You can tell me the truth.'

Tolly opens her mouth to explain how she did once do the first day of the operators' course, but she never gets the chance. The door to the bridge bursts open and a man like a giant potato in a uniform shoves his head around the door.

'Vellum,' he says, pointing to himself. 'Second to Commander Eye. You the radio operators?'

Harlon holds her breath. This is the moment when Colt could expose them as frauds.

265

Tolly leaps to her feet and salutes, and Harlon copies her, which obviously pleases the man but she notices that Colt does not salute.

'Good. Glad to see you're keen. You'll need to be ready to send Commander Eye's communications at all hours. Is that clear?'

'Yes, sir!' Tolly stands very straight and almost shouts her response.

'He may want to send a communication imminently.'

Harlon's stomach drops, but Colt speaks up and salutes at last.

'Third Engineer Colt, sir,' he says. 'I'm here to fulfil technical requirements. I'm afraid we have a few problems. Nothing serious, should only take a few hours to put right. Upper and lower diode spike rod spark settings are a bit off. But I'm sure you understand these things, sir.'

Vellum looks as if he might struggle to understand the word *switch*, but he nods knowingly.

'Oh yes. Very tricky that,' he says. 'Carry on, Engineer, Operators.'

He backs awkwardly through the door, managing to hit his head on the frame as he does so, and then is gone.

'No such thing as the upper and lower diode spike rod of course,' whispers Colt, 'but I just wanted to make sure he really didn't know anything about radio operation.'

'Thanks,' says Tolly. 'You saved us.'

Colt looks at Harlon and nods.

'Your secret's safe with me, if mine's safe with you.'

Harlon nods.

'What was that all about?' Tolly asks when Colt's gone.

'Tell you when we're back in the cabin,' Harlon replies. 'I have to lie down now or I'll fall down.'

When Harlon wakes, she can't tell if its day or night. Down in cabin 37, beyond the reach of daylight, it's impossible to know. It feels like she slept too long. She only intended to take a short rest and then carry on the search for Xeno.

'Hello!' says Tolly. 'I've had a sleep, three meals and found the laundry room while you were out of it.' She holds up two sets of clean uniforms.

'Did you find a shower?' Harlon says groggily. 'I stink and the burn on my head is oozing again!'

Tolly points.

'Across the corridor. Hey,' she adds, 'we've been chasing an ice ship with red sails.'

'What?'

'You know, a ship that takes icebergs from the White Sea to sell the ice down south? But that's not the best bit. Its captain is a tiger...'

Radio operator to the bridge. Radio operator to the bridge at once.

The tannoy is very insistent.

'I'll go,' Tolly says, shrugging on her uniform jacket. 'It's fine. Colt dropped that manual by and I read it. Cover to cover. Twice.'

She dumps the book, heavy as a brick onto Harlon's bunk. 'Your turn!' she says, and with that, she's gone. Harlon is left wondering, sleepily, if Tolly really said, 'red sails', 'iceberg' and 'tiger'.

The hot water on her skin feels incredible, even the pain as it hits her scarred scalp and arm feels good. What time is it now, she wonders? If the *Dolphin* is chasing another boat it might be a good moment to slip quietly around the ship and look for Xeno. The sound of heavy boots approaching down the corridor makes her jump. Immediately she thinks of the real Leezul and Kogi and assumes that she and Tolly have been unmasked as frauds. But the boots go past her door. It's a door down further along that gets a pounding from big, insistent fists.

'Engineer Colt?' a gruff Automator voice shouts. 'Open this door by order of the Head of Intelligence.'

There's a pause, then from the other side of the door Colt replies.

'I'm required at once in the radio room, sir. I'm just getting dressed.'

'Engineer Colt, or should I say *Listener* Colt, open this door now. Order of Commander Eye.'

The bird, Harlon thinks. The bird: someone's found out about the bird. Someone's betrayed him. Will he think she betrayed him? And if he does, will he betray their secret to try to get himself out of trouble? It's possible. Dammit. Maybe Ma was right after all.

Never trust anyone.

There's a long pause. She can imagine that poor Colt is trying to think what to do. Harlon throws on her clothes and opens the shower room door a crack. She can't see anything from here but she can hear what happens. Colt's door is forced open; there's a scuffle. Colt's voice yells, 'let go of me' and then, 'don't hurt her!' But he isn't dragged past her door. They're taking him the *other* way, through the door and towards the stairway and the locked hatch. Harlon doesn't stop to think, she follows, quiet, in bare feet. Colt is putting up a fight all the way and in the confined space of the corridor it takes all the guards' attention to hang on to him and the small cage in which the bird is now imprisoned. Good, that means the guards will not be paying attention to what's going on behind them. They leave the first door half open; Harlon crouches in its shadow until they've gone down the stairway at the far end of the corridor. They'll have to wait for someone on the other side to open the hatch at the bottom.

Harlon moves along the corridor in silence and finds the door she needs, the one marked 'Main Fuses', and goes through. Inside, a little security light comes on automatically, nicely illuminating rows of switches, fuse boxes and wires. Everything is clearly labelled; there's even a very clear diagram of the ship, showing which switches correspond to each lectric circuit. She picks the one she needs and it's a moment's work to break the fuse wire and replace the fuse in its place. The sound of cursing carries up from the bottom of the stairway, where Colt, the guards and the corridor beyond the door, have all been plunged into darkness.

Harlon waits, invisible in the dark at the top of the stairway, while the guards fumble and complain at the bottom. She hears a voice from the other side of the locked door, the sound of the wheel cranking round and the creak of metal hinges. She slides down the reverse side of the stairway and slips behind the guards as they go through the door. In the darkness they don't bother to turn and close it behind them. She lets them move away down the corridor in front of her. One of the guards has found his torch and shines it in front of them as they drag the struggling Colt along. Even in the flash of the torch beam Harlon can tell that the other guard is being extremely careful with the bird in the cage. As if he's had strict instructions that the creature is precious and must not be harmed. The third guard, the one who opened the door, is disappearing up the stairwell, gone to find someone to sort the electrical fault. Probably, Harlon thinks, the third engineer.

The swaying torch beam shows a doorway slightly open to her left, next to the one through which Colt and the bird are being shoved. She pushes it open a little and stands inside next to stacks of buckets and mops.

Two sets of footsteps approach down the metal stairway, the bright gleam of a lantern illuminates the corridor outside her hiding place. An unmistakeable voice begins to speak in a kind of slow drone.

'Really this business of going up and down ladders, sooo tedious.' Harlon guesses that this is Commander Eye himself, and there's another person with him whose white coat she can just see.

'Report please, Capo Nayda!' The commander barks.

'Prisoner Colt confined, Commander. Together with the bird, as requested.'

'Very good, Nayda. In here, is it? Hang that lantern inside so we have some light, for goodness sake. Is there anything at all to sit on?'

'Um no, I'm afraid not. Just a table for the um … equipment, sir.'

'Oh the discomforts of this wretched voyage!' complains the commander. 'Capo, just open the door.'

'Should I enter first, Commander?' A younger voice that must belong to the white-coated person.

'Well *obviously*, Doctor, yes!' the commander snaps.

There is a great deal of shuffling and bumping as the guards, the commander and the 'doctor' manoeuvre in the tight space of the corridor. Harlon wishes she could see. It would be quite comical.

'Would you like security in the room, Commander?' asks the bulky capo.

'*Obviously* not, Nayda. How do you think *you* would fit in there? Just stand by.'

'Very good, sir.'

There is a creak and a clank as the door is opened and then closed, leaving the corridor in shadow and torchlight. Very slowly, feeling her way so as to reduce the risk of any noise Harlon turns, works her way in slow motion through an obstacle course of invisible objects to the wall that stands between her and Colt. There is a tiny chink of light, the size of the end of her finger. A place where one of the rivets that hold the ship together has rusted and fallen away, leaving a small, round hole, easily enough to see and hear through. She brings her face close to the chink and peeps through.

Colt's hands are cuffed behind his back and attached to a metal hoop in the far wall. Commander Eye is draped in the corner like an elegant piece of furniture and the doctor, a dark-haired young man with large soulful eyes, bends over a table fussing with a contraption of wires and dials. The cage is hung out of the way, from a hook on the low ceiling; inside, the bird paces anxiously back and forth.

'So Colt,' says the commander. 'One of your dear shipmates reported your friendship with this little bird here. Given the very important nature of the mission of this ship I can only assume that any Listener aboard is a Green Thorn spy. Perhaps *using* our little feathered friend in some way?'

'I just rescued her,' Colt replies, his voice tight with fear. 'She was oiled, I cleaned her and I was going to release her. Nothing more. I'm not a Listener. *She* came into *my* head. She's a *Speaker*.'

'*She* came into *your* head?' Doada gives a high laugh. 'As if any beast could have the intelligence to do such a thing. How very sweet, imagining a bird can be a *her*. A bird is an *it*, an object, with no more sense or feeling than a boot or a nail. When will you people understand. Well, *we* will get that into your head won't we, Doctor?'

The doctor lifts his head and offers a nervous smile.

'Yes, Commander. Ready, Commander,' he says.

The table with its contraption is moved closer to Colt. Small pads are attached to his head and chest. He has stopped struggling now.

'Please don't harm the bird,' he pleads.

'Oh dear boy, do be quiet!' Commander Eye snaps. 'Now, I'm sure you have heard about this marvellous machine. It's called a Turner, my own invention originally but now *much* improved by my excellent colleagues. It will burn out that nasty bit of your brain, just enough to let us be able to make a useful citizen of you.'

'But I'm not a Listener!' Colt pleads.

The commander stops leaning in the corner and approaches the equipment.

'I'll control the pulse level, doctor, if you please.'

The doctor looks dismayed.

'Oh, yes, of course, Commander.'

The doctor turns the device around so the commander can access its controls. Colt braces himself against the pain he guesses is coming. Commander Eye's long finger rests on the dial that will increases the intensity of the lectric pulse and the expression on his face tells Harlon exactly how he got his nickname, the Vampire.

Harlon doesn't want to look. She squeezes her eyes shut and waits for Colt to cry out in pain. But instead there is a sudden pop and a burning smell. Harlon opens her eyes to see Colt looking a little dazed but unharmed and a small cloud of smoke hanging above the Turner. The doctor fiddles with the machine, but it is clearly broken, its wires no more than a blackened tangle now.

'I'm most terribly sorry, Commander. I think this problem will take some time to solve.'

'Oh really. This is *too* bad,' the commander exclaims. 'Go and fetch the owl handler. We'll use her to look into this bird's brain.'

The doctor swallows.

'There is a small issue with the handler also, she…'

The commander cuts him off.

'Don't tell me. *Just don't tell me.*' He opens the door of the room, and propels the doctor through it. 'Get out! Take this *equipment* and … Nayda, Nayda? Get the girl from the cell next door.'

The doctor is glad to escape. He scuttles away, trailing wires behind him. The commander doesn't look at Colt, but stares at the bird who presses herself against the bars of her cage as far as possible from him as she can get. Harlon holds her breath as they wait for *the girl from the cell next door*. The clanks of metal doors and locks, the shuffle of boots, seem to go on for an eternity. And then, as if conjured from her own imagination, there is Xeno, thin and dirty, clearly afraid, but still herself. Her eyes inside their dark circles still bright, her hands still fluttering at the end of the sleeves of the same blue jumper. Harlon jams her hands over her mouth to keep everything inside.

'Out, both of you,' the commander orders Nayda and his sidekick. 'Now.'

Xeno stands just inside the door. Watchful and alert as always. But there's something stiffer, harder, about her now that makes Harlon's heart squeeze. The pain she's been through has marked her.

'We know each other well enough now, do we not, *dear Xeno*.' The commander moves towards Colt and grabs his hair in one hand, pulling back his head to expose his throat. When Colt cries out and struggles more, he cracks the boy's head agains the wall, expertly, just enough to knock him out.

'There now,' he says, turning to Xeno, 'we can have some peace to talk, can't we? What I need is for you to tell me what is in the mind of that bird. If you do not, I will kill both this boy and his little feathered companion. Do you understand?'

Almost imperceptibly, Xeno nods.

'And you understand that I am not pretending when I say I will kill them.'

Again a tiny nod that wrenches Harlon's heart again. How has little Xeno learned such a monstrous lesson?

'Good. Then use your *power* and do what I ask.'

Xeno raises her arm towards the bird's cage. Her fingertips touch the bars and the bird's eyes turn towards her.

'Wayfarer!' she whispers to it. 'We fly one path.' Her voice is as strange and birdlike as ever. The tern's harsh voice rings out as it flaps its wings against the bars of its cage, then it quietens, folds it wings, sways a little on its feet and closes its eyes.

The heat of the small metal cell grows. The air seems ready to turn solid. Xeno gasps. A smile spreads over her face as if she's found a gift hidden inside the small, feathered head. She chirps the robin sound that was always her favourite way to speak to Ash. It is all Harlon can do not to break into pieces and fall noisily among the metal buckets.

At last, Xeno speaks.

'*Map*. A map of sky and sea and time. A map that shows all life.'

'Come along now, child,' the commander chides. 'That's all a bit airy fairy, isn't it? I *know* this boy must be a Green Thorn spy, like all you disgusting little Listeners. I *know* this bird must be enmeshed in it all somehow. Look harder. Who have

275

they been talking to? What have they been saying? Names! Details! Plans!'

Xeno drops her arm from the bird's cage and stands straighter. She rolls her shoulders free of tension and concentrates harder.

'A route,' she says. 'A trail: a space trail and a time trail. A line that gleams, a where, a when. A place that draws all life to it! An island, green in the night-blue depths of the sea.' Xeno looks up into the commander's face, her eyes shining so brightly that the commander takes a step back.

'An island!' Xeno exclaims, as if she can see this place floating in the air before her, as if she understands something for the first time. 'Like a green thorn! Gathering all the power of life on land, on sea, in air.'

Xeno's voice rises, stronger.

'A million, million lives on one trail, one place, connected there in one song, one singing. Voices to make a hurricane of life, a force, irresistible, everywhere at once, springing from this place, this time, a song to sing the world anew, to crack the sky and sweep *you* away. *They're on their way!*'

Xeno seems to glow and, like a moth with a flame, the commander can't look away, until she shuts her eyes and turns from him.

He pulls himself together; rearranges his glasses, his hair, his coat. He wipes the sweat from his brow with an exquisite blue silk handkerchief. Then, composed, leans down to put his face right next to Xeno's ear and speaks.

'Thank you *so* much, *dear child*. You have provided excellent information about the intended test site for my weapon. A fine description of the island, whose approximate whereabouts I already knew. You have confirmed its importance and strengthened my resolve to destroy it. I had guessed that something like this was afoot. Some hideous primitive jamboree, a pathetic attempt to defeat my plans.'

He whispers, hissing into her ear.

'It will not succeed. What was it you said, a million, million lives all assembled on that one, dear little island? How much power do you think they'll have when they've all been roasted, boiled? How much *singing* do you think they'll do when they are evaporated into nothing but ash and gas? A hurricane indeed, but one of death, not life!'

Harlon has never heard a voice carry so much hate and poison. But Xeno does not flinch, with her back still to him she speaks, her voice a whisper, with a razor's edge.

'The seeds are sown; you sowed them. The sky will hatch; you cracked it. The ocean will ring; you struck it. It has begun.'

The commander's self-control shatters like glass. He grabs Xeno and spins her round to face him and raises his other hand to strike her. But Xeno simply looks at his raised hand until he drops it and releases her. Once more she turns her back on him.

The commander calls out for Nayda, who opens the door at once.

'Put her back in her cell,' he snarls, then points to Colt. 'And put him and his little feathered familiar over the side. I'm sure they'll prove popular with the sharks.'

Harlon waits while they escort Xeno back to her cell a little way down the same corridor. She waits while the commander grumbles his way back to the upper decks, and while they drag poor Colt up the stairway. She waits until everything is silent then creeps out and stands outside the door of Xeno's cell.

'Xeno!' she whispers. 'Xeno?'

There's a sound behind the door, like leaves in a breeze, and a tiny scrape at the door's lowest edge, as Xeno pokes a strand of something under the door towards her sister. In the dimness Harlon can just see the blue of the old jersey. She holds the soft thread and feels Xeno, pulling back.

'Harlon?' Xeno says. '*Harlon!*'

'I'm here, little bird,' Harlon breathes. 'It's going to be OK.'

They hold on to the blue thread, feeling, through the tension that runs between their fingers, each other's strength, each other's life.

'A storm coming, made of song,' Xeno says, 'to break and make the world.' As usual her words don't make any normal kind of sense, but this time Harlon feels their truth. There *is* a storm coming; she feels it too.

'Harlon go, go. Go now,' Xeno says. 'Danger. Keep safe!'

She's never expressed anything so directly before. It makes Harlon want to break the door down and hold her little sister tight. But Xeno's right. It's time to go. With a tiny chirp Xeno lets go of her end of the strand, and Harlon tucks the little scrap of blue next to her heart.

Stealthily Harlon makes her way back through the ship, and up onto the deck. The wickedness she has just witnessed through that small spy hole sticks to her skin and she craves light and air to dispel it. She stands out on deck as the breeze freshens. There really *is* a ship, with red sails all set, that they

278

seem to be pursuing. There is no sign of an iceberg but she did not dream the part about the tiger; there it is, huge, and glowing orange at the prow. More extraordinary still to Harlon is the small figure who leans against the main mast. Impossible. *Impossible!* But unmistakably Ash. Her heart leaps with a mixture of joy and fear to see him. She can't imagine what strange route has brought him here – no stranger perhaps than her own. She wants to wave at him, to shout his name but she mustn't draw attention to herself or him. She thrusts her hands deeper in her pockets and goes below. Now, even though she can't see a way through the darkness that surrounds them, a gleam of hope has sparked in Harlon's heart. She slips her hand inside her coat to touch the strand of blue wool.

Hang on, Xeno. Hang on, Ash!

11

The Raven Tells

Ash

 The Gula's only comment when Ash explained that they would be staying on the *Ice Maiden* was to stomp into his head and tell him, *This is the trail,* as if that was perfectly obvious. But Skrimsli's attempt to improve the Gula's ability to communicate with Ash was unsuccessful.

I know how to talk to Cub. Don't need stripy cat to tell.

It doesn't matter. He and the Gula understand one another well enough and most of the time what she thinks of Skrimsli doesn't matter either. Now that they are crew, there is not much time for anything but work and sleep.

A lot has happened in a short time on the *Ice Maiden*. Each watch feels like a whole day and, with every one, Ash has had to learn new skills. The crew were not unkind, but they were watching him to see if he came up to scratch. The old Ash would have crumbled under such examination, but this time he rose to every challenge. The Gula too had been on trial, and there were a few moments of snarls, especially with Karu, the chief of the rowing crew.

Bears hate gulas, gulas hate bears, was how the Gula had

280

explained it to Ash. But they put aside their species' prejudices. Now at mealtimes Karu often chooses to sit on the bench beside them. His close friend, Bollovar, second-in-command of the rowing crew and a bear-sized human, comes too.

'We speak in the head, like you and your gula,' Bollovar explains. 'We come from far east of Nordsky, a nasty, rocky place. You would not like it. We did not, did we, Karu?' Bollovar laughs and Karu shakes his head and snuffles down his long nose.

'Was good luck we were sold, cub and boy, to circus. There we meet old stripy rogue, yes?' Bollovar laughs again, and nods in reply to something Karu says inside his head.

'Yes, yes, Karu. I know a rogue but a good rogue, yes? Yes, I think so!'

He claps Ash on the back so heartily that Ash splutters over his food.

'We like you, little Ash. Big spirit. We even like the weasel.' And to the Gula's huge disapproval, both Bollovar and Karu ruffle the fur on her head with their big paws as they stand up to leave. Ash does not tell her that she has been called a 'weasel'.

The raven is the only crew member apart from Ray and Margi who liked Ash and the Gula from the start. Ray says there are only three others who the raven likes: Ray herself, because she provides food, the captain, and Daunt, the ancient ship's surgeon who she has known from a time before Skrimsli was captain of the *Ice Maiden*. But whenever Ash and the Gula are in the rigging, the raven perches close at hand and greets them with soft cawing and bowing of her head. The Gula reacts strangely to this, like a queen tolerating the presence of a star-struck child. But Ash can tell that she secretly enjoys the bird's presence.

Like in the mountains, the Gula commented once, with her coughing version of a laugh.

Raven follow Gula, steal scraps.

Ash likes to hear the raven's musical cronking. It is the sound he woke to on so many mornings back home.

But the skill that gained the crew's respect is one that neither Ash nor the Gula had to learn. When the cry *aloft aloft* comes, both of them climb the rigging with delight. Only Inagi, and Silverback, the gorillas, are more at home up there, but they are both too big and heavy to be really nimble among the top gallants and the skysails. Ray's little son Margi will be a wonderful climber, judging by how easily he clambers into Ash's bunk, but at three he's still too small to be crew. Besides, they all dislike the cold winds that don't bother Ash and the Gula, used as they are to mountain snows. During the freezing sleet and high winds that dogged their first watches aboard the *Ice Maiden*, the boy and Gula spent hours high above the decks, reefing and unreefing sails. Her dextrous long claws made the Gula's forepaws almost as useful as hands and, with a little practice, she managed to use her teeth to help her tie knots. After the first freezing storm, when Ash and the Gula saved the gorillas from spending time in the chilling wind and sleet, Inagi and Silverback greeted them with deep respectful rumbles and gentle head patting.

'They are very happy you were in cold, not they,' Bollovar explained. 'They tell me to say thanks! Now you are truly crew.'

Today is the first calm day since Ash and the Gula joined the ice ship. They have left the deep cold of the White Sea behind and as the rising sun makes a bright path on the ocean, Ash can feel real warmth in it for the first time. Behind the ship, the berg casts a long, indigo shadow and its underskirt of ice shines turquoise through the gilded surface.

The Gula and Ash are high up in the rigging, gazing out over the sea. High in the sky there is a constant traffic of birds heading southwest out into the great blue. The schools of whales and dolphins that he's seen over the last days seem to be heading that way too. Ash wonders for a moment where they are going; surely it's too early for flying south? But what does a mountain boy know about the workings of the ocean? He turns his eyes down to watch shearwaters track the path of the ship in long slicing glides. Little rafts of puffins float and preen. Just ahead a crow of gannets fling themselves into the water one after another, like reckless arrows. The surface is boiling with fish, driven up to the surface by dolphins; the air is so still, that his warm out-breaths hang like miniature clouds above the water. Finally, two humpbacks burst through the shoal, with their huge black jaws and billowing throats.

The Gula sticks her nose into the air and breathes in the clean, salty-blue smell.

I smell far off, far far off.

She shuffles along the yardarm towards him and touches her broad nose to his hand.

I like. I like this, Cub.

I like this also, Ash tells her.

Trail is good. Trail is strong, she replies.

Down on the deck the work of the day is beginning gently. Skrimsli pads around, visiting all three decks, greeting crew and issuing orders by silent thought, to which the crew respond with a quiet, 'Aye aye, Cap'n'. He visits the oarsmen who are hard at work because there is no wind, touching each one in turn on the back with a big soft paw. His presence calms and encourages them and they start to sing a song to help them keep their steady rhythm. Though Karu cannot form the words he leads the singing, starting each line with a deep harmonising growl, like the lowest notes of an organ.

Grrrrrrrrrwwwwwwwooooooo

We ro-o-o the old ice ship in the blue

We ro-o-o the old ice ship in the blue

Some of the sailors sing in standard and some on their own languages. Inagi and Silverback add soft low hoots like the beats of a drum. The song rolls out: a pulse of warmth over the chilly water.

Ekar is dangling her legs over the side of Skrimsli's platform in the prow, watching over Margi. Ray washes her pots on deck and feeds scraps to the raven who perches on the gunwale close by. Daunt, whose job it is to tend to all the various bodies on the ship, living and mechanical, sets out the solars in the sun, lines up batteries for charging, services their ancient radio so they can contact other ice ships. It's like a family, Ash thinks, a great big family.

The breeze picks up with the sun and comes dancing playfully towards them over the ocean. Ekar cries *aloft, aloft* and two other young crew, Reddick and Mallum from the Nordsky port of Ussvoik, join Ash and the Gula in the tops. Together they unfurl the top four sails, one after another and the *Ice Maiden* leaps forward as the canvas tightens in the lively breeze.

Ship is not alive? asks the Gula as she's asked a hundred times before.

Made of wood, Ash tells her again, *dead wood.*

No! the Gula exclaims, *ship alive!*

There are jobs to be done down on deck now that their watch has begun, but all four 'height junkies', as Bollovar has nicknamed them, linger in the tops, looking out for more whales, more birds, more of the glorious, free expanse of the ocean.

'Look!' Reddick points north. 'It's the *Narwhal!*'

'Our big sister! Coming our way!' Mallum responds.

'What's the *Narwhal?*' Ash asks.

'Another ice ship. Twice our size,' says Reddick.

Ash shades his eyes to peer into the distant blue. He can make out the gleam of topsails and the shining bulk of a towed berg.

'We have many friends on her crew.' Mallum nudges his Nordsky companion. 'Reddick has a girlfriend on the first rowing crew.'

She shoves him back.

'And *you* have a boyfriend on the second.'

Now it's Mallum's turn to blush.

Girlfriends and boyfriends are a mystery to Ash but he smiles anyway, glad to see his new companions happy and excited.

The *Narwhal* is huge. She has two decks of oars and three masts. She tows a berg much larger than the *Maiden*'s, but, Ash considers, of a rather boring, block shape. He much prefers the *Maiden*'s wild, icy canine. While the paths of the *Narwhal* and the *Ice Maiden* slowly converge, Ash feels the excitement build on the ship. Although they are still in waters where the sea temperature is chilly, there is an outbreak of bathing and laundry on the deck. Brighter, cleaner clothes, scarves and head cloths are pulled from sea bags. There is singing and laughter. A row boat is dispatched to fetch stores from the berg and soon especially delicious smells are wafting up from the galley. Even Ekar wears a different green coat and when Skrimsli comes up from a visit to his cabin, his whiskers look as if they have been combed and straightened.

Finally, towards midday, the two craft are close together, moving on parallel tracks through the sea. The ropes connecting each ship to its berg are paid out to their full extent, so that as the ships slow down and approach each other there's no risk of collisions. The wind has dropped to nothing and the sea is glassily calm. The height junkies are again deployed to furl the sails. All crew not engaged in rowing are gathered on the gunwales, waving and calling out to their friends on the other side of the band of blue water. Skrimsli yowls out to Captain Var and her first-mate, a large male orang utan, whose disklike face is wrapped in layers of woollen hood. A grey parrot, part of the *Narwhal's* crew flies back and forth as if he simply can't wait for them all to be together.

But just as the ships are about to heave to, so the fiesta can begin, the raven caws loudly from the top of the *Maiden's* main mast.

'Ship ahoy! Tar ship on the port beam!'

She flaps her wings and swoops down to perch beside Skrimsli on the ship's prow.

Immediately Mallum swarms up, level with Ash and the Gula and gets out his small telescope.

He calls down to Ekar.

'Confirmed, Madam!'

'Thanks, Mallum,' she replies, then shouts to Var and Skrimsli. 'What do the Automators want with us?'

'Ha!' Var shouts back. 'The usual, I expect. You know how they hate a mixed crew.'

'Aye,' Ekar replies. 'Best we both get away from them.'

The atmosphere of excitement has gone. Although still in their best clothes, the crew is now grim and focused. It's clear this Automator ship is considered a very serious matter.

Var calls to the *Maiden*.

'Free the bergs?'

Ekar consults the captain then replies.

'Yes, Captain agrees, free bergs, and take separate courses. They can't come after both of us at once.'

'Perhaps when we come back to get the bergs we'll have our fiesta, Ekar. If not, we'll share a brandy in Angellis!'

Ekar waves her hat at the other captain.

287

'For sure, Var, for sure! Fair winds to you, fair winds.'

Then she turns to her crew, her hat replaced.

'Loose the berg!' she cries. 'Steer due west. Double on the oars there.'

Skrimsli nods and jumps up to his station on the prow.

The Gula puts her nose towards the Red Ship and takes a long breath.

Smells bad, she says, *bad bad bad.*

The Red Ship does not head north to follow the *Narwhal.* It's the *Maiden* that she's after. The mood on the ship grows serious and the raven is dispatched to take a closer look at the Red Ship. She disappears into the distance but does not return as expected. Everyone grows more tense.

'It's so far off, why is everyone so worried?' Ash asks Mallum.

'From up here on the mast head, the horizon's eleven miles away, that means the Automator ship is closer than that. Maybe nine miles. Unless we get a wind to fill our sails, she could be on us less than two hours. She's no warship; she has no cannon, but she'll have a well-armed crew.'

'What do they want?' Ash asks uneasily.

Mallum shrugs.

'Trouble? Isn't that what Automators always want?'

Ash doesn't not have to wait long to get a clearer answer. Down on the deck Daunt reports to Skrimsli and almost at once Ekar orders Ash from the topsails.

'Report to the Captain's cabin!' she commands and Ash climbs down with dread sitting in his stomach like a cold stone.

The tiger sits like a sphinx on the bed, Ekar in the carved chair beside him, her face is closed and wary.

'Sit, if you please,' she says.

Ash takes a seat facing them both and Skrimsli is at once in his mind.

The captain of the Red Ship has messaged us. By radio.

Skrimsli lifts a lip in a small, silent snarl of disgust, as if he can't bear the thought of such a thing as radio waves. Ekar picks up the story.

'Their captain says if we do not hand over the boy, Ash, they will board our ship and burn us.'

Ekar's gaze is hard and Skrimsli glows like a stoked fire.

Why do they want you, Ash?

'They believe I am the son of a rebel leader, the one they call the Boogam, the Ghost.'

Ekar gasps.

'The one that destroyed the first tar station many years ago. She was the talk of the north! *Are* you such a child?'

She looks shocked. Ash can see she feels she's been deceived.

'I don't know,' Ash replies. 'My mother was just my mother. I don't know who she was before that. The Automators attacked our home, took my little sister. My elder sister and I escaped and got separated. I was taken to the tar station. I think they killed my ma.'

'But if *they* believe she is alive,' Ekar persists, 'and she *is* the Boogam, then you are valuable to them, as bait perhaps?'

All Ash can do is nod miserably.

Ekar and Skrimsli look long at each other.

There is more here than either you or I know, Skrimsli says. *And more to this Red Ship also. Deep, deep evil is there. I feel it,*

Ekar. I smell it like the stink of a rotting corpse. I will not give up any member of my crew to evil. We will attempt to outrun them.

Ekar purses her lips.

'They have speed that doesn't depend on wind,' she says. 'And many armed crew. If they catch us, there will be little we can do to resist.'

'Wait!'

Ash stands straight and looks the tiger and his companion in the eye. It's hard to say what must be said. But it's the only right thing.

'Captain, Madam Ekar, I don't want you to risk anything for me. If it's me they want, just give me up. All I ask is that you take care of the Gula.'

Ekar looks at him for a long time, and the tiger's green eyes soften; at length Ekar looks at Skrimsli and she sighs.

'Back aloft with you then, boy,' she says. 'Watch for wind that we may escape this wickedness without harm.'

Ash doesn't wait to be told again; he runs out onto the deck, glad to be accepted as a member of the crew for at least a little longer. The Gula is waiting in the top.

What did stripy cat want?

Radio messages and rebel leaders, how can any of these be explained to her?

To ask whose cub I am, he replies.

Easy, says the Gula, *my cub.*

The chase goes on in slow motion. Each oar now has two rowers and, without the berg to tow, they pick up speed, but the Automator ship, with its puffing tar engine and big rear paddles, is still faster. Minute by minute they gain. Ash's eye begins to water with the strain of staring at the ship that keeps on coming. Suddenly he sees a black speck break free from the ship's outline and start to move towards them at speed.

'Raven! Raven,' he calls down to the deck and the crew cheer.

As the crew sees her they start to chant: 'Ray-*ven*, Ray-*ven*.'

But just like the *Maiden*, she too is being pursued. A dark shape streaks up from the Red Ship and Ash knows at once what it is: an Automator's falcon, a machine beast, that gains on the raven even as the Red Ship gains on the *Maiden*.

Ash doesn't hesitate. He slithers down the rigging, and is across the deck and into his bunk in moments. He grabs the crossbow and rushes back on deck. The raven's progress is painfully slow; feathers are missing from its wings. It cannot stay ahead, and all the time the falcon grows closer. The anxious watchers on the deck feel their fates are tied somehow to the fate of their own dear, grumpy Raven. None of them notice the boy creeping to the base of the main mast with a Celeddi crossbow.

Ash leans his back to the main mast and places a bolt in the bow. When the falcon comes within range he will have time for one shot only. He needs to concentrate.

The Automator ship is shockingly close. People are visible through the wide windows of the bridge that sits on the top of the ship like a set of teeth. Ash tries not to let that distract him. But there is a lone figure, outside, on the deck that calls his attention. It wears the uniform of the Automators, but something in its shape reminds him of Harlon.

Harlon, his heart says.

Impossible. Impossible, his mind replies.

Concentrate.

The raven struggles on, beat after painful beat, but all her head start has been eaten up by the falcon's swift, sure flight. Ash pins the falcon in his gaze. *Watch this, sister,* he thinks.

Fffwt.

The bolt zings true, hitting the falcon square in the chest with a metallic dink. The machine-creature spins out of control and smashes into the sea. The raven fairly tumbles down towards the deck where Ash has dropped the bow to catch it in his arms. He glances to the Red Ship, but the figure that he thought he saw there has vanished. Yes, quite impossible.

The crew turns to Ash astonished, cheering wildly. Karu raises him up on one huge paw and juggles him for a moment like a ball before returning him to the deck. Ekar claps him on the shoulder and leans down to whisper in his ear.

'If they want you now, Ash,' she says. 'They will have to kill us all first!'

As if the Red Ship's heard her words, bullets strike the *Maiden's* side, knocking chunks of wood from her gunwales into the air. They have come within range of the Automator's rifles. But only just. The wind may save them save yet. A wakening breeze pleats the ocean into a thousand tiny pin tucks and Ekar cries, 'Aloft ! Aloft! All sail! All speed!'

Skrimsli strides briefly into Ash's brain.

Get below. Take the bird to Daunt; she is hurt, he says, then leaps down to the mid deck to take an oar himself.

The *Maiden's* wings are spread. She gathers a little speed, and pulls away so that now the Red Ship's bullets fall short into the water. But for how long will they stay out of range if this fragile new breeze fails to blow? Ash doesn't want anybody dying to save his skin. He'll take the raven to Daunt then go on deck and offer to give himself up again. It hardly matters if he really is the Boogam's child or not if it saves the *Maiden* and her crew.

The Gula scrambles down the companionway behind him, and jumps up to sniff the raven in his arms. The bird's eyes open at the touch of the Gula's nose.

'Gula! Gula!' she croaks. 'Evil on the Red Ship. Evil in a box of glass.' Her eyes close again.

Hurry, says the Gula, *fix bird, fix bird!*

The surgeon's cabin is deep in the bowels of the ship, tiny and lined with cupboards that Daunt can reach from where he sits at his examining table. Sounds from the deck are muffled down here, and distant. Can Ash hear shouts and shots from up above? He wants to rush on deck and see what's happening.

'Don't think about what's happening up there,' Daunt tells him sternly. 'Right now, here's your business. Understand? Hold this bird steady while I stitch her wound.'

Ash nods. The Gula puts her paws on the table where the bird lies, and sniffs her anxiously.

'Don't you worry yourself, m'lady Gula,' Daunt says. 'If anyone can fix 'er, that's me.'

Daunt's hands are knobbled as old wood, but gentle and skilled and his voice is like a balm.

'She's had a life this one,' Daunt tells Ash. 'She was a Celeddi chieftain's bird, but when the Automators killed her tribe, the rebel leader found her, rescued her.'

'The Ghost?' Ash exclaims, his heart racing once again.

'That's the one. We took her south out of trouble and brought the raven with her, before Skrimsli's time that was. I stitched a nasty wound on her cheek and she told the raven's story.'

Ash is stunned. He feels the pieces of the puzzle fall into place.

'There now,' says Daunt. 'That wound is closed, should heal well.'

Up on deck unfamiliar voices shout, give angry orders, and the slack slap of water tells that the *Maiden* is no longer moving. They both know what this means.

Daunt looks straight at Ash.

'Time for you to go now, lad. Lady Gula will stop a while to mind the raven, I believe. I'll protect her and and I'll raise help. Don't you worry. We've survived worse than this on the *Maiden*.' He glances to the shelf above his bunk where a pistol sits atop a small, old-fashioned radio. It crackles softly into life, homely as Ray frying onions in the next room.

Narwhal calling Maiden. Narwhal to Maiden. Come in, please.

'That young woman didn't flinch once while I stitched. Tough as nails. You remind me of her. Brave. Determined. You'll do well enough.'

They nod at each other. Ash straightens his shoulders and goes to meet his fate.

He comes out onto the deck to find it bristling with Automators, huge people with huge guns. Standing with them is Dough Boy, in a smarter Automator uniform and with two handguns in holsters at his hips. Spot-coat man, Doada Sisal, is there too, this time dressed in a long, shiny black coat with a large fur collar into which he nestles his chin, like a child snuggling a toy.

My uncle? Ash thinks.

'Ah! *Dear child*!' Doada says as Ash approaches and two guards step forward to tie him and gag him.

'How marvellous to see you. You have saved me having to shoot any more of your *beastly* little playmates.'

Most of the crew is herded together on the foredeck with a ring of guards, their rifles raised, around them. Ekar, Karu and Ray are bound and gagged. Both Inagi and Silverback are tied to the main mast and have gunshot wounds but alive. Ash is relieved that least they didn't have to deliver on Ekar's promise. Indeed most of the crew seems to be out of the way somewhere below decks.

'There was some *very* bad behaviour at first,' Doada drawls, looking at the two gorillas, 'but when we confined the small *monkey*, behaviour improved. It would be *so* easy for it to be dropped over the side.'

He points to a sack wriggling with Margi's unmistakeable energy, lying at Dough Boy's feet.

Skrimsli himself lies on the deck, lolling, limp, somehow smaller. He is apparently lifeless, the bloody track of a bullet's graze above one eye. Seeing him, Ash cannot stop himself from crying out.

'Oh, your *special* friend, eh?' Doada grins. 'Please don't upset yourself. The cat is drugged, not dead.'

Ash notices a small man with a white coat and large syringe crouching by Skrimsli's gorgeous head. He pumps another dose of drugs into the captain's muscled shoulder. How dare he have power over Skrimsli? How dare he think he has. Only the captain's love for Ray and Margi kept him from killing all of the intruders in a moment. He never had the chance to fight. Doada walks over and crouches down to run his hands over Skrimsli's stripes.

'He'll make the most *beautiful* coat,' Doada gloats. 'I want his body delivered in peak condition to my furrier.'

Ash wants to be sick.

The man looks around as if checking the final details of a table set for dinner.

'Our business here is almost concluded. Just a few more jobs. Load the cat onto our ship. And the boy, of course. Burn the sails. I don't want to be followed.'

Dough Boy grins.

'Happy to oblige, Commander.' He turns to the ring of men around the crew. 'Lock this lot in the hold, with this.' He drops the sack with Margi inside it with obvious disgust. 'Then set fire to all of it,' he says. 'Any trouble and kill that.' He points to the sack.

Ray whimpers and Ekar gives a sound that's very much like a tiger's roar.

Doada steps delicately onto the wide gangplank that joins the two closely rafted ships and then turns to give one last instruction.

'Oh, and bring the bear. He'll make a marvellous rug. Doctor, administer the necessary drugs. We can't have rot spoiling those lovely pelts.'

Ash is blind with anger. He struggles so hard he slips from the grip of the Automators holding him and lunges towards Doada. In the moment he could kill the man and never flinch. But baton blows stop him in his tracks, raining down on his body. He hardly feels them until the one on his head that stills him.

He is dragged backwards over the gangplank looking up at the sky, where the smoke from the burning sails already curls up into the blue. Something's calling from up there. A harsh cry, piercing, sharp. A shape, scissor tail and pointed wings, delicate as a swallow, tough as steel, white as ice: a snow tern! *The* snow tern.

Greeting! Greeting! She swoops into his head. Map, stars, sky, ocean, time, *sing* in him again. He sees what she sees from high above. The *Maiden* with flames leaping in her rigging. The Red Ship with its heart of darkness pointing to a deadly course. But all around the blue of ocean and of sky laced through with a thousand, thousand gleaming trails lopped and laced and interlocking but leading in the same direction.

All trails lead lost in the ocean's deepest heart, she says.

Go there, Wayfarer.

12
The Striped Coat

Doada

Doada snaps down the blinds on the glow of an exquisite sunset. Overall, he thinks, the pleasures afforded by the natural world are limited. They have certainly not reduced his anxiety. Another day of zigging and zagging across the wretched blue waters of this forsaken ocean trench, and no sign of the island, nor of Toren's attack. He had not predicted that the deep blue, that looked so tiny on the globe in his office, could be so vast, so dull.

It is all *most* frustrating. He has the trap baited, Toren's children under lock and key; he has a force of armed Automator fighters ready to subdue her. But what is the point of a trap, if the creature it is set for cannot find it? He's had his strange little radio operators *broadcast* the ship's position, uncoded, and yet she has made no move. Perhaps she is even weaker than he thought and she can't even raise enough support to get her on a ship? Or perhaps she is already on the island; the island that Doada cannot find.

It is more than ridiculous. It is humiliating. Doada grows daily more aware of how much of a gamble he has taken on this *island* business. Is he mistaken about its significance? Is his memory of that map from his lost childhood so unreliable? Perhaps the island doesn't even exist.

No. He will not endure this agitation. A visit to the Greenhouse and her Gardeners is what is required to calm him and reassure him of the progress he has made. Doada leaves his stateroom and strides across the deck but has not gone four paces before he's intercepted.

'Commander, sir, it's the bear, sir.' It is the doctor. The hopeless and incompetent doctor.

'What *about* the bear?' Doada snaps.

'All its fur has fallen out and … it's dead, Commander Eye.' The man is fawning.

He has failed in every task he has been set so far and now *this*. That bear-skin rug was to be the centrepiece of Doada's new office. Perhaps he'll make a rug of this young doctor instead.

'Just put it over the side. And don't bother me any more.'

Doada waves his hand to dismiss this human irritation, but immediately a far more shocking possibility occurs to him.

'Wait!' he calls. 'Wait! The tiger, how is the tiger?'

Doada has no intention of losing that *beautiful* new coat.

'The tiger is well, sir. A little thin perhaps but…'

'Thin? *Thin?*' Doada shouts, 'When I commanded that this animal should reach my furrier in peak condition? *Why* is it thin?'

'It's the sedative, Commander,' the doctor babbles. 'The drugs that must be used to control the creature. They impair its ability to move and eat, of course.'

Doada looks at the doctor. He really is an imbecile.

'Then cease using them, at once.'

'But there is the risk of escape, sir,' the doctor replies.

'Don't be ridiculous. The beast is confined behind *metal bars* thicker than my arm. *Cease the drugs.* I will order my steward to send a joint of meat from my personal stores.'

The doctor stares at Doada for a moment. It's clear the commander has no conception of the terrifying intelligence that will return to those green eyes when the drugs wear off. But what can the doctor do?

'Yes sir,' he mumbles to the commander's retreating back.

Doada strides away down the deck, convinced yet again that he is the only intelligent being in an ocean of idiots.

The Gardeners' world is completely sealed off from the rest of the ship. An enclosed space, protected by two sets of steel doors and the best guards the Red Blade had available. On one side of the room are neat coils of wire, fine as hair, made of unique and secret metal alloys: phalanxes of rods of coloured glass, delicate as icicles. On the other, the tools that put them all together, pliers and blowtorches, crucibles and saws, whole dynasties of hammers, screwdrivers, planes. Everything the Gardeners need to keep the Greenhouse in perfect condition, ready, at all times, to do its deadly work.

'Good evening, Commander!' the three Gardeners speak at once, almost like a chorus. They have individual names, Doada knows, but their names do not matter, only what they do. Gardener One, Two or Three are the names he uses.

'Have the tests gone well today, One?' Doada asks.

One is the shortest of them. Possibly female, but Doada finds it hard to tell. One is in charge of records and has a clipboard with rows of precisely written numbers that describe the health of the Greenhouse.

'Perfectly, Commander,' One replies, with the closed mouth grimace that is One's interpretation of a human smile.

'Greenhouse has had an outstanding day,' adds Three, who is angular and narrow, like a skinny desk lamp.

'Yes, outstanding,' Two echos. Two is lightly bearded, soft like something uncooked, with eyes as big as dinner plates. He has the habit of standing a little too close. Doada takes a step away; Two continues.

'On today's figures the Cellular Ignition Resonance zone would have a radius of twenty miles.'

Doada takes a deep, satisfied breath.

'Describe to me the exact *consequences* Three, if you would be so good.' Doada knows what these will be, but hearing it from the Gardeners is pleasurable and reassuring.

'Within the CIR zone all living cells would self-ignite. In common terms all plants, animals and so on, would shrivel and turn to ash.' Three speaks as if she were describing nothing more important than the precise temperature of freshly brewed tea.

'There may be a little obvious flame,' One adds, 'but we estimate this would be a minimal effect.'

Three consults One's clipboard once more and adds, 'Our figures indicate that Greenhouse could reach CIR in as little as nine minutes and thirty seven seconds from activation.'

Two purses his lips.

'Nine minutes and thirty seven seconds plus *delay*,' he says nervously. 'The *activation delay*, which we will need to allow safe exit from the area.'

He nods several times, as if agreeing with himself.

But Doada stopped listening at *all living cells would self-ignite*.

He stares at the Greenhouse. It is a just a glass box, barely large enough to accommodate a child, but what glass! Its walls are layered with colour, laced with wires finer than a human hair. It is an exquisite crystal sarcophagus, delivering death.

Doada dangles his fingers over the row of shining switches, which will activate the device and finds his mood is much improved. Really, these Gardeners are *very* clever. There is just one last detail that concerns him.

'The journey from the ship to the test site will not be a problem?' he enquires.

The Gardeners turn to Doada with the same expressionless expression on their faces. Three replies, 'The exit is well suited to our purpose, and the Velocitys are prepared.' She points to where a set of double doors open, just above the water line and indicates two narrow, black craft the Gardeners have named, with astonishing originality, 'Velocity One and Velocity Two'. Small enough to exit the Red Ship swiftly and securely, large enough to take the Greenhouse and essential passengers to the island.

Two is scribbling calculations on a pad of paper.

'I calculate that Greenhouse can be loaded into Velocity One in seventeen minutes and thirty two seconds,' he says.

'It would however,' One says peering over the clipboard, 'be of great assistance to know *where* we are going and *when* we will expect to arrive.'

One's questions dispels Doada's good mood almost instantly. He refuses to grace them with an answer. As the steel doors clang shut behind him, he feels all his agitation returning in a rush. The situation is intolerable. Toren's children *must* know something more than they are telling him about the precise location of the island. If their mother was in possession of the map, they *must* have seen it. He will question the brats again, at once. There may be some *scrap* of information yet to extract.

'Open the boy's cell first!' Doada commands the guard on duty. Ash takes no notice as Doada steps in to the cell but curls himself into a tighter ball. His mother's old coat is wrapped round him like a blanket against the damp of the cell.

'It is very impolite to ignore a visitor!' Doada says, and gives the child's back a small, exploratory kick.

'I don't have anything to say to you.' The boy's tone is far from the fear and submission which Doada expects.

'Sit up at once and face me, child,' Doada orders, 'or I will invite one of the charming guards to offer some persuasion.'

Slowly Ash sits up, and turns around. His face is cut and bruised from the guards' previous efforts at 'persuasion'.

'Tell me again about the island, all you know.'

'Nothing,' Ash snarls. '*Nothing!*'

'And the map.'

'I've never *seen* a map.'

Doada sighs.

'Really, your life would be so much more pleasant if you just told me what you know.'

'Go away!' the boy actually snarls. It is so infuriating that Doada lunges at him and grabs a corner of his coat.

'If you will show no respect,' Doada cries, 'then you will lose all privileges including this, this *garment* as your blanket.'

The coat is old and worn; it rips as Doada pulls it from the boy, who takes no notice and simply turns away to face the wall. The defeat Doada feels at the child's lack of distress and complete defiance surprises him. He steps quickly from the cell and slams the door. He's just about to hand the tattered coat to the guard, with orders to dispose of it, when he sees something peeping from its ruptured seam. With trembling fingers he enlarges the tear; there, sewn into the lining, is Borden's map! He doesn't even need to look at it to know.

The wait while the captain finds how the map links to her maritime charts, and plots 'the most direct of routes', is a trial. Although many blue crew are now in Automator uniforms neither the captain nor her young first officer are among them, and the atmosphere of the bridge is still tense. They lean over the chart together poring over the map. Doada can't help thinking they are deliberately taking longer than they need with all that drawing and measuring business. He dispatches Vellum to make sure the tiger is now being fed and returns to his stateroom to pace in peace. He wants no witnesses for this level of agitation.

When he can wait no longer he returns to the bridge. The captain looks up at him with her usual cold disdain.

'Your map, Commander, shows the outline of the Marraduka Trench most clearly,' she says. 'I have been able to pinpoint the island on our own charts.'

She points to their position on the chart, and then shows the outline of the island, faintly pencilled in.

'We are very close!' she says. 'We may see your island on the horizon in thirty-six hours. What are your plans when we reach this destination?'

An hour ago her haughty questioning would have made him snarl, now he can just sweep it aside.

'All in good time, *dear* Captain.' he leans over the chart table to gloat at the small distance that separates him from his goal, and sees Borden's map clearly, laid out under the bright light. It is disconcerting how guilt and bitterness rush up to greet him from its blues and green. He reaches out to roll it up and put it out of sight again but the captain places her hand in its centre.

'There is one thing I'd like to ask, Commander, before you repossess your map. I'm intrigued as to the meaning of all the fine golden lines.'

Doada stares at her. 'Lines? I'm not certain I understand you?'

The Captain smiles. It is not a smile that Doada can enjoy.

'They are visible under the illumination we use to preserve night vision. Let me demonstrate.'

She reaches up to the lamp above the table and turns its setting so that a blood red light falls onto the chart. Immediately hundreds of fine lines, invisible in ordinary daylight, appear, glowing faintly as if lit from within.

'They are not contour lines,' the captain continues. 'They could perhaps be shipping routes of some sort, but if so then this one small island must once have been the centre of prodigious trade. All these lines, passing through this one tiny spot.'

'In fact,' the first officer has joined them now, like some bouncy ten year old. 'We tried a few colours of light on it. There are almost as many under blue light.'

The captain looks into Doada's face, as if delivering some challenge.

'It is almost as if this map was made for other kinds of eyes, that see differently from human eyes.'

Doada's stares at the gleaming lines. Some look almost as if they float above the surface of the map, other seems to swim below it. Xeno's words echo in his mind.

A million, million lives on one trail … a force, irresistible…

The lines prove that he was right, that this island is important; but important in a way Doada doesn't want to think about. He should feel triumphant but, instead, he feels afraid.

'Well, I am glad you have enjoyed toying with a precious family heirloom,' Doada snaps.

He reaches to the light and turns it back to white. The lines disappear. All that is visible now is the human world: depths and coastlines, degrees and distances. Doada's heart slows again. *That's* how easy it is to make it all of nature and her mindless workings disappear. That's how easy it will be.

'The lines are primitive decoration. Nothing more.'

He snatches up the map and curls it under his arm.

'Please keep your minds on your duty, not on idle speculation.'

Out on deck Doada stares out across the ocean. No glowing lines, no songs, no words, no hidden power. Power is a human thing, like maps, and books, and buildings, lights, veekles and machines. The only thing out there is just so much empty water, moving under an empty sky. Boring, dull and passive, like all of nature. It is all waiting to be controlled and dominated. *Used.* Turned to profit.

The seeds are sown, the sky will hatch, the ocean will ring.

Indeed, Doada thinks. Indeed, but not the way you imagined it, *dear* niece. There will be no triumph for you and your beasts. He will see to it.

It is late. The night guards patrol and more armed fighters are standing by. Whenever and wherever Toren comes, he's ready to crush her and everything she stands for. Behind the door of his stateroom, Doada imagines the moment when the Greenhouse ignites for the first time!

In the wake of the Red Ship, the waves move like muscles flexing underneath a skin, gleaming green with the phosphoresence of a million, million sparkling lives.

Fourteen Years Earlier

Toren's Story
3

Afterwards, when no one called her Breen any more but Boogam, or Ghost, rebels would talk about that raid on the first Station Gold with a gleam in their eye; how the Automators were caught unawares, rhinos and snow bears had fought willingly as equal comrades beside rebels; how the burning station had melted though the ice and took the drilling rig to the bottom of the ocean; what a great victory it was! But what Toren remembered were the burned Celeddi villages, bodies of humans, rhinos, bears, strewn like flotsam across the ice. The Automators had taken their revenge from the air and bombed every settlement for a hundred miles. Thousands had died. All she had saved had been the raven; Toren found the bird in the remains of Qimmiq's igloo, clinging to the old leader's cloak like a lost chick. She'd paddled out between the floes to intercept an ice ship, one of those that had smuggled supplies and weapons for her before.

But from that destruction, Green Thorn was born, and what could Toren do but lead them? For a time they had pierced the growing power of the Automators. They'd burned factories, blown up roads, fought beside the people whose land was taken, whose forests burned, whose villages were smashed, whose solars, wind and water mills had been destroyed. But innocent people died, including hapless Automator conscripts and always the Automators just rebuilt. They told people they were the new way, the *right* way, the way to *freedom*. Freedom from the merciless tyranny of nature that didn't care about humans at all. Nature that brought storms and ice, plagues and weeds, and gave nothing without endless struggle. What could people do but flock to the cities to be fed, when their fields and homes were ash and desolation? They made Listeners into inhuman demons, so that when they were dragged screaming from their beds or murdered in the street, no one said a word.

Toren leant her head against the window of the train and thought of how sick she was of killing, tired of grief, utterly exhausted with it all.

The carriages were full of what the Automators called 'pioneers'. They were people driven from their communities in the countryside to take up lives in new-build cities, each one exactly like the others. What was this one called? Free Town? Liberty City? New Start? Toren could barely remember. As the train lines converged on its station, she could see several trains full of 'pioneers'. A flood of despairing, powerless humanity. What could she do to stop it? Maybe this was what the people wanted?

She was just twenty years old and all she'd known was death and destruction. Somewhere Tui was bringing up their daughter alone. Would the child even remember her mother?

Toren had to admit that she almost certainly would not. The thought that her daughter was growing up without her made Toren's heart feel like a wrung-out rag. What was it all for, anyway? Nothing seemed to stop the Automators.

Stoppit, she told herself. Stoppit now!

You just need to find another way to defeat them, isn't that was this trip is all about, to find a way that doesn't need bombs and bullets?

As usual, before allowing passengers off, armed Automators came through the train, checking for Listeners or rebels. They were children really, Toren thought, children hidden behind black masks, children with no other choices, recruited at gun point. Their 'checking' consisted of walking slowly down the train, glaring at everyone and waving their guns about. She stared out of the window and tried to slow the beating of her heart.

Somehow, a butterfly had got into the carriage. It battered itself against the window above Toren's head. She sat on her hands to suppress the desire to stand up, open the top of the window and free the poor thing. The woman opposite was watching it too. She wore the black fist badge of the Automators in her lapel and her mouth was a hard line. Just as the two boy soldiers came level with their seat, waving their rifles, the woman scowled and reached up to squash the butterfly. But Toren had snapped her wrist before her hand was anywhere near the insect. It hadn't even been a decision.

The Automators chanted as they dragged her off the train, 'Listener scum, Listener scum', and kept it up until the moment she was handed over to the prison capo. He didn't even ask her name because, 'You scum just give false names.'

As it turned out, that was very fortunate.

She was thrown into a cell and the door was locked behind her. At least it they couldn't know who she was, not really. At least, not yet. They would torture her to see what she knew. She could hold out for a while. Deny. Pretend. But no one could stand torture in the end. The real danger came from the photograph. It was surprising that the prison had a camera, one of the new sort, that printed little pictures while you waited. The Automators didn't like them because rebels used them to record the Automators' violent deeds and allowed their lies to be held up for all to see. It was most unlucky that the prison capo was 'an enthusiast', determined to make his superiors see what a fine security tool a camera was. He was not very expert and she knew the tricks about moving very slightly so the image would be blurred. But he would have a good-enough likeness. And when it crossed the desk of the Automators new Head of Intelligence, 'Commander Eye' whose real name, Doada Sisal, was already quite forgotten, Toren would be done for. He'd have her murdered quietly, before she could tell the inconvenient secret that the great commander was the brother of the Boogam. It was almost enough to make her laugh. The stupid thing was that no one would believe such an outrageous thing anyway. Doada's fear, like almost everything else about him, was fiction.

There were footsteps down the corridor. A clipped efficient step between the plodding clumps of two sets of Automator boots. Toren took a breath: this was it. The torturer would come in with his smart shoes and light step, while the guards just held her down. The cell door opened, the guard stood to one side to let a woman in. She didn't look much like a torturer. She was in her fifties, perfectly dressed in a very expensive suit and woven coat, her hair professionally styled. On the lapel of her coat she wore the gold leaf denoting her as a member of the Board of Governors, a Senior Merit. She stood square in front of Toren and looked straight into her eyes.

'Daughter!' she exclaimed, 'Dearest daughter!' Her voice was saturated with controlled emotion, a lifetime of aristocratic restraint.

'Mother!' Toren responded, doing her best to match the woman's tone.

The woman took Toren's right hand in both of hers and squeezed it.

'Shall we go home?'

'That would be very nice,' Toren replied.

The capo meanwhile was fawning. Had he been a spaniel – which Toren noticed he rather resembled – he would have been rolling on the ground, displaying his belly.

'Merit Aylet. How can I apologise. Such a terrible error.'

Merit Aylet regarded him coldly.

'Let me get my child out of these premises and we'll say no more about it.'

'There is a little paperwork…' the man suggested.

Aylet gave him a look that would have frozen a volcano.

'I'm certain you can manage *that* without my assistance, *Capo.*'

312

And that was that. They walked out of the prison without a word. For a chilling moment as they approached a lovely, old-fashioned carriage, drawn by two well-matched bays, Toren thought that perhaps the Merit woman was Doada's agent and she was merely going to be whisked away to her death. But the driver leaned down to tip his cap to her and she saw that, behind the bushy beard, was Tui.

'Don't ask any questions,' Merit Aylet said as the carriage drew away. 'Better you know nothing beyond the fact that that was my *greatest* performance!'

They went straight to the docks and within the hour they had boarded the ship *Magdalena*, bound for Angellis. They travelled as Senior Gale and his wife Madame Sulis but there was no false name for their three year old, who would only answer to her own, real name.

'I have a sailboat waiting for us,' Tui said. 'She's small but she's very strong.'

'Like me!' said Harlon, looking shyly at the tired, sad woman who Pa had told her was her ma.

13
Code

Harlon

 Since the boarding of the *Ice Maiden* a week ago the Red Ship has grown ever more tense. Many of the blue uniformed crew have taken Automator uniform and every companionway, ladder and passageway has its watchful guard, round the clock. Xeno has been hidden in some new place that Harlon cannot find, and she has no idea what they've done with Ash. The bear died yesterday and they put it over the side, but the stink of its misery still lingers over the whole ship.

No one, apart from the officers on the bridge, Doada, and his fat-boy side-kick, know where they are going or what, exactly, is going to happen when they get there. Their zig-zagging is announced on the tannoy as 'manoeuvres'. But the rumours that pass around the ship like a virus say that Commander Eye has lost something; either the remote island that he said they were aiming for, or the mysterious weapon that they were supposed to be testing.

'Don't know how he thinks he'll find anything in waters this deep,' Harlon overhears the blue-uniformed sailors say. 'It's the flipping Marraduka Trench, innit? You could lose a mountain range down there!'

There are streams of creatures in the seas around them and the sky above. Xeno's strange words echo in Harlon's mind every time another flock of birds wheels overhead, or a pod of dolphins passes in the sea.

The seeds are sown. The sky will hatch. The ocean will ring. It has begun.

But no one on the crew refers to this constant natural traffic.

'Don't they see it? The birds, the fish, the dolphins?' Harlon asks Tolly.

'Yeah, they see it,' Tolly answers, 'but Automators are always afraid that if they notice anything in nature and speak of it they'll be labelled a Listener. Everyone's watching everyone else.'

With no information about the real nature of the mystery weapon or why they are wandering about this stretch of ocean where no other ships seem to go, the crew is nervous. They are anxious about what might be happening back home. They sidle up to Leezul and Kogi in the canteen and ask, *'What's happening in the capital? What is Green Thorn doing? Is there going to be war?'* The questions don't stop, in spite of the fact that the girls can only give the same answer.

'It's all sent in code. We can't make head nor tail of any of the messages.'

And that is true.

Mostly.

Doada codes all his communications himself and the sheets on which they are written are carefully monitored. They must be returned to whichever Automator officer is on the bridge after transmission is over. So even if Harlon or Tolly knew anything about codes – which they don't – there's no opportunity to crack the ones that Doada uses.

But they are called to the radio room several times each day to send some *uncoded* messages; coordinates of their exact position. Almost as if Doada *wants* to be followed.

The girls suspect that their erratic course means that Doada *is* searching for that island *green and sharp as a thorn.*

Is this Ma's island, lost in the deepest ocean? No, Harlon tells herself that would be a crazy coincidence, wouldn't it? Crazy as sending your kids to find a place that wasn't on a map! As the warm, calm days drag on, Harlon feels that she has almost become Leezul, helping the Automators instead of trying to bring them down or free her brother and sister.

It's like being stuck in a nightmare.

Then, while reading Colt's *Radio Operators Manual* for the fourth time, Harlon notices something. It hits her brain like a bolt of lightning. She jumps down into Tolly's bunk to show her.

'Look! Look.'

Harlon points to the bottom of the second page of the manual, where three words have been written vertically, close to the spine, with the finest of pens.

page line word

followed by

73 4 13

'What does it mean?' Tolly asks sleepily.

'*Page* 73, *line* 4, *word* 13! It's a message, a coded message from Colt!'

'Oh, Oh!' Tolly is wide awake, sitting bolt upright now. 'I don't know how I missed it. I've read the manual more times than you!'

'But you understood all this technical stuff, Tolly, The *only* bit I understood were those three words.'

Harlon starts to riffle through the pages of the manual.

'Here, page 73…' she scans down the lines, finds the thirteenth word: *second*

Tolly rummages at the bottom of her messy bunk to find a pad and pencil and writes down the word.

'That doesn't tell us anything!'

'Wait … see? Where to find the next word is written here!'

At the same location, on the right hand page, tucked in close to the spine, three spidery numbers that you would never notice unless you knew to look for them.

Page 8 line 56 word 5: *radio*

'A second radio!' Harlon exclaims. 'Maybe. Maybe Colt *was* a Green Thorn spy. Maybe they're planning something? To stop this weapon?'

Tolly nods.

'Alright … next word then.'

They follow the trail back and forth through the manual until they have a complete sentence.

second radio location boiler 4 upper ladder step 5

'He's hidden it in the engine room?' Harlon exclaims. 'How are we going to get in there? It's got two guards on the door day and night.'

'Same way as we got on this ship,' Tolly says. 'By being good little ensins!'

Harlon is getting to know the gleam in Tolly's eyes when she gets a really bold idea.

'You, Tollara Flix,' Harlon whispers, 'are a born rebel.'

They don't have to wait long to put Tolly's bold plan into action. Just a few hours later the blaring tannoy has called them to the radio room in the middle of the night.

'Close that door!' Vart, the second officer, barks as he enters from the bridge. 'You're not here to gaze at the stars, Ensin Leezul.'

Vart's in a bad mood. He's much grumpier now he's swapped the blue uniform for the Automator's black and red.

'Why do you *both* always come up here, anyway?' he complains. 'One should rest while the other works, so the radio can always be staffed.' He's like a bully, trying to pick a fight. Harlon doesn't know what to say to him, but as usual Tolly has a great answer, an answer that, Harlon realises, is part of her plan.

'Security and accuracy, sir. The watchwords of the radio corps.'

Well, thinks Harlon, *that* should shut him up. But it's not enough for Tolly.

'We are each other's keepers, sir, making sure mistakes are not made nor security breached. Ensin Kogi checks each character and I translate it into Morse and check it back. With messages from the Commander Eye himself...'

'Alright, alright,' Vart replies. 'No need to go on.'

'We've been thinking sir, about security,' Tolly says.

'You aren't employed to think, ensin,' Vart snaps, but Tolly ignores him and goes on, her voice quiet and wheedling.

'We were wondering whether, if Third Engineer Colt was a spy like they say, he might have concealed something – contraband signalling equipment, for example – in the engine room.'

'We could look for it, sir,' Harlon chips in.

The wheels in Vart's mind are cranking visibly. If *he* could be the one to uncover the remnants of a rebel plot, that could mean a promotion within the Automator ranks.

'Hmmm,' he says. Vart seems quite restored to his previous, blue-uniformed cheerfulness.

'The engine room is a restricted area. You can't just waltz in there, but I'll issue you a pass at once!' he says. 'You can go once you've sent this.'

He hands them the message sheet.

'Not coded, sir?' says Harlon.

'Ours it not to reason why, Ensin.'

Island located. Expect arrival imminently.

'Don't just stare at it, girl, send it,' Vart barks. 'At least it means we could all be going home soon.'

The guards on the door into the engine room have their masks on and their jackets buttoned up even though it's hot down here: a sign that they are *very* vigilant. They examine the pass that Vart has created for his radio operators for some time before allowing them through. They hammer on the door to alert the engineers, then open it to let Harlon and Tolly in. One of the engineers' mates, in oil-stained dungarees over a sweaty vest, comes to meet them at the door.

'Whaddya want?'

Automators are not popular in the engine room after what happened with Colt.

Tolly hands him their pass.

'Search the engine room? What for?'

He's about to the slam the door on them when one of the guards puts his big boot in the door jamb.

'Orders,' he says. 'Let them in. *Now.*'

'Alright. I'll tell the boss,' he replies. 'Be quick and don't get in the way.' He snarls at the girls.

The engines in the engine room are working very hard, but the engineers are not. They are playing cards round a small table beneath a giant piston that moves up and down with stately precision. They shoot suspicious looks towards the girls and whisper to each other as they deal another hand.

The engine compartment is a huge three-dimensional jigsaw puzzle, with little ladders and walkways connecting it all in a most confusing fashion.

'We can't ask where boiler four is, I suppose?' whispers Tolly.

'No,' says Harlon. 'Don't want to risk them finding it before we do.'

They search the huge space, climbing up and down and along and round. It helps that the engineers are very occupied with their game, so that the girls can peer at the tags that label parts of the machinery, without creating suspicion.

They locate boilers 2 and 3, 5 and 1a; plus valves, pistons cogs wheels, dials and monitors, and are ready to abandon their search when there it is: boiler number four, like a sort of metallic hippo. There is a short flight of iron stairs at one end. Step five is the top. Harlon peers underneath while Tolly keeps watch for any passing engineers.

'I think I can see it but I can't reach. it. Gonna have to climb round and get it.'

Harlon squeezes between the wall and under the stairs. She reaches toward the box of the radio and out of the darkness a small face looks at her, and little hand rests on hers. A monkey, like a tiny gold-furred person with huge, frightened eyes. She pulls at the box and it seems the monkey wants to come too. As Harlon emerges from behind the steps with the radio under one arm and the monkey on her shoulder, there is an explosion of steam from boiler number five that brings the engineers running.

Their faces, as they see what Harlon is holding, show that they don't care a bit about the box or the steam coming from boiler 5, but care *very* much about the monkey. For a few moments no one says anything and then all the engineers try to speak at once.

'Don't hurt him.'

'We're not Listeners.'

'He helps with the little fiddly jobs, up high.'

They are very afraid and it takes a while for Tolly and Harlon to calm them down. Harlon explains that the monkey wasn't what they were looking for; Tolly promises that they will forget about its existence the moment they leave the engine room, if the engineers will also forget about the wooden box they're taking with them. They reach agreement, shake hands and learn the engineers' names, Sol, Metti and Rak. The monkey climbs into Sol's large arms where, Harlon suspects, it spends a lot of time.

'You're the radio operators, 'int you?' says Metti, the one in the dungarees. 'You don't look much like Automators, if you don't mind me saying.'

'Colt said you were alright,' Rak nods. '*Really* alright.'

'We liked Colt,' says Tolly. 'We were really upset when...'

The engineers exchange a look.

'Well,' Rak says, rubbing an oily rag absently over his bald head. 'I wouldn't be *too* upset, like!'

'Yeah, there *might* have been a life raft lost overboard *about that time*,' adds Metti.

'Accidental like,' Sol says. 'He might just have climbed aboard it. I'll get you a sack for that box, eh?'

Tolly and Harlon hold up the sack with the radio box hidden inside.

'Dead rats,' says Harlon, to the guards. 'Quite stinky!'

The two guards step back, wrinkling their noses behind their masks.

Back in cabin 37, Harlon and Tolly lean the mattresses against the door and walls for soundproofing. The fish-frying crackle of the radio still sounds horribly loud but they muffle it with pillows. The instruction for the frequency to tune to, the call sign to use, the first message they must send, were all left for them in Colt's radio manual.

'Who will we be talking to?' Tolly asks.

'I don't know,' Harlon replies, 'but we have to trust Colt,

322

and just see what happens. Or we just go on helping the Vampire by being his radio operators.'

'Alright!' says Tolly. 'Alright!'

She taps out the message letter by dot-and-dash letter.

'I've just said...' Tolly slides one phone off an ear to translate what she's heard. Harlon finds she no longer needs it. Somewhere in all the many messages she's sat through, the dots and dashes have got into her head.

'*Small fish calling acorn,*' she whispers to Tolly. 'I know, I've been practising my Morse.'

Tolly's eyebrows shoot up in surprise and she's about to say something teasing but acorn is replying!

Acorn to small fish we receive you.

Wait.

page line word message follows

2,6,9

27,18, 31

It takes a long time to send the three numbers for every word. But as the Morse taps them out, Harlon flips the pages of the manual to look them up.

Weapon test mission must be terminated at all costs.

Help coming.

Utmost importance you delay progress 4 hours min.

Do you copy?

There are footsteps outside the door. The guard on their passageway is passing and they can't be sure how good their soundproofing is. They hold their breath and the footsteps pass.

Roger Acorn, Tolly taps.

Little fish over and out.

Acorn over and out.

'That was Colt,' says Harlon. 'It has to be!'

Tolly nods.

'But where is he? On the ice ship or is there somebody else coming to help?'

Harlon smiles grimly, and shrugs.

'Hardly matters; the important question is how do we stop this ship moving for four hours?'

'Leezul? Kogi?' It's Vart's voice right outside the door, muffled by the mattresses but still too close for comfort.

'Ensins Leezul and Kogi?' Vart is little louder now but irritated.

'Sir?' Harlon makes her voice sleepy.

'I can't hear you. Open this door.'

Harlon pulls the mattress aside and puts her face next to the door

'We aren't dressed, sir.'

Vart, shuffles, coughs.

'Oh I see, well… *Did you find anything?*' he whispers.

'No sir,' Harlon replies. 'Our search was interrupted. There was an engineering problem. We could search again though, sir.'

Tolly gives Harlon a silent thumbs-up.

'Right now if you like, sir,' she adds.

There is a moment's pause and then a hand-scribbled security pass is poked under the door.

'One of you can go,' Vart snaps. 'I need the other in the radio room at once.'

'Yes, sir!' they chorus in response.

Harlon unscrews the slotted cover of the air vent in their cabin and puts the radio into the space behind, then screws the cover back again. They both know the danger if they are caught with this radio.

'What are you going to do in the engine room?' Tolly asks.

'I don't know. Improvise,' Harlon says. 'Might be best if you didn't go to the radio room. Just hide out somewhere?'

'No point making them suspicious before we have to.'

She puts her hand on Harlon's arm.

'I'll be fine!' she says. 'Good luck.'

The guards on the engine-room door glance at the pass and let her through but Harlon stops them from hammering the door to alert the engineers.

'It's better if I go in unannounced. This is a security matter.'

They nod, wordlessly, and push the door quietly open.

Sol, Metti and Rak are not at their card table. In fact they are nowhere to be seen. How much could they really be trusted? If she explained that the rebels would like them to stop the boat please for a while, would that work? No. It's too risky. She will just improvise. Along the starboard side of the engine room is a wall covered in wheels that turn to open and close things: pipes, valves, boilers – who knows what. Above them, a line of gauges like neat clocks. This is the place to start.

Harlon isn't sure if making things tighter or looser is more dangerous, so she turns some as far as she can to the right and some as far as she can to the left. She notices smaller wheels, dials and taps and she does the same with every single turnable object. Soon a horrible juddering begins, some steam explosions, and the huge piston above the engineers' card table begins to speed up. Harlon runs up a ladder to another level and starts to do the same with every wheel and valve and button. Below her, Rak and Metti pop up from a hatch in the floor she hadn't noticed; they are yelling and frantically trying to work out what's gone wrong. Sol pops up too, squeezing his bulk though the small space, he spots her and shouts. She feels bad, they've been kind and they saved Colt. She knows they don't much like the Automators that are running their ship.

There's an alarm going off now, and flashing lights. Up and up Harlon goes, running out of things to meddle with. She finds a massive spanner lying on the floor and grabs it. Using it to do as much damage as she can as she climbs. There's no going back now. Good Ensin Pria Leezul just ceased to exist. She's Harlon again and now she's going to be on the run within the ship. How long can she keep from being captured? She doesn't know. Metti's racing up the ladders to follow her. She looks around. It's a dead end. The ladder runs up almost to the roof and stops in short metal walkway. She backs to the end of the walkway and stares at Metti, wondering what he'll do. He's skinny but he looks strong. There's a pipe she can drop onto to break her fall if she has to jump, but she'll wait until the last moment. She gets ready and watches him carefully as he comes towards her. He stops, looks down and around then smiles at her, winks and points above her head and mouths 'hurry!'

Harlon flicks her gaze up quickly. It could be a trick, but there's a hatch hidden in the shadows up there, almost out of reach.

'*Hurry!*' Metti whispers. 'There isn't another place to hide.'

Harlon nods then jumps, grabs the wheel that opens the hatch and uses it to pull herself up so she can brace her legs on the rails of the walkway. She gets the hatch open and scrambles up.

Just in time, as there are footsteps crashing up the metal stairway. Metti shouts down.

'She's not up 'ere!' he yells to the others, then looks up to Harlon and whispers something about 'not opening … at the top'. But she can't quite hear, and isn't really listening as she snaps the escape hatch shut and wedges the spanner in the handle to keep it that way.

Above her is a long, dark shaft with a metal ladder. There's nowhere to go but up. And up. And up. It's a long climb and at the top there's another red hatch. Harlon listens hard, trying to work out where she'll be when she opens it and what might be waiting for her. She can't stay where she is, like a rat in a trap. She turns the wheel, the hatch peels back and Harlon peers out into darkness. There's a wall behind her, sky visible through the bars of a cage.

Don't open the hatch at the top must have been what Metti was trying to tell her because this is…

Where the tiger is, yes!

The tiger is both inside and outside her head at the same time. His face is looking down at her, his huge green eyes, intent. Her first instinct is to pull the hatch closed, but almost before she has thought it, the tiger speaks again.

Don't. I won't hurt you. I haven't eaten a human in years, although my stay on this ship has tested my resolution.

Very slowly, never taking her eyes off the real tiger, Harlon climbs out of the hatch.

The animal sits on his haunches. He is thin and somewhat ragged, but still huge. Inside her head he glows with life.

Forgive me for this intrusion into your mind, but these are difficult circumstances. You may speak also if you wish?

Harlon can't seem to find her voice. The tiger continues.

My name is Skrimsli. I am, was, the captain of the Ice Maiden, *but apparently my true destiny is to be an overcoat for that Automator chieftain.*

Skrimsli snarls. His teeth are very white and very large.

I hate him! Harlon blurts out.

Yes, Skrimsli responds. *I also hate him. He is deeply evil and must be stopped.*

The tiger gives a low growl, full of emotion, that speaks to the place inside Harlon untouched since Enkalamba's voice reached into her. Her feelings rush up from the dark little pond where she has been keeping them all this time. Once she begins to speak, she can't stop.

I think he's trying to do something terrible but I can't quite work out what and I promised Ma I'd get to an island but I don't really know what she wanted me to do and I lost my sister and my brother and it was my job to take care of them and now they're after me because I wrecked the engine and I've left my friend Tolly all alone.

She sounds like a kid. It's embarrassing.

Sorry.

Dammit! Another thing she didn't plan to say.

Please don't apologise. You mentioned wrecking the engine? I think in that you have been successful. Listen! Observe!

The regular thrub thrub thrub of the ship's engines has stopped. No smoke is pumping from the chimney above their heads and the ship is still. There's a lot of shouting. There are small explosions coming from deep within the engine room.

But why did you want to do such a thing? You are in Automator uniform, the tiger asks.

I'm not an Automator. I'm Harlon I came aboard to find my sister. Oh, wait, Ash. Ash was on your ship, he is my brother and the reason I wrecked the engine was because the rebels on the radio asked me to and I think it was your ship they were speaking from and I think they're coming to get us and they'll catch up if we stay still for a bit but they didn't say how far away they were.

Why can't she order her thoughts?

I see.

Skrimsli responds.

Or I believe I do. May we clarify? You are Ash's sister?

Harlon doesn't want her words to run away with her again so she simply nods. The tiger points his nose towards her and sniffs deeply and thoughtfully.

Yes, he says, *indeed you are!*

Harlon realises that he can smell that she is Ash's sister.

And you have had a radio message? Skrimsli continues, *One asking you to disable this ship, so that someone – my ship you think – can come to our aid, but you do not know their position?*

Harlon nods again but some words squeeze out anyway.

They said it was imperative to stop the weapon.

The tiger in her mind darkens like a cloud.

The weapon, yes. That weapon. I feel its presence, like a weight. Yes, that must be stopped at all costs.

The tiger raises his head and smells the air.

329

The bigger picture, yes, a bigger picture indeed, he says to himself.

I am confident my crew is on its way. We must survive until they arrive. Also try to make their job easier.

He gives a small snarl, a tiny sample Harlon guesses of the power and ferocity he can muster.

Muffled explosions come from the engine room, there are shouts, and running footsteps, then all the ship's lights go off. Everything is now hidden in perfect darkness.

You did a fine job with that engine, Skrimsli comments. *But now, let us escape and go somewhere else.*

Harlon can't see how they are going to get out of this cage, but Skrimsli just walks to the door and it swings open.

Good. The doctor did as I suggested at last and forgot to fasten the bolt. The guards on this deck also have taken my suggestion, to patrol elsewhere, but they will not do so for long. Your arrival is well timed; we have just a few moments.

Skrimsli looks up to the roof that juts out over this part of the deck. He jumps up onto the curved gunwale, placing his large paws delicately to balance on the narrow edge, gathers himself, and in one huge bound, he's up. His face peers down at her, a slightly darker shape agains the cloud-filled sky.

How is your climbing, Harlon? Are you as good as your brother?

Ha, thinks Harlon. Watch me.

In a moment or two she's beside him. They crouch low together, so as not to make silhouettes against the sky.

Good, says Skrimsli.

I am not familiar with the layout of the ship. I need to be. Hold what you know in your mind and I can look.

Harlon is getting a little more accustomed to having a big

orange cat inside her head. Carefully she runs through what she knows about this part of the ship and what lies below it.

In front of them the rear funnels, with huge water tanks on and a pair of lifeboats on either side and then the foreword funnel. Beyond that, a curving deck where there's an equipment store. That's the roof of the commander's stateroom. There are usually guards up there. It would be possible to drop down onto the roof of the bridge but not without being seen. In front of the bridge is a small deck that connects on either side with the rest of that level. A companionway connects it at the rear, to the decks below, and the one above.

Skrimsli purrs.

Excellent, you think like a hunter.

He lifts his head slightly to look for their next move. Footsteps are running up the stairs leading to his cage. His escape will be discovered.

Let us move, there, between the starboard tank and the funnel.

Skrimsli flows, like a shadow sliding over the ground. Harlon moves as quietly as she can but compared with the tiger, she feels clumsy. He crouches low and she peers over his shoulder, close enough to touch his fur. For all its rough appearance it's still silky and the muscles underneath the skin are iron hard.

Two guards can be seen on the roof of the stateroom, silhouettes pacing nervously, their weapons drawn.

Harlon, I do not kill without reason but you understand that there is reason? Every armed Automator on this ship is one who may end the life of one of my crew. It is my duty to protect my crew. I will disable where I can, but these two, I have to kill.

Harlon's heart races. She has never imagined she would

331

really have to kill anyone. But Skrimsli's right. What choice do they have?

I understand, she says.

Good. I will take the larger one. The male. The other will not shoot and risk hitting her companion while I attack. Can you disarm her as quietly as possible? I will do the rest.

For the first time in a long time Harlon thinks of Ma and the endless, *endless* exercises, in taking guns, batons, knives away from hands that very much want to keep them.

Thanks Ma, she thinks.

Yes, she tells Skrimsli. *I can.*

Good. Wait until I bring the first one down, then move fast. My life may depend on it. It is best if we are quiet and do not alert others. We must be swift.

There's no time for Harlon to think that she's out of practice, or out of condition or out of luck. There is only action. After so long stuck in the loop between cabin 37 and the radio room, it's a relief.

Skrimsli moves forward, out of her mind now, wholly in the world and focused on his task. Low to the ground, shoulders rolling, feet placed infinitely carefully. It seems slow but there is no pause in his progress: silent, relentless. He passes the second funnel, moving in its shadow through the tumbled clutter of equipment, without a sound. Harlon notes Skrimsli's route as well as she can, so she can follow as quietly and quickly as possible.

The guards are leaning out, looking down at the levels below. The noises from the engine room are fewer now, and there's less shouting. Harlon can hear the thud of heavy boots: all the Automators are on alert, there could be ten or more of them on every deck.

Skrimsli's in position. So close to the guard he's targeting, the man could pat the tiger's head. But the tiger has made himself invisible, just part of the shadow on the edge of the deck. Harlon tenses, ready…

The pounce is so fast that Harlon just sees the man go down. There's hardly a struggle, he's dead before the other guard has turned around. And when she does, Harlon is already on her; one leg wraps around her body, the other kicks the gun out of her hands; one arm around the eyes, the other punching the throat with all her strength. Harlon feels how strong the woman is but she goes down, clutching at her neck. Then Skrimsli's on her and she lies still.

I will hide the bodies, says Skrimsli. He carries them in his jaws, as if they are no more than rag dolls, to the area between the funnel and the lifeboat and Harlon helps him pull a tarpaulin over them.

They have been quiet enough, but not completely silent and the thuds and scuffles have been heard on the deck below. A torch beam thrusts up towards them and a voice calls low.

'What's going on up there?'

'All good here,' Harlon calls back, trying to sound like her Automator self again. 'I tripped in the dark. What's going on down there?'

'The word is the engine's been sabotaged,' the man replies,

then drops his voice another notch. 'Turns out the radio ops with the scabby head was a spy.'

'No!' says Harlon. 'How long before the engine's fixed?'

'I haven't heard. You alright up there?'

Another set of footsteps and another voice.

'Quiet there! What part of silent operation do you not understand. You want to be chatting, when the stinking little rebel pirates slit your throat?'

'No, sir. Sorry, sir.'

'To your duty, lad! And you two up top, the same. Not another word!'

They will discover us here, says Skrimsli. *We must move.*

He's right, but where to? Every deck below them is crawling with Automator guards, armed and vigilant. Every place they can get to from here, they will be spotted. Except one.

Your cage. They won't look in your cage! Harlon says. *We can go back down the shaft to the engine room, the way I got out. No one will expect anyone to come down that way. The engineers will be occupied with their repairs.*

Skrimsli agrees.

Yes, you are right. We go.

They creep back the way they came, through the obstacle course of gear and tanks beside the funnels, back to the roof above the cage. But now two guards are patrolling the area in front of the door of the cage. Which means Skrimsli's escape is no longer a secret, and getting past them without being seen is impossible. At the same moment there are shouts of alarm from the roof of the stateroom; the guards from the deck below have come up and found the bodies. Shouts and torch beams reach towards Harlon and the tiger.

Lifeboat, says Skrimsli. There's just time. They leap into the space beside the first funnel, over the water tank to one of the starboard lifeboats. Its cover is closed tight with a rope lacing, and the seconds tick as Harlon tries to undo it. The fighters are cautious, afraid of the tiger in the shadows, but their swinging torch beams are getting closer.

We're in! says Harlon.

Like a giant striped worm, Skrimsli wriggles under the tarpaulin and Harlon follows. She pulls on the rope-lacing from the inside, trying to make it look tight and undisturbed. The guards are close now, closer still. Then passed.

'Maybe it went over the side?' one of them suggests.

'What?' his companion responds. 'It's a tiger, not a flipping mermaid. No, they have to be here somewhere. Check the lifeboats.'

The torch beams and voices fade a little as the men check the port-side lifeboats. Then they return. Skrimsli is very still, Harlon guesses he's trying to slip inside one of the guard's minds to draw their attention elsewhere. But now the Automators are standing still beside their lifeboat.

'We're know you're in there, Leezul, or whatever your name is. And we know that filthy tiger is with you.'

They've fallen silent. Harlon can imagine how they are signalling to each other.

'You've got five to give yourselves up,' their leader announces.

'Remember, head shot only for the cat. Special order of the Commander,' he instructs his comrades.

Say nothing, Skrimsli says. *Wait for them to lift the tarpaulin.*

'A count of five, starting...' A long second stretches. 'Now: one...'

Skrimsli's body tenses, ready to spring.

There are three. I will take the one on the left, he says calmly. *You, the one in the middle; the other will run, I smell his fear.*

'Two!'

The sound of rifles being settled into shoulders, feet more firmly planted.

'Three!'

Fingers working the edge of the lifeboat cover free, and laying hold of its edge, ready.

'Four!'

Rifles cocked, breathes taken.

'FIVE!'

The tarpaulin is ripped off. Harlon and Skrimsli find themselves looking along the narrow barrels of three Automator rifles. But only for a moment. Now each of the Automators has a knife to their throat, held by a tall woman in a green jerkin, a huge man with a silver nose ring and a gorilla with a bandage round his head.

'Drop your weapons, in silence,' the woman tells the Automators quietly, 'or we will slit your throats.' The tone of her voice can leave no doubt that she means what she says.

'Bollovar, Silverback, deal with these men.'

Bollovar and Silverback make short work of it and the three guards are soon lined up in the bottom of a lifeboat, trussed up and insensible.

Skrimsli has jumped from the lifeboat to greet the woman with a headbump like a fireside moggy. It's clear she too is very glad to see him.

'Ah!' she says, looking at Harlon. 'You are Ash's sister. I am First-mate Ekar, and these are Bollovar and Silverback. But we have little time for introductions now. We need to take this ship.'

There are gunshots from the lower decks, shouts of alarm. Ekar gives a sly smile.

'Some of the *Narwhal* are here also. We came in advance of the ships. The rest will be here by morning. Green Thorn also.'

Good, says Skrimsli. *Our task then is to stay alive and ensure our enemies do not. We can drive Automators below and confine them there until we have full crew.*

'Just like the old days eh, Captain?' says Bollovar. Skrimsli gives a low growl of approval, then walks briskly into Harlon's mind.

This will be bloody work we do. Find your brother and your sister. Locate the weapon if you can. My senses tell me it is on a lower deck, in the prow. But I suspect a special guarded entrance. Don't take any risks. We will deal with all else.

Ekar hands her one of the Automator rifles and a bandolier of ammunition.

'You look like you know how to use this,' she tells Harlon. 'As Skrimsli says, take no risks, but you may need to defend yourself. Wait a little, while we secure these two decks, then move.'

They drop down to the deck below, where three guards have already been silently dispatched by other ice-ship crew, and vanish into the dark like water into sand.

Harlon waits. It is absolutely dark. The takeover of a ship doesn't sound like she expected. There are little burns of gunfire, the occasional scream. But it's really very quiet, two sets of trained hunters, stalking each other in the dark.

The breeze is stiffening and with no engine to hold her in position the *Dolphin* drifts, broadside to the growing swells, like a floating corpse.

Ma's dead, Harlon thinks.

She hasn't let herself think it quite like that before.

She tries it out loud.

'Ma's dead,' she whispers. Does that feel real? Harlon isn't sure.

Do you have to keep promises to the dead? What did that crazy promise mean in any case?

Harlon shakes her head. What matters is stopping the Automators and their weapon and finding Ash and Xeno. And Tolly. *Tolly.* There's another thing she needs to say out loud. She whispers, 'I love you, Tolly,' into the night.

It's time to go. Harlon knows where to start her search – the one place thats she's definitely never looked: the commander's stateroom. The cloud has shifted and there's faint moonlight to see her way by, but she can't be certain that the ship is under Skrimsli's command just yet. There could be Automators or blue crew hiding anywhere, so she moves back over the roof, as cautiously as before, crawls onto her belly and wriggles to the very edge of the roof, right above the door into the stateroom. She listens. Nothing. The hunt is still going on deep inside the ship, down corridors and in dark cabins, but here it's already over. Harlon lets herself over the edge and drops down onto the deck, outside the door. A fallen Automator lies face down on the little deck in front of the big windows. She bends beside the lifeless figure, takes its torch and moves inside the room.

The beam illuminates a couch, a bed, lamps. But there's been a struggle in here; there are bloodstains on the carpet, a table turned over, and the wreckage of the same machine that they tried to use on Colt. A mirror catches her torch beam and makes her jump.

'Nnnnrrr.'

A groan. Someone's in here.

'Nrrrrhhh.'

Coming from the closet. Harlon approaches, opens the door and Tolly falls out, tangled in some of the commander's clothes and clutching Colt's radio. Harlon drops onto her knees. Drops the torch, can't see, picks it up, tries to hold it and Tolly.

'Tolly, Tolly! Are you alright?'

Tolly coughs.

'What d'you reckon, Harlon? I've been half beaten to death; my arm's bust. I crawled into the cupboard so no one would kill me by mistake. Can you stop shining that torch in my eyes?'

'Sorry.'

Harlon props the torch up on a small table to give the room some general lighting. She helps Tolly to sit up and looks at her face: one eye is already closing, puffy and purple; there's a cut on her temples that's bleeding and her arm is probably broken, but she's alive.

'Glad to see you!' Tolly says. 'I thought they were gonna feed you to the sharks after what you did to the engine.'

'I didn't quite plan it. Or think what they'd do to you.'

Tolly shakes her head.

'No, you did good,' she says. 'The Vampire did his nut. I could hear him smashing things on the bridge. Shouting, ranting. Mad, completely *mad*. I didn't know what he'd do; thought he might call for back up or something, so I ripped all the wires out of the main radio.' Tolly gives a mad little laugh.

'That's when I got this.' She points to the bruise on her head.

'Vart found Colt's radio.' Tolly goes on. 'Went straight to our cabin when we got the news about you. Then old Vampire made me use it to send his signals... I tried to refuse, but I think he really would have killed me.'

She coughs again.

'I wasn't brave enough.'

'Yes, you were, Tolly. You were so brave.'

Tolly waves her hand.

'You've got to go after him. He's gone. As soon as he heard the attack, he was ready. He's taken the weapon. And he's taken your brother and sister. And he said something weird.'

Tolly reaches for Harlon's hand.

'He said, "The Boogam will come and get her children". He thinks that your brother and sister are the children of the Ghost! Is that true? Are you her child?'

Harlon sits down on the floor. It's suddenly clear to her that she *is* the Boogam's child. *That's* the past Ma didn't want to speak about. But how Commander Eye came to know it she can't think. In any case that doesn't matter now.

She feels very tired. All she can do is nod.

'Perhaps,' she tells Tolly. 'Though I don't think I ever knew who she really was. She's dead in any case, but my brother and sister are still alive. Where has he taken them?'

Tolly still holds her hand.

'To the test site,' she says. 'The island. He and Vellum and some thugs took them in two fast boats. I think the Vampire plans to leave them there and then blow the whole island up with his weapon. He thinks your mother will come, but how can she if she's dead?'

Harlon doesn't answer. How the commander thinks what he thinks is beyond her. He's deranged. What matters is getting to Xeno and Ash in time.

'How far is it?'

'It can't be far. I heard the captain say we'd see the island before morning. It's on some old map. On the bed. Vampire was in such a panic, he left it.' Tolly tries to prop herself up to point to where the map is, but she winces with pain and lies back down.

'I'll find it. Lie still,' Harlon tells her.

She shines the torch on the rumpled landscape of the bed and there is an old parchment map, big enough to wrap a loaf of bread: green island, deep blue sea.

Where has she seen this before? She trains the beam over it bit by bit. There, in spider writing, in one corner, is a list of words in many languages: the island's name – Tap, Tynt, Cailete, Nabawlee and then halfway down them, Lost!

Oh Ma, you didn't mean an island lost in the deepest ocean. You meant an island, Lost, in the deepest ocean.

Xeno and Ash are on their way there. She must try to catch up. Try to stop the weapon being used. She has to go, now, to find a way to do that but it's hard to leave Tolly when she's so hurt. Harlon turns to her but before she can speak, Tolly reads her face.

'I'll be fine. It's just a broken arm. Go! *GO!*'

14

Waking the Greenhouse

Ash

 Ash is locked in the bathroom of Doada's stateroom. He is bound with his hands behind his back, gagged, battered and bruised, but he is the happiest that he's been in a long time because Xeno is here too. She's trussed up just like him, and she too has been beaten, but she's alive and still Xeno. They can't talk or even sign to each other, but they can lie close together.

The ship has stopped moving and Doada is not pleased about it. On the other side of the door they can hear him yelling and ranting. He's on about the map too: about golden lines and how he's going to destroy them. Ash has given up trying to make sense of what is going on. Doada Sisal is mad. Not just bad, like a thief who'd steal your money and then go off and spend it and leave you alone. Nothing will ever be enough for Doada. He'll always want more, and he'll break the whole world to get it.

There's someone else in the stateroom with them now. A girl. Ash and Xeno can hear her being hit. That's when Xeno burrows her head into Ash's chest.

Then the lights go out. There's mayhem on the other side of the door. Doada screaming, footsteps, gunshots... Ash and Xeno keep very still and hope that they will be forgotten until whatever is going on is over. But that's not what happens; torch beams pierce the bathroom's darkness and the two of them are flung over the shoulders of Automator thugs and carried through the ship. In the blackness, it's impossible to see where they are, so it's only when they are thrown into the bottom of a boat together that Ash realises what's happening. Doada is leaving the ship, running for his precious 'island' with the weapon and a small force of very tough-looking Automator fighters.

Ash is sure that somebody will see them and put a stop to this escape. But they're all too busy fighting in the dark to notice the two low black boats with black-clad crew slip from the side of the wallowing ship. Ash can't cry out or struggle. All he can do is press himself close to Xeno's side and hope it makes her feel a little bit better.

Everyone aboard keeps very quiet and the engines run low. As soon as they get far enough away from the ship, the boats begin to zoom across the surface leaving a tarry stink behind them, with a great roar.

'Head 220 degrees,' Doada yells to the man at the tiller. 'We'll get a sight of the top of the island in about ten miles.'

From what Ash has overheard, they are going to test a weapon, which sits in the middle of the boat, boxed and wrapped. It doesn't look like much at all, but being near it makes Ash's skin crawl. It has minders, inventors, that's what they must be, Ash thinks: three weird people who look as if they have been locked in a cave. They sit close together and whisper about the weapons. They call it 'Greenhouse'. Not even *the* Greenhouse; 'Greenhouse' as if it was a person with a name.

Why is he here? Why is Xeno here? Does Doada think that Ma is following this boat right now? That she's going to come to try and rescue them? And then Doada can just grab her, easy as taking a fish off a hook? It's all completely loony. If it wasn't so terrible and miserable and sad, it would be funny. It is like one of those nightmares where you run and run and still go backwards. Nothing makes sense.

Ash thinks of everything that's happened to him since that night on the mountain when the Automators came. All the terrible things. All because people want and want and want. Why can't they just *be?* Why can't he just *be*, with Xeno, back on their mountain? Or in the rigging of the *Ice Maiden* with the Gula. Thinking of it makes his eyes prickle. *Being.* Being is what matters.

There's another fuss. The compass that they are using to navigate with is going crazy. This seems to give Doada an excuse to do the same. For a long while, they go in circles, then they stop. At last one of the Greenhouse 'minders' suggests that there is a star that they can use to steer by and off they go again.

There's nothing Ash can do about any of it. He'd like to scream at them to stop, he'd like to overpower the big lug driving the boat and throw the lot of them overboard so he and Xeno can escape, but instead he shuts his eyes and waits.

345

Who knows, maybe this island place that Doada is so worked up about, this *test site* will be nice. So they can all enjoy the view while they get blown up, or whatever it is this stupid glass box does. After everything he's been through, he could sleep on a bed of rocks. The bottom of a boat is easy.

'Up up up up,' one of the masked Automators is shouting and dragging him to his feet. Another has put Xeno over his shoulder like a parcel and is wading through the surf. It's chaos while all the things and people that were in the small boats make their way onto the land.

But what land it is! The beach is a perfect half-circle of white. The sea is bluer than the bluest thing Ash can think of and the land is the greenest green. It looks like a huge green thorn reaching up into the dawn-pink sky. There are animals *everywhere*. The air is filled with sea birds of all sizes who take no notice at all of the humans and stream past them at head height. Whirling above the pinnacle of the green are skeins of larger birds, birds from Ma's books, as magical to Ash and Xeno as unicorns or dragons. Crabs of at least five different sorts run about on the sand and dive down little burrows to avoid the massive boots of the Automators as they unload all the boxes of gear.

Ash turns to Xeno and she is shining, through her gag. She makes a sort of 'look' sound and points with her head. Just off the bay there are whales, *lots* of them really close to shore, their blows and backs, their lovely tail flukes, all visible. As the children watch, two breach one after another, and the sound of their splash back into the sea rolls like a wave up the beach. Songbirds are calling from the trees at the top of the beach and lizards, green ones, black ones, stripy ones, zip about over the rocks.

Ash thought there could be no place on land better than the mountain, but this place feels *amazing*. He catches little zings of bird thought and crab thought and lizard thought. Not just zings, but streams and trails. Yes, *trails* like the gleaming trails the Gula showed him and like he saw when the tern took off and flew away. He looks around, the trails are everywhere and for a moment he can *see* them just the way the Gula can! The air is full of them. He thinks that maybe Xeno sees them too.

What *is* this place?

The guards from the second boat have spaced out along the beach, pacing back and forth with their guns. The guards from the first boat, the one that carried the glass box, the weird inventors, Doada, Dough Boy, Ash and Xeno, make a sort of procession, carrying the weapon and all its gear up the beach. They reach grass grazed to a lawn by large tortoises, and then walk along it, parallel to the waves. The old ruins of stone cottages are tangled in climbers and bushes. They stop at the fourth one along, and make a camp.

Once this cottage would have faced the sea, with a walled garden behind and the hill rising steeply beyond, in a tumble of huge grey boulders and tall trees. What a lovely place it would have been to live! Now the cottage and the garden are just walls enclosing two green spaces. The inventors set their boxes down inside the garden walls and Ash and Xeno are told to sit with their backs against the seaward wall. The

Automators take positions, crouching down and aiming their guns.

The inventors get busy setting up the weird glass box they call Greenhouse. It doesn't look much like a weapon with sunlight slanting through it and making little rainbows on the grass. But it's how it *feels* that makes Ash wish they could move further from it. Even thirty feet away it fills him with horror. Like those dead-eyed dogs, or the mechanical falcons, but much, *much* worse. As the wires running through it start to spark and the weapon wakes up, the feeling grows stronger, more wrong. Xeno turns her head from it and shuts her eyes, to try and block it out.

Unlife

Wasn't that what the Gula said?

Unlife

That's what this is for. It's an unlife weapon. A weapon of wrongness.

The inventors are taking photographs. Of course Doada will want photographs of his weapon for the newspapers in Fidrac. He poses beside the box and smiles. Doada's smile is one of the nastiest things Ash has ever seen.

Dough Boy brings the Automators from the beach. Most take up positions inside the cottage walls but one disappears into the tumble of boulders and trees on the slope above.

The tension grows and grows.

Dough Boy steps up to Doada and draws him away from the weapon, away from the inventors and the guards, which means they are closer to Ash and Xeno. Their voices are low but Ash and Xeno's ears are *very* sharp.

348

All Doada's 'dear boys' seem to have run out. He simply snarls. Which Ash feels is better because that's what he was really doing all along.

'What is it? Can't it wait?'

'Not really, sir,' Dough Boy replies. Compared with Doada, Dough Boy now seems quite a reasonable person.

'Alright!'

'There's a nasty smoke trail on the horizon, Commander,' Dough Boy reports. 'I think our attempt to hold onto the ship and repair the engine may have failed. So we will have to rely on Velocity One and Two to exit from the test site. We might have several days to wait before help comes. Would it be advisable to delay the test?'

Doada snarls in reply.

'*No*. No, we will not wait. I've sent messages to New Dawn Tower to send a transport for us.'

Dough Boy isn't giving up that easily.

'I am aware of that, Commander. But we had no response confirming that a transport is on its way. I really think...'

'Think? *Think*,' Doada is almost spitting now. 'You can't think. Just do what you do best, what you are *told*. Keep those children at gunpoint. She will be here any moment and then the test will begin. We will leave her and her brats to fry along with all of this ... this greenery. Now do the job I pay you for.'

Doada turns away to return to his pacing and posing beside the glass coffin.

Dough Boy scowls. He approaches Ash and Xeno and points his gun as he was asked, but there is mutiny brewing in those piggy little eyes. Ash knows it.

349

He and Xeno will not be exiting the test area. Neither will Ma if, for some *crazy* reason, Doada's plan works out. They will be staying as part of the test of the weapon's ability to make 'unlife' of them. But that's only part of it. Doada's come here because this island holds so much life. He wants to kill it all, all those looping threads, those trails and voices. If this weapon thing works, none of them – the birds, the crabs and lizards, Xeno and himself – have long to live.

Something's happening with the weapon. The inventors have stopped fussing round it. Ash listens hard and hears.

'We are ready to begin the test, Commander.'

'Cellular Ignition Resonance will be reached in 12 minutes and 37 seconds from initiation.'

'With the delay, of course,' the one with the beard says, 'to allow for us to safely exit the area.'

What is Cellular Ignition Resonance? It doesn't sound good. Cellular is about cells and thats what all living things are made of, and ignition means burning. Burning cells. That must be what the weapon does.

'Excellent. Excellent,' Doada says but his face and body say anything but excellent. 'We must wait. Until I can be certain *my guests* have arrived.'

Guests? That means Ma, the Boogam! Can Doada really believe that Ma is going to walk up the beach and give herself up?

The inventors exchange a look. Everyone thinks Doada's bonkers, Ash is certain. Why don't they just tie him up and stop all this?

Then, from somewhere amongst the trees and boulders a loud voice rings out.

'Commander Eye!' It's hard to pinpoint where it's coming from, but easy to know who it is. Ash had begun to think he dreamed seeing her on the deck of the Red Ship but he didn't.

Harlon!

He glances at Xeno but she doesn't seem at all surprised. This gets more like a dream every second. If Ash's hands were free, he'd pinch himself.

There are metallic clicks and clunks as the Automators round the walls prime their weapons. Ash's heart jumps in his throat. *Stay out of sight, Harlon, keep your head down,* he warns her in his head.

Dough Boy shouts instruction to the guards around the walls.

'Aim carefully! Make every shot count. Fire when you have a good shot.'

A volley of shots that are obviously not really aimed at anything bounces off the rocks and thwacks tree trunks. There is a moment of silence.

Harlon speaks again. 'We don't want innocent people under orders to die. Lay down your weapons, let the two children go and you can go in peace.'

Doada laughs a mad, mad laugh that sends a shiver down Ash's spine.

'And to whom am I speaking?' he shouts.

'Do you really want an answer to that question?'

Ash can see a few of the Automator guards exchanging 'who the hell is that' looks.

'Always nice to know who one's enemies are before they are exterminated,' Doada yells back.

'I'm Harlon, daughter of your enemy, the Boogam. And I've come to put an end to you.'

'Fire!' Doada screams. 'Fire! Fire!'

The Automator guards do as they're told, and fire even though they can't see who they're firing at. Who is with Harlon hiding in those trees, amongst those rocks? Whoever it is they don't respond to the wild shots from the Automators, they wait, firing well-aimed shots and picking off targets one by one. They use guns but also crossbows which strike silently and they don't aim to kill but to disable, hitting hands and legs and feet. The Automator fighters grow visibly more afraid and nervous. Each time one of them is hit they are more reckless, sending unaimed showers of fire bouncing off the rocks and biting the tree trunks. For every bullet from the trees, the Automators have sent at least twenty back. How much ammunition did Doada's fighters bring, Ash wonders? If they run out they'll have to fight without their guns and almost half of them are injured now.

There's stalemate. The Automators still able to hold rifles signal silently to each other behind the wall. One creeps out and makes it to the wall of the building next door under a rain of covering fire. More wasted bullets, thinks Ash. Good. He will skirt round and try to get behind the snipers hiding in the rocks. He *could* get Harlon. Everything goes quiet and minutes pass, while Doada and his inventors crouch beside their glass contraption. Ash wonders what would happen if it was hit. Almost immediately he gets an answer; a shot from the rocks ricochets off the wall and slams into the

352

weapon. It's tougher than it looks; the bullet skeeters off and doesn't even leave a mark.

Something's going on, hidden in the trees. Wild shots from an Automator weapon, shouts, rocks falling, branches shaking; then a scream that would freeze a cup of boiling tea. Finally a body is ejected violently from the green cover by a pair of massive black furry arms. Silverback's arms! The body tumbles down the slope and lies out in the sun. It has been bitten in the throat. Ash remembers Skrimsli's words. This is his work.

If we wish it dead, it will be so.

Ash can't help but be glad that the Automator died and not his sister or his crewmates Silverback, or Ekar, or Bollovar, as they intended.

The Automators are spooked by the sight of their dead comrade. They respond with another hail of bullets. Ash guesses they must soon be out of ammunition. And now the *Maiden* crew increase the tension by throwing bundles of burning leaves that land just short of where the fighters crouch begin the walls. Soon Ash guesses the orange fury of a Northlands tiger will burst through the clouds of pungent smoke that are starting to envelope Doada's forces.

Ash turns to Xeno to smile through his gag to give her hope, but she's not there. The rope that bound her wrists and ankles is lying empty on the ground next to him as if she just melted away. He looks around but there's no sign of her. When Dough Boy's notices she's gone, he curses. Xeno has escaped from right under his nose. He glances towards his commander but Doada's not looking because at that moment the *Ice Maiden* crew explode from the trees, making enough noise to bring a roof down.

'I've had enough orders from that madman,' Dough Boy says.

He drags Ash to his feet and out through what would once have been a front door. He waits in the cover of some tall bushes while the screams and shots and shouts erupt behind them, then moves swiftly between the walls of two more buildings, nearer to the shore. Ash can see the deep blue of the sea and the black arrows of the two boats lined up on the sand. He can guess what Dough Boy wants to do.

Oh no, not again, Ash thinks.

Ash makes himself as limp and dazed as possible, as Dough Boy drags him down the beach. He waits until the man's attention is occupied with pushing the boat and then he kicks as hard as he can, with all his strength and purpose, to the inside of the knee. Harlon taught him that, one sunny afternoon in the garden back at home. It doesn't work as well as Ash had hoped; Dough Boy's still standing but only because he grabbed the boat with both hands. But he's dropped his pistol into the water and let go of the rope. Just enough for Ash to get away.

Ash realises too late that he should have run straight for the cover of the bushes because even on the flat sand of the beach, running with your hands tied behind you makes you slow. He's not far enough away and Dough Boy has another pistol. Ash glances back and sees the man has pulled it from its holster. He has a clear shot, in good light. Ash runs on but it's no good; it looks like he might have to die here on this beach after all.

15
A Perfect Shot

Harlon

Four of the *Maiden's* crew plus Ash's Gula are on the bridge. The *Narwhal* people have taken over the fight below decks, driving Automators into corners. Ekar seems confident that they can keep control until both ice ships arrive with their remaining crew.

The map of Lost is spread on the chart table, lit by red light. The Gula has her front paws on the chart table; she snuffs at the map and looks at Harlon. Once again Harlon feels the intensity of that gaze, and for a moment the wild, golden lines that lace the map seem to blossom in the air in front of her, running from the Gula's wide snout and out over the ocean. Silverback's big hands hold it down and he gazes at the myriad golden lines that cover it. Bollovar, standing next to him, nods.

'Yes, I agree,' he says, looking into the gorilla's hazel eyes, 'it is a very, very important place, full of power.'

It is powerful indeed, Skrimsli adds, with wonder in his voice. *Snow tern was right when she told us it is the place where all trails lead. But why? Why? What does it mean. I sense this is a part of that greater picture, Ekar.*

'If it is so important,' Ekar says smartly, 'then we had better look sharp to save it!'

356

She turns the light to white so they can see the outline of the island and its topography clearly, without the distraction of the glowing spider web.

'Now is not the time for questions,' Ekar says. 'Now is the time for action. We need a plan.'

Harlon is glad of Ekar's practicality. There is so little time and the commander and the weapon have a very big headstart.

'So,' Ekar says glancing round at her crew, 'we agree that we must not wait for the ships to arrive before we act?'

Yes, the Automator chieftain and his filthy device are ahead, but perhaps will not be so far ahead of us.

'How so, Skrimsli?' Ekar asks.

Skrimsli exchanges a look with Silverback.

There are other lines that run through this island. The planet's magnetic field bends and twists here. I feel it clearly. Silverback also. The Automators' compass will not guide them true. That will buy us time.

'Good,' says Ekar. 'And we know that there is only one place where they can land their boats. Here!' She raises a magnifying glass to look at the detail in the tiny contour lines that mark the green shape of the island. She points to the curve of the sandy bay on the island's western side. 'We can land here, on the east side, and get into position here, where the land slopes down towards the west.'

There is likely to be good cover there. We can pick them off. Goad them into wasting ammunition. Then rush them. Let us go.

Skrimsli leaps from the chart table and through the door from the bridge, followed by Silverback and Bollovar. Harlon and Ekar follow but Harlon is full of doubt.

357

'Skrimsli makes it sound so easy,' she says, 'but there are five of us, and the Gula, against fifteen or even twenty armed Automators. Even if we do catch up with them.'

'We have fought with such odds before,' says Ekar. 'Besides, there is no choice. Now come! Don't forget your map!'

The craft that the ice ships' crews used to approach the Red Ship are tiny. They are not much more than a large snowboard with a sail that can swing freely around a small mast. Several are moored on the *Dolphin's* starboard side, with a rope ladder now dangling above them. 'Windslices' is what the crew call them.

'You see Skrimsli,' says Ekar, 'we brought you a windslice of your own!'

Excellent! Madame Gula will come with me. Harlon with you, Ekar.

The ice ship crew swarm down the ladder one after another and jump onto the raft-like structures. Ekar and Harlon come last.

'Stand to the rear and move when I say,' Ekar explains. 'The wind is in our favour; we will cover the distance in less than an hour. Enough time to be in position before the sun gets high.'

The windslice is more stable than Harlon feared. All the same, when Ekar pulls the sail upright and it catches the wind, Harlon almost tumbles into the water, because the slice moves like something alive and eager, a horse wanting to turn its nose into the wind.

'It's fast!' she exclaims.

'Ha!' Ekar laughs. 'Just wait!'

Harlon can hardly believe what happens next.

As the slice picks up speed, its hull simply rises above the surface on a keel as delicate as a flower stalk. Beneath the surface the keel flares into a whale tail shape. Even though she can see how it's working, it still feels like magic.

'In good winds we can make 40 knots or more,' Ekar calls above the rush of the air and the voice of the waves, 'and this is a good wind.' Harlon's feet remember the balance they found on a snowboard. With a squeeze of the heart Harlon thinks how much Ash and Xeno would love this.

'When we get there, surprise will be everything,' Ekar says as they rush over the dark sea. 'I don't know what they expect, but probably not to be picked off one by one by invisible assailants. The more afraid we can make them, the more they will waste their bullets.'

'How will we stop the weapon?' Harlon asks.

'If they have come so far to test it, it must be powerful. They won't want to be on the island once it is ready to use. We will keep them confined as long as we can. Others from the Green Thorn are on their way.'

They approach the island from the east, with rising sun behind them. An emerald peak in a night-blue sea. It is beautiful. How did Ma know about this place and how did the map end up in the commander's hands? More of Ma's long secret history, Harlon thinks.

Ekar slows their slice as they approach the island, checking where they can get close to the bottom of the cliff.

'There!' she says, pointing to a small cove just showing in the early light. 'See? Where the wind pushes against the rocks? Soon it will be too rough to land. We must be quick.'

They make the last half mile at breakneck speed. One after another the crew run their craft in, leap off onto the rocks and lift their windslices out of the water. Bollovar breaks his keel but aside from that, crew, craft and weapons are undamaged.

Once the windslices are securely stowed beyond the reach of the sea, the crew gathers at the foot of a cliff, and look up.

Now, says Skrimsli, *we climb. After you, Madame Gula.*

The Gula snuffs her approval and sets off up the almost vertical slope, fast as a fly running over a wall. They all follow, rather humbled by the smaller animal's performance.

It's a long climb and the last section is a slight overhang, which challenges everyone, even the Gula. But at last they are at the top, with the deep blue sea far below and just a short slope separating them from the brow of the hill. All along the line of the cliff where they stand, huge dark birds with long, narrow wings glide lazily on the updraft. They reach the end of the cliff and wheel round to try again.

I think they are waiting for something to begin, says Skrimsli. Harlon feels just the same. The whole island feels as if it's waiting, poised, right on the edge of something. Everywhere they look there are flocks of birds, and in the clear water at the foot of the cliff a shoal of rays swirls to the surface, amid the silvery flash of smaller fish.

'So many lives here!' Bollovar exclaims with a broad smile and Silverback nods. 'What *is* this place?'

Once more, Ekar pulls them back to practicalities.

'Silence from now,' she says. 'We must be very careful as we go over the brow. We will have a view down to where I think they will be, but in that case they may see us too. Keep to cover. Stay hidden. Surprise is all.'

Ekar's planning could not have been better. The crew creep between rocks on the rather exposed brow, but they are soon invisible in the cover of the trees and larger boulders that cover the slope below. This side of the hill is shaped like an amphitheatre, with the ruined cottages and their little squares of green clearly visible below them. The procession of fighters, inventors and the weapon is only just arriving. Skrimsli was right; they must have been delayed by the disruption to their compass bearings. They take up positions within the walls closest to the bottom of the slope. Somehow Harlon finds she knows that this was once a walled garden. Images of walking between rows of cabbages and squashes flash into her mind. There's not time to wonder at them now.

The weapon and its attendants are positioned behind the highest section of wall, closest to the bottom of the slope, hardest to see from their positions. Harlon spots Ash and Xeno bound and marched at gunpoint. They look so small, so fragile, down there. She wishes she could fly down, scoop them up and take them from all this danger. Once they are made to sit, they aren't visible to Harlon but she can see Vellum standing over them with his pistol drawn. *Hold on, hold on*, Harlon tells them, even though she knows they cannot hear.

The crew position themselves across the slope, moving slowly, taking time and care to be silent. Thanks to the curve of the hillside they can take shots from a variety of angles. The slightest mistake from any of the Automators crouched behind the scant cover of the walls will cost them dearly.

'Remember to move,' Ekar says.

'Don't make shots from the same place more than once. Don't let them get a chance to learn your position and refine their aim.'

Ekar, Silverback and Bollovar have their own weapons: compact, powerful crossbows, and also rifles taken from the Automator fighters on the *Dolphin*.

We need to goad them into wasting ammunition, Skrimsli says. *Once their fire is spent, we have them. Then I can be of use with my weapons.*

Skrimsli holds up a paw and springs the claws. Ekar gives grim smile. Harlon would not like to face either of them in a fight.

Skrimsli's right about getting them to waste their fire; from what she's seen of the commander he is easy to goad. When she suggests the way *she* might help, the *Ice Maiden* crew is very pleased.

'You are your mother's daughter, in truth,' Ekar says. 'But wait until they are settled awhile. Let them relax a little, think that they are safe.'

Harlon hopes the sound of her voice will help keep Ash and Xeno strong. This time she won't let the three of them be separated.

The plan works so well it's almost too easy. The commander is immediately unnerved by Harlon's taunts. The fear and tension down in the ruin is almost visible, and the fighters make more and more errors. They waste volley after volley while the crew keep safe behind their rocks and trees.

The *Maiden* crew spread themselves out across the slope as Ekar advised. They can't see each other and can't call to keep in touch, but Skrimsli flows like a shadow between them as their rearguard and line of communication. Each one operates as a lone sniper choosing their shots carefully, aiming not to kill, only to disable; arms, hands, legs and feet are the targets. After each shot they move position, slipping away like shadows, leaving Automators to waste ammunition on retaliation that bounces off rocks and tree trunks.

Harlon knows she has to help, but she has never aimed at living humans before. Skrimsli, sensing her concern, comes to stand beside her.

Choose your target; watch carefully. See there? The one in the middle of the right-hand wall? He keeps putting his hand on the top of the wall? Also his leg is exposed, there. Perhaps the leg is better?

Harlon focuses on the swatch of black-and-red cloth visible though the small gap in the wall. It's just a target, Harlon, she tells herself, not a leg, and takes the shot.

Good, Skrimsli says. *Very good. He will have to attend to such a nasty leg wound. Move now, Harlon. I will come to you if you need.*

He melts between the trees and vanishes to stalk about behind his comrades, guarding their backs.

Harlon moves across the slope, skirting round to give

herself a different angle. The boulder, the trees, everything about this hillside is familiar to her. More and more she feels she's been here before. She finds a good spot with a clear line of sight to the walled space below. One of the fighters has misjudged the height of the wall; the top of his helmet sticks up. She could hit it; the bullet would probably go through the helmet, but that would kill him. So she waits, he'll move in a moment, expose another bit of himself. She keeps her aim and concentration on him, waiting for her chance. Beyond him is what would have been the door of the cottage.

A blue door, Harlon thinks. Sky blue.

How does she know that?

The crack of a twig behind her comes too late. The Automator's arm is round her throat. He's big, four times her weight, and he has a knife pressed to her back; it could be through her heart with one hard push. She holds still.

'How many of you are there?' he snarls in her ear.

How does he expect any kind of answer with his arm half strangling her? She plays for time, goes limp in his grasp, and tries to shout out thoughts for help, but she's really no idea if it will work.

Skrimsli, Skrimsli. Help!

There's no answer and now she can feel her assailant tense; he's decided he might as well kill her.

I hear, sister Cub.

It is the Gula, snarling in her mind!

Two breaths more, I come.

Harlon speaks into the arm around her mouth, making her voice more like a cough than a word, so her attacker could think he hears a muffled number. It's just enough to give the man a second's pause at this offer of information. Just enough for the Gula to run from cover and sink her teeth into the back of his thigh. He screams and wheels round but the Gula is still attached. Harlon seizes her rifle and punches him in the stomach with the butt.

Stand aside, Harlon.

It's Skrimsli. Harlon has just time to jump back before Skrimsli drops from the boulder above to finish the job.

He steps from the body.

Are you unharmed?

Harlon nods.

Then move again. Madame Gula with me. Silverback will deal this body.

With the stakes so high and the advantage of numbers against them, gruesome tactics are necessary. Silverback throws the man's body clear of the trees and boulders and sends it bouncing down to land in the grass below. The Automators can see that their comrade did not die of a gunshot wound; they are too horrified to respond at once, but soon they are using up ammunition again. This time the volleys end with the sound of triggers clicking on empty clips.

I think they are almost out of ammunition, Skrimsli says, with obvious pleasure.

'Caution, Skrimsli!' Ekar whispers. 'It could be a trick. Let us test them a little more.'

She slips off her jacket and dresses a broken branch with it, then moves silently further down the slope. She moves the branch and jacket to a gap between the trees, like a fighter darting to new cover. There's more fire, and more empty clicks. Ekar slips back to Skrimsli's portion and is joined by Bollovar, Silverback and Harlon.

Now? Skrimsli asks.

Ekar nods.

'I think so.'

'I count only six still with all limbs unharmed,' Bollovar reports. 'None of the rest can hold a weapon.'

Yes, Skrimsli agrees. *Five are dead. Another six too injured to give us any trouble. Do we agree; we rush them now?*

'Smoke first, boss?' says Bollovar.

Excellent! Skrimsli answers.

Bollovar and Silverback hastily construct cannon balls of leaves. As soon as they are lit they start to billow thick white smoke.

'Throw them, Silverback, before we all choke to death,' Ekar exclaims.

The balls land in the green space enclosed by the walls, and engulf it in strands of smoke like trailing wool. Silently the crew begin to creep down the slope, the Gula flying like a small, brown shadow before them.

When they are all are on the same level as the ruined cottages, but still in the dense cover of the trees, Ekar raises a hand to call a stop.

I will take the guard at the corner, Skrimsli says. *He is the least injured. Madame Gula at my side, I believe. Secure the fighters before the weapon. We can do nothing safely until all their fighting power is subdued.*

'Agreed,' breathes Ekar. 'Bollovar, you and I will go to the right. Silverback between us and Skrimsli.'

'I'll need to protect my sister and my brother,' says Harlon.

'Of course,' Ekar agrees.

Harlon, skirt to the right, keep out of our battle. The fat one will run to the beach with your family. I am certain of it. But wait for us to engage in the battle before you move.

Skrimsli counts for them. On five they burst like a storm into the light, yelling like the wild creatures they all are. The Gula is in front, too low for anyone to notice. She has her teeth in an Automator's leg before he even saw her coming.

Now is Harlon's moment! She skirts to the right, along the edge of the trees and rocks. She breaks cover in line with another ruined cottage and stops in the shelter of its walls to assess the situation. Peeping around the wall's edge she can't see Vellum but she has her route to his position mapped out in her mind. She glances towards the continuing fighting: the strands of smoke part and she sees what the fighters haven't noticed, that the Vampire and the three attendants are escaping with the glass box. For a moment Harlon considers pursuing them. But he can't go far. No, this time she must protect Ash and Xeno before everything else. She runs low under the wall and across to the wall of the next ruined cottage. The spaces between the walls are familiar: she knows without having to look where the gateways and corners lie. She reaches the wall at right angles to where Ash and Xeno were, to find that they're no longer there.

Harlon runs on between the cottages and catches sight of Vellum up ahead. Just as Skrimsli predicted, he's heading for the beach, dragging Ash by his bound hands. But Xeno is nowhere to be seen. Vellum and Ash disappear between the end walls of two ruined cottages, closer to the beach. Harlon follows. She crouches in the shadows then moves forward. Now she can see the bright space of sand and sea framed in the gap between the buildings. There is Vellum, by the boats but she can't see Ash! Has he been thrown into the boat? No, he's got away, and Vellum's dropped a pistol into the shallows, but he pulls a second weapon from his belt and he raises it to aim. Harlon does not hesitate, she rushes forward.

Ash is running awkwardly along the open beach, his hands tied. Vellum is aiming at him, an easy shot in bright light even though Ash is a moving target. Harlon is angry with Ash; why didn't he run straight for cover? She is angry with herself; her brother could die now because she didn't teach him well enough. And then she remembers. She has a rifle, a good one, and she can shoot straight. It's a simple choice: Vellum's life or Ash's. She won't fail to protect her brother now.

Time slows. Harlon aims with great steadiness and precision. She breathes out. Squeezes the trigger slow and steady, just the way Ma taught her.

Vellum is dead before he hits the ground. It's a perfect head shot. The shot you take when you are *really* sure. The shot you take when you really want something to be *done*.

But the shot did not come from Harlon's gun. She walks from between the walls into the open, down to the water's edge and finds she has literally walked into her dream. The dream with Pa in it; the dream in which every night she promises she

368

won't forget him and as soon as she's awake she does. She shades her eyes with one long hand. This is that beach! She knows its curve, the sound of its surf, the shape of the treeline that is its boundary; all of it as familiar now as her own face.

Dazed and bewildered by the sudden strength of this recovered memory she stares down the length of the strand. In the distance at the far end of the beach, a sailing dinghy is being drawn up onto the sand by two people, neither of them Pa. They look like Tolly, with her arm in a sling, and Colt! Closer, much closer, another person is walking towards her. This isn't Pa either but now Harlon *knows* this has to be a dream. This person walks with a new limp and yet another scar on her face, but she unmistakable. Ash has seen her too and is running. But Harlon gets there first.

'Ma!'

'My girl,' Ma says and puts a hand on Harlon's cheek.

'I knew you had that shot, Harlon. I knew you'd take it too, not a doubt,' she says, 'but *you* don't have to be a killer.'

Harlon hugs Ma tight.

'Is this a dream?' Harlon asks.

'No,' Ma says. 'I will tell you all about it soon, but right now we have to find that weapon and put an end to it.'

16

No one Leaves

Doada

The Greenhouse is surprisingly heavy, and the Gardeners unsurprisingly weak. But the smoke screen that the girl and her collaborators have created has worked against them, allowing Doada and his weapon to make their escape. He *will* triumph. This place and all its pathetic little golden lines *will* be destroyed.

The Gardeners put the Greenhouse down in another small grassy clearing separated from the beach by a line of trees.

'Activate it. Activate it now!' Doada commands. Their three faces turn towards him like moons.

'Commander Eye, with all respect,' One begins. 'I feel that would be unwise.'

'Surely, it would be better to defer?' Three suggests.

'*Do as I tell you!*' Doada is almost shrieking now. Why won't they do what they are told? *Why can't anybody ever just do what he wants?*

Two steps towards him, too close again. Doada moves back but still Two comes. He has a wild look in his big dinner-plate eyes.

'Are you completely mad?' Two says. 'If we activate it now, how will *we* get away? For all we know they've holed our boats. Do you want your cells ignited along with everything else on this wretched little island?'

Three and One look suitably shocked but Doada can tell they are in agreement with their colleague. Doada feels a kind of icy calm come over him. He knows exactly what he's going to do now. If the Gardeners won't do the job, he'll do it for himself. He smooths his hair, cleans his glasses, calmly replaces them.

'That's where you are wrong, Two,' Doada says, quietly. 'An Automator transport is, even as we speak, on its way to take us to safety. I sent the order for it last night. It will have set off at once and will arrive imminently. So your activation can begin *at once.*'

Before the slow-moving Gardeners can do anything to stop him, Doada makes his move. He congratulates himself on his own remarkable agility and resolve, not to mention his understanding of how the Greenhouse is operated. He shoves aside the puny One, the hopelessly angular Three. They fall to the ground like broken sticks but as he reaches to flick the activation switches on the Greenhouse he finds that Two has finally got much, much too close and is hanging around his neck and screaming.

Fortunately Doada has equipped himself with a regulation pistol, not as beautiful as the elegant piece he has had to sacrifice, but serviceable. It certainly seems to work effectively on Two. He falls into the grass and lies there, bleeding from an impressive stomach wound. Doada guesses he will be dead in a matter of minutes. Unfortunate, but he still has the expertise of One and Three available to build the next Greenhouse.

Doada would not admit ignorance in anything but he experiences a moment of uncertainty as his fingers hover over the silver switches on the glass box. He flicks them *all* for good measure.

'Oh!' says One. 'Oh! Oh!' One repeats that same small sound. 'You have activated the weapon, but set no delay.'

'Yes,' agrees Three in a small, blank voice. 'Even with the disruption caused by the sudden relocation it will reach Cellular Ignition Resonance in fewer than twenty minutes.'

Doada stares at her.

'Well then, *activate the delay*, until the transport gets here!'

Why is it that people are always so stupid?

'That is not possible, Commander. It is a one-way street. Once all the switches have been set as you did, the delay mechanism cannot be activated. It will reach CIR and kill everything within twenty miles of this spot.'

'The Velocity,' Doada says, a note of panic rising in his throat, 'the Velocity will get us far enough away.'

'No, Commander, that is not correct.' The pitch of Three's voice is the only thing that gives away her emotion, it has risen to a squeak. 'It will take at least thirty minutes to cover a sufficient distance; we have twenty at most. If you could rise in the air to three thousand feet you could escape it. But without a transport that is not possible. We will all die along with every living thing on or around this island.'

Doada stares at the Greenhouse, glittering and alive.

'Then we will destroy it.'

He shoots at the Greenhouse but the bullets skeeter off, leaving its shining surface totally unmarked. He shoots again. Kicks it.

'Doada, put the gun down.' Doada spins around towards the sound of that once familiar voice.

Toren. *Toren.* He's pleased to see she's aged badly. Skinny, lined and scarred. Well, that's something. At least his plan has worked at some level and she'll die here too. Her son is with her, the boy from the ice ship, and his own radio operator: she must be the oldest child, under his nose all along! He's glad the bird girl is missing. He hopes that she has already come to a bad end.

'My gun will do you no good, Toren. Nothing will. My excellent Gardener here informs me that the weapon, once activated cannot be stopped. All living cells for twenty miles around will fry inside ten minutes.' It's an exaggeration he feels is justified. But the stricken expressions of the two technicians beside the weapon do nothing to contradict him.

The look on Toren's face as she absorbs this information is almost enough to compensate Doada for the loss of his own life, the cruel snatching away of his power. He laughs out loud at her horror; the way she clutches her children. How *touching*. But that moment's loss of focus is enough. He runs. It has occurred to him that a very fast boat with just *one* person in it could perhaps get far enough away, in time. It certainly seems worth a try.

He races down the beach and no one even follows. So he's alone to hear the sound of a transport, alone to savour the moment of his salvation and his triumph. Reeven Dopp, dear, dear boy, has heard his message and sent the transport.

It is a *small* transport. Very small. More like the old civilian craft now banned but who cares … it will be enough to lift him up above the kill zone. Never was there a sweeter sound. There's just time to get away. In moments he will be high, high up, able to photograph the glory of the Greenhouse and the moment when his power will be complete.

He staggers, light headed with relief and elation. He totters down the beach as the craft lands lightly on the sand and prepares to rush inside. He'll even take One and Three with him if they get here in time. He is, after all, a generous man. He turns to call them as the doors of the transport swing open. But instead of efficient Red Blade officers ready to pull him in, repel enemies and take off swiftly, there's a face straight from his past, one he hasn't seen since early childhood. The sister of his father's ostler, the man Cat Vellum and his helpers beat to death the night his own father died. Doada would know that cloud of messy hair anywhere.

'Well,' she says. 'Doada Sisal. You'd better step back from my ship. She's not for you.'

He has no time to wait; he'll just kill her. He points his gun but what at? She's become a cloud of wings and buzzing that soon engulfs him.

Doada falls to his knees in the sand. Through the pain of the stings, between the slits of his closing eyes he can still see the globe of the transport. Even *he* can hit that, even *now*. He fires the last of his bullets into the gas balloon. It's enough – the silver skin is ripped and gas inside rushes out. If he can't leave this place alive, *no one will*.

Toren's Story
4

Twenty miles off Angellis, with the sun rising over a silky sea, Tui spread Borden's map on the little chart table.

'I know where this island is,' he said. 'Look! The dark blue of the deepest water on your map fits perfectly with the outline of the Marraduka Trench!'

'So we can sail there?' Toren was like a child at the thought of really going to the place on Borden's map.

'I think we can,' said Tui. 'But what I wonder is *why* it isn't on the charts. Could be just that there's not much boat traffic in that part of the Latantic Ocean or something else...' He smiled. 'I guess we'll find out when we get there!'

There were days of being becalmed and days of storms but they reached the Marraduka Trench at last. By the time they got there, they had some answers to Tui's questions. Twenty miles from where they *should* have got their first sighting of the island the compass started going crazy. It was difficult to hold a course.

'Well, that explains the name,' Tui said.

'What name?'

'The name of the island, Toren. Look!' He pointed to the edge of the map. Tiny faint spidery letters that Toren had never noticed were written there.

'Argoll, Chamenos, Tynt, Tapt, Natowele,' Toren read. 'They can't *all* be its name.'

'They're all saying the same thing in many languages,' Tui replied. 'Argoll in the old tongue means, well, look!'

Tui pointed to a faint word in the middle of the long list.

'Lost!' Toren read. 'But we'll find it!'

In the end, they used the stars to find their way, and at last anchored in the wide bay on the island's western side by moonlight. By then Tui knew something else about the island.

'It may not be on human maps. But there are other sorts. I can feel a lot of different routes running through here. The sky, the water, the rocks, all full of them.'

From the moment the sun rose on the first day they felt they'd come to a kind of paradise. The island was deeply green with a high, wooded centre that caught the clouds, giving them plenty of fresh water. It was shaped like a half moon, the western side one long curving bay, the east, steep cliffs and grassy slopes where colonies of terns the colour of stem clouds and great dark-eyed albatrosses came to nest in summer. All around were clear, cold waters, with nutrients welling up from the deep below, nourishing great forests of kelp and clouds of fish. Dolphins came to feed, sharks and huge leatherback turtles. Sometimes swarms of rays swooped over the weed tangles for a few days before disappearing again.

It wasn't easy. Tui had brought tools and seeds, and basic supplies to keep them going for a while. But they had to catch or grow their food, or starve. People had lived on Lost once, there were the remains of stone cottages behind the beach.

But why their inhabitants had left was a mystery, and the ruins held no clues. Tui and Toren repaired three of the cottages one to sleep in, one to cook in and one for a store.

Their days were simple and full. They gathered seaweed and shellfish, they tended the little garden back from the shore, sheltered by stone walls. They collected driftwood for fires, cared for their few, precious bits of technology, like the solars that gave them light at night and a little warmth. Hid from fierce storms and the few really cold days of winter.

Every day Toren felt more connected to the world. More connected to Tui. She was amazed how she had forgotten how many colours were in his eyes. Harlon was quick, full of energy but quiet, thoughtful like her father. Toren watched her in wonder, hardly able to believe that the child was really her daughter. Although it was to Tui that Harlon turned to first for most things, slowly she and Toren remade a bond.

Bit by bit, Toren healed: healed old cuts and breaks in her body, scarred over and tight; healed the deeper wounds of violence and fear within her mind and soul, injuries whose depth only now became clear to her.

Tui's siardw blossomed. After a lifetime of having to hide it, here he could try it out on everything. He listened in to the island beetles, to the little black and white stripy fish that swam around in the shallows. More and more he experienced the island through their eyes and ears, through their skin and noses, through senses that humans did not possess. They brought him information and understanding completely outside his own perceptions. He saw things Toren couldn't see, knew things she could not understand.

One day Toren found him with his sketchbook, gazing at a jellyfish in a large rock pool.

'It is kind of map,' he told Toren, 'or rather it holds a map within its body. It can sense the pattern of the planet's magnetic field and feel currents from distant shores.'

'What's it thinking now?' Toren asked.

'Oh, that's much more simple,' Tui laughed. 'Right now it's pretty much thinking about pulsing round this pool, Blob Blob Blob.'

They laughed together for minutes on end for the first time since they'd been teenagers.

The more Tui tuned in to the island's life, the more he became convinced of its importance.

'It's not just the things that live here, it's all the stuff that passes through,' he explained. 'It's like some kind of huge train junction. It's as if, wherever else animals go, they have to come through here.' He smiled and shook his head. 'I wish understood it better.'

Among the creatures passing through Tui's junction were humpback whales. They came at the end of summer, stayed for while and moved on. Tui sailed the boat out to where they breached and sang. He made a little raft so he could float quietly above them, sliding in and out of the water at will, listening to their songs and their thoughts, making sketches of their black-and-white tails to help him tell one from another. But when Toren asked Tui what the whales were saying, he shook his head.

'Stories that tell the world; songs that sing life? I don't

understand most of it and the bits I do, there's no way to translate. I'd have to *be* a whale. All I know is that it's really important.'

One day Toren found Tui staring at her father's map pouring over its details with a magnifying glass.

'E*verything* goes through this place,' he said. 'Every song and every story ever told runs through here and reaches out across the world. If you could draw them on this map it would vanish under a million threads. Sometimes I can almost see them, look!'

Tui held the map up so it was at the level of their eyes. The evening light slanted over the map and Toren thought she saw its surface shimmer, like a spider's web in the breeze.

But it was the tiniest moment and it passed.

'Maybe,' she said. 'I can't be sure.'

'If I had the eyes of a bird, or whale or an insect I would see them,' Tui said. 'I'm certain of it and I'm certain they mean this place *matters*. That it's powerful. Maybe even powerful enough to break the Automators.'

Toren asked him what he meant but he could only shake his head and say, 'I'm not even sure myself...'

As Toren's strength returned she found herself worrying more and more about what was happening 'back in the world'. Paradise was all very well but she wanted to get back to help rebuild Green Thorn and try to defeat the Automators. But every time she mentioned it, Tui would say, 'I think this island holds the key to defeating them, Toren. This place. Just let's stay a little longer, to work it out. I need one more season with the whales. Then maybe we can go back with something that they can't defeat.'

It began to come between them. They argued.

'Then why don't you go back alone if you want to fight so much?' Tui said one day.

'I can't leave you. I can't leave Harlon,' Toren cried.

'You seemed to manage well without us before.'

The bitter words couldn't be unsaid and every day they grew more distant from each other.

Then Harlon got sick. Really sick, a fever that made her delirious. Toren and Tui argued about that too: whether to risk the strain of the long journey and try to get her to a hospital, or to stay safe and quiet on the island. By the time they walked away from their fight Harlon was unconscious, burning up, consumed by whatever was attacking her. Toren fell asleep with Harlon in her arms, rocking her tiny, hot body, feeling that her daughter's life was slipping between her fingers.

She woke to find her arms empty and Tui gone. The boat was gone too. Toren scoured the brightness of the morning sea and saw Tui's distant silhouette, the blows of whales around the boat. She saw Tui slide Harlon's tiny body over the side. So, the child had died while she slept and now Tui was bidding their daughter goodbye without her! Toren roared with grief and rage, a sound that came from somewhere underneath her feet. It rose through her, burning everything away and leaving her a stranger to herself. She didn't know that she lay face down in the sand until Harlon found her, and put her small, cool hand against her mother's cheek.

'Ma!' the child said. 'Ma, wake up. I'm all better and Pa's turned into a whale!'

All the child could say was that the whales had let her swim with them, that they sang a song to make her better. It sounded like a story to Toren. But Tui couldn't say what had happened because he had lost most of his human speech. Harlon was right: at some level now, Tui was more whale than man. He had gone so far into their minds to get their help for Harlon that parts of him couldn't come back.

Toren's heart went out to him. She felt he'd sacrificed himself to save their child. Even though he could hardly speak the gap between them closed.

Now when Toren asked to leave, Tui did not resist at all. Together they provisioned the little boat for a long voyage and set sail. Harlon cried in her bunk for three days straight.

The storm hit them when they were almost home. Rumyc's south coast was in sight. Tui felt the warning of its coming through the fish, all heading down for deeper waters. But that didn't help. The storm came too fast and too strong. No one could have been prepared for it. Wind and waves growing huge as suddenly as a sprung trap. A freak wave and a freak gust, a random lining up of nature's forces. In the space of a few terrible minutes it snapped the mast like a twig and left Tui crushed beneath it.

Toren put Harlon in her survival suit and locked her below decks. She screamed loud enough to be heard above the waves. The sails, still attached to the fallen mast dragged in the water, tilting the boat badly. Toren struck them off with an axe. Then, she tried to get Tui free. Only when she clung beside him on the pitching deck, could she see how bad it was. A wood splinter, thick as her arm had pieced him. Toren guessed it had destroyed most of his right lung. The only reason he wasn't already dead was the fact that the splinter was plugging its own wound and that he had something he desperately wanted to say.

Toren held his dear face between his hands as his mind reached for her, clutching for words that were already almost out of his grasp.

'What is it, Tui? What do you want me to know?'

He fought for every word.

When
all
dark,
take
our
children
back.
Sing
the
world
new.
Promise.

Toren promised, even though she didn't understand what he had told her. What did s*ing the world new* mean? And why did he say *children?* She held him tight, unable to believe that he was gone.

But now was no time for grief. She had a child to save from the waves. She set her face to stone and held her tears. The mast, half severed, trailed over the side, threatening to capsize them in the heavy seas. Toren hacked it free. It slid into the waves and vanished, taking Tui's body with it.

Toren lashed the rudder the way that Tui'd taught her, then went below and shut the hatch against waves and wind. All night Harlon wept, and Toren held her tight. They slept at dawn when the storm too was all but cried out. Toren ran the boat aground in a bay somewhere east of Angellis and swam for shore with Harlon on her back, before swells broke the hull to pieces on the rocks. She built a driftwood fire to warm the child and wrapped Tui's coat around the two of them. She watched the last of the little craft sink beneath the waves and thought about the island and her father's map, gone to the bottom now, forever. For the first time, Toren felt the cruel tyranny of nature that the Automators spoke of; it had taken Tui and his knowledge to its indifferent heart.

Tui's words had run out just too soon. So Toren never knew his plan to share the things he'd found about the meaning of the island and what he believed that it could do. She never knew he'd seen the golden lines that showed how Lost shone bright on many other maps; she never knew it lived for years, skin-close, sewn into the lining of her lover's coat as gradually it lost his smell and took on hers.

17
Walk the Line

Xeno

 As soon as the boat ran up onto the beach Xeno knew that this was the place. The place she'd seen in the minds of birds all her life. At first she caught just glimpses, fleeting moments of thought and flight, a deep glow of bird emotions that sometimes even Xeno didn't understand. But it was only when birds began to tell her, that she saw it clearly. A place through which all routes and stories run, where all songs sing, a place where all the threads that hold the world are woven, twined in one.

The swifts spoke through her about it. The snow tern spoke through her too. She saw the power of this place, felt it. But she didn't understand that it was fragile too. Now she's here, the fear that it could be destroyed is all but dissolving her.

She doesn't want to leave Ash again but she can't stay there while everything is calling so loud. She slips her wrists like feathered wingtips, and steps bony bird feet from the shackles at her ankles and flies away into the green and blue of the island. *Ma's island.* Yes, that's another thing she understands at last. But not safe like Ma hoped. Not safe for anybody.

Bird lives flap inside her heart and mind. What they see; what they know. It fills her up: the shape of wind, the space between one wingbeat and the next, the wisdom of the flock. The star map of an open ocean, the creases in a leaf where aphids hide; and eggs' perfection, hatching love and home. Eggs in nests on cliffs and trees, white in dark burrows, blue like the eye of the sky or mottle-blotched like captured bits of cloud.

Flight. Flight! Letting go of weight, lifting, swooping, reading details of the air, the trickster stories of the breeze, the spell of thermals and the promise in the gale. The work of it, blood and bone, muscle, lungs and airsacs, feathers, bent to that one purpose: up.

All of that is in her. How can she she hold it and not *be* it?

She is small and bruised, tired and alone. *It's too much. It is too hard to long for something so much.*

She's breaking, cracking open to the white, bright nothingness of sunlight.

No, not nothingness. *Not now.* There is something she must do. She can't quite hold it in her mind enough just yet. But she will try.

There's no time for nothingness, no time for the place that her hopeless longing to be a bird has always taken her.

Time is running out. Today she must not lose herself.

Today she must accept what she really is.

She must hold on to that fragile little thread

of here

of now

of me.

But with *me* come things she doesn't want:

    My fault. My fault that the starling saw inside my head.

    My fault it told Doada what it saw. My fault they came.

    Ma's blood, my fault. Ash and Harlon's hurt, my fault.

    Me. My.

    All of it, *my* fault.

But that's another kind of nothingness.

    She must walk the line between them.

Look at your feet, Xeno, she tells herself.

    Your *real* feet. Not bird's claws. They never will be.

    Look at your arms, Xeno, she tells herself.

    Your real arms. They never will be wings.

    You are *yourself.*

    You are not a bird, you never will be.

    You are earthbound, fragile, mortal.

    You, Xeno can act. Now. You can make a difference.

    You are not just a beak for other voices to sing through.

    Xeno climbs down from the tree, and walks into the grassy space.

    Above her in the air a chaos of singing; calling birds, wheeling, swooping, in ever wider circles over the land, over the ocean.

Xeno looks around as if she has woken up for the first time in her life.

    She sees the threads are all *around* her.

    In the air, on the ground.

    She can gather them in her hand, like strings.

Gather the birds, their lives, their voices, all they see and feel.

Gather them and sing them.

That's what the snow tern meant.

A million, million lives on one trail, one place, connected there, one song, one singing.

Xeno is a connecter.

Voices to make a hurricane of life.

She can help build the hurricane.

The seeds are sown; you sowed them. The sky will hatch; you cracked it. The ocean will ring; you struck it.

The Automators made this day, like an egg, they hatched their own destruction.

Xeno walks towards the beach, with the birds like a storm cloud over her head.

18
Worse than Dying

Ash

The weird inventor, the skinny one, has explained what the Greenhouse is about to do. But it turns out the CIR thingy doesn't go far up into the air, so if Doada *hadn't* blasted holes in Mayo's transport, some of the humans at least could have got high enough to be safe. There are the fast boats, of course, but they aren't fast enough. So that's it. They're done for.

Dying is bad. His family dying is worse, but worst of all is that everything else here is going to die too. Thousands, millions perhaps, of lives on and around this beautiful island will end. All the gleaming trails he glimpsed when they arrived, will all be cut and some big important part of the world will be destroyed.

Doada and the two inventors have crawled off somewhere out of sight. They will be dead too but that thought doesn't really cheer him up. There are more important things to do than think horrible thoughts about them.

When everyone realised what had happened, that they were trapped here just as Doada had planned all along, there was panic for a while, Ma desperately trying to think of a way to save her children. That was awful, seeing Ma so upset. It was the worst part. But now, everybody's calm. There's nothing more that they can do. Just wait to be dead. Not a long wait and in it they can just be. Ash thinks that if he could go on living, all he'd ever want is *to just be*.

Ash goes to Ma and holds her tight. Everybody is doing stuff like that. The *Maiden's* crew stand head to head, their arms around each other's shoulders. Harlon and her friend, Tolly, hug. It's weird; Harlon looks happier than he's ever seen her. People are crying but all quite calm. There's no point fussing about stuff now.

'Where's Xeno?' Ma cries. 'Where's my bird?'

'She'll be fine, Ma,' Ash tells her. 'There's so many birds here. She'll be with *them*. That's where she's happiest anyway.'

All the same, he does wish Xeno were here, and the Gula too. Harlon says the Gula's here but he can't see her. He hopes she's not lying injured somewhere, all alone.

He decides there's no time left for wanting what you don't have: he's got Ma and Harlon and Aunt Mayo. He's glad she got back to being a pilot, like she was before her bees on the mountain. Turns out Ma found her way to Mayo's house as well, after the Automators came to their home. Ma healed up there and then went back to being the Boogam!

'I just wanted to take Doada's attention from finding you,' Ma says, 'but looks like I did a poor job.'

It must be almost time. Some of the leaves on the trees are turning brown, and there's weird mist on the sea. Is that the start of it? Will it hurt? Ash imagines that it will. A lot.

Ma has her arms around him and Harlon, and Tolly too. Mayo and her cloud of insects wrap them all.

Ma is crying. Ash doesn't want crying to be the last thing that they do together. So he smiles at Ma and Harlon.

'We can keep our promise to you, Ma. We're on the island lost in the deepest part of the ocean, like you said, so we should sing our song here.'

'Maybe Xeno will come if she hears us sing,' Harlon says, 'you know, in time, before...'

Ma shakes her head. 'I don't think I can.' Her voice is shaking. 'But you know the last thing your pa said to me? He said "when all is dark, take our children back, sing the world new".'

Ma's words strike Harlon like lightning. She steps out of their hug.

'Sing the world new!' she says and grabs Ma by the shoulders. 'I know what he meant. I *know what to do to stop all this*. I've got to sing to the whales. I got a message for them.'

She shouts to the *Ice Maiden* crew.

'We've all got to sing, everybody, everything! Sing! Sing don't stop.'

Ma starts to speak but Harlon stops her.

'You know when the Automators came you said there was no time to explain? There's no time to explain, Ma, just sing.'

Harlon rushes up to Tolly, kisses her on the lips, then she runs to the sea.

'Sing!' she yells and then starts to swim.

What does this mean? Ash and Ma stare at each other. They are frozen and the *Ice Maiden* crew is too. All the calm that

Ash felt just moment ago has gone, his heart races, he's full of fear again...

Hope

Hope, cub.

The Gula races into his mind as she comes limping down the beach, her left forepaw bloody and bent. She speaks so clearly in his heart.

There is hope.

The trail does not end here, she says.

All trails sing, all trails join.

Cub, sing, sing loud.

Sing trails together, land trails, air trails, ocean trails.

Sing unlife down.

Sing!

Then Ash understands. There is a chance, a tiny chance that somehow Harlon is *right*, that *together they can stop all this.* His brain can't see how but his heart can feel it. As the Gula fairly leaps into his arms he takes a breath and the first notes of the old lullaby, that Xeno calls the song that sings us, escape, shakily, into the air. He takes Ma's hand and she joins in, Mayo too, although she doesn't know the tune. The *Ice Maiden* crew come and stand in a ring around them and add their voices. Skrimsli growls a base accompaniment and Silverback adds harmonising wails.

But Ash's heart is still full of fear and sorrow. His singing is no good. He feels it cannot work. When Ma cries out, he's sure she feels the same but what she says is Look!

LOOK!

Coming down the beach, *dancing* down the beach is Xeno!

She's gleaming as if lit from deep inside. Above her head a cloud of birds all calling, cawing, screeching, singing. All around them glowing golden threads fill the air, crisscrossing, harmonising, counterpointing into one huge symphony of noise and life.

Trails together strong strong strong, the Gula cries!

Ash's heart slows. A smile spreads over his face, his heart lifts and his voice soars, strong at last. Invincible! The air shimmers with wings and sound, the ocean surface ruffles and trembles with song.

Ash sings and sings until he's not sure if he hears the sound, or sees it or tastes it or touches it, until he can't work out what's in his head, what's out of it. He sings while the Gula wriggles from his arms to twirl along the sand on the edge of the waves. He sings while Skrimsli rolls and gambols beside her, strange and beautiful, and very, very orange. He sings in joy for this wondrous golden song of life and living, that tangles them all together in its threads.

19
The Song that Sings Us

Harlon

 The water is cool and clear. Deep as eternity. White flippers shine turquoise through the sea's prism, as the whales turn like dancers in the water.

They are are singing,

whoop whoop whooooop

ruuuuuuuurrrrrbbbubbb

iiii-ipp iii-iip.

They are telling Harlon their old, old stories; the ones Harlon and Pa learned from them years ago. Harlon has a message for them, a message that she's carried, kept safe in a dream since the day when they healed her. Healed her heart and soul, and gave her this message to bring back to them.

So Harlon sings: the song she's always sung with Ma and Ash and Xeno, the song the whales sung into her when she was sick. And then she finds a new song rising in her throat. Even in her puny human voice, she feels its power. It is the signal to the whales, the sign that they have waited for that says 'now it's time', time to sing the great unmaking, the song to end the story of the Automators and all they've done. The song to sing the world anew.

Harlon knows she did not invent this song; nor did the whales. It has been waiting to be remembered and now they've all remembered it at once, everyone and every thing who always knew there was a song that sings us. All the living things that always knew, and all the humans who forgot, until this moment. The song bends time; then and now and tomorrow all tangle in the song's thread as it spreads, all in a single instant, to every place and every being in the world.

It sings in voices, it sparks in glowing phosphoresence, it dances in the jumps of dolphins and the slow pulse of jellyfish. It twines in the tails of sea horses and blossoms in the spawning of corals; albatross snatch it from the gleaming surface and spread it over waves to the cliffs of the farthest islands. It washes onto the shore, where limpets write it on the rocks. It is taken to the sky in clouds and sung in rain, passed through roots and and leaves. It crackles in the fungal networks in all the secret darkness underground. It spreads fast as thought, quicker than a photon. It sings from throats and beaks, in the forest morning when the air holds still, from burros in the desert, and under the aurora. It crosses mountain valleys, oceans, and echos in the veins of leaves, in cells, and between one breath and the next. It trickles down the skin of elephants so they know that *we* again exists, and not only I.

Time unravels, not much, but just enough to hasten up the healing. So that a giant kapok tree grows on the place where Enkalamba fell. Snow terns flock to feed in the wake of the ice whales that swim where tar turned the ice floes black. In fields where the air and earth were silent there is a buzz, a susurration of wings, and the world mosaics in a billion compound eyes.

It reaches everywhere. Into city streets, machines and factories, into the dark minds of the abandoned Turned, into Fallen as he patrols his cells of stolen children. Into Red Blade officers pointing their weapons down darkened alleyways. Into the countryside where people pick their way amongst the ruins of the villages that Automators burned.

In the capital, the Fang and all its contents weather in a heartbeat, the way mountains wear down in an eon. By morning saplings will be full-grown trees and foxes will make their earths where it once stood. Wild roses twine the rusted cars. People stand dazed, amazed with the revelation that life's long, long history is just a family saga, written in one shared language that everybody knows. Listeners *listen*, with new ears and hearts. And minds. And for the first time people hear the words of other people and really understand.

In the eye of the song, in the elemental instant of making and unmaking, every golden thread of being is joined, one beam, one rope, one note, a power irresistible; the wind strikes, the lightning punches, and the essence of all beings becomes a molten magma in the earth's old heart. Minds meld. Across the world, humans, animals and plants – all life flows as one hot river. Understandings forge between beings who have not shared a mother for a hundred million generations. Strange and most wonderful of all, for some, are those human minds that meld with other humans. For a heartbeat that's a lifetime, every being shares the being of another, and learns the wild, untamed meaning of one kin, one song.

This is a force bigger than the sky and smaller than a grain of sand. It will not change the world forever, because that's a work in progress. Life will always have to fight against the powers of unlife. But today it's easily enough to break a greenhouse into a thousand pieces, even one with such big ideas about itself.

As the singers cease their singing and sit dazed and changed upon the sand, the shattered fragments of the crystal coffin lie forgotten underneath the trees.

Who have you been? everyone is asking. *What have you been?*

Ash, of course, has been the Gula, and slept with her kits beneath the snow. Ma has been her long-lost love Tui, travelling south on a sled with his little daughter tucked beneath his heart. Tolly has been Enkalamba walking in the grass on the bird hills with her kin.

They ask Xeno who she's been, expecting the usual commentary in robin-speak.

'Me!' says Xeno, shining. 'I've been me for the first time!'

She races her brother over the sand as if this was just any other day on earth, and laughing about the miracle of living is all that anyone can do.

Ma smiles and smiles and turns to her eldest, her warrior, her whale singer. She takes her jacket off, puts it on her daughter's shivering body and asks.

'And who were you, Harlon?'

Harlon looks at Ma, really looks, so that she sees her, Breen Avvon, Boogam, Toren Sisal and says, 'I was you, Ma. I was you!'

Epilogue

Doada

 In the morning the skinny guy with the glasses like the bottom of a bottle raked the gravel paths on the east side of the garden, and in the afternoon he raked the west. Every day the same. Crying as he raked, quietly, constantly. He was very, very old and had been in the Home for so long, people had forgotten who he was.

'Wasn't he was one of those Automators?' somebody would ask. And someone else would shrug and say, 'Maybe. I forget...'

But the old man, Doada Sisal, did not forget. He remembered everything, and all the time.

Everything he had done, and what it meant. He'd come to understand those meanings on the day people now called Song Day, the day when everyone remembers how close they came to letting unlife win.

On that first Song Day, long ago, when minds were melted open and other lives flowed in, he had become a starling. He had flown in a dense flock of thousands, making murmurations over the winter fields. He had sung, pouring a liquid chaos of silver notes into the air. He had felt, through every nerve and feather, connected to his own being and all others. Oh, the sharpness of it! A hundred times more clear and true than anything in his meagre human life.

So Doada came to understand what he had stolen from the starling he had made his slave.

The pain of that knowledge never left him, the regret, the sorrow. What could he do? He could not give back the life he took, and how could a long-dead bird give forgiveness or accept apology?

So he lived on. Not quite alive, not able to die.

Until one autumn a robin, keen to stake her claim on her winter territory, saw the opportunity that the old man's rake provided. It stood taller than any other point around and was a good size for her delicate feet. The fact that it had an old human attached did not seem to matter. She flew to it and settled there.

She was not even an arm's length from Doada's face! So tiny, so beautiful, so bold. So entirely and wonderfully herself. She looked at him, bright eyed, and she sang.

FURTHER READING, AVAILABLE TO RESIDENTS OF RUMYC

The Salt Sky Loops Blue: Poems from the World by Xenora Sisal, with illustrations by Tuidard Meyer

A Gula Aloft: Travels on an Ice Ship by Ashard Meyer

A Photographic Guide to the Wildlife of the Woken Forest by Tollara Flix

Two Worlds, One Life: A Memoir of the Bigger Picture by Skrimsli and Ekar Nordd

The Life of the Ghost: Toren Sisal and the Green Thorn by Harlon Sisal

Acknowledgements

An African proverb says 'it takes a village to raise a child', and I think every writer knows that it takes a community to write a book. Included in the community that got this book written are the many thousands of children whom I have met and worked with over the years as a children's author. Their innate love for the natural world and for the power of stories was my deepest motivation for writing *The Song that Sings Us*. Included also in that group of motivators and inspirers are the many scientists, conservationists and activists whose work I have represented in my writing and whose knowledge and passion are included here behind and between every word.

But the greatest debt of gratitude I owe is to my closest community, the small group of friends and family with whom I discussed this story and who saw it through to the end. First to Julia Green and David Almond, who listened to my plan for the *Song* in the author's yurt at Edinburgh and who were so kind and encouraging that I felt that I might manage to write it. Second, to my editor at Firefly, Penny Thomas, who trusted in the story from the start and was prepared to give me a contract to write it on the basis of a half-written first chapter. Penny, my deepest thanks for your enthusiasm, meticulous editing skills and the ability to cry more with each re-reading of the manuscript (also for not passing out when I hit 100,000 words). Third, to my first audience, my niece Katy Shooter who read the written text in its rawest form and loved it, and to Cathy Fisher, Jackie Morris and Molly Howell who listened to me read in the long nights of lockdown; I will never forget your laughter, tears, gasps and your insistence on which characters had to survive! Fourth is a second thanks to Jackie Morris for her visual genius that has made the *Song* sing so very beautifully. I have been so moved by your delight in my story, Jack, and by the time you have given to it, when your workload was already so great.

My last thanks is to my husband Dan Jones for his calm, his unshakeable belief in my ability, his steadfast devotion to my happiness and his endless talent for making me laugh. I'd never have done it without you, my darling.

Coming soon from the author of *The Song that Sings Us*

SKRIMSLI!

by Nicola Davies

'*Words changed me, shaped me, made me into something other. I am not wholly tiger now; I am part human…*'

Wind whips the snow around the tents and carts that crouch amongst the slag heaps. A ragged flag flaps in the moonlight, announcing 'CIRCUS' to the empty sky. Into this frozen scene, devoid of colour, a small orange being has come. He is the last cub in the litter, born into an iron cage, to the old tigress, Narastikeri. He is not welcomed. Narastikeri breathes her last before she can even lick his nose. His other siblings, pearly white tiger cubs, which would have fetched a great price, were born dead. Cheated of his profit, Kobret Majak, Circus Proprietor, is in no mood to nurture an orange cub. He throws the creature into the snow to die.

But there's another reject in this Circus. Owl Boy people call him. He darts out from his dark corner, scoops up the cub, darts back. He whispers to it, words from a language that he only half remembers, words that connect him to a place he doesn't know. The cub gnaws at his fingers with its toothless gums; Owl Boy laughs.

'Monster!' he tells it in that old tongue. '*Skrimsli.*'

So begins a friendship that will change this boy, this cub, forever…

Firefly Press, ISBN 978-1-913102-80-7